Happily Ever Ninja

A Married Romance

By Penny Reid

http://reidromance.blogspot.com/

Caped Publishing

Caped Publishing

Made in the United States of America

Print Edition: January 2016
Print ISBN: 978-1-942874-16-4

DEDICATION

To soul mates.

A Short Foreword

Dear Reader,

Three businessy items:

1) Fiona and Greg have a prequel/origin story (Knitting in the City book #4.75) entitled *Ninja At First Sight*. If you haven't already read *Ninja At First Sight*, I highly recommend you do so prior to starting *Happily Ever Ninja*. You can download it for free (from Amazon, Kobo, iTunes, Barnes & Noble) or read it serialized on Wattpad for free (www.wattpad.com/user/PennyReid).

2) A few months ago, I asked my readers to send me letters or written exchanges between them and their spouse/partner/imaginary future partner. With the exception of the Prologue, at the beginning of each chapter is an excerpt from a real letter (or Post-it® Note, or text message, etc.) between real people.

3) Three years ago, when I decided to continue the *Knitting in the City* series beyond Janie Morris's random factoid spewing, this book (Fiona and Greg's story) was the one I wanted to write the most. Is anything more romantic than enduring love? However, I knew—in order to write the action as I imagined—I would need to wait until Elizabeth, Sandra, and Ashley had been partnered off first. Once you finish *Happily Ever Ninja* you will understand why.

Best, Penny Reid

PROLOGUE

Dearest Fiona,

It occurs to me that today is Valentine's Day. As far as holidays go, this one is absolute rubbish.

I'm surrounded by maudlin men who miss their girlfriends, wives, and Internet porn (perhaps not necessarily in that order). They've all arranged delivery back home for overpriced bouquets of reedy flowers and substandard chocolates.

You would be proud of me. I didn't once point out that a woman who demands gifts on Valentine's Day is almost as intolerable as a man who only gives gifts because it's Valentine's Day.

And yet, it is Valentine's Day.

And I miss you.

I don't know how else to write it other than, I miss you.

These months apart grow unbearable. Each passing second is a moment filled with the absence of you and it suffocates me. I realize I promised I would be less morose in my correspondence, but I grip these empty sheets at night and curse them. They are cold where your body is hot and soft and so infinitely mine.

Perhaps I miss the feeling of you beneath my fingertips and belonging wholly to me. Perhaps I miss how you tense and relax in my hands, how you look at me with trust and want. If I'm honest, it's the want in you I miss the most. The need you have of me. Because it echoes the insatiable and feral nature of my need for you.

I miss you.

At this point you've no doubt already gathered I have sent neither chocolate nor flowers for Valentine's. I do not believe in obligatory gifts any more than I subscribe to compulsory love.

As such, I send you nothing but this letter and my longing for you, neither of which I can contain. I love you.

Yours forever, Greg

CHAPTER 1

Dear Husband,
I love you today more than yesterday. Yesterday you were a real jerk.

-Debbie
Dry-erase board on fridge
New Jersey, USA
Married 28 years

~Present Day~
Fiona

"ARE WE GOING to have sex tonight? I have stuff to do and it's already nine thirty."

"I only have fifteen minutes before I need to go pick up Grace and Jack from ballet." It may have been 9:30 p.m. for Greg, but it was only 2:30 p.m. for me. I glanced at my watch to confirm this fact. I had less than fifteen minutes. Actually, I had ten. "And we're not doing anything until you tell me why you haven't signed the transfer paperwork for the new retirement accounts."

I didn't add, *And I have a headache.* I did have a headache. I'd had a headache and no appetite for the last week, and off and on for the last month and a half, but I kept this information to myself. I didn't want to worry him.

I watched my husband sigh, his face falling into his hands. He looked tired, burnt out. He worked sixteen-hour days and usually didn't shave when he was gone. None of the rig workers did. But he must've shaved a few days ago because his chin was covered in two-day-old stubble, which only made him look more tired. But it also made him look devilishly sexy. I wished I could reach through the computer screen and give him a hug. And a kiss.

"Fine," he growled, finally lifting his head and gathering another large breath. His eyes narrowed and they darted over my form, or what he could see of it from his side of the video call. "Could you at least take off your shirt?"

"Greg."

"Show me your tits."

"Greg."

"I miss your skin, just . . . flash me."

"Greg, be serious."

"I am serious. Do I not look serious? Nothing is more serious to me than your body, specifically your tits and legs and mouth. And vagina, but the vagina goes without saying."

I gritted my teeth so I wouldn't smile, or worse, laugh. I wasn't sure how he managed it, but even when I was in a foul mood and feeling overwhelmed—like today—he always found a way to make me laugh. "Greg—"

"And your brain. Sorry, I can't believe I didn't mention your brain."

I allowed myself to give in to his sweet silliness. "I love that you mentioned my brain, because I love your brain."

With a hint of vulnerability, he asked, "But you don't love my vagina?"

I did laugh then, thankful I hadn't been sipping my coffee. Had I been drinking, it was the kind of laugh that would've sent a spray of liquid out of my mouth and nose.

The sound of his slight chuckle met my ears and was welcome; but it was also a reminder, he was trying to distract me.

I shook my head at his antics and tried to refocus. "Okay, enough about your lady closet. Mr. Jackson needs your approval to transfer the money into the new accounts. He emailed the forms three weeks ago, so why haven't you signed them yet?"

He sat back in his chair and crossed his arms, sighing for a third time. When he finally answered, his voice and expression were free of all earlier playfulness. "I'm not happy with his fund choices."

I blinked at the vision of my husband, the stubborn set of his jaw. Confused, I sputtered for a full minute before spitting out an incredulous, "You approved it last month."

"But then I researched the global fund further. Over eleven percent of the principal is invested in a Monsanto subsidiary."

My headache throbbed; I nearly growled, "Then pick a different global fund."

"That's not the point. I don't like that he suggested that fund to begin with. I want to go with a different financial advisor."

My brain was going to explode all over my bedroom, which would be inconvenient since I'd just vacuumed.

I meticulously modulated my voice so I wouldn't shout my response. "Are you kidding? I've been through every investment house in Chicago and there is no one left, as according to you, everyone is either incompetent or corrupt. This has been going on for eighteen months, and meanwhile our retirement has been sitting in a low return savings account."

"Better it return nothing than we invest it in malicious corporations." He shrugged. "You know my thoughts on Monsanto."

I . . .

I just . . .

I just couldn't . . .

I took a deep breath, pushing the rage down. Greg had no way of knowing, but today was one of the worst possible days for him to deliver this news.

In addition to the unexplained headaches, I was extremely low on sleep because our daughter, Grace, had been having nightmares all week. The garbage disposal stopped working two days ago, as had the dishwasher. Both kids had science projects due and every store in Chicago was out of poster board. Plus our son, Jack, had forgotten to give his teacher the money and slip for his field trip later in the week—he'd lost both—and I hadn't yet found five minutes to contact the woman about sorting it out.

Added to all this, I'd started contract work for my old engineering firm two months ago and was already behind in my latest project. Everything I touched was breaking, or broken, or a failure.

Therefore, I endeavored to be reasonable . . . or at least sound reasonable. "Pick a different fund."

His eyelids lowered and he shook his head slowly. "No. I'm not investing my money with a corrupt wanker."

"He's not a corrupt wanker. Mr. Jackson is a grandfather who volunteers his free time with the Boys and Girls Club and organizes the South Street Soup Kitchen. Alex checked him out—like *checked him out*—and he's completely clean." Alex was my good friend Sandra's husband, and also a world-class computer hacker. When I said Alex had checked out Mr. Jackson, I truly meant it. The man was a saint.

"Then why would he suggest a fund with an eleven percent stake in Monsanto?"

"Probably because he's trying to do his job, which is invest our money where it'll have the best return. We can pick a different fund."

He said nothing, just continued to shake his head slowly. Meanwhile, I was holding on to my composure by sheer force of will. But when we ended the call I was likely going to dismember Greg's favorite boxer briefs and hide his cell phone charger. He always did this. He always found a reason not to sign.

Desperate and beyond aggravated, I scoffed, "If I show you my breasts will you sign the papers?"

Greg's eyes narrowed until he was squinting. He turned his head to the side, glaring at me as though he were both trying to discern whether or not I was being serious and whether seeing my boobs was worth compromising his morals.

"Add an emailed photo of your ass and you have a deal."

I did growl then, and this time my face fell into my hands. If he didn't sign those transfer papers, then I would send him a picture of an ass. Maybe lots of asses. Only they wouldn't be mine. And they wouldn't be human. They would be equine.

"Fiona, darling, I'm not trying to aggravate you. You know where and how we invest is important to me." His voice was soft, beseeching, and he knew exactly what he was doing. I loved his voice; I loved his posh British accent; I loved it when he called me darling, which—after fourteen years of marriage—he rarely did anymore.

Usually I could laugh off his churlishness and bring him around to my perspective using well-reasoned arguments and my wifely wiles. But I didn't have the time or the mental energy at present to entertain my forty-one-year-old husband's plethora of opinions—opinions I usually considered endearing and charming.

For some reason, in this instance, his opinion didn't feel at all charming. It struck me as burdensome and self-indulgent. Like he was being dismissive of the work I'd done, the massive amount of time and effort I'd spent on resolving this vitally important issue.

"I have to go," I finally said, because I did have to go. But also because my head hurt and I couldn't talk to him anymore without losing my temper.

"Okay . . ."

I wasn't looking at him, my brain was full of fire ants, but I heard the reluctance and surprise in his voice.

"Okay. Bye, Greg." I lifted my gaze and scanned the screen for the location of the cursor, moving the mouse to the *end call* button.

"I love you, Fiona," he said, his voice still soft, coaxing, and maybe a little confused.

I gave him a flat smile and nodded, responding reflexively, "I love you, too."

"Don't be angry."

I shrugged. "I have to go."

"Okay, love."

"Bye."

"Wait, Fiona—"

I ended the call before he could complete his thought and immediately regretted it. I would apologize to him later. Staring at the desktop icons for a full minute, I contemplated what to do next.

I wouldn't dismember his boxer briefs. I loved it when he walked around in just his boxer briefs. He'd maintained the lithe runner's build from our college days. Even if he hadn't, I would still enjoy watching him walk around half-naked, because he was my husband, he was mine, and I was his. I truly adored him . . . most of the time.

But if he didn't pick a different fund and sign those papers, I was seriously considering hiding all the cell phone chargers he kept in the apartment.

I shook my head, dispelling the childish impulse, and checked my watch again. It was time to go.

As I grabbed my bag and left our apartment, a sinister voice in my head—tired of being covered in fire ants—reminded me there was another option. I could fake his signature and never tell him, invest the money without him knowing. Just contemplating it made my stomach hurt. It was a line I wasn't ready to cross. I'd already allowed Grace— who is five-years old—to have a princess costume to wear to a slumber party, and Jack—who is eight—to play soccer without Greg's consent.

I hadn't even asked Greg because I'd known what he would have said.

That's right. Greg had an opinion about princess costumes and boys playing sports—he was against both. I knew for a fact he hated princess culture, loathed the *Disney machinery of patriarchal oppression and objectification* as he called it. He'd also said in the past if Jack played sports then Grace had to as well. Which was why Jack was currently taking ballet with Grace—because if Grace took ballet, Jack had to as well. Jack didn't mind learning to dance, as long as he also got to play soccer.

But Grace didn't want to play soccer. She wanted to wear pink and play with dolls. She also loved superheroes, Legos, drawing, Darth Vader, and astronomy. She was a great kid, who happened to love dressing as a princess. So while he was gone, I bent the rules. Just a little.

"Hey, earth to Fiona. Anyone home?"

I started blinking as I brought my neighbor into focus. He was holding the elevator doors open, had likely said hello, and I'd been so lost in my thoughts I hadn't noticed. This level of distraction was *very* unlike me; awareness and the cataloging of my surroundings was typically second nature. Apparently, I was extremely upset.

I rushed forward into the lift and turned to give him an apologetic smile as he walked in after me. "Oh, hi. Thanks. Sorry, Matt. I'm a little preoccupied. Sorry."

He pressed the button for the lobby and stepped back to face me, tilting his head to the side, his light brown eyes assessing as they moved over my face. "Are you okay?"

"Yes. How are you?"

"Just fine," he responded slowly, openly inspecting me according to his habit.

I'd first met Matthew Simmons when I was nine. He'd been two. His parents and my parents were both unhappily married and belonged to the same country club. I babysat him a few times over the years, one of the few normal teenage activities I'd been allowed.

Matt had moved in next door to the kids and me two weeks after Christmas. I hadn't realized it was the same Matty Simmons until I'd brought him a welcome-to-the-building dinner and he'd blurted, "*Peona!*" The name he'd given me when he was a toddler.

This habit, openly scrutinizing people, was something he'd done even when he was still in diapers. And after living next door to Professor Matthew Simmons for the last two months, I knew evaluating and calculating were his adult default as well.

My smile grew more sincere the longer he scrutinized me. Matty—now Matt—had grown to be adorably peculiar and nerdy. In fact, he was brazenly nerdy; but he was also nice and genuine. He'd always been nice and genuine.

Regardless, I'd had Alex run a background check on the professor—I might have been a little slap happy with the background checks, but suspicious was my default. Grace and Jack had warmed to him so quickly. The man was an open book. Undergrad at Caltech, post grad at MIT, computer scientist, associate professor at the University of Chicago, divorced two years ago and presently married to his work, terrible cook. He was also surprisingly good with kids, though he had none.

And my parents and his parents still belonged to the same country club.

"How's Grace's science fair project coming along?"

I pulled on my gloves and bobbed my head back and forth. "So-so. She convinced the kids to taste the PTC strip, but can't get them to eat the broccoli." Grace was trying to determine how many of the children in her second grade class were "super tasters," meaning more sensitive to certain foods than the rest of the population.

"Well, let me know if you need any help."

"I appreciate the offer."

"I'm not being altruistic." His dark eyebrows lifted high on his forehead, a display of pointed sincerity. "I'd do almost anything for another of your roast chicken dinners."

My grin widened. "Then why don't you come over and help Grace with her science fair project on Saturday? I was planning to make roast chicken anyway."

Matt nodded before I'd finished making the offer. "I accept," he blurted as the elevator dinged, as though marking his acceptance rather than our arrival to the lobby. We both laughed and filed out, parting ways at the entrance to the building after another few minutes of small talk.

Despite the distraction of nerdy and nice Professor Simmons, I was soon stewing in my discontent again. I stewed as I catalogued the inhabitants of the train, making note of threat likelihood, the location of exit points, and potential weapons. One man near the end of the train was holding an umbrella tucked under his arm; this was odd because it was snowing, not raining.

I kept my eyes on him when the train stopped—still stewing in my earlier frustration—and watched him as we both departed. When we exited the train station, he opened the umbrella and turned left. Apparently he didn't want any snowflakes to fall on his waterproof nylon jacket.

Delores Day's Dance Studio was on the third floor of a mixed-use brownstone, and I arrived on time. Several mothers, fathers, and nannies—all of which I recognized—were crowded around the door between the practice room and the waiting area. Kids, mostly little girls in tight buns, pink leotards, and stockings, skipped out of the classroom to their caregivers.

I nodded and smiled, chitchatted with the gathered parents about nothing in particular, and craned my neck for a glimpse of my munchkins. When they didn't appear after a few minutes, I excused myself from the circle of adults wrangling their own children and poked my head into the classroom. Grace was sitting on the floor trying to tie her snow boots and waved at me immediately; Jack was sitting on a bench in front of a piano. His back was to me, and he appeared to be in deep conversation with their ballet teacher. Miss Delores Day was eighty, at least, and in better shape than most thirty-year-olds I knew. She was also sassier than most thirty-year-olds I knew.

Letting the door close behind me, I crossed the room, the sound of my footsteps drawing Delores's and Jack's attention. The older woman gave me a broad smile and glided to meet me halfway across the room with the grace of a life-long dancer.

"Mrs. Archer."

"Please, call me Fiona." I waved away the formality, my attention moving between Jack and his teacher. "Is everything all right?"

"Oh, yes. Everything is excellent. Jack was filling in for Mrs. St. Claire again. He is such a dear boy. A disinterested dancer, but a dear boy."

"Filling in?" I frowned at Delores then looked to Jack for a clue; he wasn't looking at me, his dark eyes were affixed to the keys of the instrument and I noted his cheeks were red. "Doesn't Mrs. St. Claire provide the piano accompaniment?"

"That's right. He has a real gift, though he's a bit rusty on the "Dance of the Four Swans." More practicing at home should straighten all that out. Now, I do want to talk to you about—"

"Wait, hold on." I held my hands up to keep her from continuing. "I think one of us is confused. Jack doesn't play the piano. He doesn't play any instruments."

Delores squinted at me, as though she didn't understand my words. "What was that, dear?"

"Jack doesn't play the piano."

"Yes, he does."

"No, he doesn't."

"Well then he does a good job of pretending to play Tchaikovsky."

"Wha-what?" Why was it suddenly hot in the dance studio?

I turned my confused frown to my son and found him watching me with a gaze too much like Greg's. His face was angelic, but his eyes held a hint of devilry and guilt.

"Jack?" I appealed to him. "What's this all about?"

He shrugged. "I've been messing around a little." I didn't miss how his fingers stroked the white keys of the piano with affection.

"Messing around?" Delores and I asked in unison.

"My dear boy, one does not mess around with Tchaikovsky's *Swan Lake*." Delores straightened her spine and sniffed in his direction, as though he'd offended her.

"When? Where?" My head was swimming and I needed to lean against something sturdy. I walked to the upright piano and placed a hand on it.

He shrugged again. "Here. At school. At Professor Simmons's."

"Have you been getting piano lessons? At school?"

"No. But Ms. Pastizo lets me in the chorus room during lunch."

"Ms. Pastizo lets you in the chorus room . . . ?" I repeated. I was so confused. Jack was only eight, never had a music lesson, never—to my knowledge—displayed any interest in music or taking lessons. I glanced between him and the instrument. "Play something, please."

He swallowed, his gaze wide and watchful . . . and wary. "I still want to play soccer."

"What?"

"If I have to choose between music and soccer, I want to play soccer." Jack crossed his arms over his chest.

"I promised you, you can play soccer this spring and I will keep my promise." My gaze flickered to Delores, who was now watching us with dawning comprehension.

"He's never had a lesson." She made this statement to the room rather than to any one of its inhabitants, and with no small amount of wonder and awe.

Her wonder and awe made me nervous. "Jack, play Tchaikovsky. Play the Dance of the Six Ducks."

"The Dance of the Four Swans," Delores provided gently, coming to stand next to me.

"Yes. That one." I knew nothing about Tchaikovsky's music other than what I heard on the local NPR classical radio station. I couldn't believe my young son was capable of playing chopsticks, let alone anything so complicated.

Jack narrowed his eyes with protest, so I narrowed mine with warning. My mom-glare must've been sufficiently threatening because he sighed loudly and placed his hands on the keys. He gave one more dramatic sigh before his eyes lost focus and he began playing.

And *ohmydearGodinheaven*, my son was playing the Jig of the Even Numbered Birds by Tchaikovsky. And he was playing it well. Remarkably well. Without sheet music. My jaw dropped and I covered my open mouth with shaking fingers.

"Oh my God."

Delores's hand closed over my shoulder and I turned my gaze to hers. She was smiling at me, a knowing smile, an elated smile. And it terrified me.

"He's never had a lesson?"

I shook my head.

"Then you know what this means."

I shook my head again—faster this time—not because I didn't know what his spontaneous piano playing meant, but because I didn't want her to say it.

"How lovely," she said, obviously not understanding the ramifications of her next words, "Jack is a prodigy."

***

"YOU HAVE TO take a bath."

"But the water is wet."

"That's the point of water."

"Can't I take a sand bath?"

I looked to the heavens beyond the ceiling of our apartment. "What are you talking about?"

"Jack says people who live in the desert take sand baths." Grace's little voice adopted an accusatory edge, as though I'd been keeping this vital piece of information from her. As though I'd been needlessly subjecting her to the horror of wet baths for the last five years, like some sort of barbarian water-pusher.

"We don't live in the desert. We live in snowy Chicago, where water abounds—not sand."

I heard the distinct ring of my cell phone over the rush of the faucet and Grace's protests.

"But—"

"No. No more arguing, Grace. Get in the bath."

"But—"

"If I have to tell you one more time to get in the bath . . ." I turned to leave, rubbing my forehead, the sharp spike of pain radiating from my temples. If Greg were here he'd know how to get Grace into the bath without a fight. He was the master of convincing our children to brush their teeth and go to bed on time, all the while making everything fun.

Greg hardly ever being home meant it was only me who was failing miserably at convincing my children personal hygiene was important.

Out of nowhere I was overwhelmed by a sense of longing for my husband, a need so visceral I had to stop for a second and lean against the wall, close my eyes to rein in my emotions. I wished Greg were home. I wished for him all the time.

I quickly banished the wish. He was where he needed to be. Doing good work, making a difference in the world, providing for his family. Wishing only served to make me sad. I didn't have time to be sad.

I needed to stay focused.

"I don't want a bath—"

"GRACE, GET IN THE BATH!"

"Fine," she grumbled to my back. Then I heard her pathetic wail, "I hate baths!"

And I hated yelling at my children.

I inwardly cringed as I left the bathroom and jogged to the living room. I swallowed the lump of regret in my throat as I searched for my phone. My head was full of too many thoughts, none of which brought any clarity. The fire ants had been joined by bees. The bees brought their viscous honey, slowing all processes to a virtual halt.

Shell-shocked after what I'd discovered about Jack this afternoon, I'd ushered the kids out of the dance studio and gone through the motions of escorting the children home, making their dinner, and assisting with homework. As usual, I argued with Grace about taking her bath and I negotiated with Jack to a half hour of playing Minecraft, and only after reading one of his chapter books for a full hour.

It was a typical evening in the Archer household: Just the three of us, me tripping over little shoes, Grace preferring dirty to clean, and Jack complaining about the distressing lack of pizza on his plate.

Except my heart was heavy with worry and my head was pounding.

I swiped my thumb across the screen of my cell phone after identifying the caller as our babysitter; my worried heart sank further. "Hi Jennifer. What's up?"

"Hi Fiona, this is Jennifer's mom. I am so sorry but she can't babysit tomorrow night or take the kids in the morning. We just got back from the doctor's and she has strep throat."

"Oh goodness!" I dropped to the couch, rubbing my forehead with my fingers, more worry rising in my throat. I would have to find an alternate babysitter for the next night. A member of my knitting group, my good friend Ashley Winston—nurse and book worm—was moving to Tennessee.

Our close-knit band of friends had planned a going-away party for her, scheduled for tomorrow night. I'd made the cake. I'd spent all morning on it, toasting mountains of coconut for the special meringue frosting. But the real issue was Jennifer had babysat two days prior. "Well, I hope she's okay."

"The antibiotics should do the trick. You might want to keep an eye on Grace and Jack. The doctor said she might have been contagious for the last few days."

I nodded, her warning an echo to my thoughts. "I'll do that."

"Thanks. And about tomorrow morning, I am so sorry. I know this is bad timing."

It was bad timing. Jennifer was supposed to wake the kids and take them to school so I could be at the hospital by 6:00 a.m. I had an early morning MRI scheduled, part of my once-every-two-years tumor screening. I was going on sixteen years in remission, but I'd been having headaches recently, headaches I hadn't given myself permission to think about.

I had too many other things to think about.

"Don't worry about it. I hope Jennifer feels better soon."

After a few additional pleasantries, I ended the call as another of Grace's wails sailed through the apartment. "Why can't we live in the desert?"

I huffed a frustrated laugh and shook my head, collapsing back against the cushions. First things first, I needed to leave a message with the hospital about rescheduling my MRI. Then I would go through my list of alternate babysitters and try to find a replacement for Ashley's going-away party. Then I would pour myself a Julia Child-sized glass of wine—so, the entire bottle—and wrangle my adorable children who I loved (*I do, I love them, I love them . . . I do, truly*) through their bedtime routine.

Then and only then would I sort out what to do about Jack's miraculous musical acumen.

I dialed the hospital and was immediately placed on hold. While I waited, a knock on the front door pulled me from the classic rock wait music, specifically, "Every Rose Has Its Thorn." But before I could stand from the sofa, Jack bolted from his room.

"I'll get it!"

"No, you will not get it." I was hot on his heels and stopped him with a hand on his shoulder. "What are you thinking? You don't answer the door without asking first. You know that."

"But it's Professor Simmons."

"How do you know it's Professor Simmons?"

"Because he said he was going to bring me his space atlas."

"When was this?" I stepped in front of Jack and peeked through the peephole. Sure enough, it was Professor Matthew Simmons.

"Yesterday. When we came home from school, remember?"

Nonplussed, I frowned as I opened the door. I didn't remember. Well, I remembered seeing Matty yesterday morning, but I didn't remember any conversation about a space atlas.

"Peona." Matty nodded his head at me in an efficient greeting, his use of the nickname inspiring a wave of nostalgia. I was pretty sure I'd never be able to look at him without seeing the toddler he used to be. Of course, since he was always wearing a vintage Star Wars T-shirt—no matter the time of day—it was difficult for me to see him as anything other than a big kid.

Matty pulled a large, hardbound book from under his arm and presented it to Jack. "Jack, the promised space atlas."

Jack grabbed it from Matty, his eyes wide and excited. "Whoa! Thanks!"

The peculiar professor grinned at my son's enthusiasm. "No problem at all."

I stepped to the side and motioned with my hand. "Won't you come in? I'm sure Jack would appreciate a tour of the atlas."

Matty didn't hesitate and quickly stepped into our apartment. "Sure, just for a bit. I don't suppose you have any leftovers from dinner?"

"Oh good Lord! You are a food addict."

"No, I'm a *good* food addict. And you make good food."

I shut the door behind him and gave him an indulgent smile. "We had spare ribs, twice-baked potatoes, and broccoli for dinner. Help yourself to anything in the fridge."

"Twice-baked potatoes!? Good God, woman." His eyes bulged, he didn't need to be told twice. Matty quickly shuffled by me and sprinted for the kitchen.

Meanwhile, Jack was already on the carpet in the living room, flipping through the massive pages of the atlas. "This is so cool."

I heard the fridge open and close, the telltale sounds of jars and dishes rattling as he rummaged. "Are you sure I can have anything in here?

Anything at all?" Matty called from the kitchen.

"Yes, help yourself." My eyes snagged on a pile of mail I must've left forgotten on the coffee table yesterday. I frowned at it, feeling rising frustration at my increasing forgetfulness.

"Anything? Anything at all? Even the ca—"

"Go for it, but don't make a mess in the kitchen. Use a paper plate," I interrupted, responding absentmindedly, flipping through the mail and relieved when I found it all to be advertisements and credit card offers.

"Your kitchen is so clean, it sparkles," Matty marveled, and I heard the fridge close. "How do you do that?"

Of course he hadn't seen the kitchen yesterday. Yesterday it was a disaster deserving of a biohazard warning. I'd spent all day yesterday and this morning picking up, cleaning, and doing laundry. It was my only chance to get the place straightened up before my Tuesday night knitting group descended. It was my week to host.

Now I just had to keep it clean for the next week . . .

"What's an alabeado?" Jack struggled to pronounce.

"Albedo," I corrected as I stood and walked to the shredding bin. "It's an attribute measurement, the reflective property of an object that isn't a source of light. Right, Matty?"

"More or less," Matty said as he shuffled back into the living room, his words garbled as he was obviously trying to talk over a mouthful of food.

I smirked as I lifted my eyes from the shredding, but then the smile fell away and a cold panic hit me in the chest when I saw what he was eating.

It was cake.

It was Ashley's cake.

He was eating Ashley's cake!

Jack must've looked up and noticed the contents of Matty's plate as well, because he gasped loudly then said, "Ooooohhhh! You are in soooooo much trouble!"

CHAPTER 2

Dear Husband,
You are my home. Which is astounding, since I've never really had one
before. I didn't even know the meaning before you walked into my life.
You give me things I never even knew I was missing.

-Morgan
Letter
Iowa, USA
Married 4 years

~Present Day~

Fiona

THE FIRE ANTS in my brain were back. My face must've
communicated my despair because the look on Matty's face and his rush
of words were effusively apologetic. "Oh no. I am so sorry, I'm so, so
sorry! You said anything in the fridge and I love coconut and . . . oh shit,
this is fucking fantastic cake."

"Ooooooooohhhh! You cussed! He cussed!" Jack stood and bounced on
his feet, pointing at Matty like I might need assistance deciphering who
exactly had said the expletives.

"Ahhhh!" Matty's face contorted with remorseful horror.

Jack's eyes were wide and excited. "He said fu—"

"Don't say it!" Matty and I cut him off in unison.

Jack clamped his mouth shut, looking thwarted and frustrated.

Matty groaned. "Sorry. I'm making a mess of things." Then he turned on his heel and rushed back into the kitchen. "I'll go put it back."

It took me a few seconds to move past my despairing shock, and another few to process his words—he was going to *put it back.*

"Wait, what? What are you doing?" I called as I jogged to the kitchen, "You can't put back cake. There is no putting cake back, and you've already taken a bite."

I found Matty hunched over the cake. He'd slid his wedge back into place and was using his finger to blur the line he'd made in the meringue frosting. He was making a mess.

"Stop—"

"I am so sorry, Fiona. Sometimes my stomach does the thinking and I'm powerless against it. Some people have a devil and an angel on their shoulders; I have a stomach on one side and a tongue with giant papillae on the other. And then there's my irrational love for coconut."

I grabbed his hand and removed it *and* his person from the vicinity of the cake; then I turned to assess the damage. It was beyond repair. The meringue was crushed, and he'd flattened the coconut in his haste to return his piece. I sighed sadly. It looked old and tired, rumpled and ruined.

And I had an odd thought: the cake was me.

I was the cake.

I was a mess.

And I had a piece missing . . .

Peripherally, I saw Jack peek into the kitchen, his big eyes moving between Matty, the cake, and me; and then he said, "It's ruined."

"Yes. Yes, it is," I said.

Jack hesitated, stepped into the kitchen, and licked his lips; hope permeated his question as he asked, "Does that mean we can eat it now?"

I looked at my son and unexpectedly laughed. And once I laughed I couldn't stop. I gripped the counter and held my stomach. But with the laughter also came tears. And soon there was no laughter, only tears.

The two males in the kitchen were paralyzed by my outburst, and I was aware of their eyes on me, confused and panicked. Eventually, Matty stepped forward and wrapped his arm around my shoulders, turning my face to his chest.

"Jack, make your mom a cup of tea, please." As he said this, he escorted me out of the kitchen and into the living room, awkwardly patting my back and guiding me to the sofa.

We didn't speak. I cried for another minute, but no longer. I was able to rein in the tears by pulling away, gathering several deep breaths, and mentally rearranging my schedule for the next day. Since I had to cancel the doctor's appointment, I would be able to make another cake.

No big deal.

I could handle this.

No problem.

Everything happens for a reason.

I was not a crier.

I didn't know why I was crying now.

No need for these ridiculous tears.

"I'm really sorry," he said again, a note of desperation in his voice.

"No, I'm sorry." I shook my head, wiping my eyes. "I don't know what came over me. It's just a cake, and I did say anything in the fridge was fine. I think I'm just tired. Grace hasn't been sleeping well this last week and I've . . . well, I haven't been sleeping well either, and there's a lot going on."

I felt his scrutinizing gaze moving over my features as I stared at a spot on my jeans, trying to remember how much coconut I had left in the pantry. I would skip my glass of wine, get my contract work done tonight, and make the cake in the morning after taking the kids to school. I could talk to Jack's teacher about the field trip, purchase the rest of the cake ingredients, and stop by the hardware store for a new garbage disposal . . .

Neither of us spoke for a long minute until Matty asked, "What's that music?"

I glanced at the phone in my hand I hadn't realized I was still holding; "Every Rose Has Its Thorn" had been replaced with "Welcome to The Jungle."

"Oh, I'm on hold with the hospital."

"The hospital?"

"Yes. My sitter just cancelled as she's sick with strep throat."

"Is she in the hospital? For strep throat?"

"No. She's at home with antibiotics. I have to cancel my appointment for tomorrow."

Matty's confused frown smoothed but was replaced with concerned surprise. "Your appointment?"

"Yes. I had an MRI scheduled for six thirty a.m. I've been having headaches. Anyway, the sitter was going to take the kids into school for me, but since she's sick I'm going to reschedule. Which is why I'm on hold now."

Matty reached for my hand holding the phone, drawing my eyes to his. "Fiona, please let me take the kids in. I am so sorry about the cake; let me make it up to you. Then you don't need to cancel your appointment."

"No, no. I can't ask you to do that." I waved away his suggestion.

"You're not asking. I'm offering. It's no trouble at all. I don't have office hours tomorrow until three. It'll give me a reason to wake up before noon."

"No . . ."

"You'd be doing me a favor. It would give me another opportunity to raid your fridge—legal food this time. Mine only has moldy cheese of questionable origin. It's green, but I'm pretty sure it started out orange, and unless it's actually oxidized copper, I should use a hazmat suit for its disposal."

I shook my head. "It's not merely getting the kids to school. I have to talk to his teacher about his field trip, stop by the store for new coconut cake ingredients and poster board for the science fair. Plus the garbage disposal is broken and I need to pick up a new one."

"I can do those things, plus I'll install the new disposal for you."

"And the dishwasher is broken, I need to—"

"Let me take a look at it."

"I know what's wrong with it, I just need some time to fix it."

"I'll do it."

"But—"

"The water is too hot! It's TOOOOOOOOOO HOOOOOOOOOOT!" Grace wailed from the bathroom. Instead of inspiring my sympathy, I huffed another sad laugh.

"Just a minute, Grace. I'll be right there," I called, trying to keep the frustrated laughter out of my voice lest she think I was relishing in her anguish.

"Let me help," Matty said gently, tapping my knee with the knuckles of one hand. Before I could respond, he shook his head and spoke over my protest. "Listen, we've known each other forever, right? When I moved into the building two months ago, you brought me a welcome-neighbor dinner before you knew who I was. Remember that? You had Jack and Grace bring drawings, in case I didn't have anything for my walls. Those drawings are now framed and hanging in my dining room. It was the first time I'd had a home-cooked meal in seven years, since my mother's cook left to go back to Croatia. You know how it was growing up in my family. You're more family to me than they are. It was maybe the first time I'd *ever* felt truly welcomed."

I huffed, feeling torn and tempted. It would be so nice, *so nice*, such a welcome break to accept the help he offered.

His smile turned teasing. "Let me do this, otherwise I'll drown in guilt. Honestly, I wouldn't offer except your children are pretty awesome. Besides, how hard could it be?"

"Now it's TOOOOOOOOO COOOOOOOOOOOLD!" Grace's renewed bellowing arrived as Matt finished speaking. I lifted my eyebrows at him, silently challenging his last question.

Matty shrugged. "Well, I'll do my best."

The music originating from my cell phone switched from "Welcome to the Jungle," to "Pour Some Sugar On Me." The shift in tempo reminded me I was still on hold with the hospital. It also made me wonder who was responsible for choosing the wait music.

"I don't know." My words were reluctant, not because I didn't trust Matty but because I hated asking for help. I hated the idea of needing it. I knew I could do everything myself. I didn't *need* his help . . . but the offer to share my burdens was so enticing.

Plus I wasn't certain Matty would actually succeed in getting the kids ready, make it to school on time, and still be on speaking terms with me afterward.

"I don't mind." He grinned like it was all settled, placing his hand on my knee and giving it a quick squeeze before standing. "What time do you need me?"

I studied the screen of my phone for a few seconds, then finally ended the call and stood as well, giving Matty a resigned smile. "Five thirty. And I'll leave detailed instructions for you. Grace and Jack can get ready on their own, but they just need a bit of prodding when they start daydreaming instead of putting on their snow boots. And the school isn't far, two blocks."

"Sounds good." He said this earnestly, like he was truly looking forward to taking the kids to school.

I studied his cheerful expression for a long moment as his eyes moved to Jack, who was currently absorbed in his space atlas. Matty's small smile held true affection as he looked at my son. My chest filled with warmth and gratitude. When another person, especially one not related by blood, takes a sincere interest in the wellbeing of my kids, it makes my heart go soft.

I decided Matty Simmons was more than nice. He was a good guy. He was a good friend.

***

GRACE WOKE ME by climbing into my bed at 3:27 a.m., another nightmare. We cuddled and I soothed her. Once she was sleeping peacefully, I started my day.

After skipping my shower and quickly getting dressed, I responded to several work emails, typed detailed directions for the kids, and had three minutes to apply a little makeup before Matty arrived at 5:27 a.m., looking bleary-eyed, nervous, and enthusiastic.

I made it to the hospital by 6:00 a.m. and then waited. And waited. And waited.

But I put the waiting to good use. First, I secured an alternate babysitter for the evening. Then I whipped out my laptop and caught up on my schematics for work. I was feeling good about the status of the project when I was finally told at 10:06 a.m. the hospital was having problems with the MRI machine and the scan would have to be rescheduled.

Beyond irritated, I stemmed my inconvenient urge to (figuratively) shoot the messenger. It wasn't the medical assistant's fault the machine wasn't working, he didn't deserve my ire.

So I took several calming breaths and mumbled to myself, "It is what it is."

Then I waited some more before having my blood drawn and meeting with my oncologist. I calmly told him about the headaches. He promised to get me in for a new MRI appointment as soon as possible.

I was friendly with his nurse, Liz Shaffer—average height and build, sandy-blonde hair, brown eyes, married with two kids, nosy but well-meaning—and she knew both my knitting group friends, Sandra and Ashley, from working at the hospital. Sadly, Liz didn't knit. But she was funny and kind and had known me since I moved out to the mid-west from Virginia eighteen years ago. She was my first nurse at my first cancer-free follow-up appointment in Chicago. We'd grown up together in many ways.

Unfortunately, I didn't have much time to visit. So after chatting for about ten minutes, I sprinted out of the hospital. I made it home by 1:00 p.m. and figured I had barely enough time to take a shower and bake the cake before leaving to go pick up Grace and Jack from school.

As soon as I shut the front door, I heard Matty's voice call from inside the apartment. "Fiona?"

"Yes, I'm home. How did it go?"

"Great! I'm in the kitchen."

I jogged to the kitchen, impressed that the apartment was still clean, and found my neighbor's long, jean-clad legs and half of his bare torso sticking out from underneath the kitchen sink. I realized with some surprise that Matty Simmons had a six-pack. In fact, everywhere I could see was chiseled muscles and bronzed skin. This realization made me feel old because I used to babysit for someone who now had a six-pack.

"The kids were okay?"

"Yes. No problem. And I spoke to Jack's teacher about the field trip."

"Thank you."

"And the ingredients for the cake are on the counter, but I stopped by the bakery and secured a replacement cake just in case you run out of time. Obviously, it pales in comparison to your coconut genius, but better to be safe than sorry. I also noticed you were out of ketchup and some other things so I grabbed those as well."

See? Genuine and nice!

"Whoa, this cake is huge."

He'd purchased a giant sheet cake, enough for fifty people or more.

"Then there will be leftovers. Everyone loves leftovers."

"Thank you, Matt." I surmised he was counting on being the recipient of said leftovers. "And thanks for keeping the place clean. I don't know how you managed it. But I have friends coming over Tuesday night and I truly appreciate the lack of mess."

"No problem. I had them use paper plates for their breakfast. Oh! Also, there was no poster board," Matty paused and I heard him grunt. His abdominal muscles flexed in conjunction with the sound of channel locks turning. "So I stopped by my office and grabbed five from the supply cabinet."

"Ah, thank you!" I walked to the counter and inspected the bags of groceries; everything I needed was present and accounted for. "Finding the poster board has been impossible."

"The dishwasher is fixed. Your suspicion was correct, it was the solenoid."

"This is the third time it's burnt out. I think I need a new dishwasher." I pulled off my jacket and hung it on the back of a kitchen chair, mentally calculating how soon I could afford a new dishwasher. The extra income from my contracting work would definitely help.

"Probably not a bad idea," he agreed, sounding distracted.

"Thank you so much for all your help, Matt." I said this to his legs as his upper body was still hidden under the sink. I observed, in addition to his shirt, he'd removed his shoes. He had a tattoo of the pi symbol on his left foot. I smirked at this. He was such a nerd. "If you need to go, I can take over from here."

"No rush. I think I'm about finished with the disposal. Go relax or something."

I smiled wistfully at the idea of relaxing. "No time. I need to take a shower and get this cake baking."

"Then go take a shower, I'll be a few more minutes."

"Thank you, so much, for—"

"Stop thanking me. Instead I'll take the ruined cake—the cake *I* ruined—and we'll call it even."

"You have a deal." My eye caught the time on the wall clock hanging over the table. I needed to hurry. Darting from the kitchen, I made for my bathroom, swiftly undressing as I shut the door behind me. When I was in my birthday suit, I reached into the shower to turn on the water.

Nothing happened.

I stared at the inactive showerhead and frowned. I'm ashamed to admit it took me a full ten seconds to realize nothing was happening because Matty had obviously turned off the water to the apartment in order to fix the dishwasher. Sighing when I couldn't locate my bathrobe, I pulled an oversized towel from the rack and wrapped it around myself, then speed-walked to the living room. All the while making a mental list of the things I needed to accomplish before leaving for Ashley's party at 4:00 p.m.

"Hey, Matt," I called, "Did you turn the water off?"

"Who's Matt?" a voice at my left asked, making me jump and crouch into a fighting stance as my eyes flew to the source.

And then I saw him.

I saw Greg.

He was . . . here.

Standing in the entranceway to the apartment, a small duffle bag on his shoulder. His day-old scruff was gone. He looked exhausted, but happy.

My confused heart stuttered then leapt, beating excitedly before my confused brain could figure out what was going on.

We stared at each other for several seconds, his grin growing wider, until I finally managed to breathe out, "Oh my God!"

"No, darling. It's just your husband."

Not giving me three seconds to recover, he dropped his bag to the floor, crossed the room, and wrapped me in his arms.

I returned the embrace as I was too stunned to do anything else but sputter, "How-when-how . . . ?" And, inexplicably, my eyes stung.

Greg backed me against the wall in the living room and kissed me, groaning when his mouth met mine. Meanwhile, my eyes were wide as I watched him, blinking away the unexpected rush of liquid emotion, unable to process the truth of his presence, here, home, and not off the coast of South Africa on an oil rig.

"Stop staring and kiss me, would you?" His hand fisted in my hair and he tugged, angling my head back, then bending to bite my neck, sending wonderful sensation shivers racing over every inch of my skin. "Ah, you're delicious."

I shook my muddled head and placed my hands on his shoulders, pushing him away so I could see his face. I needed to see he was real and not a figment of my imagination.

Before I could speak, Matty's voice carried to us as he exited the kitchen. "Yes, sorry about the water. I'll run downstairs and turn it back . . . on."

Greg stilled then tensed. I watched as he twisted and glanced at Matty over his shoulder. Still feeling astonished and confused by the sudden appearance of my husband, I stared at his neck and jaw for a long moment. I blinked, half expecting him to disappear. When he didn't, I peeked around Greg's large frame to where Matty was suspended just inside the kitchen.

I sensed Greg stiffen further and straighten. He turned from me to face our neighbor. "Who the hell are you?"

Matty's eyes were wide, clearly confused, and more than a little concerned when they met mine briefly, then flickered back to my husband's. "Uh, I'm Matt."

"Mat? As in, a small rectangular piece of carpet made for the express purpose of cleaning dirt from one's shoes?"

Greg's impolite words and clipped tone pulled me from my stupor and I smacked his shoulder. "Greg!" I pulled my towel tighter and walked around my rude husband to stand in between the two men.

"Oh, you're Greg," Matty said, sounding less confused, but more wary.

"Yeah. I'm Greg," he growled, making no attempt to disguise his hostility; but then, he never did.

"Greg, this is Matthew Simmons. He is our next door neighbor."

"Is that so?"

"Yes," I ground out, "that is so."

Matty, holding a kitchen towel, gave his palms another wipe before reaching out his hand to Greg. "Nice to meet you . . . ?"

Greg made no movement to accept the handshake, instead opting to narrow his eyes threateningly. "Why don't you have a shirt on, Matt?"

Matty's eyes widened and he dropped his hand as he glanced at his bare chest. "I, uh-I was just—"

"He was replacing the garbage disposal," I supplied, irritated with Greg's bad-mannered behavior. Furthermore, I was irritated that I was irritated, because my husband was home. He was home! He was here and I'd missed him and, instead of taking advantage of his presence, I was standing in my towel in the living room being irritated.

"My garbage disposal?" Greg's frown was severe as his gaze moved to me, ripe with accusation. "You let him replace *my* garbage disposal?"

"*Your* garbage disposal? What are you talking about?"

"I just installed that disposal."

"No, you didn't. It's been three years. And Grace ruined it in January."

"How did she do that?"

"She put Jack's rock collection in the sink and turned it on as revenge for him hiding her Barbie dolls."

Greg blinked and he appeared to be digesting this information with some difficulty. At last he said, "Grace has Barbie dolls? When did she get Barbie dolls?"

Sigh . . .

I glanced at the ceiling and shook my head, then turned to poor Professor Matthew Simmons. "Thank you for your help, Matt. I really appreciate it."

Matty's eyes moved between us, then finally settled on me. "No problem. I'll just get my tools and . . . other stuff." He tossed his thumb over his shoulder, lingered awkwardly in the doorway for two seconds, then disappeared back into the kitchen.

I slid my eyes to Greg and found my husband still staring at the spot where Matty had been standing, an angry frown creasing his tired features.

"What is wrong with you?" I asked in a tight whisper, gripping the towel at my chest.

"What is wrong with me?"

"Yes. What was that?" I motioned to the kitchen, to Matt, keeping my voice low.

My husband's eyes flashed and he spoke through gritted teeth, "A man, who happens to live next door to my family, takes off his clothes in my home while my beautiful wife is walking around in nothing but a towel . . ." Greg's typically dry delivery was intoned with an extra helping of scathing sarcasm as he added, "Yeah. Seems legit."

It took me a few seconds to recover from his insinuation, but when I did I forgot to lower my voice. "I used to babysit him, Greg! I changed his diapers."

"Babysit him? What?" He looked truly perplexed, like I'd revealed Matt was responsible for all the *Star Wars* prequels, but then his eyes narrowed again as though he'd just realized something important. "Wait, so you've seen his penis?"

I gasped, then inadvertently laughed my frustration. "Really? That's the take-home message? That I've seen his penis? If it makes you feel any better, it was about this long." I held my thumb and forefinger apart to indicate an inch.

At the same moment Matt reappeared in the living room—shirt on—and unwisely said, "Hey! I was only two years old. It's at least fifteen times larger now."

"Fifteen times? Prone to exaggeration, aren't you?" Greg drawled, giving Matt a look of plain disbelief.

"Not longer, larger." Matt shrugged innocently, like he was clarifying the size of his sofa and not his man parts. "I was referring to volume, not necessarily length—though it is—"

"Oh good Lord." I spoke over him, my fingers coming to my forehead. I rubbed the space between my eyebrows where a new headache flared, causing me to wince.

"Not helpful or pertinent information, Matt." Greg's eyes sliced to Matt, but then he did a double take. "Hey, wait a minute. Is that a cake? Who said you could have that cake?"

Matt looked from me to Greg, then took a step back and toward the front door, shifting the cake in his hands like he might make a run for it. "Fiona. She said I could have it. It's my cake."

Greg's eyebrows jumped, his mouth fell open with livid shock, and he turned his glare back to me. "You made him *the* coconut cake?"

Pointedly not looking at my husband, I turned to Matt and said sincerely, "Please, take the cake. And thank you again for your help this morning. It made all the difference. If you wouldn't mind, could you please stop by the basement and turn the water back on in the apartment?"

My neighbor gave me a quick smile, opened his mouth to respond, but then seemed to think better of it. Instead, he nodded solemnly and quickly made for the exit. The sound of our front door opening and closing was followed by a long silence, during which I took several deep breaths, attempting to calm and arrange my thoughts.

I decided I wouldn't waste time being angry. I would ignore Greg's boorish and slightly insulting behavior. Seeing him, having him here in person was a rare gift. I would determine how long he'd be in town and make the most of it.

And then I was going to distract him while I hid all the kids' contraband in their rooms, including but not limited to Grace's Barbie dolls and princess dress, as well as Jack's soccer bag and uniform.

"So . . . you babysat him?" Greg was the first to speak, his tone laced with the barest hint of an apology.

I sat on the couch and gathered a deep breath. "I did. I babysat him for four years until he was eight."

"He's how much younger than you?" A shade of curiosity colored his words.

"He's seven years younger. I was nine and he was two when I helped his nanny change his diapers, but I didn't start watching him on my own until I was eleven and he was four."

I felt Greg's eyes on me, though I wasn't ready to meet them. I was still upset. I needed another minute to bottle my feelings of offended frustration.

"I see. And he, what? Tracked you down and moved in next door?"

"No," I responded evenly, though what I really wanted to do was call Greg out on his apparent jealousy. But what good would that do? I might feel better for three seconds—vindicated, superior, outraged—and then what? If I'd learned one thing over the course of our relationship, it was to pick my battles with the utmost care, because our greatest commodities were energy and time.

So I swallowed the urge and explained, "He moved in next door in January without realizing who I was. The kids and I took him dinner—as you know is my practice with every new person on the floor—and he recognized me."

"And he's been hanging around since?"

"No, Greg. He hasn't been *hanging* around since." I was abruptly exhausted and lifted my tired eyes to my husband. "Give me more credit than that. I had a doctor's appointment this morning. Jennifer cancelled last minute with strep throat, Matt offered to pitch in—with taking the kids to school, and with the garbage disposal and dishwasher and grocery shopping. The kids like him and I needed the help, so I accepted." I refused to feel guilty about accepting help . . . I refused. Yep.

Regardless, I still felt guilty for accepting help.

We stared at each other, me sitting on the couch, him hovering behind the large club chair. My throat was tight with regret because we could have been enjoying each other. Instead, we were studying each other, waiting for the other to react. I had to remind myself, it was always like this at first. The first few days and weeks when he returned from abroad were typically strained, like we needed to relearn how to be married. But usually I knew when he was coming home, and I would have time to mentally prepare for it.

"I'm sorry," he said, sounding and looking remorseful. "I've been traveling for almost twenty-four hours, and I'm out of sorts."

I nodded, giving him a small smile. "Thank you for apologizing."

"I'm sorry I was . . . rude to the child you used to babysit."

I barked a small laugh and shook my head.

Greg continued, "I mean, he looks like he's sixteen. How old is he again?"

"He's twenty-nine or so."

"Poor chap hasn't hit puberty yet."

"Greg . . ." I made a warning sound in the back of my throat.

"I'll go easier on him next time. Must be difficult walking the earth as a man-child."

"He's only a few inches shorter than you."

"But with men, a few inches makes all the difference."

This, of course, made me laugh. Despite my headache, despite the stress of the month and week and day, despite his terrible behavior, I was laughing. Thus was the magic of my husband.

Grinning like he'd won something, Greg moved to the sofa and put his arm around my shoulder, pulling me to his chest so I was laughing against it.

"I miss your laugh," he whispered as my laughter tapered, his lips next to my ear. I heard him hesitate before adding with dark desperation, "I've missed you."

His tone gave me pause, the ferocity of the simple sentiment. It sounded like a warning, or a call for help. I lifted my head from his warm chest and glanced at him, searching his face. He wasn't smiling. In fact, the intensity of his eyes, the hard set of his jaw, the slight frown hovering around his mouth sent a wave of alarmed concern through me.

I lifted my hand to his cheek and gently brushed my thumb over his temple. "Greg, honey, are you okay?"

He stared at me for a long moment. Stormy eyes were rimmed red with exhaustion . . . or maybe something else. As though he couldn't hold my stare any longer, he pulled me tighter against him and reclined on the couch, pressing my ear to where his heart beat.

"Just lay with me. I want to . . ." He sighed, squeezing me tighter before his hand caressed me through the length of the towel—my back, over my bottom, pausing at my thigh—slipping beneath the parted fabric. "I need to feel your skin."

We lay together for several wordless minutes, his fingertips skimming over my upper back and shoulders, my thigh and hip in an absentminded caress. I curled against him and kept my eye on the mantel clock, making sure we didn't loiter too long and neglect picking the kids up on time.

This exit and re-entry into each other's lives never grew easier. Rather, it became ritualistic, and this first silence was a sacred part of our ritual. We'd been doing this dance for fourteen years: voluntarily leaving each other, then coming back together after a prolonged period. Usually we would lie together, cuddling in silence, until we fell asleep. But we didn't have that luxury at present, because the kids' dismissal time was drawing precariously near.

Unfortunately, our wordless cuddling would have to be placed on hold. I was about to break the news when Greg, without any sign or warning, shifted to his side and peeled away the corners of the towel from my chest, stomach, and legs.

"Gorgeous. . ."

I frowned, trying to watch the progress of his hands and his face simultaneously. "What are you doing?"

"I'm going to get you off, before I leave to collect our delightful children."

My eyes widened in surprise. "As much as I appreciate the offer, we don't have time for that."

"Challenge accepted." He placed a kiss on my chin, then traced the line of my jaw with the tip of his tongue, ending his exploration by sucking my earlobe into his mouth.

I shivered, tensing. "You *just* walked in the door. And I haven't showered yet."

"You know I don't mind."

"But I do."

"Then I'll lend a helping hand."

I was pleasantly trapped between the couch and the wall created by my husband's long form. I watched as he leaned away, his eyes hungrily moving over my bare skin. He gently brushed the underside of my breasts with the back of his knuckles, making me shiver again.

I sighed, wanting to protest, but finding I had no will to voice a refusal. We hadn't been physically together since just after Christmas, seventy-nine days ago—but who's counting?

He felt so good, he knew me too well, was too intimate with the canvas of my body because he'd been the original—and the only—artist of my desire. I loved how he wanted me.

And this was especially true, and heady, during the first few weeks after his return.

"You have three minutes." I spread my legs and draped one over the back of the sofa, trying to keep my tone light. "You really think you can make this happen in three minutes?"

"No." His mouth dipped to my collarbone, nipping, licking; his hand, already between my legs, his softest touch making me instinctively arch against him. "I think I can make this happen twice in five minutes, and sprint to the school instead of walk."

"You'll be out of breath."

"So will you."

I started to laugh again, but then stopped, gasping as he touched me. My chest and stomach were now tight, my limbs growing heavy with warm tension. I gripped fistfuls of his shirt and suddenly needed—*needed*—to feel his skin. Therefore, I clawed at his clothes, tugging the fabric from his pants and moving my fingers to his stomach.

He bent slightly away from me and grabbed my wrists with his other hand. "No, darling. We're concentrating on you right now."

"I need to—"

"Later."

"No, not later—"

He covered my mouth with his, swallowing the rest of my demand, and driving away all intelligible thought. His hot, languid tongue taking and giving in an echoing rhythm. As we kissed and he worked his Greg voodoo, my breath hitched, and I was caught in the twisting beginnings of my orgasm.

He was right, of course. Five minutes, two orgasms, one right after the other. It was always this way when he came home.

Over the years I'd learned absence doesn't make the heart grow fonder. The heart becomes wary, somnolent and cynical during periods of prolonged absence, burdened with cares and fears borne in solitude. However, absence *does* make the body greedy and irrationally amorous with frustrated need.

Greg must've felt or recognized the signs of my precipitous completion, because he pulled his mouth from mine and whispered harshly against my lips, "You belong to me. Say it."

"I belong to you." I repeated the words he craved, believing them as I always did when lost to the moment. I shut my eyes and gave myself over to it, craving the singularity of sensation, the brief halting of time and thought.

In the back of my mind I knew he would leave again and I would be alone. But for now, for better or worse, my wary heart awoke. No longer lethargic, but alive to this man, and how much I loved him.

"I need you, Fiona." The dark desperation had returned to his voice, and the sound cut through my lingering fog of fulfillment.

His words sounded like the tip of an emotion iceberg, so I twisted my arms around him and held on tightly. "Hey, I love you."

Greg shook his head and breathed out, ragged and fatigued. He pressed his face to my skin for a long moment, then abruptly released me.

Pulling my arms from his torso, he turned and sat on the edge of the couch, glancing around the apartment. "Right . . . here's what we'll do: I'll get the kids. You take your shower. After homework and playtime, I'll challenge them to shots until they pass out. Then we'll eat the rest of their Halloween candy while binge-watching Game of Thrones."

I sat behind him and wrapped my arms around his shoulders, still trying to pull myself together. "The Halloween candy is long gone. And what kind of shots are you talking about?"

"Apple juice." He squeezed my arms, then stood. I watched him cross the room with long strides to where he'd dropped his duffle bag; he retrieved a coat from the floor and faced me, his eyes giving my body a quick perusal, like he was taking a mental snapshot. "Or, the hard stuff, if you prefer."

I narrowed my eyes and stretched. "We don't keep Kool-Aid in the house, you know that. It makes Jack hallucinate."

"He doesn't hallucinate; don't be so melodramatic."

"He talks to the walls."

"Only because they talk to him first."

He was right; Jack didn't *actually* hallucinate. The one time he drank Kool-Aid he did talk to the walls, then he laughed uncontrollably until he passed out. Basically, Kool-Aid made the kids crazy and loopy and caused them to run around like sugar-high savages.

"Although your plan sounds delightful, we can't do that tonight. I have Ashley's going-away party at four, and you're invited, of course." I yawned, my eyes flickering to the mantel clock. He needed to leave in the next thirty seconds and I needed coffee.

"Is that tonight?" Greg zipped his winter coat, frowning like he was disappointed.

"Yes. Why? What's wrong?"

He studied the gloves he'd retrieved from the pockets of his jacket. "No, nothing."

I pulled the corners of the towel back around my body. "She's leaving on Wednesday, for good. I'm bringing the cake. I had no idea you would be home and this isn't something I can miss or skip."

"Of course. We need to go. We'll go. We must go," he said resolutely, as though he were trying to convince himself. Then he lifted his gaze to mine and I felt better, seeing it was clear of conflict.

"By the way, why are you here? Obviously I'm not complaining, but how did this happen? I thought there were no breaks on this assignment."

He walked backward to the door, checking his watch. "I'll tell you all about it when I get back."

"Oh! I also need to speak with you about Jack. Something happened yesterday—"

Greg stiffened. "Is he okay?"

"Yes, but—"

"I have to go, we'll talk about it later. Speaking of which, when I return, it would be super great if you were still mostly naked, mmm-kay?'

"Mmm-kay." I stood, giving him a goofy grin. "I'm sure the kids won't mind their mother walking around the house naked. That's not weird at all."

"Good." He nodded once, a smile brightening his eyes, then turned. I was halfway to our bathroom when I heard him open the front door then bellow at me, "And by mostly naked, I mean completely naked. And wet!"

This made me smile, until I heard Greg say, "Oh, hi neighbor Matt. I didn't see you lurking there in the hallway. Awkward."

And then I laughed.

Good Lord, I'd missed him.

CHAPTER 3

Dearest Wife,

I really thought love at first sight and soul mates were bullshit. But the second I saw you, nothing else seemed possible. How could I not spend the rest of my breathing moments with you? I needed to be with you. I was in love with you from the moment I saw you, and every time I see you now it's that same feeling of, "NOW I am complete."

-Mark
Letter
Ohio, USA
Married 7 years

~18 years ago~
Greg

"SHE'S A SIX."

Frowning at the class syllabus for English Composition 101, I endeavored to ignore the males of my species directly behind me.

"What? No. Look at that rack. It adds three points. She's *at least* a seven. Maybe even a seven point five."

This statement was deserving of an eye-roll. Thus, I rolled my eyes.

Barely functioning, hormone-addled cretins were my punishment for putting off first year English until my third year at university. I ought to have CLEP-ed out of the class—which was where one takes a proficiency test in lieu of three credit hours spent weekly in a classroom.

This approach hadn't come to fruition for two reasons.

First, I got drunk the night before the exam last summer and failed it. I fell asleep halfway through the essay portion.

I'm not a drunk, not yet at any rate, but I do enjoy a night of oblivion from time to time. I'm haunted, mostly by ghosts of blokes I used to know. Watching other people die requires turning off a switch within oneself. When everything was illuminated and yet still dark—shadowy with regret and the knowledge of true pain, true suffering—my ability to live and function in the present was compromised.

How I longed to scream at people, how I longed to wake them to the world around them, and not their petty concerns of TV dinners and the cancellation of their favorite TV shows . . .

But alas, no one likes a harbinger of truth. So I opted for infrequent periods of drunk debauchery in an effort to curb my killjoy proclivities.

The other reason I'd enrolled in English 101 was because I needed a boost to my grade point average. My humanities teacher had given me a C last semester. Note the distinction: It hadn't been deserved. It had been *given*. Like a present. Or a sexually transmitted disease.

I'd had the audacity to call him an insufferable twat. He was an insufferable twat. But then what did I expect from a ponytail-wearing pacifist who spent five dollars on a cup of coffee, yet complained daily about his paltry adjunct stipend?

Also, he was a philosophy Ph.D. candidate. The most pretentious and worthless of all college degrees, where nothing was made or produced or accomplished, except endless discussion of feelings and thoughts. So, again, nothing accomplished.

In retrospect, I ought not to have called him an insufferable twat in front of the entire class. That was on me. My bad.

English Composition 101 was my penance.

Apparently the hormone-addled cretins behind me were part of that penance.

"She's a six point five and no higher. Butterface. Put a paper bag over her head or fuck her from behind and she goes up a half point."

I gritted my teeth.

Lord, give me strength.

"What about her?"

"Which one? The fat one?"

"No. The short one; she just walked in. I'd totally fuck her face to face."

My attention flickered to the side, to the young lady at my left. She wasn't the subject of their objectification, but she had obviously overheard their comments. Her youthful face was flushed and stricken, clearly horrified. From the looks of her, she was in her first year, likely fresh from some corn farm in Iowa.

And now she was going to think all men were insufferable twats. I felt sorry for her. But mostly, I felt sorry for the nice boy who would one day want to court her attention, only to find her prejudiced against all men, and living with a flannel-wearing lesbian.

Then again, I considered the matter and concluded, *flannel-wearing lesbians are pretty awesome.* I decided the wankers behind me might be doing her a favor.

"Whoa . . . I see her. Christ. I'd let her suck my dick."

I gripped the edge of the desk. Where the hell was the professor?

I hadn't checked to see who they were speaking of. It didn't matter. No one deserved to be subjected to such filth and degradation. If the next statement out of their mouths wasn't in reference to their cherished mother, I would have no choice but to ruin their day.

"I would come all over her face."

"She has small tits."

"But that ass."

"Anal, with a mirror."

That's it.

Straightening in my seat, I glanced over my shoulder at the boys behind me, eyed them up and down, then laughed lightly. They were as I imagined they would be, barely out of diapers.

Wait for it.

One of them, a pale-complexioned fellow with nostrils betraying his pig-nature and pockmarks betraying his juvenile mind, smirked. "You see her too? She's got a sweet ass."

"No. I smelled your desperation. It stinks."

His smirk fell.

"What?"

"Your desperation," I repeated. "You stink."

His vanilla cheeks flushed red. "What did you say?"

"I said you smell of callow youth and masturbatory semen, also known as desperation. And I'm not the only one affected by the stench." I lifted my chin to the young girl at my left, some seats away. Her eyes were fastened to the front of the room, though I knew she was listening to the exchange. "Perhaps save your infantile babble for someplace more appropriate, like a play yard, or your crib."

"You want a fight, asshole?"

"Not particularly. But if you children come across any other adults, I must caution you. Not every man is as forgiving as I." Holding the chatty one's feeble glare for a long moment, I added, "Boys, if you insist upon your current course of innate thought pollution, I'm liable to lose my temper. Cease or I shall have to punish you."

His eyes wavered to the side, to the girl. His fragile ego threatened, he lifted his hand as though to strike me and blurted, "Hey, fuck you, man."

I caught his hand, twisting his wrist easily, and constricted my fingers around his fist, eliciting a sharp cry of pain. "I don't want to beat you senseless—not today at any rate, perhaps tomorrow—but allow me to speak clearly since your comprehension of the English language is apparently deficient."

I paused, squeezing his hand, feeling the bones crunch together. He cried out again. Thankfully we were at the back of the giant, bustling lecture hall, and he had enough pride to muffle the involuntary sounds of pain.

"Stop. Talking." I shifted my attention to his little friend; his eyes were wide and panicked. "Never speak again in my presence. Or in the presence of any woman. Everything out of your mouth shows that you are vile and insignificant. If you died tomorrow, the world would be a better place. You are filthy little beasts and I shall not hesitate breaking all the bones in your hands. And that would certainly be devastating because we all know the only two types of sexual satisfaction you're ever likely to receive is of the self-serve variety, or the four legged variety."

After another long stare and threatening squeeze, I released his fist and turned back to the front of the class, glancing at my watch. The professor was already several minutes late. I hoped this teacher didn't expect us to stay longer in recompense for his poor planning.

Telltale sounds of the boys vacating their seats, scurrying out of the room like the vermin they were, calmed me considerably. I made another attempt to study the syllabus, but then I felt the weight of someone watching me. Lifting my eyes, I found the girl at my left giving me a shy smile of reverential gratitude.

I nodded once, noting that—if her eyes were any indication—she possessed some intelligence. But she was very young. I had no desire to be worshipped. No desire to be fawned over or—God forbid—needed.

Most importantly, however, I already had a girlfriend. And Vanessa suited me just fine.

She was the shrewd, practical sort who enjoyed frequent orgasms and liberally employed me as arm candy. Intelligent, independent, reasonably even-tempered, Vanessa required very little maintenance. Her self-sufficiency left me plenty of time for my preferred solitary pursuits—namely long-distance running and voracious reading.

Plus, Vanessa was tall. I preferred tall women. I liked not having to stoop when carrying on a conversation.

"I'm Madeline." Introducing herself, the girl to my left gave me a little wave.

"Greg." I pressed my lips together, issuing a tight smile, relieved she hadn't extended her hand for me to shake.

"Do you know her?" Madeline asked, lifting her chin toward a spot a few rows below us. "The girl they were talking about? Is she a friend of yours?"

"I don't . . ." I shook my head, my attention straying absentmindedly to where Madeline had indicated.

Her.

There.

She.

You.

Stunning.

Are.

Woman.

Want.

I lost my train of thought.

I lost my words.

In truth, I lost my ability to speak.

And think.

I'd been addled insensible by the vision before me.

Dark eyes lined by thick lashes set in an extraordinarily exquisite face—she was a painting. A marble statue, set apart and untouchable. Yet a moving, breathing object of artistry. Everything grace and elegance and beauty.

Her red lips pursed thoughtfully. The unknown woman was searching for something, eyeing the space around her desk, unaware she was being watched, the subject of intense fascination.

My mother had been an object to my father, a means to an end. A tool for a purpose. He was handsome, unfaithful, and soulless. His cold lack of regard eventually killed her. As such, I'd never allowed myself to be blinded or corrupted by a façade. I'd trained myself to search for signs of authenticity and intelligence beyond the false and oftentimes misleading stucco of appearance.

But this woman . . . she was blinding.

Enchanting.

And she was bending over.

And now I was gaping at her remarkably perfect ass. It was the Helen of Troy of asses, the kind wars are fought over.

"You know her?" Madeline's repeated question pulled me from my brazen gawking.

Ashamed, I forced my eyes away and cleared my throat twice before answering, "I don't know her."

"Oh. I thought she might be your friend. Why did you defend her if you don't know her?"

"Mutual flirting and willing seduction are one thing, but forceful leering and being the target of unwelcome objectification are quite another," I answered offhandedly. "I defended human decency."

Unable to help myself, I re-centered the woman in my vision, appreciating the curve of her narrow waist, the bewitching line of her jaw and neck, as I might admire the handiwork of an exceptionally gifted artist. She'd twisted around again, sending me chasing my breath. Her loveliness again jarring and startling.

"She's pretty," Madeline said. It sounded like a fishing lure, a comment meant for me to contradict.

I ignored it, instead focusing on the woman's sad eyes. But also curious. And wise. They held depth of thought, of *knowing*.

No. The thought was unbidden. *She's a reminder that true and brilliant beauty exists in this world.*

I shrugged, dazedly watching the captivating creature as she slipped into her seat, and replied clumsily, "I have a girlfriend." It was more a reminder to myself than a response to the girl's remark.

Madeline said nothing else.

I heard nothing of the lecture.

And when the class ended, I battled my guilt, keeping my eyes pointedly downcast in atonement for looking.

But mostly for noticing, and allowing myself to be intoxicated by the sight.

CHAPTER 4

Dear Husband,
You know I love you because I don't murder your mother.

-Jenna
Post-it Note
United Kingdom
Married 22 years

~Present Day~
Fiona

GREG AND I arrived at the party five minutes early. This was a miracle because we'd left our apartment fifteen minutes late; the kids were ecstatic to have their dad home and didn't want to let him go. Also, we encountered blizzard-like conditions on the streets of Chicago. Recognizing the plight of our tardiness, Greg suggested I call Janie— another of our close-knit group, though she crocheted mostly—and ask if she could send a car to pick us up.

I rationalized this frivolity by reminding myself I was bringing the cake. It was the cake, not us, that warranted the fancy car ride.

Greg saw nothing frivolous in asking Janie to send a car, remarking, "What's the good of having friends if you can't exploit them for their resources?" This statement earned him a stern look because he was only half-joking.

I'd known Janie—savant, guileless, tall—in college; when I was a master's student she was starting her freshman year. I was the resident advisor on the dorm floor. We'd kept in touch over the years. Janie and her husband Quinn—resourceful, stoic, covertly noble—live in a penthouse apartment in a building he owns, at the north end of Millennium Park. He is in the security business.

In addition to Janie and me, the remainder of our knitting group is as follows:

Dr. Elizabeth Finney, emergency room physician, twenty-nine, blonde hair, blue eyes, average height; Janie's roommate from college; stubborn and, similarly to Quinn Sullivan, covertly noble. Married to Nico Moretti—aka Niccolò Manganiello—celebrity comedian, thirty, black hair, green eyes, medium build, and enough charisma to indiscriminately paralyze women, men, and house pets.

Dr. Sandra Fielding-Greene, child psychiatrist, thirty, red hair, green eyes, five foot seven; works with Elizabeth at the hospital; altruistic, fun-loving, wickedly clever. Married to Alex Greene, genius, world-class hacker, twenty-three, black hair, dark blue eyes, six foot two; mistrusting and resourceful.

Ashley Winston, pediatric intensive care nurse, twenty-six, brown hair, blue eyes, five foot eight; worked with Sandra and Elizabeth at the hospital until recently; sassy bookworm. Involved with Dr. Drew Runous, federal game warden, PhD biologist, thirty-one, blonde hair, blue eyes, six foot four; reserved and intense.

Marie Harris, freelance journalist and artist, thirty, blonde hair, blue eyes, average height, headstrong, food enthusiast. I met Marie when she was doing an article on women of the CIA and brought her into the knitting circle. She was involved with a chef for a prolonged period, David Carter, but they'd split about a year ago.

And lastly, Kat Tanner—aka Kathleen Tyson—administrative assistant, twenty-three, brown hair, brown eyes, five foot four. Kat had worked with Janie for a number of years at an architecture firm before Janie went to work for Quinn at his security company. Little known fact: Kat is the heiress to a vast pharmaceutical fortune, and her family was based out of Boston. She doesn't speak of it, or them.

"You're early!" Sandra rushed forward as soon as she spotted me and stopped short of wrapping me in a hug. I understood her surprise. I was never early. People with children are only ever early by accident.

"Goodness, Fiona. What's the deal with the cake? That's the largest cake I've ever seen."

"My neighbor accidentally ate a slice of the coconut cake I made yesterday, so he went out and bought this one to replace it." I handed Greg the cake so I could accept Sandra's hug.

"He has a habit of overcompensation," Greg added with a note of cheerful sarcasm.

I gave him a warning look. He winked at me, the stinker.

"Well, hello, Mr. Fiona." Sandra grinned at my husband, using the name she'd assigned him years ago. "I didn't expect to see you here. Are you still trying to teach Grace how to code?"

"If she doesn't learn about data structures at home, she'll just learn about it on the streets."

Sandra laughed. This was Greg's stock answer for all the age-inappropriate activities he tried to teach the kids. Most of them were odd, but benign, like computer programming. However some—like coaching them to win every argument by declaring, *That sounds like something Hitler would say*—were much less benign.

"Are you back for good?"

Back for good meant a month, maybe two, if we were lucky.

"No, just twenty-four hours."

"E-gads! How long was the flight?"

"Twenty-two hours," he answered smoothly, like it was no big deal. For him it wasn't a big deal. His longest trip home had taken three days. That was four years ago when he'd traveled home from Nepal. One leg of his journey was by pack mule.

Greg had informed me in the car on the way over that the company had evacuated all rig workers from the site for four days and given them comp time. Instead of staying in South Africa, he'd decided to jump on a plane so we could spend a day and a half together. The older I get the more I understood everything is relative. One person's travel horror story is another person's dream vacation.

"Why are you holding them hostage at the door?" Elizabeth appeared and reprimanded Sandra, reaching for my arm and pulling me forward.

"I'm not holding them hostage, I'm welcoming them."

"For the record, I do not feel adequately welcomed," Greg piped in with his typical contrariness.

I patted him on the shoulder. "You'll survive."

"I will suffer through. Where are the men folk?"

"Around," Elizabeth said distractedly as she guided me away. "Sorry, Greg, we need Fiona. We're having a crisis."

"No one is better in a crisis than Fiona." I glanced at Sandra as she said this, lifting her chin toward the cake in Greg's possession. "Be a dear and put the cake in the kitchen?"

"Fine," he mock-grumbled. "But if you don't return my wife to me in a half hour, I will orchestrate a new crisis."

"Such as?" Elizabeth paused, obviously wanting to hear whatever humorous thing Greg was about to say. He had this reputation with my friends—hilariously wrong in the head—and they often compared his jokes to a clown car accident, unfortunate but funny.

"Where's Alex?"

Sandra gave Greg the side-eye. "What do you want with my husband?"

"I thought we might check out what the Senate has been up to."

Elizabeth didn't comprehend his horrid threat. "Meaning?"

"Don't you dare." Sandra narrowed her eyes, administering a piercing squint at my husband; of course she would catch on at once because terrible minds think alike.

I gave him a withering look and tossed over my shoulder, "No hacking into government websites again, Greg."

"I'll see you in a half hour, dearest."

There was a short pause before Elizabeth gasped, finally understanding his meaning, "*You* did that? You put up those pictures of that senator? The naked selfies on the house dot gov main page?"

"I did no such thing." Greg sounded and looked insulted, then added, "Alex did it. I was merely the Pinky to his Brain."

Sandra gave Greg one more dirty look before pushing us around the corner and out of earshot. Meanwhile, Elizabeth was laughing.

"I can't believe he did that. Where did he get the pictures?"

Sandra's irritated expression quickly dissipated and she chuckled lightly. "He is so delightfully wrong."

"It's not funny," I said. It wasn't funny, not really. Granted, this senator was responsible for passing laws making federal programs negotiations of drug prices with Big Pharma illegal, which cost taxpayers millions. And this senator had been slated to become a lobbyist with Big Pharma—so, basically, he was corrupt and had sold his vote.

Still, the end doesn't justify the means; hacking into cell phones isn't funny. And yet . . . Greg made it funny. He made people both wince and laugh, feel guilty and good at the same time. As Sandra might say, it was his superpower.

"What's the current crisis?" I changed the subject, unzipping my coat and allowing Sandra to help me remove it.

"Janie is hiding in the bathroom." Elizabeth turned me toward a hallway.

I frowned at this news. "Again? Why?"

"She isn't precisely hiding, but she won't come out. And she sounds . . . not well," Sandra clarified.

"Not well?" I spotted Marie and Kat directly ahead of me, standing on either side of the closed bathroom door, and gave them both a quick hug.

"I think she's throwing up again." Marie's forehead creased.

Elizabeth shook her head at this news. "If she'd told me she was sick we could have moved the party to my apartment."

"She keeps insisting everything is fine," Kat whispered to our circle. "But she's been in there since I arrived twenty minutes ago to help set things up."

"What does Quinn say?" I lowered my voice to match Kat's pitch.

"He's not home yet."

"Did you try calling him?" I asked, glancing at the closed door.

"I called him." Elizabeth showed me her cell as though to prove her efforts. "So did Sandra."

"He said he was on his way home and told us to *mind our own business.*" Sandra did her best Quinn Sullivan impression, which would have made me smile if the situation had been different.

"What do we do? Ashley and Drew will be here in a few minutes and the rest of the guests will start arriving at five. Do we move the party?" Marie asked, and all eyes were pointed at me to provide the answer.

I surveyed my friends' worried expressions, then the door where the sound of Janie coughing was just audible. I walked around Kat and Elizabeth, crossed to the door, and knocked gently.

"Janie, it's Fiona."

"Oh, hi Fiona." She sounded weak, unsteady, and I heard her sniff. "I'll be right out, I just need to . . .'"

When Janie didn't finish her sentence, but instead made a horrid dry-heaving sound, I retrieved two bobby pins from my pants pocket. "Janie, I'm coming in."

"You can't. The door is locked. I need another minute."

"Elizabeth, can you bring me a glass of juice? Not apple. Lemonade if she has it." I picked the simple lock while I made this request.

"If she's got a stomach flu, flat ginger ale would be better," Elizabeth suggested.

I shook my head. Based on the facts presented, I was fairly certain Janie's illness wasn't as transitory as a stomach flu; Quinn's response and lack of overt concern being the most damning of the evidence. He knew what was up . . .

"No. Lemonade. And Saltines."

Sandra squinted at me. "Are you thinking what I think you're thinking?"

I shushed her, which had the opposite effect I'd intended. Sandra gasped, covering her mouth, her eyes growing impossibly large. "Oh my apple pie! Do you really think—"

I shushed her again and waved her back. "Give me a minute?" Before any of the other ladies could give voice to their questions, I slipped into the bathroom and locked the door behind me.

Janie was lying on the tile floor. Her long body was folded into a ball, her curly red hair in disarray around her head and shoulders. Her eyes opened and met mine. She wasn't in pain, she was nauseous. Tremendously nauseous.

Yep. She was pregnant.

I tried not to smile, and failed. For better or for worse, parenthood is a club. It's based on shared experiences, usually having to do with either indescribable joy and/or unspeakable suffering. I'd been the solo member of the parent club amongst my good friends for the last eight years. Therefore, I couldn't help but feel a deep camaraderie with—and maybe also gratitude for—Janie now.

"We'll move the party," I said simply, and continued before Janie could protest. "We'll move it to Elizabeth's place. You stay here and rest. When it winds down, we'll all come back to see if you're feeling better."

"I'm not sick, though most insurance companies and the AMA consider it a *disease state.*"

"I know." I nodded once, then moved to the sink, wetting a clean washcloth with cool water and grabbing a dry fluffy towel. I knelt beside Janie, helped her lift her head so I could fit the fluffy towel beneath it, then dabbed at her forehead with the washcloth. "But apparently you also can't host a party when you're in your first trimester."

Her eyes widened and grew more sober, watchful. "How did . . . never mind," she croaked. "You know everything."

"I do not know everything."

She ignored me and continued, "I didn't want anyone to know. We found out last week and, with Ashley leaving, this is her party. I didn't want . . ." Janie swallowed weakly and her eyes fluttered shut.

"You didn't want to hijack her party with your news?"

"Exactly." She tried to swallow, then made an involuntary gagging sound.

"Janie?" Quinn's voice called from the other side of the door. "Kitten, are you okay?"

She tried to push to her elbows, but I placed a hand on her arm to keep her in place and responded for her. "She's okay, but she needs those

Saltines."

"Ugh, I can't eat."

"You need to eat, otherwise the nausea will get worse. Elizabeth is bringing you lemonade and crackers. Citrus helped me with both Jack and Grace."

"Elizabeth is here with the food. Fiona, let me in." Quinn sounded appropriately concerned. His anxiety made me smile. Greg had been of a similar disposition for our first pregnancy—like I was made of both glass and plutonium.

I gave Janie one last smile of commiseration, then turned to the door, taking a deep breath before I opened it. I wasn't surprised to see everyone—and I do mean *everyone*—hovering anxiously on the other side.

I addressed Quinn first. "She has to eat. If she doesn't eat, she'll keep getting sick."

He nodded gravely, like I was giving him directions to save her life. "Okay. I'll make sure she eats."

"I will too," Dan—Quinn's second in command—chimed in, looking almost as anxious as Quinn.

Daniel O'Malley, six foot, stocky, brown eyes, brown hair; Quinn Sullivan's childhood friend and now business partner; candid, loyal, and unrequitedly in love with Kat Tanner (aka Kathleen Tyson) . . . unrequited because she is in denial.

"Why didn't she tell us?" Elizabeth addressed this question to Quinn, as though she held him responsible.

Based on the way he was grinding his teeth, I surmised he was going to repeat his earlier answer, *It's none of your business.*

Therefore, I interjected, "She's not that far along, and they just found out last week. Plus, she didn't want to be the focus of tonight, what with Ashley leaving on Wednesday."

Ashley and Drew had arrived while I was in the bathroom; they were standing at the back of the gathered crowd, and she shook her head at this reasoning. "She is a nut. I don't care about having a party—seeing y'all is enough for me. I wish we could cancel the whole darn thing and just hang out and knit."

"And crochet," Nico—Elizabeth's husband—added with a grin. He and Janie were the crocheters in our group, though I suspected Nico did it primarily as a way to spend time with his wife, and secondarily to bond with her friends.

"Elizabeth, please take the food to Janie's room." I motioned with my chin down the hallway, then turned to Quinn. "It would be good for you to carry her, but lift her gently."

He nodded solemnly and started for the bathroom, then stopped and turned to me. His typically glacial gaze was tempered with gratitude, but also something else.

"You'll come back, right? You'll come back and check on her?" he asked.

I frowned at him, confused, especially since Elizabeth was an ER physician and Ashley was a nurse.

I was about to point this out when Elizabeth said, "Maybe you should make a list of foods, the best kind for her . . . condition."

"She doesn't have a *condition*. You make it sound like she has gonorrhea." Sandra shoved Elizabeth's shoulder, grinning with gusto. "Janie and Quinn are going to have a baby! Why is no one doing cartwheels?"

"I agree," Marie nodded enthusiastically. "This is a reason to celebrate. I'll mix cocktails."

"I'll help," Kat offered.

"Let's all help." Nico herded everyone toward the kitchen; he must've understood the strained expression on Quinn's face and wisely decided to move the crowd.

Greg loitered behind, waiting for our friends to shuffle past, then came to my side.

Before Greg could speak, Quinn tugged me by the arm and turned me to face him again. "Listen, I need your help."

I blinked at him blankly for two beats before I found my voice. "What do you need?" Quinn wasn't the type to ask for help, ever.

"Janie has been sick for weeks, and the doctors keep saying it's normal and everything is fine as long as she's not dehydrated or doesn't lose too much weight. It doesn't seem normal to me. They gave her a prescription for Zofran, but she doesn't want to take it."

"Why not?"

"She's worried it hasn't been adequately studied in pregnant women."

"Pregnant women take Zofran all the time."

"Yeah, but you know her. She says she wants to see a randomized, double-blind clinical trial." Quinn and I shared a look of commiseration; this was classic Janie. He continued, "She's tried everything to stem the nausea and nothing works. Ginger, peppermint, Preggie Pops—whatever the hell those are. Do you have any ideas?"

I thought on this for a moment, then asked, "Is she craving anything?"

"She hasn't mentioned anything."

"Maybe try bringing her different kinds of foods, all with strong flavors. Citrus helped me with Jack. With Grace, mustard or anything vinegary did the trick."

"The other thing is," Quinn's eyes darted to Greg, then back to mine, "she won't listen to me. She's been—"

"Irrational?" Greg supplied. "Crazy? Emotional? Exhausted?"

Quinn nodded. "All of those things."

I covered Quinn's hand with mine and squeezed. "I'll talk to her for you. Have her take a few days off work and I'll come over, bring different foods. Something will help."

"Thank you." Quinn turned his hand so he was holding mine, and his typical stoicism was replaced with the sincere warmth of relieved gratitude. "Thank you. I mean it."

"No problem."

Quinn let go of my fingers and pulled his through his hair. "Okay, I'm going to get her."

He gave us both one more distracted head nod before disappearing into the bathroom. Greg tossed his arm around my shoulders and turned me toward the living room, placing a kiss on my forehead and whispering, "Are you thinking what I'm thinking?"

I gave him the side-eye. "I think so, Brain. But where are we going to get rubber pants?"

Greg grinned at my reference to *Pinky and the Brain*, a cartoon that originally aired in the 1990s, and one that Greg had forced me to watch repeatedly during his senior year of college. He'd left Iowa to finish his degree in Texas right after we'd become engaged. Every Tuesday and Thursday we'd sit on the phone together and watch *Pinky and the Brain*.

"I missed you, Pinky," he said, staring at me like I might disappear.

I returned his smile, though I was inexplicably sad.

No . . . not sad. Nostalgic.

When I was pregnant with Jack, Greg had taken a desk job for a year so he could be with me, so he could hover and worry and fret daily in close proximity. It had made me crazy at the time, as we'd been apart more than we'd been together during our engagement and marriage. But now I looked back on those twelve months as some of the happiest of my life.

Greg's grin diminished the longer I stared at him. Wanting to keep the moment light, I redoubled my effort to smile and lifted to my toes, giving him a quick kiss.

"I missed you too, Brain. I always do."

***

". . . AND SO I took Enis out of the soccer program and added him to the little league waitlist." Ashley's co-worker finished her lengthy monologue—regarding the trials and tribulations of the local co-ed youth soccer league—with unbridled exasperation.

"Fascinating." Greg nodded intently, his eyes narrowed in a way that told me he hadn't been listening to a single word she'd said.

Granted, he'd joined the conversation just minutes ago, stepping close to me, and shoving a plate of food into my hands, saying, "Please eat something."

Kat and Sandra, who were also present, had nothing to add. Sandra scanned the crowd while Kat smiled politely. Kat's superpower was being polite.

Meanwhile, I had been listening to the woman. I was keenly interested in the league's dynamics since Jack was about to start practices next month. "Thank you for the information. You've given me a lot to think about."

We'd moved the party to Elizabeth and Nico's penthouse, which was down the hall from Janie and Quinn's. The blizzard-like conditions kept many people from venturing out, opting to send regretful texts instead. Ashley's phone kept buzzing with messages, so she eventually turned it off. If she was disappointed by the turnout, she didn't show it.

Ashley's co-worker looked at her watch. "Like I said, soccer wasn't the right environment for Enis. But your son might have a better experience."

"Jack won't be playing football," Greg said distractedly.

"Right . . ." The woman gave Greg a questioning frown, but didn't address his statement; she obviously wasn't aware that, to the British, *football* meant *soccer*. Since I had no plans to tell Greg that Jack would be playing soccer, I made no effort to clarify. I felt Sandra's eyes on me; obviously, she had caught Greg's meaning.

I decided to change the subject. "What time is it?"

"It's almost nine. I should be going." The woman scowled at her watch, like she was irritated at the time.

"It was nice to meet you." I passed my plate back to Greg.

"You too. Please do call me if you have any more questions." She shook my hand, then pulled a card from her pocket and passed it to me. "This is my work number, but it's probably the best way to get hold of me."

"I absolutely will. Thank you."

After a few more pleasantries, Ashley's co-worker left us to search for her husband.

As soon as she was out of the room, Greg tugged lightly on my elbow. "Did she say her kids' names are Penis and Vagina?"

Kat coughed, her eyes bulging. Luckily she hadn't been drinking her red wine as he spoke. Kat was known for her spit-takes.

Sandra smirked, not even trying to suppress a goofy chuckle.

I whipped my head back and whispered to Greg harshly, "No! It's Enis and Ragina. Their names are Enis and Ragina."

"Sorry," he shook his head, leaning away, shrugging, and not looking sorry, "I'm still hearing Penis and Vagina."

I lifted an eyebrow at this. "I think those are your two favorite words. It's the only explanation for why you're constantly saying them out loud."

"Or maybe," Greg's eyes widened to their maximum diameter and he adopted his mock serious face, "they are my favorite words, which is why I constantly want *you* to say them out loud."

I laughed at his likely theory. He pushed my untouched plate back into my hands. I accepted it distractedly, picked up a baby carrot and took a bite. It tasted like sawdust. I put it back on the plate and surveyed what was left of the party.

We had the weather channel on in the background, and when the meteorologist announced things were going to get worse before midnight, most of Ashley's work friends had left. We hadn't yet served the cake.

"Poor Quinn."

I glanced at my husband, and found him shaking his head mournfully.

"Why *poor Quinn*?" Kat asked.

"Dan still has his crush on Nico, and Quinn isn't here to defend his bromance."

I snorted because this was true. Dan had a bit of a crush on Nico. But then, we all did.

As though reading my thoughts, Sandra mock-whispered, "We all have a crush on Nico. Even you, Greg."

He didn't deny it; instead, opting to say, "I'm going to start a rumor that Dan and Nico bought tickets to the Cubs opening game, they're going together, and are hoping to get on the kiss-cam."

I clicked my tongue in mild disapproval. "You are a gossip, Greg Archer."

"Yes. I am. Annoyingly, Alex is worthless at spreading rumors because he's smitten with Drew."

"And you're smitten with no one," I stated.

"Untrue. I'm smitten with you."

This earned him an appreciative grin; I lifted my chin. "Well played, husband. Well played."

Looking remarkably satisfied with himself, Greg bent and gave me a kiss on my cheek, whispering, "How much longer are you looking to stay?"

My heart sank. I wasn't ready to leave yet. My attention shifted to Sandra and Kat and then back to Greg.

Kat cleared her throat and touched Sandra's arm. "Come on, Sandra. Help me get another drink." She turned to us and asked, "Can I get either of you anything?"

"No thanks, Kat," I answered for both of us, thankful we would have a moment of privacy.

I was torn. On one hand, Ashley was a good friend. She was leaving for good. This was one of the last times I would see her in person, unless it was a special occasion or a vacation. I was going to miss her, having her here.

On the other hand, I hadn't seen Greg—if you don't count Skype calls, which I didn't—since the end of December. His surprise visit was a gift and I couldn't help feeling like I was being selfish, squandering our time together.

When Kat and Sandra were out of earshot I turned to Greg, "Do you mind if we stay another hour?"

"Not at all," he said, openly studying me. I didn't believe him. Something about the way he was looking at me said differently.

"I know you enjoy Alex's company, but you've barely talked to him tonight." He needed to mingle. Greg had been orbiting or hovering over me for most of the night.

"They're trying to talk me into a camping and fishing trip over the summer. Drew says I should bring the kids."

"Oh! You guys should go."

Greg pressed his lips together in a flat line. "I can't. I'll still be on assignment."

I contemplated his statement for a long moment. It seemed terribly unfair to Grace and Jack. They shouldn't miss out on a camping and fishing trip because Greg was going to be gone.

So I spoke and thought at the same time, "Maybe I'll go. Maybe I'll take the kids and we'll go."

My statement surprised him; but his surprise morphed into an unhappy glare before he could disguise it. He straightened and, sounding like he was fighting to keep his voice even, said, "Absolutely. I mean, why not?"

"I like to camp," I rationalized, my eyes settling on where Drew and Alex were chatting across the room.

"I know."

Not liking the edge in his tone, I further explained my thinking. "It would be fun with Drew and Alex. I bet Drew could teach the kids all kinds of things about foraging and wilderness survival."

"I could, too. If you recall, I *was* a Marine."

"Yes, you could. But you're never here." I winced as soon as the words were out of my mouth, realizing too late how they might be interpreted. "I mean—of course you're not here. You're working. I didn't mean it like—"

"I know. You didn't say anything untrue. You're right, I'm never here." Not looking at me, Greg crossed his arms then uncrossed them, and stuffed his hands in his pockets.

"Honey—"

He cut me off again, pointing a massive frown at the dish full of food in my hands. "Is there anything on the buffet that looks appetizing to you? I'll get you another plate."

Not waiting for me to respond, Greg took the food out of my hands and turned toward the kitchen, walking away before I could sort through my mess of thoughts. My words sounded accusatory. Accusatory hadn't been my intention. Not at all. Not even a little.

At one time, his job—more precisely, the location of his job—had been a source of anxiety in our marriage. But we'd resolved those issues years ago. As far as I was concerned, this subject was closed and I'd moved on, accepted his absence as a constant, inescapable fact of our life together.

"I love how he loves you." Kat's statement—imbued with more than a hint of wistfulness—alerted me that she and Sandra had returned. I glanced at her and found her eyes were following Greg's retreating form.

I paused to examine her before asking, "Because he took my food away?"

"Because he noticed you weren't eating the food on your plate, and you're looking a little pale," Sandra clarified, her green eyes alight with mischief. Though, to be fair, she almost always looked like she was up to something.

"I'm just tired," I admitted. The last few weeks were catching up with me.

"He noticed that, too. That's why he asked how much longer you wanted to stay. He's worried about you," Sandra said, further explaining her interpretation of Greg's actions. Sandra's interpretations were typically correct.

Now I paused to examine Sandra, considering the likelihood that she was correct. I replayed the last several minutes with Greg based on this new perspective.

At length I asked, "How do you do that?"

She lifted her eyebrows. "Do what?"

"We've been married for almost one and a half decades and I didn't pick up on any of that."

"It's because you're tired, and . . . " she titled her head to the side, her eyes moving over my face, her brows slowly drawing together as she studied me, "you're overwhelmed."

"When people are overwhelmed, they can't see past their own campfire." Ashley sauntered up to our trio, saying these words like she was quoting someone. She confirmed my suspicion by adding, "My momma used to say that, and if you want my opinion, Greg is right to be worried. You've been pushing yourself too hard."

I opened my mouth to protest, but no sound came out. I didn't know how to respond, because I'd never discovered a satisfactory response to this kind of statement. Maybe I had been pushing myself too hard, but what was I supposed to do instead? What was the alternative? Not take care of my children? That was lunacy. Not work? We needed the money. Not keep the house running and in working order? None of my obligations were optional. Neglect personal hygiene? I doubt that's what they were insinuating.

Eventually, I closed my mouth and shrugged. "It is what it is."

Sandra wrinkled her nose at me. "Sometimes I wonder about you, Fiona."

"How so, Sandra?" A rueful smile slowly claimed my features as my friend and I studied each other.

"You are so wise. And yet, I think sometimes your wisdom blinds you to the obvious."

Ashley pushed Sandra's shoulder. "Stop making those fortune cookie comments and just say what you mean."

Sandra and I continued to regard each other, her eyes narrowing by millimeters until they were slits.

Marie chose this moment to jog over and interrupt, her tone infused with urgency. "Okay, all of Ashley's work people are gone. It's just us knitters and the husbands-slash-significant others, plus Dan the Security Man and his boring date. I say we go back to Janie's place and see how she's doing. If she's up for it, let's divide that humongous cake into seven equal parts and chow down."

Sandra and I stared at each other for another beat before she shifted her attention to Marie, her expression clearing at once as she said, "Yes. Let's go eat cake."

Sandra surprised me by letting the matter of my blinding wisdom drop so quickly. Typically, she was like a cat with yarn when it came to psychoanalyzing people for their own good.

But then she stepped forward and looped her arm through mine, turning us toward the kitchen. "Come on, Fiona. I'm taking you to your husband."

"Why?"

She squeezed my arm with hers and inclined her head toward mine. "Because he's going to take you home. You need to get laid more than you need cake."

CHAPTER 5

Dear Future Husband,

Here's the thing, future husband, if I'm marrying you, then you must be a pretty awesome person. I promise to love and cherish you always. But if I annoy you, just walk away, but don't leave. Don't get mad at me and then don't speak to me.

- Kristen
Ohio, USA

~Present Day~
Fiona

I FELL ASLEEP on the ride home.

We were talking about the night, snuggling in the backseat, and apparently I collapsed against him. He must've carried me upstairs and put me to bed, because when I woke up I was naked.

Typical.

I glanced at the clock on the nightstand. It was 3:04 a.m. and I was awake. I was awake because Greg was home, and the knowledge that he was here made me restless. I typically slept less when he was home because I didn't want to miss a minute.

Not helping matters, Greg's equally naked form was wrapped around my body, his hands on my stomach and breast. Slow, even breaths were hot against the back of my neck. Add to this cornucopia of matrimonial extravagance, the super-soft cotton sheets warm against the bare skin of my side and legs, and I was all tingles and hopeful, impatient desire.

And yet . . . I needed to brush my teeth. And I hadn't shaved my legs in weeks. Or tamed my *lady closet* as Greg was prone to call it. I didn't take the time to groom before the party and now I was regretting my inaction. Staring into the darkness, I debated whether to make a move on my husband or take care of business first.

"Fe . . . are you up?" His voice was a low whisper, roughened by sleep, the sound sliding over me like a silk sheet.

It stole my breath. I'd missed him so much. So. Much. The ache was physical and constant, vacillating between a sharp, stabbing pang and a dull, simmering tightness.

"I'm awake." I closed my eyes, concentrating on where our bodies touched, trying to memorize every texture and sensation.

He moved, released me, and the heat from his body shifted away, causing my eyes to fly open.

I twisted to look at him. "Where are you going?"

"Just a sec."

I heard him briefly rustling and moving items on his side table before he was back, and his hand reached for one of mine.

"Take this." He placed a small, smooth rectangle in my palm.

"What is it?"

"It's that dental chewing gum. I know you're thinking about getting up and brushing your teeth. Don't."

I grinned into the darkness. "Thanks."

"You're welcome." I heard him unwrap his own piece, followed by the sound of him chewing. "You have two minutes."

I popped the strongly flavored gum into my mouth. "Two minutes?"

"I have questions. And you have two minutes before you're interrogated."

I turned to my other side, so now we were facing each other. His hand moved in unhurried circles on my body, caressing me from my shoulder, down my arm, hip, thigh . . .

"What kind of questions?" I whispered, though it might have sounded like a pant.

His movements stilled and I could just make out his eyes by the dark grey light filtering in through the closed drapes. He was staring at me. My palm was pressed against his chest and I felt the uptick in his heart rate, the change in his breathing.

"Fe . . ." He said it like a plea.

"I miss you."

He gripped my wrist before I could move it lower, guessing my intentions correctly. I didn't want to talk, not yet. Maybe later.

. . . maybe not.

"I miss the sound of your heartbeat," I continued, because I did. I missed it. I craved it.

"You must stop," he growled and groaned.

"Why?"

"Because I am worried. You cannot fathom how much I need you."

"That sounds like a reason *not* to stop."

His hold tightened as I halfheartedly tried to pull out of his grip.

He ignored me, instead clearing his throat and changing the subject. "You know I'm not one of those weird bastards that fixates on my partner's eating habits, but I can't help noticing you're not eating at all. You've lost nearly a stone."

"Remind me, how much is a stone? In pounds?"

"Fourteen pounds."

"Hmm . . ."

"Hmm . . ." he mimicked, threading our fingers together and bringing our joined hands behind my back.

I hadn't lost fourteen pounds. It was more like eleven pounds. And the reasons were simple: nothing tasted good and I was busy.

"What's going on, Fe?"

I shrugged, lowering my eyes to his lips. "Nothing out of the ordinary. Things are . . . busy."

"So busy you're not eating? What can I do to help?"

Staring at his lips, my first thought was, *kiss me.*

My second thought was, *touch me.*

And my third thought was, *hire me a nanny, chef, and housekeeper. . . and never leave me again.*

I didn't give voice to any of these thoughts. I was enjoying his nearness too much. The resultant combined warmth of our bodies wrapped around my limbs, heart, and mind, thawing the frigidity of loneliness.

While he was gone the bed was cold. Even in the summer, I would bring hot water bottles—three of them—into bed with me. I'd knitted them cozies. In a state of mild drunkenness one night, I'd sprayed the knitted cozies with his cologne.

Even though we were married, I had to admit the wool cozies that smelled like Greg were a little weird. I hadn't told him about their existence. I wondered what, if anything, he did to battle the solitude.

"Momma?" Grace's sad little voice pierced the blanket of warm silence that had fallen between us.

I lifted my head and waited. When she called out again, my head dropped back to the pillow and I sighed.

"I'll get her." Greg was already rolling away.

"She's been having nightmares. I think she's growing."

He pulled on his boxers and grabbed his pajamas. "You think she's having nightmares because she's growing?"

"Yes." I snuggled deeper into the bed, my hand gripping the sheet where he'd been laying, wishing I could grab and hold and keep the residual warmth of his body. "She gets emotional when she's growing—temper tantrums, crying, nightmares—I think it's low blood sugar. Give her a banana."

"I got it." Pajamas in place, Greg leaned forward and kissed my forehead. "Stay here and sleep. I'll get the kids in the morning and keep them home from school."

"No school today. It's Saturday." I stretched and yawned, thankful it was the weekend. Jack and Grace would go crazy if they thought Greg was at home without them. I reached for his pillow and hugged it.

Greg loitered at the edge of the bed, hesitating like he wanted to say something else. I stared at his greyish outline, blinking tiredly.

"Momma!" Grace's urgent voice was closer than before. She must've left her bed.

"It's good to be home," he said finally. Reaching forward again, he cupped my cheek and brushed his thumb across my lips. "It's good to touch you."

Then he turned, pushing his fingers through his hair, and left the room. He closed the door with quiet carefulness. I pressed my face into his pillow and inhaled, because the weird wool cozies were paltry imposters in comparison to the lingering scent of him on his pillow.

***

I WOKE TO the sound of the front door slamming, followed by Greg's voice urging in a harsh whisper, "What did I tell you about slamming the door? Your mother needs her sleep cycles, otherwise she'll keep malfunctioning and we'll have to take her to the mechanic again."

"Dad, Mommy is not a robot." Jack sounded reluctantly amused.

"I never said she was a robot. I said she's one-quarter robot. And as I've told you a hundred times, you're one-sixteenth robot—why do you think you're so good at math?"

"Dad . . ."

"It also explains why your grandmother has no soul. She's one hundred percent robot."

"Am I a robot?" Grace whispered her question; she must've been standing very close to our bedroom door.

"You have the same percentage as your brother," Greg responded very gently, "and that's why you don't like baths."

Relaxing into the pillows, I folded my hands behind my head and listened.

"But, Gracie, baths are good for you. They keep your circuitry working. And dirty robots can't dance."

"Can they do the robot?" Jack asked, his tone exceptionally dry. He'd been growing more and more sarcastic over the last few months.

"No. Dirty robots can't even dance the robot, but they can do the skunk."

"What's the skunk?" Grace asked.

"It's where you stand really, really still . . . and then you fart."

Both children launched into a fit of hysterical laughter, with Grace exclaiming, "That's not a dance!"

"It is so a dance. Here, watch me."

"Dad, no!" I could almost see Jack roll his eyes.

"Jack, where's your mute button? Or did you have it taken offline?"

"I don't have a mute button."

"What? Well then, we'll need to have one installed as soon as possible . . ." Greg's voice faded, as did Gracie's giggles. I heard the front door open and close, then silence.

All at once I realized I was smiling; I also didn't have a headache. I couldn't remember the last time I woke up smiling. It was probably the last time Greg had been home.

I allowed myself another few moments of luxury—lying in bed, in the morning, surrounded by quiet—before I sat up and glanced at the alarm clock.

My mouth dropped open.

11:57 a.m.

I couldn't believe it.

I'd slept for over twelve hours.

Greg was leaving for the airport at 1:00 p.m.

I jumped from the bed and darted to the bathroom, tripping over his shoes and nearly face-planting into the carpet. I caught myself against the wall, noticing the mess of clothes all over the place. A few were mine— the ones he'd removed last night—but most were his.

Two pairs of jeans were on the floor in front of the hamper; his socks, boxers, pajamas, and shirts were strewn like confetti all over the place. I frowned at the mess, but decided to ignore it for now in favor of taking a quick shower.

Though I did mutter to myself as I waited for the water to heat up, "What is so hard about putting clothes in the hamper?"

Ten minutes later, I was showered and dressed and feeling like it was Christmas morning. I quickly walked to the living room and was about to call out to see if anyone was home, but I abruptly lost my ability to speak.

The apartment was a disaster.

A consummate disaster.

If mess-making were an Olympic sport, this mess would have won the bronze medal, maybe the silver.

Apparently, every toy Grace and Jack owned was scattered—again, confetti style—all over the living room. The cushions had been pulled from the couch. Grace must've been painting at the coffee table—which I never allowed—because the water jar for her paint brush had tipped over. Dirty brown water had spilled all over the carpet.

Breakfast plates and cups were where the sofa cushions had once been. Three boxes of miscellaneous cables and broken machinery—which, last I knew, were in storage downstairs—were spread out on the dining room table along with Greg's soldering gun and the kids' toolboxes.

A stack of clothes, clothes I'd just folded the day before yesterday, were piled in a disordered jumble by the entranceway.

I closed my eyes against the visually violent mess assault. I was afraid to check the kids' rooms or the kitchen. I felt like crying.

I might have just slept for twelve hours, woken up refreshed and reinvigorated, but this chaos had effectively undone two and a half days of work. My knitting group was coming on Tuesday. I'd been so careful about keeping everything clean.

Pragmatic me knew, in the scheme of things, it was no big deal. It was just a mess. My friends wouldn't care. I could clear the dishes, replace the cushions, and push the toys to one side of the room. I could strong-arm Grace and Jack into putting their belongings away tomorrow. I could refold the laundry while listening to an audiobook. The carpet would be stained . . . so what? It happens. Shit happens.

And yet, why was it necessary for shit to happen all over the apartment I'd just cleaned? Why couldn't they have shit outside?

The front door opened and I shook myself, trying to figure out what I should do and who I should be. Defaulting to pragmatic me was easiest because it was where I lived most of the time. I was good at bottling my frustrations and disappointments, especially when they didn't really matter.

Later, I would scream into my pillow. I would run thirteen point one miles while the kids were at school. I would go to the gym and beat the stuffing out of a punching bag. I would work out with one of the other black belts at my mixed-martial arts studio.

But, pragmatically speaking, right now—right before Greg left again for the airport and disappeared for the next four months—was not a good time to be angry. I endeavored to soothe the angry, feverish fire ants in my brain.

Breathe in through the nose, out through the mouth. . . and repeat seven thousand times.

Grace jogged into the apartment and made a beeline for the dining room table. She fished around in one of the boxes and pulled out two coils of copper. She was wearing a welding mask; it was pushed up and away from her face.

A welding mask . . . ?

"Grace?"

She stopped short, searching the apartment and grinning widely when she spotted me.

"Mom! We're making something for you. Come see!" She turned on her heel and sprinted out the front door.

I picked my way through the toys, stepping over partially constructed Lego buildings and a discarded muffin wrapper surrounded by a halo of crumbs. Clearing the obstacle course, I left my apartment in my bare feet and found Grace propping open Professor Matt Simmons's door. She waved me forward and I followed her through Matt's apartment to the balcony.

What I saw then would forever be etched on my brain.

Everyone was wearing welding masks, Greg, Matt, and Jack. Which was a good thing, because Jack was welding.

That's right, eight-year-old Jack was welding.

Granted, Greg was helping.

But Jack was welding.

It was too much. I lost my mind.

"Stay here," I ordered. I grabbed Grace's mask and marched to the balcony door.

I knocked on the glass, loud enough for them to hear. Matt turned his masked face to the door and waved cheerfully. I glowered at him. He dropped his hand. He moved to Greg and tapped him on the shoulder, then pointed at me. The welding gun turned off, Greg glanced over his shoulder. He waved. I glowered. He dropped his hand.

I watched his chest rise and fall with a bracing breath—that's how *I* knew *he* knew *I* was mad—and he leaned forward, saying something to Jack. Jack nodded and leaned back in his chair, placing his hands on his knees.

Greg stood, lifting the mask and pulling the gloves he was wearing from his hands. He gave me a tight and contrite smile as he approached the door.

"Grace," I said, holding my husband's gaze while I spoke to my daughter, "go out on the balcony with your brother. And under no circumstances is anyone allowed to *weld*."

"Okay, Mommy."

I took two steps back and Grace walked swiftly by me as soon as Greg opened the balcony door. He waited for her to pass before entering. When the door was firmly shut, we stared at each other for a long moment. I didn't speak, not yet, because my urge was to place him in a chokehold.

He lifted his hands and said, "I was hoping to be finished before you woke up. It's taking longer than I expected."

I still couldn't speak because I was expecting the first words out of his mouth to be, *I'm sorry. I shouldn't have allowed our eight-year-old son or our five-year-old daughter to weld. I realize it's very dangerous and their wellbeing is important to me. Please forgive me.*

Since that's not what he said, I still wanted to place him in a chokehold.

He scratched the back of his neck and shifted on his feet, watching me cautiously like I might explode. Hesitantly he asked, "Is this about the mess?"

"The mess?" My question was shrill; it reminded me of a police siren.

Was that my voice?

"In the living room. We were in a hurry, but I did clean the kitchen."

"You cleaned the kitchen?" *That can't be my voice. I don't sound like that.*

"We made muffins this morning. I saved you some, they're on the counter."

The resident fire ants in my brain were trying to singe their way out of my brain using a tiny ant-sized blowtorch.

"No, Greg. This isn't about the mess. It's about our eight-year-old son and our five-year-old daughter, who are now apparently proficient welders."

"I wouldn't call them proficient, at least not at TIG welding. It's safer in some ways, but it's more complex on the whole."

"Greg—"

"And besides, if we don't teach them about welding at home, they'll just learn about it on the streets." He grinned. He was grinning at me.

Fire ants.

In my brain.

With a TIG welder.

Matt opened the door; he, Jack, and Grace filed in. My eyes darted to the trio and I took a calming breath.

"It's not snowing, but it's cold outside. I thought I'd make the kids some hot chocolate," Matt explained, his smile apologetic.

Jack asked, "Are you guys arguing?"

"Yes," I said.

"No," Greg said.

We stared at each other, Greg's grin morphing into a wane grimace.

Grace came to my side and wrapped her small hand around my index finger. I glanced down at her just before her little voice declared, "That sounds like something Hitler would say."

Matt gasped. Greg barked a laugh. Jack, unfazed, walked over to the piano. And I closed my eyes, reminding myself to keep my voice level and calm.

"Are you angry, Mommy?"

I nodded my head. "Yes, Gracie. I'm angry."

"I'm sorry."

I pressed my lips together and lifted my eyelids, issuing my daughter a small smile. "Thank you, Grace. I'm not angry with you, but when we get home I need you to pick up your toys, okay?"

"Okay," she said, then gave me a kiss on my hand.

"Can I get anyone something to drink? Hot chocolate? Vodka perhaps?" Matt offered.

"No vodka for me," Jack said, sliding onto the piano bench.

"Come with me, Gracie. Maybe you can find some marshmallows while I boil the water." Matt disappeared into his kitchen like Al-Qaeda was on his heels, likely relieved to escape, and Grace skipped after him.

"Darling," Greg closed the distance between us, taking my hand in both of his and kissing my palm. "I'm sorry about the mess in the apartment. I can go back right now and clean it up. But the kids and I wanted to make you something, and the Professor had a TIG welder."

I felt myself soften. "Are you and Matty best friends now?"

"I'm not going to braid his hair anytime soon." Greg's eyes moved to the right and he tilted his head back and forth in a small considering movement. It was funny. I softened a little more.

Seeing my temper disarm, Greg lowered his voice. "Listen, Jack isn't too young to weld, not when I'm sitting right next to him. I wouldn't do anything to endanger . . . to endanger . . ." Greg frowned and turned, glancing over his shoulder to where Jack sat at the piano, playing Tchaikovsky.

Playing Tchaikovsky. . . !!!

"What the hell?"

"Oh my gosh!" I squeezed Greg's hand, bringing his attention back to me. He looked utterly confused. "I forgot to tell you."

"Forgot to tell me?"

"About Jack. About his piano playing."

Greg studied me for a long moment, obviously trying to piece everything together on his own. "Has he been taking lessons?"

"No. He's playing by ear."

"By ear?"

"Yes. I just found out, two days ago."

I quickly told the story of discovering Jack's aptitude for music. Greg stared at me, disbelieving as I related the facts.

Greg crossed his arms over his chest, struggling to understand. "He was playing at the dance studio?"

I nodded, feeling perplexed and overwhelmed all over again. "Yes."

"Well, what did you do about it? I mean, what are we going to do? This is serious, right?" Greg shifted his stare to Jack, who was still playing.

"She went to the doctor," Matt said, entering the conversation with a non sequitur.

"What?" Greg's gaze flickered between Matt and me. "You took Jack to the doctor?"

"No. Fiona went to the doctor. For her headaches. But the MRI machine was broken, so . . . That's what you're talking about, right?" Matt placed a cup of hot chocolate in my hands, adding, "I did put some alcohol in your cup, Fiona. But I was out of vodka. I hope you like rum."

***

"WHEN WERE YOU going to tell me about the headaches?"

"I didn't want to worry you."

Greg was pacing back and forth in our bedroom, his hands on his hips, more furious than I'd ever seen him.

"You didn't want to . . ." He shook his head, his eyes skimming over my form like I was unknown to him, a stranger who'd suddenly appeared before him. "I can't believe you didn't tell me."

Grace and Jack were still next door. As soon as Matt had mentioned the headaches, Greg grew very quiet and still. He looked at me. I flinched because I knew my husband and I saw that he was enraged. With a tremendously cold voice, he asked Matt to watch the kids. He grabbed me by my hand and marched me back to our apartment, and into our bedroom. He paced back and forth, obviously panicking, for several untenable moments.

And here we were.

I was sitting on the bed, hoping he'd sit next to me. I reached out to him and he recoiled, moving out of my reach, and continued his pacing. My heart lodged in my throat and my stomach dropped to my feet.

"Will you sit next to me please?" Despite my distress, I endeavored to keep my tone calm and reasonable.

"No!" he thundered. His tone was neither calm nor reasonable, and the single word made me jump.

"I'm sure it's no big deal."

"Do you not remember having a brain tumor?"

I ignored his heated question, instead opting to impassively explain. "I haven't been sleeping well, Grace is having bad dreams—nothing I can't handle—and I'm sure that's it. Once she starts sleeping through the night again, everything will go back to normal."

He stopped his pacing. Instead, he glared at me like I was a terrorist. "Nothing you can't handle?"

"That's right." I nodded once.

"So, you don't need me."

"Right. I don't need you," I assured him automatically, hoping he would calm down.

Greg blinked once, his jaw ticked, and I didn't miss the renewed inferno blazing behind his eyes. He said nothing, but I couldn't help feeling like I'd done something wrong. A heavy ache settled in my chest, peppered with heavy helpings of guilt and doubt. We stared at each other across the ocean of our king-sized bed, both frowning.

Perhaps I should have told him about the headaches . . . but to what purpose?

He'd been thousands of miles away on a different continent. He couldn't do anything from an oil rig in South Africa.

We'd never argued about the nature his work, about his leaving. After Jack was born and Greg's year-long desk assignment was over, we'd discussed his job and the logistics of his absence like two rational adults. We'd made a pros and cons list, and money had been the deciding factor, on paper.

But in real life—so, not the cold, logical facts written in list format—Greg loved his job. He loved the important work only he could accomplish on-site. He made a difference to the world. The techniques he taught saved lives, and not just human lives. He was a pioneer. His methods for oil extraction were making a difference in the global environment. His ability to ingratiate himself to local governments and convince them to do the right thing was invaluable.

I'd decided years ago I wanted children, and I'd recognized at the time I'd likely be raising them mostly by myself. I'd made the choice and accepted the consequences. I was on my own.

I didn't like the shuttered quality to his expression, nor the withdrawn, measured way he glanced around the bedroom. I debated what to do, what action to take, what I could say to make things better. In the end I decided to give in to the impulse to apologize.

"I'm sorry."

His gaze flickered to mine and he held very still. "For what?"

"I'm sorry if you're upset about the headaches. But if I thought they were important, then I would have told you."

"And Grace's nightmares? Are you sorry you didn't tell me about those?"

I searched the ceiling, my bedside lamp, table, and the pillows on the bed. I didn't know how to answer him, so my thoughts tumbled from my lips. "Grace has nightmares. Sometimes Jack has nightmares. Am I supposed to tell you every time one of the kids has a nightmare? Or scrapes their elbow? Or gets a paper cut?"

"What about Jack's sudden aptitude for music? Or were you going to surprise me when he turns eighteen and is playing at Carnegie Hall?"

I pointed a wagging index finger in his general direction. "That's not fair. I *just* found out about Jack playing the piano two days ago. He didn't say a word to me. And when would you and I have had a chance to discuss it?"

Greg's cloud of unhappiness darkened at my words. "You found out two days ago that our son is likely a musical prodigy. That's a big deal, Fiona. That's not a paper cut. He can play complicated pieces without actually knowing how to read music, after hearing it a few times. And I found out ten minutes ago. Do you not see anything wrong with that disparity?"

"What do you want me to do? Send you psychic messages?"

"Yes, via the magical internets. Send me an email, how about that?"

Swelling anger and bitterness twisted in my stomach and burned my throat. I longed to remind him I was doing everything on my own, that I was doing the best I could. Then he comes home and can't even be bothered to put his laundry in the hamper. He didn't have a right to real-time updates on, or arbitrary opinions about children he wasn't actively raising.

But I didn't remind him.

Greg was leaving in less than five minutes. He likely wouldn't be back in Chicago for three or four months, during which I would take the kids camping with Alex and Drew. Alone. I would drive Jack to soccer practice and cheer him on during his games. Alone. I would go to Grace's dance recital and applaud when she took a bow. Alone. I would help them with their homework, give them baths, shuttle them to doctors' appointments, play-dates, and birthday parties.

All of this alone.

Arguing was pointless. It would change nothing. At the end of the day, I was still the one raising Grace and Jack, and he would still be gone.

So I swallowed the anger and bitterness, kept my tone even and carefully civil, and indulged him. "You're right. I'm sorry. I should have emailed you. From now on, if something important happens, I'll send you an email as soon as possible."

He stared at me, examining me as though my words were a puzzle. The longer he stared, the colder and more remote his posture grew. At length he cast his gaze to the floor and scowled at our carpet. I watched as he swallowed, seemingly with effort, his eyes unfocused as though he were attempting to tame unkind impulses.

"You know . . ." he started, his voice rough. But then he shook his head and clamped his mouth shut, biting back words. He turned away from me and moved to leave. When he grasped the handle, he paused and said to the door, "I love you, Fe."

He left the room.

A moment later I heard the front door open and close.

He was gone.

And I was alone. Again.

CHAPTER 6

Dear R.

I honestly believe that you were completely and totally clueless to the fact that I was and had been head over heels in love with you from the day we met. It wasn't a secret to anyone else. When you catch me "creepy" staring at you now, all I'm really doing is silently appreciating all that you are and all that you mean to me. Forgive a man if you will for wanting to cherish something a little more openly after having to hide it for twenty years.

-D
Letter
USA
Friends for 20 years, currently engaged

~17 years ago~
Greg

"**I'M NOT GOOD** enough for you, Fe. But . . ." I shrugged, unable to do anything but smile at this woman who'd become my entire world, "no else one is either. So I might as well take you for my own. Marry me."

She stared down at me, captivatingly astonished. Though I couldn't tell if she was merely shocked, or both shocked and horrified. She'd covered her mouth with her hands and was standing still, motionless, too stunned to even move.

I'd effectively pressed her proverbial pause button.

Obviously, I was completely and utterly mad.

Too early.

Too soon.

She wasn't ready, not for a proposal of marriage.

At eighteen, Fiona was wise beyond her years. And yet her wisdom was as tragic as it was beautiful.

So I waited. And waited.

And waited.

Just like I'd waited all those months after seeing her for the first time, keeping my distance despite seeing her everywhere—at the gym, the café, the library, in the dorm lobby—endeavoring to convince myself I was merely infatuated with her façade. *In lust* was an easier concept to manage than some fanciful rubbish like *love at first sight,* or *soul mates,* or *cosmically meant for each other.*

So I waited. And waited.

And waited.

Kneeling in front of her, holding my offering between us, my heart in a little blue box.

"Fe?" I prompted, because a creeping uncertainty had taken up residence at the base of my throat.

She flinched, her eyes jumping between the ring and me.

And then she said, "Yes."

Though it was more of a,

!!!! ♥ ♥ ♥ ♥ Y E S ♥ ♥ ♥ ♥ !!!!

Because she'd yelled it—screamed it at me, actually—with a shade of hysterical delight. I didn't have even a split second to recover, to grin, to rejoice in her response before she launched herself, tackling me to the plush carpet. Quick thinking had me closing the ring box before it was knocked from my hand in her exuberance.

Straddling my hips, Fiona covered my face and neck in kisses. She punctuated each press of her soft lips with another "Yes," the volume and intonation varying wildly.

I laughed and then groaned as she moved over me, lithe and eager, her body clamoring for intimacy.

"Wait-wait, darling." I sought to still her movements, but she was surprisingly strong. Though, if I dwelled upon it, her strength wasn't at all surprising. She could climb walls. And do backflips. And walk on her hands for an indeterminate period of time.

She rocked against my growing erection, driving caution from my mind and the breath from my lungs. Her dress was the problem, because the skirt was virtually nonexistent. The only impediments to a hasty coupling were her inconsequential panties, and my suit pants and boxers.

And, you know, her virginity.

"Make love to me, Greg," she whispered hotly against my ear, now driving good judgment away. In fact, all noble thoughts and feelings packed their bags, loaded up, and decided to take a vacation for the evening. Selfish desire had pushed them out.

Good riddance.

I flipped her onto her back, and her hands were everywhere—in my hair, pulling at the hem of my shirt, scratching my sides, reaching for the buckle of my belt. The only sign of nerves was the slight trembling of her fingers as she cupped me through my pants.

I batted her hand away because I was prone to make a mess in my boxers if she continued to stroke me with her eager palm.

"Fe, we have to get off—"

"Yes! Let's get off!"

"—the carpet," I finished as I straightened away, laughing at her wide, impatient eyes and opportune remark. "We have to get off the carpet."

She gave me a determined glare, then did that thing only gymnasts know how to do, where one springs off the ground in a blatant display of strength and flexibility, kicking off her shoes as she did so.

As soon as we were both standing she was on me again, backing me into the bed. I grabbed her hands between us.

"Darling, is this your way of telling me you're feeling sexually frustrated?"

"Frustrated? No." Now she was trying to climb me with just her legs. "Starved? Yes."

"Though I'm thoroughly enjoying your exuberance, I really must insist we slow down." Not because I intended to stop. But rather, much like the first time we'd kissed, I wanted to prepare her for what came next.

"No slowing down." She rubbed her thigh against my cock, crippling both my ability to think and move. "I don't know if I'm doing this right, but I honestly don't care anymore. I want you. I want you so very badly. And I want those bad things you promised . . ."

Well, okay then.

". . . and I want—"

I cut her off by capturing her mouth with a kiss, turning her such that the backs of her legs were against the mattress, then pushing her on top of it. I reached under her skirt, found her extraordinarily inconsequential lace panties, and pulled them from her legs.

Her wide eyes, though still rimmed with excitement, had grown anxious as well.

Standing over her, trailing my fingertips back along her bare legs, luxuriating in the feel of her, her nervous little exhales, I grinned.

"Prepare yourself. I'm going to kiss you now."

A panicked question formed between her eyebrows as I knelt to the floor, pressing the flat of my palms against her inner thighs and opening her to me with my thumbs.

"You're going to . . . ?" She didn't finish the sentence. Her chest moved up and down with violent breaths.

Here is the truth: I love pussy.

And hers was petal pink and sensitive and secret, and entirely *mine*. I lowered my mouth and licked her just once, loving her tortured sounds of shock and awe, the instinctive rolling of her hips, and her mindless abandoned desire. When I began to move in earnest, her hips bucked off the bed, drawing a rumbling laugh from me, and a strangled, feral moan from her.

She was strong. I was stronger. I pressed her back to the bed, held her there with one hand while I drew small circles on the back of her thigh with my fingertips.

I'd barely found my rhythm when she squeaked, "Something is happening," as though I required a status update, as though this were an experiment and not the most natural thing in the world between two people in love.

Watching her lose control, feeling it, knowing I was the master of her pleasure, the proprietor of her trust, and cultivator of her appetites intoxicated me with an intense and heady sense of power.

Just as it humbled me.

Just as it made me remember why I'd insisted we wait to begin with. I stretched next to her, petting and stroking her as she continued to tremble, gathering her in my arms. She was completely vulnerable to me. Noble thoughts and feelings returned in a flood of protectiveness and certainty of possession.

I'd bought the ring the week after Valentine's Day, more a compulsion than an impulse, and I'd carried it in my pocket whenever we were together.

The ring had been a promise to myself.

One day she would be mine.

One day I would be hers.

Until then, I'd decided I would be patient. We would take things slow, discover each other's minds, foster the seed of love and mutual respect before satiating each other's bodies.

The promise was enough. I'd planned to wait years before asking, before claiming her skin as mine.

Instead, during this first week of May, just three months after we'd agreed to be the only source of romantic situations for each other, I'd just asked Fiona to marry me.

And she said yes.

Again, it had been more a compulsion than an impulse, just like teasing her in the car earlier in the evening, or bringing her to this posh hotel, or proclaiming that I was in love with her.

I was in love with her. I had no choice. I *needed* her. She was as vital to me as the heart I'd offered and she'd accepted just moments ago. We bantered, teased. Everything felt good, better, meaningful. No doubt I was completely enamored. No doubt she owned me.

I was coming to understand fear was found in waiting. But that meant bravery was also found in waiting. I've never been very good at being brave.

Yet for her I would be. We would wait. We would explore and discover, take our time, learn to love delayed gratification. Because we were building a foundation to last a lifetime.

CHAPTER 7

Dear Husband: I am one more dog bark away from shaving my head and leaving everything behind. Your son was not good at Target. Or when we got home. There's mud all over my life and salmonella all over my soul.

Dear Wife: I promise to do all I can to get you to stay. I am sorry it is hard right now. If you leave, know I will follow. With chocolate. And muffins. And movies. And yoga pants.

-Heidi and Charles
Text Messages
Iowa, USA
Married 7 years

~Present Day~
Fiona

"**I DON'T THINK** it was actually a real thing. I can't imagine any Christians I know getting all worked up about renaming Christmas Wreath to Evergreen Wreath. It's like, come on! Who cares? We have bigger fish to fry, namely frying fish and distributing loaves to the hungry." Sandra waved her knitting needle in the air like it was a baton, emphasizing her point.

Elizabeth nodded. "I'm convinced the war on Christmas is actually just one atheist named Dave spreading rumors on the Internet from his parents' basement in Rochester, New York, trying to make Christians look like super nuts."

"Poor Dave. You should pray for him." Marie giggled.

"I will, Marie. I will pray for Dave." Sandra poked Marie with a finger. "Aren't you an atheist?"

Marie shrugged. "More or less. I'm agnostic. And it's not contagious, Sandra. You can't catch it."

"That's not what Dave said," Elizabeth muttered under her breath, eliciting various heights of laughter from the group.

It was Tuesday knit night, but we weren't at my apartment. Elizabeth had called me Monday and suggested we move the meet-up to her house as Janie was still under the weather. I readily agreed. My place was still a disaster. Severely lacking in energy, feeling morose and mournful, I hadn't made the time to do any cleaning.

The first twenty-four hours after Greg's departure were typically the worst. My chest hurt like I had unassailable heartburn. This time I was more heartbroken than usual.

I hated fighting with my husband. Nothing felt good or right or normal until we felt good and right and normal about each other.

After the kids fell asleep on Saturday, I'd composed an email. He wouldn't receive it immediately, but I needed to apologize. He'd been worried about me and I'd patronized him instead of acknowledging his concerns.

So I wrote down all my thoughts, apologizing for my behavior. Apologizing for keeping him in the dark about my headaches, promising to redouble my efforts regarding the kids and keeping him in the loop. I also confessed to Jack's upcoming soccer season and Grace's princess dress. The email took me two hours to write, and I felt marginally better after I hit send.

It was now Tuesday night and he hadn't yet responded, so I was still feeling pretty crummy.

Kat leaned forward. "As the token Jew in the room, can I just say I don't get offended when I see a Christmas tree in an airport. I like all the decorations, it's like the entire country goes Liberace for a month."

"Well, as the token agnostic in the room, can I just say nothing offends me," Marie added while studying her knitting pattern.

"Nothing that you *know of* offends you," Nico corrected with a smirk.

"Ha ha. Very clever." Marie rolled her eyes.

Sandra poked Marie again. "But don't you celebrate Christmas?"

"Absolutely. I guess I'm what's called a "Holitarian." I'm an equal opportunity holiday celebrator, especially if the holiday or special occasion involves cocktails and presents."

"I'm thinking of becoming a Buddhist." Janie held a cold glass of lemonade in her hands, taking frequent sips. "Their respect for life, all lives, appeals to me."

"I can see you as a Buddhist," Marie said in such a way that made it sound like she believed religion were an item of clothing or a costume to be tried on and worn on the outside, rather than a deeply held belief.

"Well, as the token southern Baptist in the room, I can confirm that there *are* some Christians who get irritated about relabeling things as generic that were once Christian-specific. But I suspect that's because early Christians did the same thing to the pagans as a means to dilute pagan religions and evangelize."

"That's right, they did. And it worked." Marie studied Ashley with a thoughtful frown. "Like Halloween and All Saints Day."

"Correct." Ashley nodded once. "And if—no transgression implied to my dear agnostic friend—if Holitarians dilute the meaningfulness of Christmas by making everything generic, then it's the same thing. Christmas and the traditions around it lose their meaning, so I understand the irritation, even though I don't think most Christians pay attention to it, having better things to do. But I can also confirm that the media makes a big deal out of it when they should be covering more important issues—like our hungry brethren, and homelessness, and neglected children."

"I'm going to miss you, Ashley Winston," Nico said to the hat he was crocheting. "Your perspective is always well researched and well rounded."

We all paused for a moment, the rhythm of our hands ceasing, because tonight was Ashley's last evening with us before she moved to Tennessee. The landscape of our group was changing. Over the last two years, Janie, Elizabeth, and Sandra had all gotten married, now Janie was pregnant. Ashley's move to Tennessee felt like the end of an era.

"It's because I'm a reader. Readers have open minds; they have to. Otherwise they wouldn't read. And I'm going to miss you too, Nicoletta." Ashley gave Nico a small grin. "By this time next week I'll be Skyping in from Tennessee, surrounded by my degenerate brothers. God help me."

"Speaking of degenerates, where is Drew tonight?" Nico asked. This question caused a few chuckles because Drew Runous was the least likely of our crowd to be labeled as degenerate. He was the strong and silent type, and he looked like a mountain man. Probably because he was a mountain man.

"He and Alex went to the sporting goods store to look at fishing supplies. I think they're planning a trip for the summer."

"I'm not done talking about the last subject," Sandra chimed in.

"Let it go, Sandra." Marie had set her knitting aside to help Kat untangle her yarn. "We all know what you're doing. You're in denial about Ashley leaving, so you're trying to change the subject."

Sandra ignored Marie's valid analysis of the situation and pointed her knitting needle at Nico. "You're Catholic, right? What do the Catholics say?"

Nico lifted an eyebrow and regarded Sandra with sparkly eyes. "I'm not the Lorax of Catholics. I don't speak for the trees of the faithful. That's why we have the Pope."

Kat giggled. "The Lorax of Catholics, I like that."

Sandra squinted at Nico, but her next question was for me. "What about you, Fiona?"

"Fiona is more of a lead-by-example kind of person," Elizabeth remarked, reaching for her whiskey-spiked hot chocolate.

"Fiona would be a lead-by-example kind of person," Sandra nodded her agreement, but then added, the problem is, she's too quiet about it."

"Isn't that the point of leading by example?" Kat frowned at her ball of yarn, more of a tangled mass of yarn than a ball.

"Yes, mostly. But if you don't ever say anything, then how can others follow your example? All the good works get lost in the background noise. I think there are two parts to leading by example: do what you say, and say what you do."

"Am I supposed to narrate my life? Add captions to all my actions?" I grinned, not looking up from my work in progress.

"No. But tooting a horn every once in a while wouldn't hurt—and it doesn't even have to be your own horn. But making no noise at all when you, oh I don't know, need help, or see others in need, isn't leading by example. It's living with your head in the sand, or . . . No, that's not right. It's living with your emotions bottled up. You shouldn't let people walk all over everything you believe, take advantage, or discount your feelings. If you don't prioritize your feelings, no one else will."

Everyone had stopped knitting and was staring at Sandra, including me. I'd learned long ago to always pause and reflect whenever Sandra offered an opinion; I was doing that now.

So I was surprised when Elizabeth said, "That wasn't very nice."

"What?" Sandra cast a wide-eyed gaze to Elizabeth.

"You just accused Fiona of living her life with her head in the sand," Marie supplied, frowning at Sandra.

"No. I didn't. I just accused her of living with bottled-up emotions," Sandra countered.

"Well, that's not nice either." Marie poked Sandra, her frown deepening.

"She didn't say it to be mean," I defended my friend. "She said it because she's concerned."

"See?" Sandra lifted her hand toward me. "Look how reasonable she's being. That's not normal. And she doesn't have the excuse of being a psychiatrist, like I do. Non-psychiatrists shouldn't be that well-adjusted, it's a problem."

"Still . . ." Marie continued to glower at Sandra.

"Don't give me that face. I know you care about Fiona, too. I know you've noticed how exhausted and stressed out she is. Someone had to say something."

I knew I wouldn't be able to get a word in edgewise with those two arguing. Yet, even if I could, I wouldn't know what to say. Of course I needed to prioritize my own feelings, but I hadn't quite figured out how to do that, not yet, not with two kids and a frequently absent spouse. In truth, I thought I'd been doing rather well over the last few years handling everything on my own, and still squeezing out time for myself.

For example, Tuesday night knit night was sacred, something I did for me, for my sanity, and I recognized how essential it was. I never missed a week if I could help it.

Presently, I was convinced recent events beyond my control—interrupted sleep being the major factor—had disturbed the delicate balance, which in turn had caused the headaches, which in turn had caused the exhaustion, which in turn had caused the loss of appetite.

I just need an extra eight hours in every day for the next four weeks to get everything back on track. Yep. Just eight hours.

"It's her own business." Marie shook her head.

"Says the agnostic." Sandra stuck her tongue out at Marie.

Marie giggled. "Real mature, Christian."

Marie and Sandra continued to mock-argue. I took the opportunity to marinate in Sandra's observations and check my phone for messages from Greg. Still nothing.

His lack of response was starting to piss me off.

And based on Sandra's observations about me, I decided to give in to those feelings. I was pissed off. I was angry with Greg. I was angry because I'd apologized and been honest, and he was giving me the silent treatment, and that was unlike him.

Not cool.

Not only that, but Greg hadn't done the dishes on Saturday like he'd professed. He'd made muffins with the kids then piled everything into the sink to soak. *That* wasn't doing the dishes. That was leaving the dishes in the sink for someone *else* to do the dishes.

As I was scowling at my phone, it rang, the number read RESERVED. My heart leapt to my throat; international calls frequently came through as reserved numbers. All thoughts of unwashed dishes fled.

I didn't excuse myself from the conversation, knowing my friends would understand; instead, I jumped from my chair and moved to the window as I accepted the call.

"Hello? Greg?"

A short pause followed, a slight hissing coming through on the other end, and then, "No, Fiona. It's Spenser."

I frowned, standing straighter, glancing out the window and backing away from it. The last person I'd expected to hear from was Spenser Banks. He'd been my handler at the CIA when I'd resigned. I'd considered him a friend, but when I left the service nine years ago he'd cut me off, and stopped returning my phone calls.

Over the years I'd heard bits and pieces about his wellbeing from mutual friends. He'd never married, never had a family; I wasn't surprised. He was a company man all the way.

"Oh, uh . . . Hi, Spenser. What-I mean . . . how can I help?"

The line was quiet for several seconds, I heard him sigh. Now I was worried. Spenser Banks never sighed. He was the least expressive person on the planet. If there were an Olympic sport for being the least expressive, he would win the gold medal.

"There's no easy way to say this, so I'm just going to say it."

"Okay. Say it."

"Greg was abducted Sunday after arriving at Lagos International Airport. We have reason to believe he . . ."

Spenser continued speaking, but I did not continue listening. I was stuck on the first sentence and wasn't ready to move to the second, or a third.

My first thought was to check the calendar. We were perilously close to April Fool's Day, maybe it had snuck up on me.

. . . but no. It was still the middle of March.

And Spenser Banks was still talking.

"Wait!" I held my hand up even though he couldn't see me. "Stop. Stop talking."

Peripherally, I became aware that the knitting group girls had stopped talking when I gave this order, and they were looking at me.

I turned my back to them and tried to rearrange my thoughts. "Spenser, is this an April Fool's Day joke? Did Greg put you up to this?"

"Fiona, when have you ever known me to joke or voluntarily interact with Greg Archer?" he responded grimly.

I nodded and tried to swallow, but my throat was dry. Greg and Spenser never got along. My hand started to shake and my knees were weak. I sank to the floor, pressing my side against the wall under the window, and closed my eyes. I needed to focus. I needed to think.

It took a full minute to quiet my mind, to bottle up the chaotic tangle of panic and anxiety and fear. A long dormant facet of my personality came out of nowhere, forced me to focus, to breathe, to calm the fuck down. And I did.

"Okay, start from the beginning. What's going on?"

"Greg was abducted after leaving Lagos International airport. We believe he was taken off the coast of Bayelsa."

Bayelsa . . .

Bayelsa was in Nigeria. Not in South Africa. My heart constricted with hope.

"No. No wait, he's not in Nigeria." My eyes flew open. "He wouldn't have left the airport in Lagos. His assignment is in South Africa."

"Fiona, he's been in Nigeria for the last two months. We suspect he and six others were tracked from the airport at Lagos to the crew boat. They were swarmed on their way to the rig in the Gulf of Guinea."

Focus. Breathe. And calm the fuck down.

"No, Spenser. He told me—"

"Then he lied, Fiona."

The room was rocking, and then it was spinning. I closed my eyes again and braced myself against the wall at my side.

Lied? To me? Every molecule of my being rejected this claim as impossible. Greg would never lie to me, not about something this important. Nope.

Spenser cleared his throat and continued, "He lied to you. Greg has been in Nigeria since January."

Since January?

"He was just home. He was home for twenty-four hours. I just saw him."

The room was spinning faster. I forced it to stop.

"This isn't a phone call I wanted to make, but when it came across my desk I thought you should know."

"What are you doing . . . I mean, what is the CIA doing to get them back?"

Spenser cleared his throat a second time, and I knew at once what his answer was going to be.

Nothing.

They were doing *nothing.*

I gripped my stomach because it lurched. I forced it to stop.

Focus. Breathe. And calm the fuck down.

"Greg is a private contractor for Nautical Oil, Fiona. As you know, Nautical Oil is a British company. He's not there in any capacity for the US government. Greg is part of a special task force to clean up the ecological damage created by Big Oil over the last twenty years. Buhari, the Nigerian president, is demanding action, cutting off access to supply lines until Big Oil cleans up their mess."

"Greg is part of a task force in Nigeria," I repeated, trying the words on for size.

I felt a hand close over my shoulder and a presence at my side. I opened my eyes briefly to determine who was standing so close to me. It was Quinn. But he wasn't standing. He was crouching next to me, his glacial gaze piercing into mine, silently asking me if he could help.

I nodded yes, answering the question in Quinn's eyes, as Spenser continued. "For the last few months, the local police have been successful negotiating the release of foreign nationals—specifically oil workers—for ransom."

"Negotiating? The US doesn't negotiate."

"You know there's been a relaxing of US policy on negotiating ransom. We're not authorized to negotiate or intervene, that's true. But family members won't be penalized, not anymore."

"Just a moment, Spenser. Let me make sure I've got this straight." I caught Quinn's eye again, making sure he was listening. "You believe Greg was abducted Sunday after leaving the Lagos airport in Nigeria. He and six others were followed and their boat was overpowered on the way to a rig in the Gulf of Guinea. The US government is doing nothing to recover the hostages. Instead, it's been suggested that we rely on the local police to negotiate a ransom for his release. Do I have that right?"

"You have it right," Spenser confirmed.

From his place next to me, Quinn didn't say *Fuck* so much as breathed it. He closed his eyes and shook his head, grinding his teeth.

I stared at the carpet, quickly debating and discarding potential plans of action. I said and thought at the same time, "I have to go over there. I have to get him."

"That's not advisable." I heard Spenser shift in his seat, his voice lower, as though he didn't want to be overheard. "Your discharge contract with the CIA is standard, and mandates you're disallowed from foreign travel without State Department clearance. I can guarantee, you will not be given clearance for travel to Nigeria."

"How can you guarantee that, Spenser?"

"Because I would personally make sure of it," he replied, sounding determined, and not even a little sorry.

I gritted my teeth and breathed in and out through my nose. "Spense—"

"And even if you were eventually given the okay, it would take months. If you disregard the terms of your contract, you will be arrested and held for treason."

I heard his words, I understood his meaning, but I also knew I gave no fucks about what the CIA, or the State Department, or Spenser Banks said I could or could not do.

I was going to Nigeria.

I was going to rescue my husband.

And no one would be able to stop me.

***

"NIGERIA AND THE Gulf of Guinea rank fifth in kidnappings of oil workers." Dan set a hot cup of coffee in front of me and claimed the chair at my right.

Elizabeth pushed the cup of coffee away from me. "She doesn't need that. She needs food."

"It's decaf." Dan pushed the cup back within my reach. "And, I know nobody asked me, but if I were in her situation I'd be a basket case, looking for something a lot stronger than coffee."

The four of us—Dan, Quinn, Elizabeth, and I—were at Dan's place. Elizabeth insisted on staying with me; she'd been monitoring my heart rate and blood pressure since I fell to my knees in her apartment. Dan also lived in the same building as Quinn and Janie, Nico and Elizabeth, and Alex and Sandra. It made sense, since Quinn's company owned the building, or at least part of it.

I nodded, ignoring Elizabeth and Dan's squabble, and processed the information about the kidnapping statistics. I knew Nigeria ranked in the top ten, but I had no idea they were so high on the list. I hadn't been keeping up with the CIA factsheets, having traded global crises for kid crises nine years ago, upon discovering I was pregnant with Jack.

"I thought Boko Haram had been marginalized over the last year." Quinn sat on Dan's other side. He'd refused a cup of coffee in favor of a glass of whiskey.

Boko Haram was a terrorist group that had infiltrated Nigeria, easily done since the government had been riddled with corruption fueled by oil money.

That was, until recently.

Dan shrugged. "Yes and no. Buhari has been effective in driving them back and mostly out of Nigeria, but they still have their hands in things, at least that's what my contacts in the Agency tell me."

Buhari—aka President Muhammadu Buhari—had vowed to crush Boko Haram when he took office in Nigeria. Furthermore, rumor had it he was determined to clean up the oil industry.

I hated being out of the loop, being the least knowledgeable person in the room. I had to remind myself that Quinn and Dan lived and breathed these topics every day. International corporate security was their business. When I was a field agent, national security was my every day.

Now my every day was folding laundry, kissing boo-boos, and working on engineering schematics in the middle of the night.

"I don't think this is Boko Haram." Quinn's mouth flattened into a grim line. "They haven't been behind any of the recent kidnappings, their numbers are dwindling. It's been mostly pirates and privateers holding foreigners for ransom."

It didn't matter to me who had Greg. The issue wasn't the who or the why.

I placed both my hands flat on the table. "We need a plan. How are we going to get me into Nigeria?"

Quinn and Elizabeth traded a look while Dan studied the contents of his coffee cup.

Quinn twisted his whiskey glass in what I recognized as a nervous habit. "Fiona, look—"

"No." I shook my head. "We're not wasting time discussing whether I should go. I'm going. Now, how are you getting me into the country?"

Silence stretched, and was only broken by a knock on the front door. Dan sighed and stood, walking to the entranceway to see who was in the hall. He returned a moment later with Alex trailing after him.

Alex started talking as soon as we came into view. "How far have you gotten? Because according to the CIA intel sheet, it's not Boko Haram, if that's what you're thinking. CIA thinks they were taken by a corrupt faction of the government." Alex sat at the table, taking the spot across from me, and opened his laptop.

Alex the hacker, getting down to business. His perfunctory attitude made me smirk. I really liked this kid.

"Have they made any ransom demands?" When I spoke, my voice was coolly collected and my emotions were duct-taped, gagged, and locked away.

"Yes." He didn't glance up from his laptop. "But they made the demand to the United Kingdom, not to the US."

"They think he's a British citizen?" Elizabeth studied me. "Does he have dual citizenship with the UK?"

"He probably told his captors he's from the UK, which was smart. Up until recently, US citizens were killed more often than not because the US didn't negotiate. But EU countries do negotiate," Quinn hypothesized.

I agreed with him, Greg had probably been trying to buy time.

"I don't think they're actually interested in negotiating. I think they'll take the ransom, but I don't think they'll let him go." Alex's gaze flickered between Quinn and me. "Your contact at the CIA, Banks, he said Greg was part of a task force, contracted by Nautical Oil."

Dan frowned at Alex. "How did you know that? Didn't Sandra just get hold of you?"

He shook his head. "I record all cell phone calls coming in or out of the building. I listened to the call."

"And you turned down that job with the NSA why?" I could tell Dan was trying to keep his temper.

"Irrelevant," Alex said, dismissing the question, and continued with his previous train of thought. "I believe this all boils down to oil . . . that rhymed. Boil and oil."

Sandra always pointed out when she would make an inadvertent rhyme. He must've picked up this quirk since they'd been married.

"How so?" Elizabeth pressed.

"Well, Nigeria has been oil rich for decades, but very little of that money makes it to the people of Nigeria. And the ecological damage to the country has been significant, with Big Oil companies ignoring the devastation, and corrupt factions of the government turning a blind eye while lining their pockets. Knowing Greg," Alex paused, meeting my gaze, and for the first time since he'd entered the apartment, allowed a hint of emotion to penetrate his mask of efficiency.

"Go on," I prompted.

His voice was softer when he continued, as though he were speaking just to me. "Knowing Greg, he's not going to pander or pull any punches. He was probably going to recommend some very harsh reforms—if he hadn't already—and shed some light on the corruption, both within Nautical Oil and the Nigerian government. His first priority would be the people of Nigeria and the environment. I'm guessing he wasn't very popular with corrupt officials."

Everything Alex said made sense. Greg was passionate about doing the right thing. He was gifted at swaying hearts and minds because of this passion. But if those hearts and minds were corrupt, his message wouldn't be welcome.

"Even if we pay the ransom, you don't think he'll live," I said, stating the obvious, fighting a tidal wave of nausea as I did so. I couldn't panic, I couldn't think about it, I couldn't allow myself to feel. Not yet.

Alex nodded, holding my gaze. "We need to go in and get him. I think the ransom is a red herring."

Elizabeth took a deep breath and leaned back in her chair. "I have some friends in Nigeria, from med school, part of Doctors Without Borders. They might be able to help, give Fiona a place to stay, provide a cover."

"Wait a minute," Quinn interrupted, glaring at the three of us, but addressing his comments to Alex. "If you heard the phone call, then you heard what Banks said about Fiona going to Nigeria. She could be arrested for treason."

"I've been arrested lots of times." Alex shrugged. "It's not so bad, once you get used to it."

"And what about Grace and Jack?" Dan grumbled. "Fiona, you know I like you, but how can you risk your life like that? What if neither you nor Greg make it back? You can't leave those two kids without any parents."

I considered Dan's comments and wondered how I could possibly explain my perspective without sounding like an unfeeling mother. How could I explain to someone who'd never been married or never had children? I had to get Greg because of the children. I owed it to them. Because if Greg died, I would. . . I'd be dead too.

The look I was giving him must've been intense because he flinched and held his hands up between us. "Don't shoot the messenger."

"I'm not going to shoot you, Dan."

Under his breath he added, "Christ, you're scary sometimes."

"But here's what you don't understand about me: in a street fight, in a gun fight or a knife fight, or even hand-to-hand combat, I would annihilate you. Quinn, too. No problem."

Silence greeted my revelation. Dan stared at me like I was weird, then snorted, looking to Quinn for commiseration. In my peripheral vision I saw Quinn nod his head slightly, confirming my words.

I knew Quinn had run background checks on all of us when he'd proposed to Janie. He was suspicious by nature. But now I realized how extensive the background checks must've been.

Dan turned sober brown eyes on me, as though he were seeing me for the first time. He swallowed. Loudly.

"Police officers—with children—go out on the streets every day. Soldiers—with children—are asked to sacrifice for their country. I will not be made to feel guilty or judged about risking my life to rescue my husband, because I don't do so lightly or with flippant disregard for my kids. I am very well trained. I was part of an elite extraction team as a field agent. I can do this."

I leaned forward and Dan leaned away in a mirroring motion. Alex smirked and dipped his head to his chest to hide his smile.

"Quinn is right. The greatest risk to me *when* I go to Nigeria is capture by the US government. So we have to make sure that doesn't happen. But allow me to address your words about Jack and Grace. If Greg died, I would die too. I know I would. We have been married for fourteen years. He is my soul."

He truly was. He'd been my first real home, my first unconditional anything. And he still was.

Perhaps my need of him was unhealthy, made me weak, but I didn't care. I was weak for him. I always would be.

I'd spent fourteen years as a *we*. An *us*. And becoming a *me* at this point was entirely out of the question.

"I don't know if you can grasp that—and I mean no offense," I continued, "I don't know if you've ever loved and needed someone like I love and need Greg."

Dan's mouth compressed and his eyes moved between mine, a flicker of understanding behind his expression.

"So I can either sit on my talents and skills, wait for someone else to save the other half of myself, to save Jack and Grace's father." I leaned away, turning my attention to my hands where they rested flat on the table's surface. "Or I can put those considerable talents to use, and do it myself."

"What's the plan? After we get you into Nigeria?" Quinn—finally recognizing the futility of trying to dissuade me—took a large gulp of his whiskey.

"Depending on the facility where he's being held, I'll either go in on my own, or ask for a volunteer to accompany me. We extract him and the other hostages."

"I volunteer." Dan lifted his hand before Alex could speak up, and pointed at the hacker. "You need to find Greg, and do all the hacking . . . weirdo voodoo stuff . . . that you do."

"I agree." Quinn gave his glass another twirl. "And we need to open negotiations as soon as possible, let them think there's a lot of money to be made if they hold out for ransom. We'll channel it through the United Kingdom, try to draw out the ruse. Then we can ask for a proof of life."

The promise of a significant ransom might keep Greg alive long enough for me to extract him.

"You should ask Marie and Kat to help." Alex's fingers flew over his keyboard, his eyes affixed to the screen.

Dan stiffened, a dark cloud of disquiet passing over his features. "With what?"

"Kat can front the ransom."

"No," I disagreed. "Quinn should fly down to Lagos on my behalf, to negotiate the ransom. His bank account will check out."

"His bank account is peanuts compared to Kat's. If she were to go down there—"

I saw Dan growing agitated at the mere idea of Kat flying to Nigeria, so I decided to change the subject. "How can Marie help?"

"She can put pressure on the government, write an exposé, flash her AP credentials all over the place."

"Marie?" Elizabeth scrunched her face. "I thought she wrote for Cosmo. She has AP credentials?"

"Yes . . ." I hadn't thought of asking Marie for help, but the idea definitely had merit. "She's freelance, but she's also contract staff with the Chicago Sun, and they're a member of the AP. She could do a human interest piece on Greg, on the abduction."

"Human interest piece? This shit is straight-up news," Alex snorted, shaking his head. "She might win a Pulitzer."

CHAPTER 8

Dear Husband,

I was thinking about you and decided I would write you a little letter to let you know how much I love you. We used to write each other love notes often when we were dating and early on in our marriage. I know that life has become super hectic, especially with our two little blessings' schedules keeping us on the go and worn out, but I want to try to be better about taking time to let you know how I'm feeling, even if it's just a quick note every once in a while...

-Allison
Letter (written during lunch break at work)
Texas, USA
Married 18 years

~Present Day~
Fiona

I WAITED. AND waited.

And waited.

Just after 2:00 a.m. on Friday, local time, I was released from my crate.

I was happy to be out of the crate.

I was thankful for the crate, but—after twelve hours—I also hated the crate.

"Are you okay? Do you need water?" a faceless female asked, accompanied by gentle hands reaching into the box.

"No," I whispered, grasping her fingers and allowing her to help me from my hiding place, my felt-lined rubber soles soundless as they connected with the floor. "When do we leave?"

I heard the smile in her voice as she responded, "Elizabeth said you would be all business." And then with a more serious tone, she added, "We leave within the hour. I'm sorry about your husband."

"Thanks," I nodded, even though she likely couldn't see the small movement. The room we were in was pitch black, and the smell of disinfectant and bleach permeated the air.

I had to trust this woman, Elizabeth's friend, to keep me safe and hidden for the next six hours on a medical transport until she dropped me off one hour south of Enugu. She would continue on with her team to conduct clinic visits in Enugu. I would hike three miles south through mostly jungle to the camp where Greg was being kept.

The official story: I'd decided to accompany Ashley and Drew on their drive south. I was helping Ashley get settled in Tennessee.

Professor Matt Simmons agreed to keep an eye on the apartment.

Elizabeth and Nico took Grace and Jack. I promised I would return—from Tennessee—within two weeks. Jack liked the idea of staying in their penthouse, especially since Nico always owned the latest and greatest gadgets. Plus, Elizabeth was Grace's favorite person ever since she'd given Grace a Build-A-Bear kit two years ago.

Saying goodbye to the kids had been difficult. I knew it would be. I'd prepared for tears—theirs and mine—but they were fine. They waved goodbye with smiling faces. I cried in the car afterward.

I called work and explained I had a family emergency. I told my contract supervisor I'd be off the grid for a while and couldn't accept any new work until mid-April.

Unofficially, I drove to Tennessee with Ashley and Drew. From there, I used Ashley's mother's passport—same height, same weight, same eye color, just ten years older—and flew to Puerto Rico. Luckily, US passports aren't cross-referenced with the social security death database. Therefore, Ashley's mother's passport was still valid.

In Puerto Rico, we used one of Quinn's contacts to get me on board a FedEx carrier bound for Paris. In Paris, I hopped on a Red Star mail carrier flight bound for Lagos, Nigeria, as an employee of Grinsham Banking and Credit Systems —one of Quinn's corporate clients based out of London.

I didn't enter the country of Nigeria as a person. I entered as a parcel, a wooden crate delivered to the north Lagos triage center of Doctors Without Borders.

"I'm Dr. Evans." The woman's grip on my hand turned into a handshake.

"It's nice to meet you. Call me Fe."

Our fingers entwined again as she led me out of the room where my crate had been delivered. I assumed it was a storage room, or an internal delivery dock. She paused just as we approached a door-shaped strip of light.

"Put these scrubs on. I've included a headscarf." She handed me a bundle, which I accepted. But I hesitated.

Within my tool belt had been several vials of Ketamine, courtesy of Dr. Drew Runous, federal game warden of the Smoky Mountains National Park in Green Valley, Tennessee. Also in my possession were a satellite phone, a Ketamine-loaded dart gun and a hundred rounds of Ketamine darts, a SIG DAK—Greg's preferred weapon of choice, a SIG X-Five—my preferred weapon of choice, a switchblade, and a survival kit. The goal was to get in and out with no bloodshed. Nothing that would make the news, draw any attention to my presence in the country, or inspire retaliation.

I didn't need a body count. I just needed Greg.

However, that meant the tool belt and harnesses strapped to my bodysuit would look bulky and suspicious beneath fitted clothes.

"What size are these?"

"Small. Elizabeth gave me your size."

"I need a large. And a lab coat."

Dr. Evans vacillated for a moment, dithering like she wanted to ask why I would need a bigger size, but then released my hand, reclaimed the bundle, and shifted away. I listened to her as she blindly searched for the larger scrubs and requested lab coat. Even though the room smelled like a hospital, I gathered a large breath and held it in my lungs, thankful for any air beyond the confines of the crate.

I'd received word from Alex while I was in transport on the Red Star mail carrier that he'd located Greg and the other hostages. Apparently, his captors hadn't tried to hide their whereabouts or cover their tracks, adding fuel to the theory Greg had been abducted by a corrupt government faction.

Meanwhile, Quinn—accompanied by Marie and Dan—had arrived two days ago via a commercial flight and were staying on Victoria Island at one of the luxury resorts in Lagos.

The biggest issue we'd encountered so far related to private citizens and firearms. Private citizens could not carry firearms in Nigeria. This meant all security, private or otherwise, had to be contracted with the local government. Quinn opted to hire a team of guards through central military channels, trusting the advice of a local contact and old friend, who just so happened to own the luxury hotel where he was staying. His friend handpicked the guards, but I could tell Quinn was still uneasy trusting anyone with his wellbeing and safety.

Last I heard, Quinn, Dan, and Marie had already met with the local police and initiated the process for ransom negotiations.

Dr. Evans passed me a new bundle, which I accepted, and quickly set to work pulling on the baggy attire.

"When we leave this room, we're going to pass through the hospital, then exit via a set of double doors. We'll be taking one of the triage vans—a mobile clinic unit—and two of my colleagues will join us in about thirty minutes. They're locals, trained medical assistants. I'll tell them you're a visiting physician, but don't be surprised if they address you as Oyibo."

"Oyibo?"

"White person. Whereas they call me Akátá, it means African American."

I slipped on the lab coat. "One more thing."

"What's that?"

"Is there a toilet on the way?"

She chuckled. I heard her steps move away, toward the outline of the door. "Yes. No problem."

I did have to go to the bathroom. But more than that, I hadn't yet received word whether proof of life had been obtained. I was itching to reconnect my satellite phone and check for an update.

***

I WAITED. AND waited.

And waited.

And while I waited, I watched.

The camp wasn't heavily guarded. Not at all. I observed neither rhyme nor reason to the guard's movements. Obviously, they had no expectation of being raided. And this angered me.

Initial overhead schematics sent by Alex misrepresented the size of the structure. I'd assumed it was a warehouse. It wasn't. It was an old refinery, likely illegal, and the ceilings couldn't have been higher than twelve feet. The tin roof was rusted, caving and peppered with gaping holes in several places.

Alex sent a second data package just before sundown with several rough architectural sketches, presumably of the structure some fifty feet away. I was thankful for the additional specs, because the refinery had a lower level, a basement carved into the rocky earth. A single staircase led down to a long hallway with six ten-by-ten offshoots.

That's where he was. He was in the basement, in one of those cells.

By midnight, I still hadn't received any update from Quinn, but I was tired of waiting. I also knew, in my bones, Greg wasn't dead. I just knew. He was alive and he was within reach.

So, after watching two of the guards for thirty minutes share a bottle of liquor, finish it, and open another—all the while playing cards on a picnic table—I made my approach.

They were already drunk. No challenge there. I did take their weapons though, emptied the magazines, and slid their semiautomatics under a rusted-out Buick LeSabre. I also picked up the half bottle of Ogogoro liquor. If anyone were to come by, they'd see two of their comrades passed out from imbibing too much distilled juice of Raffia palm trees.

I forced myself to go slow, counting to thirty between each position, listening, waiting, watching. I had to take out three more guards between the side entrance and the stairwell leading to the lower level. One of the men must've weighed three hundred pounds and required two Ketamine darts—one in the neck, one in the leg. I had no way to move him so I propped him against the wall and placed the half-drunk bottle of Ogogoro liquor in his fist.

Despite my training, despite all the mental preparations and subduing of emotions, the last week was catching up with me. Anxiety bloomed in my chest, a hot impatient weight. I needed to see Greg. I needed to touch him and see him and scream at him for putting me through this nightmare.

My heart galloped on adrenaline and it tasted metallic on my tongue. I was sure I'd been operating mostly on adrenaline since learning of his abduction, because my headaches were gone—or at least I hadn't noticed them. But my hands were steady as I opened the door to the basement.

The hall was clear, lit by hundred-watt bulbs placed twelve feet apart. Several had burned out.

I itched to move, to act. My skin was too tight, stretched over my bones. Yet I waited.

A man appeared, exiting one of the cells. He had a Heckler & Koch MP5. The strap was around his chest, the gun on his back, and he was locking the cell door.

I needed those keys.

While he was distracted and his hands were occupied, I allowed my body to numbly operate on cruise control, going through the necessary motions. I slipped through the stairwell door, and sprinted to him on light feet. I was a shadow. He didn't see me coming until it was too late. He dropped the keys in startled fright, and I dropped him before he could get a hand on the gun.

He was small, easy to lift and move, and he hadn't finished locking the door. I turned the key, crouched, and peeked in. I perceived no direct light source, only greyish lines of illumination provided by a circular vent in the ceiling of the cell.

I waited.

And as I waited, straining to listen, my muscles and tendons coiled, burning with tension and frustrated inaction. I realized how much I hated waiting. Waiting completely sucked.

And then someone moved within the cell.

And coughed.

And my heart skipped.

Before I could stop myself, his name tumbled from my lips, an urgent hopeful whisper. "Greg?"

Three seconds of stillness met my query, followed by an urgent hopeful whisper. "Fe?"

I wanted to run into the cell, throw my arms around him, and—again—scream at him. That part was key, he was going to be thoroughly screamed at sometime soon.

If we made it out of this alive, I was going to kill him. But I couldn't. Not yet.

"Are you alone? Is there anyone else in here?" My whisper was barely audible to my own ears.

He didn't answer. I waited. My heart beat loudly between my ears. I could taste my panic.

I was about to call out to him again when he said, "Am I dead?"

"What? Greg?"

"How can you be here?"

Relief coursed through my system. He was confused, which was understandable. Truthfully, I was just grateful he was lucid enough to talk. I dragged the guard's body back into the cell, pocketing the keys, and shutting the door as quietly as possible.

I saw Greg at once, a bound heap in the corner, lying on his side with a bag over his head. My stomach lurched, my eyes stung, and suddenly I wished I hadn't been using anything so benign as Ketamine on my way in.

I quelled the rush of violent emotion and knelt beside him, moving my hands over his body. "Greg, it's me. I'll explain everything later. Are you hurt?"

When he spoke it was with obvious hesitation, like he didn't trust his senses, like he expected me to disappear. "No. Well, not much. Maybe a few bruised ribs. My hands are cuffed, so are my legs."

I nodded. Seeing this was true and that the handcuffs were standard issue, I quickly picked the lock behind his back.

As soon as my hands were on him, working his restraints, he seemed to gain more confidence that I was real and not a figment of his imagination. "They separated me from the others this morning." His whisper was gravelly, like he wasn't used to using his voice. "Do you have any water?"

"Yes." I finished with his wrists and moved to his legs. "When's the last time you had water?"

"Earlier today. They ration one cup every twenty-four hours." He pulled the bag from his head and pushed to an upright sitting position. He began to reach for me, like he wanted to pull me into his arms, but then stopped when I placed the small canteen of water from my belt into his hands.

"Have they fed you?"

"Thank you," he said, opening the canteen with greedy fingers.

I wanted to both laugh and cry at his ingrained politeness. Even now, starved and thirsty, he'd said thank you.

"No," he belatedly answered between small sips, drinking slowly. "My Hausa is rusty, but I think they were starting to suspect I'm a US citizen."

"Okay. Okay . . ." I nodded, sitting back on my heels and drinking in the sight of him. I swallowed past the mixture of relief and fear cinching my throat. Alex had been right. They hadn't fed him or given him much water. They had no intention of releasing him, not for ransom, not ever.

"Let's get you out of here. Do you know where the others are being kept?"

"Yes," he responded immediately, then paused before asking, "why?"

"Because we have to get them."

Greg abruptly pushed to his feet, leaning heavily against the wall behind him, unfolding his long form. "No. No, we don't."

"Yes. I have it all worked out. I came in through the east entrance and it's clear all the way to the exit. We can get the rest of the hostages and—"

Greg's long fingers wrapped around my shoulder, his grip much tighter than necessary. "No, Fiona. We're leaving them. We have to get out."

"We can't leave them."

"They'll be fine."

"Fine? Fine? Are you crazy?"

"Only EU citizens are left, I checked when we were housed together. Their countries will negotiate and pay the ransom. We leave them."

"But you can't know for sure they'll all make it. I'm telling you, we can—"

"No."

"Greg—"

"We're not arguing about this. We need to move."

"Greg, this place isn't an impenetrable fortress, it's a shoddily guarded illegal refinery. We can save—"

"You are my wife!" He cut me off with a harsh whisper. "If they capture you and dig *at all* they'll find out you're ex-CIA."

I could only stare at his outline as I tried to rethink my strategy, find a way to maneuver around his unexpected reticence.

But before I could find the right words, he continued, "I'm not sacrificing you for strangers. I wouldn't sacrifice you for the Dalai Lama or the Pope or Steven Hawking. Those old enlightened wankers can fend for themselves, as can the others. We're leaving. Now." He reached for my hand, apparently his strength returning in full force.

"You wouldn't be sacrificing—"

Greg turned me, backed me against the wall, and placed his hand over my mouth, his voice—though still a whisper—deepened. "Fiona, nod yes or no. Is there anything I can say to change your mind about rescuing the other hostages?"

I couldn't see his eyes, just the shadowy silhouette of his large frame and unshaven jaw hovering over me.

I shook my head no, because there was nothing he could say to change my mind. I was confident—more than confident—we had a clear shot out. I needed him to listen to reason.

His hand slipped away from my lips and his voice was angry, tight when he next spoke. "Okay. You said the east side is clear. But how do we transport eight people?"

"There's a trail through the jungle, a straight shot north to the main road. It's only six miles."

He leaned back a few inches. "You have a weapon for me?"

I withdrew the SIG DAK from the back of my belt and handed it to him, hilt first, along with two additional magazines.

Greg snatched my offering and paced away from me toward the small sheath of light in the center of the room. He checked the chamber and placed the extra magazines in his back pocket. "What about you? What are you using?"

"I have a SIG X-Five and—"

"I didn't hear any shots."

"No, I didn't use it. Drew lent me one of his prototype dart guns. I've been using that so far."

"A dart gun?"

"Yes, it's for subduing bears and other large game. I equipped it with livestock-grade Ketamine."

"Where'd you get that?"

"Again, Drew. I flew out of Knoxville. Everyone thinks I'm in Tennessee visiting Ashley."

He nodded once and stalked back to me. "So you've been drugging the guards?"

I shrugged, shifting on my feet, feeling antsy. This could all wait. We needed to get moving. "Knocking them out then drugging them, yes. It's fast acting, they'll be out for hours. But we need to—"

"Let me see it." Greg tucked his DAK in the back of his pants and held his hand out between us.

"Greg." What the hell was he doing this for?

"Give it to me."

I huffed as I withdrew the petite apparatus from the holster at my thigh and handed it over, trying not to growl my impatience. "Why are you stalling?"

"How does it work?" He turned it over in his hands, angling it toward the light, giving me his profile.

"It has a chamber for three darts." I pointed to the cylinder where the darts were housed.

"Only three?"

"Yes. Like I said, it's a prototype. I've used seven and have ninety-three more rounds in my hip holster."

"It's safe? They'll wake up?"

"Yes, it's safe."

"Are you sure?"

"Yes, Greg. I'm sure. Now we need to get going." I reached for the prototype and he held it away, out of my grasp.

"How do you fire the dart?"

"You have to be close, and it has to hit a major artery if you want it to work quickly. Otherwise it can take up to a minute. Like I said, I've been knocking them out then administering the drug after to buy us additional time, so we can *all* escape. The red button releases the dart."

Greg shivered. I felt it and saw it, just before he whispered, "How close?"

"Very close. A foot or closer. It works best if you can press it against the person's skin. But you should give it to me, I'm much faster and—"

I didn't see him move, probably because I wasn't expecting it. But I did feel the small sting of the needle as it entered my leg, straight into my femoral artery.

I opened my mouth in surprise, but had the wherewithal to stifle my gasp before it escaped. Greg's hard features filled my vision. I could suddenly see him clearly, as though someone had flipped on a light. He glared at me with unrepentant resolve. He looked mean. I hardly recognized him.

"Greg? What did you—"

"I'm sorry, darling," he said. He didn't sound sorry.

Yet his arms wound around me and he brought me to his chest with infinite gentleness. I felt his hand stroke lovingly from my neck to the base of my spine before I went numb. The sound of my blood pumping filled my ears and drowned out any additional apology or words he may have offered.

By the count of ten, the room tilted.

Time slowed.

I blinked.

And everything faded away.

CHAPTER 9

Wife,

Do you know why I touch any part of you whenever I can? Walking past each other in the kitchen, while watching TV, tangling our feet together in bed? I need to make sure you are real, and you are really mine.

-Aaron
Text message
Indiana, USA
Married 18 years

~17 years ago~
Greg

NO ONE FINDS my jokes funny."

"Greg . . ."

"It's true. I told that joke about the G-spot, and my professor gave me a blank look. You could hear crickets, at noon, on a Wednesday. A dog barked in the distance. I don't know who I should be more concerned for, him or his wife. Obviously he doesn't know where her magic button lies."

"Greg . . ."

"As a driller of oil, one would think he'd be spot on." I wagged my eyebrows at her and grinned. "See what I did there? *Spot* on?"

She shook her head, a happy and reluctant smile tugging at her lips. "I know what you're doing."

"And what am I doing?"

"You're trying to distract me."

I studied her features, memorizing her in this moment, her bravery and strength.

This was the third time I'd driven up to visit her since moving to Texas for my last year of undergraduate studies. But instead of going out for a movie or ripping each other's clothes off, we'd driven to Chicago. Specifically, we'd driven to the Robert H. Lurie Comprehensive Cancer Center and spent the day together, waiting.

We'd waited. And waited.

And waited.

Today was her annual oncology checkup. She'd had blood drawn and an MRI. Lots of people asked her the same questions over and over. She was poked and prodded and pushed and pulled. Each time she answered them politely, with infinite patience. She was courageous in a way I never would be. She was grace where I would have been irritable and exasperated.

Through it all, I could do nothing but hold her hand. I stifled my desire to rave like a lunatic, buried the fear and frustration under teasing remarks and terrible jokes.

So far so good.

"Is it working?"

"Yes." Her brilliant eyes twinkled down at me from her spot on the exam table. I was entirely too far away, trying not to appear anxious where I sat in a remarkably small and uncomfortable chair.

Unable to tolerate the distance any longer, I left my jacket on the chair and moved to stand between her legs. "Good."

"But you don't have to." She titled her head to the side, her dark lashes sweeping against rosy cheeks. "I'm not going to have a breakdown."

"I didn't think you were, darling." I squeezed her waist and added under my breath, "But I might."

Her grin waned, grew soft and sympathetic, and she wrapped her arms around my neck. "I feel fine."

"Good. That's good. You look mighty fine, too."

Fiona's smile was back and she laughed, scratching her nails on the back of my neck. "What do you want to do when this is over?"

"Oh, the usual. Grab sardine sandwiches, give you multiple orgasms, walk the park, get married, maybe grab a drink at that new bar on Michigan."

"Sardine sandwiches? Again?"

I grinned wildly. "You know you liked them."

She gagged, screwing up her face. "It's like eating mushy, scaly salt on toast."

"Fine. You eat your brain soup and be wrong and loathed. I'll eat my sardine sandwiches and be delightful and admired."

"Plus," she added thoughtfully, "I didn't know you made a habit of getting married when you visited Chicago."

"I haven't, not yet. But I'm open to adopting any new habit that forces you to move down to Austin with me."

She glower-smirked. "For the record, I'm entirely in favor of getting married right now. But you already knew that."

She spoke the truth. Ever since we'd become engaged she'd wanted us to elope. But I wanted to wait. I wanted a long engagement. I wanted us to take our time.

"We don't have to get married in order for you to move to Austin."

"I can't move to Austin," she replied mournfully. "But you already knew that, too."

At the beginning of last summer, just as we'd become engaged and Fiona considered a move and transfer to Austin, she'd been tapped for a very important and impressive internship through the college of engineering. Some super, top-secret partnership with the Department of Defense.

She'd said, *I'd tell you what it's all about, but then I'd have to kill you* more times than I could count, finding the phrase hilarious. Obviously her sense of humor was just as twisted and odd as mine, though wrapped in a petite and sexy package.

I adopted a glower; mine was entirely false. "I don't see that I'm asking too much by demanding you give up your career, all your friendships, and extracurricular activities, and make me—and the chicken pot pie you'll be cooking every night while barefoot—the center of your universe."

"I just miss you." The words were thought and said in unison. I didn't want to imply she or her success were responsible for our separation, so I quickly added, "I wish I hadn't transferred to Austin."

"It's just one year." She shrugged and added offhandedly, "Plus, I like the phone sex stuff."

An automatic growl rumbled from my chest. "I wish I could see you, though. Someone needs to invent phones with video."

"I could always just send you pictures—"

"Yes! Do that." I nodded enthusiastically, making her laugh again. "Do that every day. Genius. Best idea ever. You're brilliant."

She laughed harder, but I wasn't joking. I wanted something tangible during the stark loneliness of her absence.

Again, I was speaking and thinking in unison, clawing fear flaring in my chest. "If something happened to you . . ." I trailed off, not quite able to complete the thought or the words.

Fiona's merriment tapered and she blinked at me, clearly recognizing the desperation behind the words.

She sat straighter, pressed her lips against mine for a quick kiss, and then gazed at me with such open love and affection, I felt immediately unworthy and selfish.

"No one lives forever, Greg." Her hand smoothed from my neck to cover my heart. "If something happened to me, you would be sad. In fact, you would be completely and utterly heartbroken, crying for days, unable to eat anything but sardine sandwiches." Fiona shoved at my shoulder lightly, giving me a bright, teasing smile before adding, "But eventually, you would be fine."

"I wouldn't. I wouldn't recover." I shook my head, adoring her, loving her, and knowing my words were true as soon as I spoke them.

"You would." She wasn't teasing anymore, and the statement sounded like an order.

Holding her stunning gaze, I gave Fiona a bitter smile. "You don't understand. But how could you . . ." I tilted my head back and forth, considering, trying to determine how best to confess, explain, yet ignore the pounding of fear in my veins. In the end I decided just to say it. "I've lost everyone, Fe. I lost my soulless father to suicide. My mother to addiction. I lost my aunt to gang violence, and my best friend to a forgotten war in Africa."

I held her gaze for a long moment. Startled concern made her eyes wide and watchful.

My voice was as flat as my expression as I added, "Loving you, needing you, has happened quite against my will. I can't lose you, too."

Her stricken features spoke volumes, an echo of her impeccable heart, a testament to the intensity of her empathy. "Greg, did you . . ." She started haltingly, then stopped. Finally, as though making a decision, she said in a rush, "I wish you would tell me about your time in the Marines, how you came to have that scar." Her cool fingers pressed against the mangled flesh of my neck, just under my ear. Where I'd been burned. It still hurt.

"I wish you would share your sorrows with me, allow me to carry your burdens. Because I want to."

I said nothing, my vocal chords paralyzed by warring desires. In truth, I didn't want to burden her with the details. I liked that she knew a depth of pain and suffering, and yet remained untouched by violence and war. My Fiona wasn't naïve, yet she was paradoxically an optimist *and* a realist.

She made me want to believe in good because she was good.

She was a reminder that true and brilliant beauty exists in the world.

And I wasn't ready to ruin her, expose her exquisite mind to the helplessness of brutality.

Not yet.

Not ever.

CHAPTER 10

Wife: Do you want a laptop or a desktop?
Husband: I want a divorce.
Wife: ...
Husband: F*%@ing autocorrect! I want a desktop! DESKTOP!!
Husband: Hello?
Husband: I'm bringing home wine, a dozen roses, those Dove chocolate things, and please allow me to give you a foot massage. Please.
Husband: I love you.

> -Henry and Gail
> Text Messages
> North Carolina, USA
> Married 9 years (and still married)

~Present Day~
Fiona

MY FIRST TWO thoughts—as I broke through the surface to concrete consciousness—were *I need to brush my teeth,* and *Where are my kids?*

"Grace? Jack?" I croaked, struggling to open my eyes. My arms were heavy, useless.

"Shhh, slowly, my darling." A voice shushed me, originating some distance to my left. It sounded a lot like Greg's. A hand was at the back of my neck, rubbing it and my shoulder. "How do you feel?"

"Where's Jack and Grace?" My words were slurred.

"At home. They're safe. We're safe."

Safe . . .

I fought to swallow but found I couldn't. The world swiveled and swayed, tossing me against a wall or barrier to my right, and continued bouncing. I tried to brace myself but my limbs weren't properly responsive.

"Drink this. It's just water. When you feel well enough, I have food." Something was pressed against my chest. I fumbled for it.

"We're an hour outside of Cameroon. Are you okay? How do you feel?"

Cameroon . . .

I opened one eye and recognized the object in my hands. It was a water canteen.

"I think I'm okay." I nodded automatically because I wasn't fully awake. I squinted at an unfamiliar dashboard. We were in a car. A Jeep. It was moving. Beyond the dashboard the landscape was equally unfamiliar. We were in a jungle on an unpaved road.

Maybe I was dreaming.

"Please, drink something."

I moved my eyes to the left, finding Greg splitting his attention between the gravel road and me. He steered the car with one hand. His other arm reached out to me. It was in my hair, his thumb stroking my neck.

"Don't drink too fast. Just take sips," he warned, his hand coming to rest on my shoulder and giving me a soft squeeze.

I nodded again and did as instructed after I confirmed that Greg was in fact the person who had passed me the water. My survival training—training which had been drilled into me until it became instinct—told me to first take stock of my surroundings for imminent threats. I mechanically made of list of facts.

I checked the back seat, then checked the mirrors. There were no cars visible in front or behind us. We were alone.

I scanned the interior of the car and identified three weapons: a Heckler & Koch MP5 behind his seat, a SIG DAK in the driver's side door pocket, and a stiletto with bayonet-style blade —switched closed— in the cup holder between us.

After my surroundings were catalogued and classified as benign, I took stock of my physical state.

My throat was dry. I sipped from the canteen. My extremities tingled with diminishing numbness. I was lethargic. I took another sip of water, screwed the top back on the canteen, and reached forward to pat down my feet, legs, and hips.

"What's wrong? Are you looking for something?"

"No. Checking for injuries." I flexed my fingers and continued exploring my hips and stomach.

"You're not injured. You were . . . asleep."

Asleep.

I thought about that word. It didn't feel right.

"No." I checked my back, then my arms. "I was drugged," I said and thought at the same time.

Greg said nothing. He brushed my hair away from my cheek, his long fingers remaining on my neck.

Now that I was certain we were in no immediate peril, for the moment, and I was free of any gaping wounds or broken bones, I endeavored to piece together the how and when and where of our predicament.

"Fiona?"

My last memory was Ashley's party, Janie on the floor. Greg had come home. I fell asleep. Grace called out. I slept in. The living room . . . *the living room. The epically messy living room.*

"Fe? Are you okay? Talk to me." Greg's tone was cut with urgency.

He left. We fought and he'd left Chicago. And then . . .

"Just a minute." I wasn't quite awake, but almost, and my brain was on the high cliff of awareness, on the precipice of pummeling headlong into the present. "Where did you say we are?"

He released what sounded like a relieved breath. "We're an hour north of Cameroon, in Gashaka Gumti National Park. We'll make—"

"Oh shit!" I shot up in my seat, instantly regretting the sudden movement when spikes of pain and stars filled my vision. It all came back to me, a violent and sudden recollection of the last several days. I closed my eyes and rubbed my forehead.

"What? Are you hurt? Can you see?"

"Why are we in Cameroon? We shouldn't be in Cameroon!" My heart thumped in my chest.

"Calm down. Close your eyes and sit back. We're not there yet. I estimate we have another—"

"No, no, no! Listen to me!" I kept my eyes shut until the flickering silver shards dissipated, and then peeked at Greg's profile. "There's a plane waiting for us in Enugu, a mail carrier puddle jumper through Red Star. It's going to take us to Lagos, where Quinn arranged for transport. Everything is set, but we need to get back to Enugu."

Greg cleared his throat, his expression hardening. "It's too late."

"It's not. The plane leaves at sundown. We have time."

"Fe, you've been out for fourteen hours. We're eight hours from Enugu. It's too late."

A sinking vertigo sensation required that I lean against the seat and brace against the door. "Dammit."

He nodded, apparently agreeing with my one-word assessment of the situation. I opened both my eyes and stared at my husband's grim profile, ignoring the pain in my head. He'd showered and was wearing seemingly clean clothes, a navy blue T-shirt that read, *Seattle Seahawks 2015 Super Bowl Champions*, and blue and grey Navy-issue cargo pants. He still had his week-old beard, which meant he hadn't taken time to shave.

I wanted to panic, but I wouldn't. Like a good soldier, I took another sip of water and forced the bile rising in my throat to recede. He drove and I stared out the window, collecting my thoughts. The collection of thoughts took much longer than usual because I was also processing how to feel about . . . everything.

He'd lied to me.

He'd lied to me for over two months.

Then he'd drugged me.

I had no idea how to cope or even order my resultant feelings.

Perhaps I shouldn't waste energy on feeling anything at all. Not yet. Not until we're alone. Not until we're safe. .

"Fe?"

"We're almost to Cameroon?"

"Yes . . . at least we should be."

"What does that mean? *We should be.*"

"It means Cameroon is south of Nigeria and we've been driving long enough that we should be there soon."

"Wait a minute . . ." I glared at him then searched the Jeep once more, my hands coming to my waist, searching for my tool belt. "Where is my belt?"

"I took off all your gear. It's on the floor behind you."

"Are you using GPS?" I twisted in my seat, searching the floor for my belt.

"No."

"What about the phone? I had a satellite phone on my belt."

"The phone is dead."

"Did you grab my gear bag? I left it on the trail. It has a solar charger for the phone."

"How could I have grabbed your bag? I didn't know you had a bag." He said this through clenched teeth.

"Well, you would have known if you hadn't drugged me."

"I wouldn't have drugged you if you had just listened to me."

Now I was clenching my teeth too. I closed my eyes and breathed through my nose. I needed to think.

"A map?" I opened my eyes and searched the glove box, feeling for a map.

"No. No map."

I stared at my husband, dawning comprehension like a slap to the face, my self-imposed control and prohibition on feeling starting to fracture. "You have directions?"

His hands opened and closed on the peeling vinyl of the steering wheel. I could tell he was biting back a sarcastic retort. "No, Fe. Not in the way you mean."

The interior of the car grew eerily silent. I don't think I was even breathing.

I swallowed, knowing the answer before I asked, "A compass? Do you have a compass?" My voice cracked on the second compass.

He didn't respond, instead pressing his lips together. His lack of response was his answer. The situation was officially ridiculous and I was losing my mind.

At length, unable to suppress panicked hysteria any longer, I blurted into the silence, "BEANS!"

He started. I'd obviously surprised him, and he gave me the side-eye. "Beans?"

"Magic beans. Please tell me you traded a cow, map, and compass for magic beans. We'll climb the bean stalk and triangulate our location from the clouds." I was laughing by the time I finished, holding my empty stomach.

"Oh, this is funny to you?"

"Yes. This is funny." I continued to laugh, and if I were more hydrated I would have been wiping tears from my eyes. "This is fucking hilarious."

"I know exactly where we are."

"Right," I nodded, the single word dripping with sarcasm. I reopened the canteen and took another sip. "Right, right, right. Just like when we took the kids to Disney World and ended up in that swamp."

"I wasn't lost. I was just free of societal notions of the names of the places where I was. It was a shortcut."

"Why couldn't you have asked for directions? Would it kill you to get directions?"

"I didn't need directions."

"Not then, Greg. Now. Ask for directions now."

The dam broke on his temper. "Who the hell would I ask? The giant jungle snails? Do you want me to water-board it out of them?"

"No, no, no. No CIA torture jokes allowed. Not when my training is the only reason you are sitting here, with me, and not back in that cell."

"I don't need directions. Like I said, I know exactly where we are."

"That's right. I forgot. You and the aboriginal speakers of Guugu Yimithirr were both born with an infallible innate sense of direction."

"The gugu-what?"

"One of Janie's factoids." I waved my hand in the air. "It's a language with no word for left and right, up and down, behind—that kind of thing. So kids grow up with north, south, and southeast in terms of directional cues. They have to be aware of their position as it relates to the earth at all times from a very young age, so they grow up with an extremely strong sense of direction."

"Oh . . ." He nodded, obviously considering my words. "We should do that with Grace and Jack."

"What?" My single word question arrived sharp, impatient, and incredulous.

"We should make them describe things in terms of north, east, and etcetera. Think of how valuable of a skill that is, to have an infallible innate sense of direction."

He was serious.

He wasn't joking. He was serious and he thought this was a good idea.

The fire ants in my brain were back. How could he possibly think this was good idea? It's not like raising the kids on my own wasn't already difficult enough. Now he wanted me to remove prepositions from their vocabulary?

I huffed. Loudly. Not just loudly, obnoxiously.

"What was that? What is that sound you're making? Are you deflating? Have you sprung a leak?"

"I was just thinking, we don't need to do that with Jack and Grace, because they've probably inherited your infallible innate sense of direction. I mean, here we are in the middle of Nigeria—"

"We're in the south of Nigeria. Not the middle."

I ignored him and continued to speak. ". . . and you know exactly where we are."

"Sarcasm. Nice. Real nice."

"Says the Supreme Ruler of Sarcasm Land."

"I'm not the Supreme Ruler of Sarcasm Land, Fe. I'm the Earl of Cynicismshire," he countered flatly.

A short laugh burst forth from my chest, followed by more laughter—a lot more laughter. I held my stomach. It was real this time, not driven by panic. And it was cathartic. Greg must've been able to tell the difference because he cracked a smile.

Seeing his crooked grin, reluctant but genuine, splintered the wall I'd built around my emotions in order make it through the last few days. Raw feeling—latent regret, fear, sorrow, hope—swelled within me, my eyes burned with what would soon be a tidal wave of tears.

"I love you, Greg," I said, already crying. "I love you so much. You can't—"

"Shhh, shhh, darling. We'll get through this." He reached out to me again, grasping my hand and squeezing.

I brought it to my lips and kissed his knuckles, holding on to him and endeavoring to speak through sobs. "When we get home, I'm going to kill you. You don't know-you don't know . . ."

He grinned again, wider this time, and chuckled. "I think I have some idea."

"You lied to me." I glared at him, allowing the accusation to carry the entirety of my fear and rage. I cried against his hand, holding it with all my strength. I'm sure my grip was verging on painful, but I couldn't let go.

His grin fell away, his eyes round and sober, and he nodded. "I did. I lied to you. But you must know I had good reasons."

I warred with myself, not knowing how to feel or what to do next. Part of me wanted to scream and yell and rant and rave. Another part wanted to curl into a ball and cry forever. And still another part just wanted yoga pants and an ice-cream sandwich.

When I couldn't stop crying after several minutes, Greg pulled the Jeep over and drove several feet into the jungle. With soothing sounds, he coaxed his hand out of my grip and unfastened my seatbelt. He lifted and pulled me onto his lap. I straddled his hips and he wrapped me in his arms.

I burrowed against his neck and held him, breathing him in, wanting to be closer. I frantically kissed his bearded jaw, his temple, his fuzzy cheek, his lips. He allowed me to kiss him, but I could tell he was holding himself back. Greg smoothed his hands up and down my back, making gentle promises.

You're safe. I'm safe. I've got you. I love you. Everything is okay. We're okay.

Two thoughts were on repeat in my head, intrinsically linked, one causing the other: *You lied to me. You almost died.*

I couldn't stop thinking about it, wretched images flashed behind my eyes, worst-case scenarios. What if I'd been too late? What if he'd been unconscious? What if . . .

After a good ten minutes of crying, and unable to sort through the tangled mess of thoughts and emotions—because apparently my husband always left me with epic messes to clean up—I collapsed against his chest, spent.

My breath hitched at intervals, caught on sobs like a child after a prolonged cry, and my mind was blank. But I was thirsty.

Apropos of nothing, I thought and said, "I just drank all that water, and now it's coming out of my eyes."

This comment made him laugh in earnest—though it sounded strained—and squeeze me again. "We have more water, and you should drink it. You also need to eat."

"You have food?" My voice was scratchy and nasally, and my brain was in a fog. "And where did you get this Jeep? And when did you take a shower?"

"I'll tell you everything." He kissed my cheek, lifted my fingers to his lips, and brushed a kiss on the back of my hand. His eyes were rimmed with traces of anxiety and I knew he didn't like that we were sitting in a car, easy targets for anyone who might pass by. "When we get to the safe house and you've rested properly. But right now, you need to eat, and we need to move."

"Safe house? You have a safe house in Nigeria?"

"It's near the border of Cameroon and Nigeria, but yes. Of course I have a safe house."

I wrinkled my stuffed nose, completely confused. "Why do you have a safe house?"

"Darling, I went to high school in Compton. I spent three years in the Marines. My wife was a CIA field agent. We are the paranoid sort who have safe houses. Just accept it."

"Fine. I accept its existence. But we can't go to the safe house. Quinn, Dan, and Marie are in Lagos. They're negotiating your ransom. What do you think will happen to them when it turns out that you—just you and none of the other hostages—have escaped?"

Greg scowled at the road, grumbled something I couldn't hear.

"And don't give me your Dalai Lama, Pope, Hawking speech again, because Quinn and company are here because of you. They helped me get you out. We can't leave them. We have to get a message to them as soon as possible."

"I *will* give you my Dalai Lama, Pope, and Hawking speech as many times as I see fit." Greg pointed his scowl at me, his tone exacting. However, his features softened as his gaze moved over my face. "But I agree. We need to get a message to them. And we'll be able to do that from the safe house, we're almost there."

***

GREG REALLY DID know exactly where we were, much to my astonishment.

His safe house was in the middle of the jungle. At least that's how it felt to me. We had to drive the Jeep off the road, into the forest, and walk about a quarter of a mile to reach it.

The exterior appeared to be exposed cinderblock and the interior wasn't much better. A single room measuring about eight by eight, a cot, a square rug, and that was about it. I'd finished assessing the space when he moved the carpet out of the way to reveal a door in the floor.

"During the Nigerian Civil War these bunkers weren't uncommon. But discovering one out here and still intact was a real find."

Greg opened the wooden door, revealing what looked like a combination safe. He entered the combination, turned the metal wheel, and lifted the hatch.

"I just finished welding this hatch three weeks ago." He stood back to admire his work for a moment before grabbing the bag of supplies I was carrying—supplies he'd stolen from the corrupt mainline sentinel—and motioned for me to climb down the ladder into the bunker.

"How did you find it?" I asked as I lowered myself into the ground.

"Luck, actually. I'd already found a place in Lagos, a safe house in a mostly Oyinbo neighborhood so I wouldn't be conspicuous. I did that the second weekend in January as soon as I had free time. The next weekend I spent my day off hiking. I got lost—"

"What? You? Lost?" I teased lightly, feeling more awake after my cry-fest. I reached the end of the ladder and stepped to the side so Greg could finish descending.

"I know. I can hardly fathom it myself. Look to the left side of the ladder, there's a switch for the lights."

"There are lights?" I asked and felt for the switch, flipping it. Compact fluorescent bulbs illuminated the space, which was at least twenty by twenty feet. Newly constructed shelves lined the walls laden with canned goods, non-perishables, computer equipment, and miscellaneous supplies. A large soaking tub took up an entire corner, and next to it was a toilet and basin sink. A single cot claimed the other corner and a table with one chair was pushed against the wall.

"The blue tub was already here. But I had to replace the other fixtures, clean the whole thing out. The power runs off a solar generator with backup batteries I installed in mid-February. They're rechargeable, like a car battery. The solar cells are a mile away in a suitable clearing, so I had to bury the lines and the generator."

Greg walked around me as he spoke, moving to what looked like a breaker box next to the shelves and flipped two switches.

"I just turned on the water heater and satellite hookup. We'll have hot water in half an hour, and Internet in ten minutes."

"Where does the water come from?"

"There's a well, behind the shed up top."

I stared at him with openmouthed wonder. "You did all this?"

He nodded, glancing around the space. "Well, I didn't build it. But I fixed it. I gave up the other house three weeks ago, as soon as this place was finished."

It wasn't fancy. Not at all. It smelled like new paint and Lysol. Except for the big, powder-blue porcelain soaking tub, it looked like a miniature military barracks. It was efficient and tidy. Everything had a purpose and I perceived nothing that could be labeled as extraneous.

But then my attention snagged on a cluster of photographs stuck to the wall next to the bed. As though pulled, I walked over to it, leaning down so the frame would be eye level.

I was smiling before I knew it. Grace and Jack's faces filled my vision. The picture had been taken over Halloween and I'd emailed it to Greg because he was on assignment in Russia at the time.

Unwelcome and unbidden thoughts bubbled to the surface of my mind: *Had he really been on assignment in Russia? What else has he been lying about?*

I batted them away, not wanting everything to be tainted by his recent deceit, not until I gave him a chance to explain. I wanted to give him the benefit of the doubt. I wanted to trust him. I wanted his reasons to be justified.

Yet, despite my desire to be fair, I was left with a bitter taste in my mouth.

I refocused on the image in front of me. Grace had no front teeth. Despite being in a Princess Leia costume, she looked a lot like the pumpkin she'd carved. Jack, dressed as Luke Skywalker from *Return of the Jedi*, was giving her bunny ears; his mischievous grin an echo of his father's—Greg's, not Darth Vader's.

My gaze moved to the other picture and my grin wavered, but only because I was surprised. The picture was of me, one of his pencil sketches, from the chest up wearing a black dress. I was glancing over my shoulder and smiling at something in the distance.

I straightened and turned to Greg. "When did you draw this?"

His answering smile was small and secretive, and his eyes were foggy with remembering. "I took it with my phone over Christmas. Jack was standing at the door telling us knock-knock jokes. You were sitting on the edge of the bed, looking over your shoulder and laughing. I sketched it on the plane back in January. Whenever I see the picture—the photo or the drawing—I can hear your laugh."

I studied him for a beat. "You should have showed it to me."

He shook his head. "No. I quite like my private memories of you."

"Private memories?" I lifted an eyebrow at this. "You mean there's more?"

Greg crossed to me, his gaze moving in a slow, cherishing path over my features. "If you knew how I saw you, how I think of you, your ego would become unmanageable."

I laughed even though I was exhausted and still enormously angry with him. I had a crying- and Ketamine-induced headache and my thoughts were chaotic. We needed to talk about why he'd kept his assignment in Nigeria a secret. We also needed to discuss his drugging of me rather than listening to and trusting my judgment.

But for now, because I was exhausted and needed a bath—and he'd just said something funny and lovely—I responded with a fond, "You're ridiculous."

And I loved that he replied as expected. "It's pronounced *remarkable*, darling."

CHAPTER 11

Dear Husband,

Sometimes when you're at home, you call me on your cell phone just so you can whisper, 'I'm calling from inside the house,' like one of those old scary movies. This basically sums up why I love you, and why we're still married.

-Lucy
Email
Virginia, USA
Married 17 years

~Present Day~
Fiona

AS SOON AS the Internet was up, Greg sent a message to Alex with the essentials: We were safe; we were together; we hadn't freed the other hostages.

I wasn't ready to give up on the captives we'd left behind. However, based on Greg's level of vehemence regarding the Dalai Lama, Pope, and Steven Hawking, I decided to bide my time.

Alex responded immediately: *10-4 good buddy. Glad you're not dead. Check back in at 06:00.*

"He's like mini-you." I smiled wistfully at Alex's message. "Except, with less tact."

"And bigger brains," Greg added.

"And weirder."

"And less street cred." Greg then proceeded to bite his bottom lip and made a weird symbol with his hands, as though this would impress me.

It didn't. He looked absurd. But then, that was probably the idea.

"What is that?"

"It spells nerds. See how my thumb and index finger make the 'N'?"

When I didn't display the appropriate amount of wonder and awe at his demonstration, he said, "Well, I can see when my mad skills aren't appreciated. I'm going to go grab us some dinner." He said this like we were in Chicago and he was running out to pick up Italian beef sandwiches from Al's.

Before leaving, Greg showed me where the towels and extra clothes were kept. I would have to hand-wash my bodysuit and underthings— which was fine—and don one of his alternate reality sports T-shirts in the meantime.

The hot bath was heavenly. My body was sore and sweaty, my face tight and puffy. Taking my time, I allowed my mind to rest and wander.

Unfortunately, when it wandered, my thoughts invariably turned to his lie about being stationed in South Africa instead of Nigeria. And also drugging me instead of listening. And also, strangely, the dishes he didn't do last week. And the clothes he'd left on the floor in our bedroom. And the mess in the living room, most of which would still be there when we returned. And the retirement documents he hadn't signed.

I decided I was going to make him clean up the mess in the living room when we returned to Chicago. It was the least he could do after drugging me with Ketamine.

These were my thoughts when Greg returned, carrying a canvas bag over his shoulder, and pulling his dirty boots off near the ladder. He set them neatly next to the wall. I frowned at his boots, wondering why he could put his shoes away in his man-cave bunker in Nigeria, but he couldn't be bothered to do so in Chicago.

"I have dinner. I hope you like giant snails. And sardine sandwiches." He gave me a winning grin, which immediately fell when he saw my expression.

It wasn't the snails.

I could deal with giant jungle snails.

It was him.

He was the cause of my acerbic mood.

Greg and his tidy bunker verses his epic Chicago messes, and his not listening to me or trusting my judgment.

I didn't try to temper my glower. Instead, I gave into it. Perhaps it wasn't the best time to be angry, but then . . . it never was. I was always choosing to suppress my inconvenient feelings, and I didn't want to do it anymore.

"What's wrong?" He stared at me with wide eyes.

"I don't know where to start."

"How about at the beginning?"

"Last Saturday, you made muffins," I blurted.

So, maybe not the beginning, or the most important of my grievances. But it's a start.

His gaze moved from side to side, like he was searching for a trap. "Yes?"

"You didn't do the dishes."

His frown was immediate. "Yes, I did."

"No, you didn't. You left the dirty muffin tin on the counter. And you left several dishes in the sink to soak. And then, the counters weren't wiped down."

"Oh my God. You're right." He clutched his heart like he'd just been stabbed. "How can I ever make it up to you? What will be the appropriate restitution? What will we do? How can you possibly go on?"

I ignored his sarcastic dramatics, which usually would make me laugh, and stayed my course. "And wiping down the counter—not sprinkling it with Comet and leaving it overnight. That's just making more of a mess. That's not doing the dishes."

"This should have been your thesis topic in college."

"And then the dishwasher—"

"Here we go." He rolled his eyes and turned away from me, crossing to the cot and taking off his socks. I'd brought up how to load the dishwasher before, so his reaction didn't surprise me.

"Everyone knows plates go on the bottom and glasses go on the top."

"Everyone? Really? Every person in the world knows this?"

"Everyone but you."

"You are harboring an unhealthy amount of dish-related resentment." Greg tossed his socks into a bucket by the shelves and stripped off his shirt, throwing it into the bucket as well.

"There is no magical dish fairy," I grumbled. But I knew my anger wasn't really about the dishes.

Well, it was. And it wasn't.

It was about . . . *a lack of respect for my time.*

I was just about to voice this conclusion when I realized Greg was approaching the bathtub. And he was shirtless.

"What are you doing?"

"What do you think I'm doing?" He unbuttoned his pants and unzipped them.

Perhaps it didn't make any sense, but I didn't want Greg to see me naked. Not when I was still furious with him. Not when he was angry with me. Even though we'd been together for eighteen years, married for fourteen, and made two children together, when we were arguing I didn't like the vulnerability of bare skin.

"Oh, no. No, no, no." I sat forward in the tub, hiding my nakedness. "We haven't talked through everything yet. I'm angry with you, and I know you're still upset with me."

He shrugged. "Then we'll have angry intercourse."

"We're not having intercourse."

"Then I'll give you angry cunnilingus."

Damn him, but that made me laugh.

Greg's eyebrows bounced once on his forehead and he grinned, his pants falling to the ground.

"I don't want any of your angry oral sex, thank you very much." I crossed my arms over my chest, endeavoring to keep my expression stern . . . and failing.

"Of course you do. Angry oral sex is the best kind of oral sex. And we are so rarely angry with each other. We should take advantage of this opportunity." His thumbs hooked into his boxers with the intent of pulling them down.

"Do not take off your boxers."

Greg didn't remove his boxers, but he didn't withdraw the threat of his thumbs either. "You know, I've heard it's a good idea to fight while naked. I think I read that in a very important medical text book written by Albert Einstein's cousin, Dr. Olga Einstein."

"You are a dirty liar. You did not read that in a medical book and you did not tell me that your assignment was in Nigeria. I'm not ready to forgive you for lying to me."

"I didn't ask for your forgiveness, Fe." His expression and voice hardened, losing its trace of teasing.

"I noticed." My tone was equally harsh. "And that's why I haven't given it to you."

Greg crossed his arms over his bare chest, gritting his teeth, his eyes flashing fire. "Okay. Fine."

He glanced around the space; finding the chair, he dragged it to the side of the tub. He sat on it, leaned forward, his elbows on his knees, and glared at me.

"I couldn't tell you about the assignment in Nigeria. I accepted it on the condition that I wouldn't be able to divulge my whereabouts or the purpose to anyone, even you."

I stared at him, waiting for him to continue. When he didn't, I connected the dots. "So you lied to me."

"Yes. I did."

"And you don't see anything wrong with that?"

"Of course I see something wrong with that. Do you think I wanted to lie to you? Do you think it was easy for me?"

"So you, what? Hoped I wouldn't find out?"

"In a word? Yes."

I smacked my palm against the surface of the water. "No! That's the wrong answer. You shouldn't have lied to me, especially not about something so important."

"Fe, how can you—" He growled, cutting himself off. "You did the same thing to me."

I stilled, bracing myself for his next words. "What are you talking about?"

"Your headaches?"

I released a silent sigh of relief because he was referring to the headaches.

Once upon a time, early in our marriage, I'd lied to my husband about something huge. He'd forgiven me. But more than that, he'd promised to forget as well. Right now, this argument would've been the perfect time for him to wield this weapon of my past mistake.

And yet he didn't. And I loved him for it.

I drew my knees to my chest and refocused on our present debate. "Nigeria ranks fifth in the world for kidnappings of oil workers. Accepting this assignment was dangerous and you should have discussed it with me first. The headaches are completely different."

"Are they?" His eyebrows shot upward expectantly. "It's the same thing. You don't think the headaches are a big deal even though I see them as dangerous."

"You didn't see this assignment as dangerous? Somehow I doubt that."

"It was triple the money, Fe."

I was about to launch another volley, challenge his assessment of the situation, when the meaning of his last statement crystallized.

I gaped at him, staring at his grim expression. "Triple the money?"

"Yes. Triple. This assignment was going to give me the ability to stay home for longer periods, maybe two months at a time for the next few years."

I blinked at that. I realized my mouth was hanging open, so I shut it. Of course I wanted him home for longer stretches of time. The kids would be ecstatic. But a little voice, a desperately angry voice, in the back of my mind whispered, *Two months isn't long enough. I need him home.*

I watched his chest expand with a large inhale, and as he released it a good deal of his anger dissipated, leaving him looking remarkably tired.

"When I was home this last time, last week, do you know what Grace asked me?"

I shook my head, studying him, his desolate tone causing my chest to constrict.

"She asked me if next door neighbor man-child, Professor Matt, was her new dad."

I flinched, felt the corners of my mouth curve into a startled frown.

"And Jack answered before I could. He told her that just because they saw Matt more than they saw me, it didn't make him their dad." Greg paused, holding my gaze for a moment before finishing hesitantly. "He said it made Matt their stepdad."

I couldn't help it, I laughed because Jack's conclusion had been so innocently logical and ludicrous; then covered my mouth with my fingers. "Oh no."

"Oh no is right." He gave me a commiserating, sad smile and scratched the back of his neck.

"You took this assignment so you could be at home more?"

He didn't precisely respond to my question, instead admitted, "I hate being away from you and Jack and Gracie. I hate watching you do everything on your own and pushing me away all the time—because you don't want to be a *burden*." He said burden as though it were the most repugnant word in the English dictionary. "We are not your parents, Fe. Everything I have is yours. You are not a burden."

"I know, I know." I reached forward and grabbed his hand, needing to touch him. "But you work so hard, Greg. I never wanted you to think I don't recognize that. I know you still enjoy the work, and I know you make a real, tangible difference, but I also know it is work. You provide for your family, so we can live in a nice neighborhood, in a beautiful apartment, in my favorite city. And I appreciate you, what you do for us."

He held my hand in one of his, and traced the lines on my palm with a fingertip. "I know . . . but it's nice to hear you say the words."

I gave him a slight smile. "I should say them more often."

"You should. You should hire a skywriter and write me a song."

I laughed lightly. "Ode to Greg Archer, Earl of Cynicismshire."

"Technically, I'm the seventeenth Earl of Cynicismshire. The fourth Earl was a cannibal; did I ever tell you that? He used to eat his housemaids, or so the legend goes."

I shook my head at him and his silliness, and I realized just how much I missed him. Really and truly missed him. This version of Greg, this man I married when I was far too young to be making such important decisions. The man who challenged me to do backflips, called me a misogynistic hermit, and teased me about liking lentil soup.

Even when he was home, between assignments, I missed him. We never caught our breath. We were hardly ever a couple, because we were too busy being a family. Selfishly, I wanted more than two months at a time.

But, I reminded myself, two months would still be a vast improvement.

Greg's tone was considerably less teasing and considerably more contrite as he stated, "I should tell you the same, shouldn't I? I'm not terribly good at expressing my appreciation for all that you do, for me, for our children."

Feverish warmth blossomed in the vicinity of my heart and claimed my cheeks; I felt myself smile widely. "Thank you. I think . . . I think I needed to hear the words, too."

"I should say them more often. Or at least send you a pile of diamonds."

"I'd settle for a greeting card."

"You should never settle, Fe. You should never have to. And you must tell me if I'm a source of unhappiness for you."

A lump formed in my throat because my husband was so entirely and epically adorable when he was being sincere. Without thinking about his words too long or too hard, I gave into my instincts to assuage his worries. "You aren't a source of unhappiness."

"I don't think that's true." He frowned at me, studying my features for a long moment before adding, "I am sorry I lied to you, about Nigeria. It was an act of a desperate man, a man desperate for his wife and family. And I'm sorry my dish-doing isn't up to regulation standards. I promise I'll do better when I'm home. I'll watch a YouTube video on the proper way to clean a kitchen, maybe I'll even buy one of those sexy maid costumes."

I gave him a small smirk. "You're going to wear one of those sexy maid costumes when you do the dishes?"

"No. You'll wear the costume whenever you'd like me to do the dishes."

"So I'll wear it all the time?"

"Ah, good point. I'd have to get a second job just to afford the fishnet stockings required. Scratch that. We'll have to come up with a different method of communication, when the dishes need doing. Maybe flash me?"

"How about you look around the kitchen and if it's dirty you clean it? All of it."

Greg's eyes narrowed on me, but this mouth curved to one side. "I don't know . . . that feels like something Hitler would say."

I tried not to laugh as I added, "And wipe down the counters."

"Fine." His attention strayed to my mouth. "I will try to do better, and make every effort to remember to wipe down the counters. Though I still reserve the right to stack the dishwasher how I see fit."

"Even though it's inefficient," I grumbled.

He grinned, his eyes moving back to mine. "Even though it's inefficient, and wrong, and horrid, and a crime against humanity."

"Glad we're in agreement." I returned his smile with a small one of my own, relieved he'd listened to my gripe about the dishes and promised to try harder. This was a step in the right direction. This had me feeling hopeful.

Greg's expression sobered as he held my gaze and I could tell he was struggling, wanting to say something he wasn't certain I would be willing to hear.

"Whatever it is, say it," I encouraged. "You might as well, because we're here until tomorrow morning and there are no kids in the other room vying for our attention."

He nodded once and said, "The truth is, my poor dish-doing skills notwithstanding, I hate you taking responsibility for decisions that should be shared, not consulting me because you don't think I care or have the right to an opinion."

I felt his words resonate in my chest and in my neck, because he was right.

Even though I knew he was right, my first instinct was to explain my actions, because I never consciously tried to hurt him. "What was I supposed to do, Greg? I'm the one who wanted children. How could I ask—"

"No. You're just the one who brought up the subject. Do you think I would've had children with you if I didn't want them? Of course I wanted children with you. They are *our* children, Fe. And I need you to stop freezing me out."

I pressed my lips together, my attention drifting to where he held my hand. My ingrained instinct was to apologize, be reasonable, let it go.

But the situation was more complicated than me freezing him out. He'd cut himself out by never being home. I was partially responsible, but we hadn't arrived to this place solely because of my choices. Decisions had been made, actions—or inactions—had been taken by both of us.

"What are you thinking?"

I gathered a deep breath and pulled my hand from his. "The water is cold."

"That's not what you're thinking." His tone was laced with frustration.

"I'm tired, Greg. This last week has been crazy. I'm tired and . . . I need some time to think about what we've discussed. I need some time to think about everything."

His jaw ticked and I could see the gathering tempest behind his expression. He was on the precipice of reacting.

I shook my head before he could speak. "No—you're not allowed to do that."

"Do what?"

"Give in to your pushy impulses. I will not be surrendering to your demands this time. I will not. You need to wait, because I need time to think. And no amount of pressure from you is going to make my thinking process go faster."

"I'm not pushy." He crossed his arms again.

"Yes, you are. You're impatient; you want everything *right now*. You want all the answers immediately, and you mow down everyone in your way. You rush into things, and it's worked out for you so far because you're smart and wily. But I'm not like that. I need to contemplate and consider. And if you don't want me to freeze you out, you need to give me some time."

He frowned and issued a perfunctory nod. "Fine. You have an hour."

I laughed, irritated and amused. "I'll take all the time I need."

"An hour and ten minutes. That's my final offer." His frown had grown fake; he was a faking frowner.

I laughed again, less irritated and more amused. "Hand me my towel, the water really is cold."

He grabbed the towel, but didn't hand it to me. "Can you do me a favor?"

"What's that?"

"Stand up."

I shrugged, then stood as requested, not immediately grasping the nature of his request. I blamed the post-Ketamine grogginess for my belated understanding.

I watched my husband blankly as he swallowed with difficulty, his eyelids growing heavy as his gaze traced over my body. I was suddenly self-conscious and considerably less cold.

I wondered; are there women who grow accustomed to being the subject of such longing?

I've found, as a general rule, the longer women are married, the more judgmental they become of other women, especially about sexuality and desire. But I've yet to meet a monogamous person who is an expert on sex, nor have I ever met a polygamist who is an expert on love.

Each marriage is a living thing, just as complex as the two individuals within it.

After eighteen years together and two kids, nothing about the way my husband wanted me in that moment felt ordinary or calm. And as thrilling as his desire was, the realization also saddened me.

We'd never been allowed to grow bored of each other. Time was a commodity, and time together had become the ultimate luxury. Perhaps if we spent infinite hours in each other's company I'd eventually tire of his companionship. Maybe . . . but I doubted it.

He held his hand out. "Come here."

"Greg, I'm very tired."

"Come here," he commanded, and yet there was a note of desperation in his voice.

I shivered and fit my fingers in his palm, goosebumps erupting over my skin. When I stepped out of the tub, he tugged me forward. I stood between his legs. His hands moved to my hips, his fingers digging into my wet skin. Mine rested on his shoulders. Both my feet were on the ground, and yet I felt unsteady.

Inclining his head, he licked a drop of water from my stomach, his hot tongue velvet against my chilled skin.

"Can you blame me?" he asked, his warm breath fanning over the wet tip of my breast, the combination of sensations coiling my insides.

"Blame you for what?" I asked, feeling remarkably winded.

He didn't answer. Instead he covered my ribs and breasts with hot, wet kisses, causing my toes to curl, my neck to flush, and my lower abdomen to tighten and twist with a pulsing ache. His hands stroked my bare body, damp and slick and sensitive.

I was so tired. And he felt so good. I wanted to be selfish, and give myself over to him. But I didn't want to confuse him, or me.

"Nothing is resolved," I whispered, even as I pressed him against me, wanting more, wanting to be devoured.

"I resolve to make you come with my fingers." His fingers moved to my center, making me gasp.

"You're not being fair."

"I further resolve to make you come with my mouth." He swirled his tongue low on my abdomen, sending a shock of heat to my core.

"Husband, this isn't a good idea. You're not listening."

His hands slid to my bottom and he lowered his head, saying, "I will, darling. I resolve to listen to all your sweet sounds, be they sighs or screams . . . each and every one."

I shivered again, a quaking capitulation, a submission.

The sound of Greg's voice, dark and thick with promise, was just as potent as his touch. I knew soon he would be speaking salacious nonsense. Demanding, exacting phrases that revealed his baser instincts and desires. Possession. Ownership. Carnal infatuation. I welcomed it.

I welcomed his provoking and zealous vulgarity.

Greg's grip grew restless and he bit me, making my breath hitch and hiss. He surged upward, stood, and I hooked my thumbs in his boxers, frantically pushing them to the ground, the tips of my fingers and the bite of my nails skimming along the coarse hair of his thighs.

He grabbed me, stroking and caressing my body. Single-minded and greedy, he pushed me against the wall, his hands rounding on my thighs, preparing to lift me.

But I didn't want the loss of control. I didn't want a rapid coupling against the wall. So I maneuvered him to the chair, pushed him down, and climbed on his lap, his skin now as wet and slippery as mine.

"I miss this," he growled against my lips.

"What?" I hastily reached for him, guiding him, sucking in a breath as he entered me.

He palmed my ass with both of his hands and squeezed. "Fucking you."

The throaty coarseness of his words, his blunt and erotic brutality, sent sharp ripples of sensation to my thighs and twisted deliciously in the dark center of my belly.

"Is that what we're doing?" I rocked back and forth, taking him within me slowly, his savage, frustrated lust an aphrodisiac. "Fucking?"

"Yes. Oh God, yes. Like two mad animals," he groaned, his head falling back as I quickened my pace.

"Do you want it rough?" I asked, scratching his bare chest and biting his bottom lip.

His hips jerked in response and he grunted at the sting of my nails. "No."

He grabbed my wrists, bound them behind my back with one of his powerful hands. The position thrust my chest forward and he took advantage, nipping and sucking the sensitive flesh into his mouth.

"How do you want me?" I panted, struggling to maintain my rhythm. I felt overheated.

"How I want you . . ." he groaned against my naked skin, lifting his hips while endeavoring to guide mine. What his thrusts lacked in finesse he made up for with ruthless control, his thumb moving to stroke my center.

His ragged breath, my hitched sighs, the sound of our bodies meeting and retreating, became a seductive and impassioned symphony of sex. The hot friction of mating quickly built to a crisis. He released my wrists and I immediately pushed my fingers into his hair, wanting him closer, wanting him.

I was on the edge of the chaos of my climax when he stilled my hips and demanded, "Say you belong to me."

"I belong to you," I repeated the words mindlessly, shifting restlessly, enamored with the feverish, aching need of release, of being claimed. "I've always belonged to you."

He flicked his thumb and pulsed forward, anchoring me to him and biting the side of my breast. "I love you wildly, madly, completely, Fiona Archer," he growled, then groaned on a broken breath. "I love you always."

His words, so desperately spoken, paired with the coarse texture of his beard against my sensitive skin sent me beyond thought, to a place of selfish shamelessness. My body bowed, every cell, every atom magnetized and provoked with frenetic ardor, and I lost control.

Yes.

Oh God.

Please.

Now.

Fuck.

Yes.

Please.

Greg . . .

Slowly, by degrees, the rigidity of my body released, and still he moved. As I rode him I grew languid, rocking, no longer taking. Tenderly, I kissed his jaw and tongued his ear, breathing hotly against his neck and arching into him.

"I love you, Greg Archer." Our chests brushed and he sucked in a sharp breath, his grip now punishing and needful.

"Fe . . ."

"You belong to me," I whispered, biting his shoulder and meeting his quickening thrusts.

His eyes closed, his jaw clenched, and his body was hard and taut as he came. I watched, reveling in his surrender to the oblivion of passion.

And his surrender to me.

CHAPTER 12

Dear Wife,

I hope you know that I miss you and that my love for you doesn't stop at the last time you heard from me. Especially when that last time turns from days to weeks and sometimes months.

-Frank
Letter
Serving in Iraq
Married 5 years

~14 years ago~
Greg

ART EXISTS BECAUSE situations exist wherein all words are underwhelming.

The words "senseless tragedy" may define a situation, but can never describe with any accuracy or poignancy the truth of raw feeling, emotion, chaos, darkness, anger, and pain.

I'd been up for two hours when the first plane hit the World Trade Center on September 11, 2001. Returning from an early morning run, I'd flipped on the television in my downtown studio apartment.

I lived alone, though reminders of Fiona were everywhere. She'd left a toothbrush in my bathroom, her lotion next to the bed we shared when she was in town. Sometimes I'd smell it and miss her even more acutely, more desperately.

Our separation was supposed to last only a year. Yet stellar career and academic opportunities kept me in Texas and her in Iowa. We made it work, always with the promise of coming together at the end of the academic year. The most time together we'd managed was a full two months last summer. It had been divine. But then I'd been offered a fellowship with Dr. Louisa Franklin's team in Houston, a pioneer in the field of environmentally friendly oil extraction.

Fiona urged me to take it. It was the smart thing to do. The opportunity was too valuable to pass up. We'd already proven we could handle a long-term separation. We'd been apart more than we'd been together over the last three and a half years.

I moved away from the racket of the morning news, crossing to the kitchen. Because I lived mostly without her, I liked the background noise to mute my loneliness. But the words *World Trade Center* and *explosion* effectively cut through my preoccupation with my to-do list of mundane tasks for the coming day.

Coffee was soon forgotten. I watched the news with both rapt fascination and abject horror for ten minutes. Then I saw the second plane hit in real time.

I stared at the TV screen, hearing nothing, seeing nothing, shocked beyond sense or sensation. I could not comprehend what had just happened.

I didn't appreciate it at the time, but looking back, my level of shock was a testament to how lucky I was as a citizen of the United States. Since my medical discharge from the Marine Corps, I'd felt relatively safe. US citizens, for the most part, existed in this bubble of doldrums, of first-world problems. We lived apart from the rest of the world, a world where the words *explosion* and *terrorist attack* are as common as making the morning coffee.

But my first concrete conviction as I broke through the eerily numb surface of my thoughts was: *Fiona and I are getting married. Today. Or Tomorrow.*

And we would. Every time we'd been together during the last three years she'd suggested we elope. She hadn't been pushy. She'd typically cloak the suggestion as teasing, but I knew she was serious. I'd been the one holding out. But not anymore.

I didn't shower. I didn't pack. I grabbed my truck keys and passport, and I left.

It didn't matter that our wedding was scheduled for January, a big extravagant affair planned entirely by her mother. We'd been engaged for three years, and in this moment it felt like three years too long. Too much wasted time. Too much waiting. And waiting.

And waiting.

Too much caution, courage, and bravery, and not enough seizing the fucking day.

The drive from Houston to Iowa took sixteen hours and I listened to the news throughout, gorging myself on repeated sound bites until my brain felt rubbery and bruised.

I stopped at a payphone around midday and left a message on her answering machine.

"Fe, darling, it's your betrothed. I'm driving up right now. I know we're not scheduled for another visit until October, but I've decided it would be best if we got married today or tomorrow. Can you call the clerk of the court and check on the requirements? I have my passport with me."

I hung up, then immediately redialed.

"Also, I love you."

I hung up again. I stared unseeingly at the dusty expanse of the Texas desert, focusing instead on the oil pumpjacks—the visible portion of a reciprocating piston pump—moving up and down in the distance.

Oil.

Oil felt like both the question and the answer to the question I hadn't asked yet.

The why and the how: Why had they attacked the World Trade Center? And how had they obtained the resources needed? A growing sense of purpose, resolve to do whatever was necessary to keep this kind of senseless tragedy from happening again, infiltrated every part of my sentient thought.

I'd always wanted to do right by the earth, leave the world in a better state than when I'd arrived. Yet now I was struck with a new sense of determination, to make every action count for the better good. Oil was a corrupting influence, but it didn't have to be. It could be a liberator instead of a tool for oppression. But people needed to be taught. They needed an advocate.

It was after midnight when I pulled into Fiona's dorm parking lot. Using the phone outside the lobby, I picked up the receiver and dialed her room number. Before it connected, one of the girls from her floor recognized me from my visit last week and permitted me entrance to the building.

"Thank you," I said, taking the elevator with her to the fourth floor.

"No problem," she said, sounding dazed. I studied her for a long moment. She'd been crying. Crying and walking around in a daze struck me as an appropriate response to the horrors of the day.

Appropriate, but completely unhelpful.

I scowled at her back as we exited the lift and I stepped quickly to Fiona's dorm room.

As the resident advisor (RA), she wasn't required to share a room or a suite. But the RA's quarters were located in the center of the floor. She was afforded very little privacy. I preferred her visits to Houston, where we could be completely alone, where she wasn't frequently sought out by college co-eds for her conversation and sage advice. The constant interruptions grated. I wanted her—time, attention, and focus—for myself.

I rapped quickly on her door, then tried the handle. It was unlocked. I frowned, irritated with her lack of security, but then realized why she'd left it open as soon as I peeked inside.

Girls. Crying. Everywhere.

Aghast, I stared at the sad figures. They were clustered on her couch, huddled by the hallway, floundering on the floor. And Fiona was moving from group to group, pouring tea. I watched her for a long moment, listened as she served wise words of consolation and encouragement.

"The best course of action is to channel these feelings into something constructive," she was saying, smoothing her arm down the shoulder of a young blonde woman. "Be sad. Be angry. But don't be silent. Find ways to help, seek out opportunities to make a difference. Otherwise all this emotion will yield only helplessness."

"It's such a senseless tragedy," someone said with an achingly hollow voice.

Fiona frowned thoughtfully, having not yet discovered my intrusion. "It was sensible to someone. It was planned and executed with meticulous and cold efficiency. Allowing our emotions to dictate our response is understandable, but unwise. We should be looking for ways to solve the problem of terrorist cells, not give them more hate-fuel for their fire."

She was the voice of passionate reason in a storm of muddled misunderstanding. An optimist realist.

God Almighty, I loved this woman.

"Fe," I called, watching her start, her wide eyes swinging to mine.

She blinked, momentarily baffled.

And then she smiled for the barest of seconds.

And then her face crumpled.

"Oh, Greg . . ." The words were unsteady and her chin wobbled. Her usually bright eyes were dim, rimmed with anxiety, worry, and fear.

My stomach dropped and I saw what I'd been blind to just moments prior. Fiona was being brave for these young girls, proving herself to be a source of strength. She'd likely been handing out advice, offering a strong shoulder to cry upon, all day.

I crossed to her, stepping over the legs littering my path, and opened my arms. "Come here."

She nodded, not allowing a single tear to fall, and placed the teapot on a nearby table as she moved to me. I seized her in my arms, cursing when I felt her tremble.

"What are you doing here?" Her tone was both strained and relieved.

"I've come to marry you," I announced, more loudly than was strictly necessary. The space fell into a perplexed silence, followed by a low hum of startled excitement. I took the opportunity to guide her out of the room and into the hallway.

Once there, I whispered, "The world might be ending. As such I'm here to rescue you and worship your body."

I felt her huff a laugh just before she buried her face against my chest. I pressed my back against the hallway wall and gathered her against me once more.

"I needed you today." She sniffled. Her hands gripped fistfuls of my shirt and her voice was muffled.

"I needed you, too." I tilted my head backward and waited until she lifted her eyes to mine. "Marry me. Tonight. Or early tomorrow at the latest. We'll honeymoon here, in Iowa. I'll find the most romantic bomb shelter in the state."

"Yes!" She smiled up at me, beaming. "Yes, yes, yes! That sounds wonderful."

"We'll dine on sardine sandwiches and brain soup."

She laughed again, though it also resembled a sob. "Yes, okay. Finally."

"Good." I kissed her nose, then rubbed mine against it. "But first we must get rid of these hangers-on. Do you want me to pull a fire alarm?"

"No." She sighed and frowned, as though suddenly remembering the thirty or more young girls in her room. "No. Instead I need you to help me. Help me help them."

Fiona's exquisite eyes, abounding with faith and love and hope—all for me—captivated and subdued my selfish instincts. I acquiesced, because she needed me. So we stayed and helped, talking of thoughts and feelings until the wee hours of the morning. Accomplishing with philosophy what could not be readily accomplished through making and doing.

And the next day, accompanied by thirty or so hastily dressed bridesmaids and no groomsmen, we were married at city hall.

CHAPTER 13

S: Looking forward to having a lovely beer with my lady tonight.
R: You mean, you look forward to having a beer with your lovely lady,
not the other way around.
S: I mean, I'm looking forward to having a mediocre beer with my
beautiful lovely woman because essentially everything else is bang
average in comparison to you.

.

-Somerled and Rosie
Email Exchange
Brisbane, Australia
Dating 18 months

~Present Day~
Fiona

WE FIT ON the cot, but just barely.

When I awoke I was sprawled over his body, my head over his heart, his fingers playing in my still-damp hair and clutching my lower back.

"Go back to sleep." His voice was alert, like he hadn't yet rested. "It's only one."

I squinted until the dim room came into focus. He'd turned off the overhead lights save one. "You need to sleep, too. Let me take a shift."

"You would deprive me the joy of watching you sleep?"

I squeezed him and was about to tell him he was sweet.

But then he said, "You know that's why I married you, right?"

"So you could watch me sleep?"

"Basically. Being married is the only time I can say or do that sort of stuff and not sound like a stalker."

"You still sound like a stalker."

His chest shook with a rumbly laugh and his fingers danced over my neck. "Good. Glad I haven't lost my touch."

I shifted to his other side and bent my knee, folding my hands over his chest and peering up at him. "Since you're up, and I'm up—"

He smirked, lifting a single eyebrow and saying suggestively, "*Gooooo on.*"

I grinned and opened my mouth to respond, but he interrupted me again.

"Please tell me you want to knit an afghan. I've been dying to try out my new set of sharp Hiya circulars."

I was astonished he'd gleaned enough about knitting terminology to say, set of sharp Hiya circulars; nevertheless, I ignored this surprising information and pressed forward. "No. I want you to tell me what happened after you drugged me."

He grimaced, and I felt his abdominal muscles tighten, like he felt the words on a visceral level. "Do you have to say it like that? It sounds so untoward."

"You *did* drug me, Greg."

"I know. But can't we frame it differently? How about we say I poked you?"

"That makes it sound like we had sex."

"We did have sex." I heard the smug smile in his voice.

"You know what I mean. And I'm not going to use the word poke for both drugging and sex. You can see why that wouldn't be a good idea. I don't want to request a poke and have you spike my coffee with Ketamine, misunderstanding the request."

"Fine. But for the record, I would always assume you meant sex."

"Getting back to the original question, what happened after you drugged me?"

"First you need to know what happened when we were captured."

"Okay, start there."

Greg's chest rose and fell with an expansive breath and his hand smoothed down the length of my back, settling possessively on my backside.

His eyes grew unfocused as he recalled the memory. "They swarmed the boat, boarded, and immediately cuffed our hands and feet, duct-taped our legs together and arms to our sides. They were more concerned about us escaping than about us knowing where we were going. I was propped up in a seat and was able to look out the window when they transported us. I mentally mapped the route."

"I thought you had a bag over your head?"

"They didn't put that on until they suspected I was a US citizen. Regardless, I saw the route they took and knew where we were, more or less."

"So you knew which direction to take when you left the building?"

"Yes, with the help of your guidance. I left out the east door—like you recommended—but I didn't take the trail. I walked south."

Greg went on to explain that my suspicion had been correct; the structure where they'd been held had been an illegal oil refinery. He'd recognized the need to find and follow the siphoning pipe. It would (and did) lead him to the main oil line.

"The company is supposed to keep the main products line secure, especially since it's not buried, but siphoning offshoots aren't unusual. Opportunists—and by opportunists I mean thieves—tap into the mainline and steal the oil. They refine it and sell it. Nautical Oil will look the other way as long as it isn't too much, unless it cuts into their bottom line. But the problem is these siphoning taps aren't well made, they spill oil all over the place. And these illegal refineries are even worse, wrecking local ecosystems, polluting water supplies. It's a bloody mess."

Greg described how the oil company maintained postings along the line, small houses where sentinels were supposed to be stationed to guard the line. But he'd discovered over the last two months that the company couldn't keep trained personnel in these positions. The sentinels would either be bribed to look the other way, or be terrorized by local thugs until they left.

He'd carried me three miles until he'd found one of the postings. Then he'd broken into the house.

"It wasn't abandoned. The sentinel inside—a man, about my age—was asleep."

"What did you do?" My stomach clenched as I braced for bad news. I'd been so careful to subdue the guards rather than leave a body count.

I'd discovered years ago the problem with marrying a Marine—or a former Marine—was that his answer to everything was usually brutal focus, and single-minded, comprehensive annihilation.

Is that a spider? Shoot it.

Your phone isn't working? Smash it with a sledgehammer.

Your mother is making you crazy? Drop a house on her, and her little dog too.

Whatever you do, commit to the set course. Never hesitate. Never falter.

"I knocked him out with your wee dart gun, tied him up, gagged him, and stuffed him under his bed. Then I stole his clothes, food rations, and his car. But first I took a much needed shower."

I grimaced. "I hope somebody finds him."

"They will. The siphon line was right next to his post. He had to be working with the same greedy bastards that abducted me."

Now I cared less whether anyone found him.

"I stuck around for an hour or so, and I . . ." He paused, glanced at me then away.

"What? What did you do?"

Greg cleared his throat. "Mostly I hoped you would wake up. Ultimately, though, I decided we couldn't wait; we had to move. I grabbed what I could and took off, using only back roads."

Why would the guards allow him to see the route? This detail was troubling; felt like more confirmation his captors had no plans to return him—or any of the others—alive.

He was inspecting a spot on my shoulder, rubbing his thumb back and forth; he leaned forward and kissed it. "You have a new freckle here."

I examined my husband, my eyes narrowing on him. He appeared to be relaxed, drowsy even. Now was as good a time as any.

"We need to talk about the other hostages."

He closed his eyes and grew rigid beneath me. "Don't give me that look."

"What look? Your eyes are closed, you can't see me."

"I *feel* the look. It's the Fiona death stare of cruel disappointment."

"I have a cruel disappointed look?"

"Yes. It's like getting a spanking, and not the good kind."

"We need to talk about them. They're not safe."

His earlier softness disappeared. "They'll be fine."

"What if they're not?"

"They will be. Kidnappings are a business down here. Pirates take advantage of the European Union's lax laws on ransoming." He opened his eyes and shrugged. "They negotiate all the time; the pirates get paid, the hostages are released. As long as these groups can reliably make money off abducting EU citizens, and the citizens are released unharmed, they'll keep doing it. It's a vicious cycle."

"Alex seemed to think that the ransom was a red herring. That they had no plans to release you even if we paid the ransom."

Greg stewed in this new information for a long moment, looking confused. "He said that?"

"Yes. He did."

I went on to explain Alex's theory about the corrupt government faction and how he'd "retrieved" the information from the CIA.

Greg grew very still, a surfeit of emotions passing over his features. I could see his level of discontent rising, as was his regret.

"Bollocks." He pulled his fingers through his hair, and then rubbed his forehead, obviously speaking and thinking in tandem, "Still, it wouldn't have mattered. We had to leave them."

"But why?" I pushed myself up, straddled him, and crossed my arms. "I could have gotten everyone out."

"First of all, two of them were injured." His gaze swept over my body and he peeled my arms from my chest. "One broke his leg when we were captured, and the other was shot in the calf two days ago while trying to escape. The bullet passed right through, but he couldn't walk. Even if we'd tried to take them with us, we would have had to leave those two behind. But even if they'd all been mobile, we wouldn't have made it. These guys, they're not subtle guys. They're used to working on a rig, not sneaking through a prison."

I absorbed this information, sending a selfish prayer of thanks Greg hadn't been injured, that he'd been able to walk unassisted.

"You thought it was—and pardon the expression—a run of the mill kidnapping?"

His sigh was flavored heavily with self-recrimination. "I should have known. They let us see the route. They were more concerned with us escaping than anything else. I should have known."

I waited until he was quiet, staring into space, before stating what I hoped he was thinking. "We have to go back and get them."

"Someone does, I agree . . ." Greg hesitated, his gaze unfocussed. His mouth curved into a grave line as he amended, "I agree, and I just hope it's not too late."

***

ALEX MESSAGED AT 06:00 with instructions for a video chat. Ten minutes later we were looking at his and Sandra's smiling faces.

"It's so good to see you! I've bitten off all my fingernails due to worry. See?" Sandra was sitting on Alex's lap and she showed us her nails. "I'm not usually a worrier, but you had me worried."

"How are Grace and Jack?" I was leaning over Greg's shoulder, too wound up in knots to sit.

"They're doing really well. Alex and I took them to the Natural History Museum yesterday then out for pizza. Jack ate just as much pizza as Alex. You need to enter him into a contest or something."

"What about Quinn, Dan, and Marie? Are they out of the country yet?"

Greg tugged on my hand, bringing me around him, and pulling me to his lap. He rubbed soothing circles on my back.

Alex's smile disappeared. "Not yet."

Sandra twisted and glanced at her husband. "Is this my cue to exit?"

His face was devoid of emotion and he shrugged. "Whatever you want to do."

She stared at him for a beat, and then pushed to her feet. "I think I'll hover in the background, eavesdrop and try not to freak out."

"It's good to see your face, Sandra." I leaned forward, wanting another glimpse of my friend and the normalcy of home.

She bent at the waist and blew me a kiss. "You too, my beautiful friend. Please come home soon."

I nodded, but was unable to speak. I hadn't been prepared for the intensity of my homesickness.

As soon as Sandra faded into the background, Greg asked, "What's going on with Quinn? Why haven't they left yet?"

"They've been delayed. Some bullshit excuse about their entry visas. Immigration is claiming they applied for a tourist when they should have filled out the paperwork for a business visa."

A spike of alarm and guilt cinched my throat. "Where are they? Have they been taken into custody?"

"No. They're still at the resort. I think having Marie there saved Dan and Quinn a trip to detainment. The Chicago Sun has been all over her updates and her first article was picked up by the Associated Press."

Greg and I glanced at each other and he asked the question I was thinking. "What article? What did she write?"

"She wrote an international news piece about the kidnapping, heavily implying Nautical Oil was behind it. Their shares tanked—excuse the pun—yesterday, and in the last twenty-four hours the pundits on CNN, Fox News, etcetera have picked it up. They really like that Greg is a former Marine."

"And so gosh-darn handsome!" Sandra hollered from someplace unseen.

"And you have cute kids. People care about other people with cute kids," Alex added distractedly.

"What do Jack and Grace have to do with this?" I leaned forward unthinkingly, blocking Greg from the screen.

"Oh yeah, sorry. Marie used a picture of Greg with Grace and Jack, *Chicago Former Marine Abducted by Nautical Oil Pirates*—that's the name of the article that ran Friday." Alex read from a newspaper next to his laptop then lifted it up so Greg and I could see. "But the picture she used was taken a while ago and she didn't use their names, just Greg's. I don't think Jack and Grace will be easily recognized."

He was right. The picture was taken over four years ago and the kids looked a good deal different. Still, Greg's name was splashed all over the place. I hated to think Grace and Jack would find out about the abduction from someone other than me.

"I think *Nautical Oil Pirates* has a nice ring to it. They should sponsor a Pittsburg hockey team," Greg said absentmindedly, pulling me away from the screen so he could see the newspaper.

"As long as the media is focusing on the story, Quinn, Dan, and Marie are relatively safe." Alex set the paper down and crossed his arms. "If something were to happen to them, the US would have to step in on some level. These oil privateers want less scrutiny, not the CIA poking around."

Both Greg and I stiffened at Alex's use of the word *poking*. I wondered which kind of poking he was thinking about.

"Alex, there's another problem. We didn't rescue the other captives, I didn't give Fiona the chance."

Greg's arm squeezed me around the waist and I took it as a symbolic *you were right and I'm sorry* squeeze. I leaned back and against him in a symbolic *thank you for your apology, now let's figure this out together* lean.

"Yeah, can't say I blame you. If Sandra showed up trying to rescue me from an illegal oil refinery in Nigeria, I'd likely gag her and remove her by force."

"Gagging would be important." Again Sandra's voice carried to the call from some unseen place. "Because you'd get an earful from me."

I felt Greg's smile against my hair.

Alex smirked and continued, "So, I checked on the other hostages when you messaged last. Looks like they were moved and the building where you were held had been abandoned, or at least I can't find any signs of life other than the refinery workers. I'm still trying to figure out where they were taken. But, even if we found them, you should consider the possibility that another rescue attempt is a lost cause. You won't be able to break them out this time because their captors will be expecting it."

I felt Greg shift in his seat before he asked, "What if we had leverage?"

"What kind of leverage?"

"Lots of money, and . . . something else."

Alex's eyebrows curved upward with curiosity and I turned to look at my husband.

"Lots of money?" I asked. "What are you talking about?"

A glimmer of something imbued Alex's voice, resembling enjoyment, but not quite. "Define whose lots of money and how much?"

"I'm not sure whose money it is, precisely." Greg split his attention between both Alex and me. "I'm guessing it's money from the illegal refineries, and usually that leads back to corrupt government factions and/or extremist groups. But it's at least a million, if not more."

"So you want to take their money and ransom it back to them? In exchange for the hostages?" I connected the dots and turned back to Alex.

Greg nodded. "When I was scouting the mainline postings last month I found large quantities of cash in several of the abandoned sentinel houses, all US denominations. Obviously I didn't touch it, but all together I estimate it's at least a million."

"Can you move it?" Alex asked. "How large are the denominations?"

"We can move it. They're in stacks of hundreds. But I'd like a different car."

Alex frowned, but acquiesced. "I'll try to figure something out. So, Greg, what's the *something else?*"

"What?"

"Earlier you said you had leverage, 'lots of money and something else'."

I felt Greg's chest expand at my back, and his arms tightened around me. "Ah yes. About that . . ."

Greg fell silent. When he didn't continue after several seconds, I twisted to face him again. I found him pressing his lips together, like he had a secret and dreaded having to share it.

"What did you do?"

"I may have," he tossed his head from side to side in a considering motion before finally admitting, "I may have rigged the refinery to explode."

It took me a full minute to recover from his statement, that he *may have rigged the refinery to explode*. When I finally found my voice I said, "Start from the beginning."

"I added acetone to their spliced line."

"Meaning?"

"Meaning . . . it's highly probable that the refinery will explode."

"Greg!"

"I know, I know." He lifted both his hands as though surrendering.

"Greg!"

"I'm not sorry. These are the wankers who have been stealing from the people of Nigeria for decades, not to mention ruining farmland, fragile ecosystems, and terrorizing innocent civilians. People are left with no usable water. No water means no fish, no farmland. And no fish and no farmland means no food." He lowered his hands and wrapped his arms around me. "Yes, it was a small refinery—as far as refineries go—but it was impressively large for an illegal operation. And it was obvious to me that they'd invested a good deal of money in its construction. Extensive automation, latest technology."

"I didn't see any impressive technology. The place looked dilapidated, like it was falling down," I countered.

"You wouldn't have, not the way you entered the building. When they brought us in it was through new control rooms."

I glared at him. I heard Alex clear his throat. Seconds ticked by.

Greg glared back, but ultimately he broke the stalemate. "I was angry and I wanted to make sure I hit them where it hurt."

"But where did you get the acetone?"

"At the sentinel house by the mainline where I stole the Jeep. There were drums of it in the garage. Acetone is used to clean up soil after oil spills, specifically a hexane-acetone solvent mixture. I'm guessing he had such a large quantity in order to hastily remove environmental evidence of the spliced line."

"So you did what exactly?"

"I rolled the drums out and emptied them into the line. At the time, I estimated it would take seventy-two hours to reach the refinery, betting that they'd move the hostages once they awoke and discovered me missing. I calculated the fluid mechanics while you were asleep and the number is closer to seventy-eight hours."

Alex's stifled laughter met my ears and I glanced at the computer screen, found him bent to the side, covering his mouth with his hand, his shoulders shaking.

Of course Alex would find this hilarious. Of course.

Of course.

I crossed my arms and continued questioning my husband. "Acetone is volatile and flammable, but how can you be sure it will ignite?"

"When you refine crude oil, you use a distillation tower. The crude oil goes through a heating furnace or a boiler on its way to the tower, and temperatures are in excess of one thousand degrees Fahrenheit. Acetone auto ignites at just under nine hundred degrees."

I gazed at him with wonder. "So as soon as the acetone moves through the boiler. . . ?"

His eyes brightened with excitement, like a little kid who has just discovered firecrackers. "Kaboom."

"Kaboom?" I parroted.

Greg made a mushroom cloud motion with his hands, his grin widening. "Big kaboom."

"*Big kaboom*? Is that the technical term?" Both Greg and I turned our attention back to the screen, finding Sandra's face filling the window.

"See, this is why I won't let you play with Alex, Greg. He likes to blow things up figuratively, and you like to blow things up literally," she chided.

Alex was still smiling as he gently pushed her out of the way, "I like to blow things up literally, too."

"All men do." She sounded exasperated.

We needed to get back on track. "How much time do we have left? Before the acetone reaches the refinery?"

"Thirty-six hours, give or take."

"How are we supposed to get a message to these people in thirty-six hours?"

"Leave that to me," Alex said, no longer looking at the camera. He must've minimized our window because I could see that he was typing and reading and clicking. "We need to be able to stay in contact. Do you still have the phone?"

"Yes, but the solar charger was lost," I reminded them.

"I'll arrange for a different car and have a compatible charger placed under the driver's seat. Give me an hour and we'll touch base again. But I'll need more time to send the message about the refinery, I'll say you planted a bomb, but leave it vague, and channel it through the CIA. Hopefully this will distract them from the sentinel houses so you can grab the stashes of money."

"Sounds good. We'll pick up the new car and go to the sentinel houses, collect the money while they're distracted." Greg's large hand moved in a slow, caressing, absentminded circle on my lower back.

Alex nodded his agreement. "Then we'll leverage the money for the hostages, get Quinn and company out of Nigeria, and figure out how to get you two on a Red Star flight bound for the EU or Caribbean."

I felt both Greg's perfunctory nod and his pinch of my bottom as he said, "I vote Caribbean."

***

"DO YOU NEED more time?"

I paused checking our weapons and counting the remaining rounds to meet my husband's gaze. We were packing as we waited for Alex's next call. Greg stood before me, dressed in another of his weird sports shirts, his hands on his hips. My gaze lingered on the text of the T-shirt, *2014 New York Rangers Stanley Cup Champions.*

"More time for what?"

"Do you need more time? To think about that thing we discussed?"

"What thing? And I'm pretty sure the Los Angeles Kings won the Stanley Cup in 2014. What is with all the bizarre shirts?"

Greg glanced at his chest, his hand automatically coming to the letters. "Oh, don't you know? Africa is where all the leftover clothes go from the USA. When sports teams play for a championship, both sets of T-shirts are printed so they'll be ready immediately, to meet demand. When a team loses, the T-shirts advertising their non-existent win are sent to Africa."

I did not know this random bit of trivia. "Huh . . ."

"I make it my mission to find all the alternate reality shirts I can find. It makes me feel like I'm living in a different dimension, where the Rangers beat the Kings and the Red Socks never won the World Series."

"You're the only person on the planet who wasn't cheering for the Red Socks in 2004."

"Not true. There are about one million St. Louis Cardinals fans who would disagree. But back to my original question—are we in agreement, about you freezing me out? No more making decisions without me? Yes?"

I considered my husband for a long moment while he stared at me expectantly, his hands on his hips. I hadn't finished mulling over all the issues.

"It's not that simple."

"Yes it is. Just stop doing it."

"I can't. Not when you cause turmoil with your mandates."

"I don't cause turmoil. I cause only happiness rainbows and shoeboxes of delight wherever I go."

I pressed my lips together and waited for him to recognize the ridiculousness of his last statement. When he continued to gaze at me blankly, I said, "You don't want Jack to play soccer."

"He can play soccer, if Grace also plays soccer. End of discussion."

I started to wave my hand through the air, then remembered I was holding the gun. I lowered my hand, deciding that waving a gun around during an argument wasn't the best way to encourage polite discourse.

"See? That's what I mean. Why can't Jack just play soccer? You make these decrees that make no sense and can't be applied in real life."

"They make perfect sense."

I ignored that statement, because . . . because. Because it was patently false and deserved to be ignored.

"You don't have to live it, Greg. You come home for weeks, a month if we're lucky. You're not there every day, watching Jack practice in his room, bouncing the ball all over the apartment, taking it with us to the park every single time we go. He watches soccer on television, rewatches matches on YouTube. He wants to play, and you're being unfair."

"Like I said, he can play. If Grace also plays."

"Why?"

"Because she needs to be pushed beyond the boundaries forced on little girls by society. Our culture tells women they need to wear pink, and base their self-worth on looks, and need rescuing, and that's bullshit. We have to rally against—"

"The modern machinery of patriarchal oppression, yes. Yes, I know. But she is five years old, Greg. And Jack is eight. Can't we just let them be five and eight? Can't we give them a normal childhood? Why does everything have to be a statement?"

"Is it the soccer you're objecting to?" Greg's gaze grew scrutinizing, suspicious. "Or is it something else?"

"I don't object to the soccer, if she wanted to play then I'd be all for it. But she doesn't and I don't want to force her, or punish Jack as a byproduct."

He shook his head. "That's not what I meant. Are you sure you aren't making this about you?"

I frowned at him, waited for him to explain. He didn't. He continued to examine me.

"What are you talking about?"

"Your childhood wasn't normal."

"So what?" I shrugged, feeling unaccountably irritated by the direction of this conversation. "Neither was yours."

"You know what I mean, and it's not the same. I grew up going to a posh boarding school, which *is* normal for a subset of the population. But you grew up practicing gymnastics six to eight hours a day. That's normal for maybe two hundred people in the world. By all accounts, your giftedness in gymnastics might be called a rare disease. Are you sure your desire to give Grace and Jack a normal childhood isn't about you overcompensating for what you missed? What you lost? Rather than what's in their best interest?"

I straightened my back, lifting my chin, leveling him with an incendiary stare. With measured coolness, I responded, "No. I'm not."

He seemed to be deliberating my words—and me—as though attempting to navigate a minefield.

"Now, darling—"

"Don't call me darling."

"Why not?"

I kept my voice monotone. "Because it's manipulative. You only do it when you're trying to get your way. And I'm tired of being manipulated by you."

He flinched, frowning, but his tone was combative as he challenged, "Did I hit a nerve?"

"Yes, of course you hit a nerve, but you were trying to. You just flat-out accused me of raising our children without their best interest at heart. You are being spiteful and mean, and I don't deserve that kind of treatment."

"Fe—"

"I am your wife. I love you. I love our children. I do my best. I'm not perfect. This is not a debate about who is wrong and who is right. I agree, we need to come to a consensus together. But you are being a bully, and it needs to stop."

Greg snapped his mouth shut, and the muscle of his jaw ticked. We watched each other, exchanging wary stares across the length of the bunker. The longer the silence stretched, the harder I had to fight my ingrained urge to apologize.

But then the laptop dinged, interrupting our standoff. Greg gave me one last hard look—one that promised we were not yet finished with the current topic—and moved to the table. I set the gun down, I hadn't realized I was still holding it, and crossed to stand next to him as he accepted Alex's call.

"Okay, here's what we got." Alex began speaking as soon as the video connected. "I will have a truck—four-wheel drive—waiting for you in five hours. You need to get to the outskirts of Enugu. There will be a compatible charger under the driver's seat, as we discussed. Once you secure the money, get to the airfield by midnight the day after tomorrow. I'm IM-ing you the directions to the truck and the airfield now."

"We're leaving the country before the hostages are released?" I started to cross my arms over my chest, but Greg reached for my hand. Not looking at me, he laced our fingers together, then brought my knuckles to his lips, absentmindedly brushing soft kisses against my skin.

It occurred to me in that moment: marriage is an ultimate sport in emotional multitasking. I'm never *only* mad at Greg. I'm mad and madly in love; angry and concerned for his wellbeing; he frustrates and delights me in the same second. We were arguing, but we were still a team.

"Yes. Once the money is secured, there isn't any reason for you to stay. Negotiations can occur without you having to be in the country. Once they release the hostages to their embassies, we'll tell them where the money is," Alex explained. "But I'll need you to booby-trap it."

Greg glanced at me, then back to Alex. "The money? You want me to booby-trap the money?"

"Yep. Just in case they don't follow through."

Greg nodded. "Okay. Sounds like fun."

I rolled my eyes but smiled. Part of me loved that booby-trapping millions of dollars with explosives was Greg's idea of fun. Maybe one day he would teach our children how to booby-trap millions of dollars, because if they didn't learn about it at home, they would just learn about it on the streets.

"Also, the mail carrier flight will take you through Egypt. From there you'll be unpacked and will take a FedEx carrier to the Cayman Islands." Alex read from a screen to his right.

"Egypt?" I frowned.

Alex glanced at his webcam. "Yes. What's wrong with Egypt?"

"Nothing . . ."

"What?" Greg pushed.

"Well, their latest protests, the environment seems dangerous. Weren't the police raping both men and women?"

Greg lifted an eyebrow, appearing thoughtful, and nodded his head. "I believe so. But to be fair, it's about time rape stopped being so sexist."

"Greg!"

"What?"

"There is nothing funny about rape."

"I agree. And there's nothing funny about sexist rape, either."

Although I could appreciate the ironic nature of his statement, I had to draw the line someplace. No jokes about rape, even if they were effective in highlighting a double standard. "You are so terrible, I don't-I can't-you should be ashamed of yourself."

"It's pronounced *astonished*. And I am."

"He has a point, Fiona," Alex chimed in, steepling his fingers as he leaned back in his desk chair. "It's about time men were raped. Why should women bear the entire raping burden?"

I glanced askance between the serious visages of my husband and Alex, and sputtered, "How about no one is raped? How about that? How about: no more rape, period."

"Motion passed, no more rape," Greg announced. "And no eating Irish babies, either."

I narrowed my eyes on him, not missing his reference to Jonathan Swift's infamous satire, *A Modest Proposal*. He mirrored my expression, squinting his eyes, and a subtle smile lingered over his lips.

Troublemaker.

Alex nodded and hit his desk once with his fist, as though he were a judge. "Excellent, we all agree, no rape. So . . . we good with Egypt?"

CHAPTER 14

Dearest Husband,
I don't think I loved you the way I love you now when I said, "Yes, I'll
marry you." Back then I thought I knew what love was, what love was
supposed to be. But each and every day you show me it's so much more.

-Helena
Letter
Ontario, Canada
Married 10 years

~Present Day~
Fiona

"**IT'S DYING, GREG.** The Jeep is on its way out."

"Shhh." He pressed his index finger against my lips and said in a harsh whisper, "She'll hear you."

I ignored his silliness (for the most part), but I did give him a faint smile. "There's no resuscitating it. The Jeep needs a new radiator and we obviously don't have the parts. All we can do is wait for it to cool, keep adding water, and see if it starts in an hour."

I cleaned the grease from my hands with a rag I'd found in the trunk, and used my wrist to wipe the sweat from my forehead. We were a good ten or so miles from the new vehicle Alex had arranged, and still on the outskirts of Nigeria's most populated city. We'd been driving all day—mostly in silence—and the sun was setting; Enugu on the horizon, streaks of orange, purple, and fiery red painted the sky.

Neither of us had reintroduced the topic of Grace not wanting to play soccer, my alleged overcompensation for the lack of normalcy in my childhood, or Greg's bullying proclivities. Mostly, we stewed in our own thoughts. If his deliberations were anything like mine—and I suspected they were—he was focusing on maneuvering through the next forty-eight hours, making it safe and sound back to Chicago, and freeing the hostages in the process.

"When the time comes," Greg stroked the hood and sighed mournfully, "will you give me some time to say goodbye to the car?"

"Do you need some privacy now? Slip inside the driver's side door and I can cover it with a tarp, give the two of you a minute?"

"No. Not now," he responded solemnly. "I'm going to drive it to a cliff, shoot it while it's not looking, then push it into a lake."

My faint smile became a full one. As though pleased with himself for making me smile, Greg stood a little taller, his eyes lingering on my mouth.

"Good plan. But do we want to stay put and wait?" I asked, eyeballing the road behind him. "Or should we grab our gear and make a run for it?"

"A literal run for it? You mean run the last twelve miles?"

"Is it twelve? I thought it was closer to ten." I was undecided which course of action would be best.

Greg scratched his neck and studied the horizon. "It would take us two and half-ish hours by foot, if we ran the whole way, but if we can get the Jeep running we'll save both time and energy."

"But if we can't get the Jeep running, then we'll have wasted an hour."

"True." Greg bobbed his head from side to side, his eyes moving over my shoulder. "But I think we have to risk it. Two Oyibos running together on the side of the road will be conspicuous no matter the time of day. We should wait until nightfall regardless."

His logic made sense.

"Fine, but we can't stay by the Jeep. We should push it off the road at least, and cross to the other side, hide in the grasses for an hour."

Greg was already moving, releasing the emergency break, and motioning me over to the driver's side. "Agreed. You steer, I'll push."

Once we finished maneuvering the Jeep some ways into the tall grass, we grabbed our gear and jogged to the opposite side, careful to remain hidden.

"As long as we stay within a quarter mile of the road, we should be safe from snakes." Greg stamped his feet before he crouched to the ground, removing his backpack.

"Good to know," I said. But what I was thinking was more like, *filet of snake actually sounds really good right now.*

My stomach rumbled. Loudly.

Greg lifted a single eyebrow as I sat next to him. "Hungry?"

"Actually . . . yes." The realization was surprising. I hadn't been hungry for the last two and a half months, not since just after Christmas. And I didn't have a headache.

"We have First Strike rations in my bag."

I made a face, because I was craving snake or something like it. *Maybe shrimp. Shrimp and butter. Yum.*

But ultimately I said, "Sure. Hand it over."

Greg passed me the rectangle of rations. I opened the sealed plastic and absentmindedly munched on the contents while I sat cross-legged next to him. The route we'd opted to traverse on our way to Enugu was mostly unpaved, which was likely how we'd ended up with a hole in the radiator. But that also meant it was considerably less traveled. Several minutes would pass between any noise or indication of a solitary car in the distance.

The sonata of sunset insects, the darkening sky above dotted with emerging stars, and the wind rustling the tall stalks were our only companions.

Surrounded by peace and calm, I found myself having deep thoughts, and I gave voice to them abruptly, before spending too much time considering the subject matter. "Why do people get married, Greg?"

Greg's attention lifted from his ration pack and settled on me, inspecting both me and my question, his handsome face betraying bewildered interest.

I sought to clarify. "You said once it made sense to partner off so burdens could be shared. But that's not what I'm asking, because I don't think shared burdens are why people get married. Shared burdens are a byproduct, not a cause."

Greg munched on a square of foodstuff that resembled a Triscuit. "You'll have to be more specific. Do you mean, why get married as in why make it official? Or do you mean, why get married as in why be monogamous and commit to spending the rest of your life with just one person?"

"The latter one. I don't even understand the desire in myself." I leaned back on my hands and studied the sky, leaving the rations in my lap. "I know, growing up, it was expected of me. Culturally, for the most part, girls are told their map of life includes partnering off, getting married, having kids."

"Men are as well, you know. Our generation, at any rate. It was understood, part of growing up is getting married."

"Exactly. That's exactly it." I turned my attention back to my husband. "*Why* is it a part of growing up? Why do we want it so badly? Why do parents want it for their children?"

"If you throw away all the first-world pundit-esque pretentious answers—like societal pressures, oppression of one sex or the other, a patriarchal construct meant to maintain order, etcetera—and assume the desire to partner is a real thing, then I think . . ." He trailed off, staring unseeingly at something in the distance.

I waited for him to continue, giving him time to compose his thoughts, and found myself enjoying the moment, and his profile. He still hadn't shaved and looked a bit wild, his hair falling across his eyes. Over the course of the day he had pushed it off his forehead again and again—like he used to do when we were first married—and the simple movement had me feeling nostalgic.

I longed to run my fingers through it and twist the silky strands around my fingers. I hadn't. Not yet. Things weren't right between us. Yes, we'd made love, made use of each other's bodies. But playing with his hair when I still carried a lump of discontent around in my stomach felt insincere.

"I think," he finally continued, his voice soft and thoughtful, "there are fundamentally two kinds of people: those who need to be loved, and those who need to love. Now, not to say the desires are mutually exclusive, quite the opposite. I believe most people are a mix of the two, with one desire outweighing the other."

"Some people need to nurture, some crave being nurtured."

"Exactly. And marriage, exclusivity, monogamy—when done right—feeds both needs in a way nothing else comes close."

I turned my attention back to the sky and marinated in his words, finding truth in my husband's wisdom. It may have been an oversimplification of a complex issue, not taking into account the many special snowflake needs of each individual member of humanity, but it resonated with me.

Conversation and debate of any kind not related to our children, and universe of worries, were luxuries. I couldn't remember the last time Greg and I had discussed anything other than the kids, the household, money, our friends, or our marriage.

I was about to ask him which of us was the nurturer and which of us needed nurturing, when he surprised me by asking, "Why did you marry me, Fiona?"

I didn't think too hard about my answer. "Because I loved you. And because you showed up and demanded we get married without delay because the world was ending."

I moved just my eyes to his face, found him smiling at the memory, or maybe at his youthful impulses. "I was frantic, I admit. I didn't want to spend another day without you as my wife."

"So you said at the time." I laughed lightly, recalling how zealous he'd been, how impassioned. We'd been so young.

We'd been too young.

"That's why you married me?"

I nodded once.

Greg cleared his throat before asking, "But not because you wanted to spend the rest of your life with me?"

The question and his voice struck me as both vulnerable and accusatory. Frowning at him, the rigid, unhappy set of his mouth, I leaned forward and placed my hand on his thigh.

"Honestly?"

"No. God no. Honesty is for the proletariat. Lie to me, of course." He was trying to disarm the moment with humor, but despondency permeated his tone and his features.

"I wanted to spend the rest of my life with you," I said, thinking at first that would be the entirety of my answer, but then—without forethought—I continued speaking. "That's not really what happened, is it? How could I have known 'the rest of my life' didn't really mean the rest of my life? Marriage, for us, means sometimes. Sometimes, over the course of the rest of our lives, I get to be with you."

We watched each other, as much as was possible under the blanket of blue-black sky and twinkling stars. And the longer we swapped stares, the more wretched I felt.

Because my suspicion that *sometimes* no longer being enough solidified into a fact.

Sometimes wasn't enough.

It hadn't been enough for several years.

As though reading my mind, Greg said, "Just because we're not in the same city doesn't mean we're not *with* each other."

"Actually, it kinda does. Geography has a lot to do with being *with* a person."

"But it's not everything."

"But it's a lot. Looking back, I see a lot of me being alone. I see a lot of me without you. I see a lot of dinners for three, not four."

He grimaced, packing up the remains of his rations. "Are you trying to make me feel guilty?"

"No. I'm pointing out that you've been missed. Being present is one hundred percent more meaningful than being there in spirit. You've been there in spirit for Grace's first words and Jack's first day of kindergarten. But when they look back, they're going to remember the absence of you, of your tangible presence. You may have been thinking about them, but you're not in the pictures."

"What do you want me to do, Fe? Quit my job?"

I removed my hand from his leg and recited robotically, "You being happy makes me happy. Your job makes you happy."

"Does it?"

"Yes. Yes, you love it. You love the difference you make in the world. You love making drilling safer and more efficient and the effect it has on the environment. You love doing something meaningful. And you're good at it."

"Then what? What's the solution?"

"It is what it is," I said rather than, *It'll just have to be enough.*

"You know I hate that phrase, 'It is what it is.' The motto for indolent, phony do-gooders everywhere."

"Yes. I know you hate it. But what else is there to say?"

"This isn't acceptable to me."

"What? What isn't acceptable? You can't be in two places at once."

"No. *You* could say, 'This isn't acceptable to me.' You're becoming invisible under the weight of unhappiness and yet you say, 'It is what it is' like you're powerless to change it."

Directing my face away from him, I was thankful for the dark, for the veiled shadow of the moonless night. I considered his words, *You're becoming invisible under the weight of unhappiness.*

Is that what is happening? Was I becoming invisible?

I didn't particularly want to share the struggle going on within me. The angry voice was back, reminding me again that two months wasn't enough. Two months would be better, but better didn't necessarily equate to adequate. And adequate definitely didn't equate to what I wanted . . . or what I needed.

"You're a bloody ninja superwoman, and I'm just one of your many admirers," Greg grumbled, pulling my attention back to him.

"Pardon me?"

"I said—" he started, but then stopped, straightening and twisting around toward the road.

I followed his line of sight and cursed under my breath.

Two cars were stopped on the opposite side of the road; men were shouting, both within the cars and outside of them. They'd left their beams on high, shining them into the concealing grasses.

The Jeep had been discovered.

"How did they see it? It's pitch black out here." His irritation was obvious.

"We're going to have to run," I said unnecessarily, more to get him moving than anything else.

"Okay. Okay. Let's go." He nodded and reached for my hand, like he needed reassurance I was still alive and well.

I held on to him tightly, thankful for the strength of his grip, finding I needed the physical connection just as badly as he.

***

OTHER THAN BEING exhausting, the next five hours were without incident.

We located the promised vehicle. The charger was under the driver's seat. We were able to leave the outskirts of Enugu without any trouble, circumventing the main city by taking the bypass route and messaging Alex as soon as the phone held a charge.

Two hours into the southward drive, Greg took a gravel turnoff I would've missed in broad daylight.

"This is the way to the sentinel houses?"

He nodded once. "Yes. There are four off this road along the pipeline, set back and obscured by the landscape."

"You found them by following the pipeline?"

"Back in January, when I started the assignment, I didn't announce my intention to survey the houses to Nautical Oil, so no one knows I've been poking about."

"Really? You've been poking about?" I gave him a mock suspicious glare.

"Actual poking." He flashed me a grin. "Not sexy poking."

I chuckled. "So you, what? Found the money strewn around in the houses?"

"Not necessarily. I wanted to trek the length of the products pipeline, determine how we could improve security and/or discourage thievery. Most of the sentinel houses are occupied, but the sentinels don't do their job. The house where we're headed now was vacant. I decided to spend the night before trekking back and that's when I discovered the cash in the empty garage, stacked in a corner."

"How odd."

"Yeah . . . well, maybe not. If the money is from illegally refining oil—and I'm assuming it is—then the cash I found has likely been laundered. The corrupt members of the government responsible for this mess need to store the money someplace before it can be deposited or used for bribes. These sentinel houses are out of the way, and since the thieves in charge apparently control most of the sentinels, where better to hide the money?" He steered us off the unpaved road and a short ways into the underbrush before cutting the engine.

"Do you think it'll still be there?"

"Only one way to find out."

I frowned at our surroundings, not seeing any sign of the house or the pipeline. "Are we here?"

"No. We're a half mile from the main products line, and another mile from the sentinel house. But this is as close as I'm willing to park. Once I determine whether it's occupied, I can jog back for you."

I'm sure my facial expression was in communion with my words as I said, "What are you talking about? Jog back for me? I'm not staying here."

Greg grumble-sighed. "Fine. But you let me scope the house first before you approach."

"It's like you're talking, but everything out of your mouth is nonsense. If one of us should scope the house it should be me."

He gritted his teeth and even in the dark I could see the unhappy lines around his mouth. "Fe, this isn't about who is more capable, this is about how I will lose my fucking mind if you're hurt. So, in the interest of my sanity, will you please do me this favor?"

"You don't think I'll lose my sanity if you're hurt? Who do you think nailed herself into a shipping crate to rescue you from an illegal oil refinery guarded by goons? A sane person?"

He closed his eyes and his head fell backward, against the headrest. "Please, dar—" He audibly exhaled. "Please."

I didn't agree. I didn't disagree. Instead, I opened my door and grabbed my equipment belt and holster. Greg also exited the truck and armed himself, casting me furtive glances. When we were locked and loaded, he led the way and we jogged in silence.

Actually, I jogged in silence, my feet and movements soundless. Greg jogged like a large man who used to be a Marine.

Crunch.

Crash.

Smash.

Snap.

Crack.

Amateur.

He also looked over his shoulder every so often to make sure I was still there.

A little over fifteen minutes later we were standing outside a dark house. I could feel Greg's eyes on me from where I ducked, scanning the windows. The porch was lit, but no other light source was visible.

"How about you do a sweep of the outside, see if there's any cars parked on the street or near the garage," my husband whispered in my ear.

I knew what he was doing. He was trying to keep me out of the way so he could get in the house first. He was making me crazy.

I leveled him with a narrowed glare. "If you promise to stay here, I will do a sweep around the house."

"Okay. I promise." He nodded once, pulled me forward for a quick kiss, then set me away. "You are very sexy when you're in commando mode. I think we should resurrect this look when we get home, maybe replace the spandex with leather."

"It's not spandex, it's a Kevlar blend."

His voice lowered to a growly whisper. "I'm so turned on right now."

Despite the situation, I had to stifle a laugh. "Can we discuss boudoir costumes later?"

"Fine. Just throwing it out there." His hand was on my upper thigh and he trailed his fingers from my hip to my knee. "Okay, go do the sweep. I'll stay here."

I hesitated. He'd agreed far too quickly. And he was trying to distract me with talk of sexy times. Ultimately though, having no reason to linger, I skipped off and circled the house.

I found no cars parked on the street and none in the driveway. But the garage door was lowered. As well I detected no movement in the house and no cameras on the façade. Twenty minutes later, I returned to the spot where I'd left Greg only to find him gone.

Of course. Of course he was gone. He was probably already in the house. I clenched my jaw and rolled my eyes. He was incredibly infuriating. I couldn't go in after him, because he might mistake me for a hostile. I had no choice but to wait.

So I waited. And waited.

And waited.

And while I waited I felt myself simmering in resentment, daydreaming about putting him in a chokehold and demanding he stop discounting me. I was also going to demand that he put his socks in the laundry bin. *Why must he leave them everywhere? Why?*

Eventually, he emerged from the front door and jogged to my location. I sat back on my heels and watched his approach, swallowing my desire to scream at him about his tendency to break promises and confetti our apartment with dirty laundry.

And why was I equating broken promises with dirty laundry?

"You promised," I accused in a harsh whisper as soon as he crouched next to me.

"I lied," he said distractedly, rushing to add before I could berate him further, "there's no one in the house, but we have—"

He wasn't expecting me to move, therefore his resistance was minimal when I pinned him to the ground, his position such that he could easily escape. I didn't want to intimidate; I wanted him to listen.

"Darling?" he asked, his wide eyes moving between mine.

I growled, "Stop lying to me. Stop discounting my contribution. Stop treating me like my opinion is nonsense."

"Fe—"

"You are really starting to piss me off."

His gaze dropped to my mouth, and his twitched like he was trying not to smile, his voice beseeching as he said my name. "Fe—"

"Laughing is only going to make me put you in a clasped-hand variation of the rear naked choke. If that happens, I *will* put pressure on your carotid artery."

"Sorry, sorry. I'm not laughing, I promise." His eyes turned dreamy. "It's just—"

"Just what?"

"It's just, you're alarmingly beautiful when you're being a badass. And it's difficult to concentrate when you're straddling me."

I felt growing pressure against my inner thigh and I rolled my eyes, huffing. "What do I need to do in order for you to take me seriously?"

"I do take you seriously. I promise."

"Just like you promised not to go in the house until I returned?"

"No. I didn't mean that promise, but I mean this one."

I bit my tongue and closed my eyes, shaking my head. And I laughed because I was frustrated. "I am so angry."

"Don't be angry."

"Don't patronize me."

"I swear I'm not." I felt his fingers thread into my hair. When I opened my eyes I found his sincere and serious. "I'm not. I needed you to stay put—not because I'm more capable, but because I'm familiar with the house, where to look, and in this situation it made sense."

I narrowed my eyes on him. "Then why didn't you say so earlier?"

"Because I am dreadfully tired. And I know I'm responsible for putting us in this mess. The thought of you getting hurt because of me and my choices isn't something I can live with."

I frowned at him, studying the handsome planes of his face, which were—blast him—etched with earnestness. I sat back and crossed my arms over my chest.

"What did you find inside?"

"Do you forgive me?"

"No. I don't know. Maybe . . . I don't know."

"Darling—"

"What did you find inside?"

He heaved a heavy sigh. "We have a problem."

"What kind of problem?"

"I found—"

"Did you find the money?"

"Yes. And that's the problem. It's—"

"What's the problem?"

"If you would stop interrupting me, I would tell you what the problem is."

I snapped my mouth shut and glared at him, waiting for an explanation.

"Thank you, my dear beautiful, brilliant wife. Now, the problem *is* the money. I found it, it's inside, but it's more than what I'd estimated. I don't think we'll have to go to any of the other sentinel houses, at least not tonight." Greg pushed himself up into a sitting position; I didn't move from his lap.

"That doesn't sound like a problem."

"We won't have to go to any of the other sentinel houses because instead of one or two million dollars, I found," he pulled the satellite phone from his pocket and showed me the screen, "two pallets of money."

"Two pallets of . . ." I scanned the image and, indeed, he'd found two pallets of money. Two, huge, pallets of money. They'd been placed in the garage side by side, apparently by a forklift.

"Oh my goodness," I exhaled, stunned.

"Hundred-dollar bills. If my math is correct, estimating based on volume, that's one hundred million dollars, give or take a million."

I split my attention between the image on the phone and my husband's calm features. "Greg, what are we going to do?"

"Well, I've always wanted a pony," he said tiredly before letting his head fall into his hand and laughing quietly.

It wasn't a nice laugh. It was a bitter, angry laugh and I could see he was terribly upset. I reached for his face and kissed him on the lips.

"I'm sorry, darling. I'm wiped. And finding two tons of illegal oil money in a house that's supposed to be used to keep these corrupt, cockered measle-warts from stealing oil is just a steaming pile of horse manure on a hot fudge sundae of shitty absurdity. It's so offensive, it's hilarious."

I gave him a commiserating smile and another quick kiss. I was also exhausted, but we were working against the clock. We needed to reach the airfield in less than twenty-four hours. We didn't have time for Shakespearean insults or wallowing in the dejected ridiculousness of the situation.

I kept my voice gentle and patient. "Greg, help me think through this. Why would they leave it unguarded?"

"I don't know." He shook his head, staring blankly forward. "Unless it's a drop site. Unless someone is on their way to collect it right now, I don't know."

"Well then, what do we do? Do we take some of it?"

"No. I was expecting a large briefcase or a box. If this group has enough money at their disposal to leave two tons of it sitting in a garage, in an unguarded house, where anyone could come upon it, then they'd definitely never ransom the hostages for a mere million or two. We have to take all of it or none of it."

"So . . . U-Haul?" I asked, half-joking, removing myself from his lap. Whatever vehicle we used, it would have to be big.

He shook his head. "We can't risk renting a vehicle. And besides, we don't have time. We need something close by, something large, something no one would suspect or question."

I stared at him as he peered unseeingly at a spot over my shoulder. I hated to think we'd come this far, come this close, and would fail because of two metric tons of cash. I'd spent twelve hours in a crate just to . . . to . . . *wait a minute.*

I gripped his hand and shook him. He stared at me blankly while my mouth curved into a triumphant smile. "Greg, I think I have a way for us to move the money."

CHAPTER 15

Wife: What is the password for the Amazon account?
Husband: I can't send it to you via text, it's not secure
Wife: Send me the password or I will cut you
Husband: I don't negotiate with terrorists
Wife: Send me the password and I will send you naked pictures
Husband: Here is the password...

-Penny and Mr. Penny
Text Messages
Florida, USA
Married 14 years

~Present Day~
Fiona

DR. EVANS WAS scowling at my husband.

"You want to do *what* with my mobile clinic vehicle?"

"Move one hundred million dollars of corrupt oil money."

Her eyes bounced between Greg and me, her eyebrows suspended on her forehead. After a protracted moment, she shook her head. But before she could speak, Greg cut her off.

"Think of it this way: you use the mobile clinic to save lives, yes?"

She didn't respond, just stared at him like he was a fool.

"I'll take your absence of outward affirmation as a yes," he pressed on, slurring his words a little. The kidnapping and subsequent lack of rest was catching up with him. "That's what we want to do. We want to use your mobile clinic to save the lives of six people."

"By moving one hundred million dollars belonging to a murderous and corrupt faction of the Nigerian government?"

"That's right," he agreed quickly, then amended absentmindedly, "except it doesn't really belong to them, does it? It belongs to the people of Nigeria."

For the first time since we'd woken her up, her expression softened. Dr. Evans's gaze traveled over Greg once more, like she was seeing him anew.

I didn't blame her for her reluctance. After Alex responded with the address for Doctors Without Borders in Enugu, we hadn't merely woken her at two in the morning. We'd broken into the hospital, found her sleeping quarters, placed a hand over her mouth to keep her from screaming, restrained her limbs, and—hovering over her bed— announced our presence. Our methods were sloppy, but well-intentioned.

Now we were sitting in the small staff kitchen and she was hovering over us.

In truth, we were tremendously tired.

I hadn't been this tired since Grace was three months old and Jack was two and a half; I was at home with the kids by myself, and I'd just been diagnosed with mastitis (breast infection). CIA SERE training (Survival, Evasion, Resistance and Escape) had actually been quite helpful preparing me for the exhaustion of motherhood.

"What are you going to do with the money?"

Greg looked to me and I braced myself for her reaction. "We can't tell you."

Her face hardened again and she straightened her back. "You can't be serious."

"We're not giving it back to them, I promise," Greg interjected, wiping his hand over his face. "We need to use it as leverage for the hostages still in their possession, but we're not giving it back."

As far as I knew, Greg's statement was patently false. My understanding of the situation was the opposite. We were, in fact, going to leverage it for the hostages and return the funds once they were released. However, Greg's promise to Dr. Evans sounded so convincing it caused the hairs on the back of my neck to prickle with warning.

"Then what will you do with it?"

"Other than arrange it into a throne of money for photo ops, we're going to booby-trap it. Then, once the hostages are released, we're going to alert the US embassy and let them deal with the ninety-nine million dollars."

"I thought you said it was one hundred million?"

"It is. But it'll be one hundred minus one million when the US is notified, as Doctors Without Borders will be receiving a substantial donation from the corrupt tossers of the Nigerian government."

Dr. Evans lifted her chin with a suspicious and prideful tilt. "Are you trying to bribe me?"

"Yes. Is it working? I would offer sexual favors, but my wife is sitting right here and I'm too bloody tired for a lap dance. I might be able to manage the Roger Rabbit if you give me a Gatorade."

Her eyes narrowed, flickering to me for a brief moment as though to gauge my reaction.

I shrugged. "I'd take the money, his sexual favors are *meh.*"

Greg's mouth fell open in shock and, thank God, Dr. Evans laughed.

"That's it, Fe. No lap dances for a month." He crossed his arms over his chest, trying to look offended. But then he moved them to the table and allowed his head to fall forward into his folded arms, muttering, "So tired. So very, very tired."

The good doctor gave him a sympathetic smile, obviously her ingrained healing instincts were taking over, and she sighed. "Yes. All right. Take the mobile unit."

His head shot up, but before he could speak she lifted a finger. "But, you have to get some sleep first."

"We don't have time."

"Make time. You will sleep for no less than three hours. Then you will both eat, shower, and dress in clean scrubs. Then and only then will you take my mobile clinic." Under her breath she added, "I don't need you falling asleep and crashing it into a tree on the way to get my million dollars."

***

LESS THAN TWENTY minutes later, Greg and I were situated in a private hospital room. Once Dr. Evans had departed, Greg rolled the bed against a wall and lifted the side rail.

"Wife. Let us sleep," he said, collapsing onto the mattress and opening his arms to me.

I didn't argue. I flopped down next to him and scootched backward, my back to his front. He pulled me into a strong embrace, kissing my temple, and insinuating his leg between mine. Though I was tremendously tired, it took me a while of staring and blinking before my mind quieted enough to truly consider surrendering to unconsciousness.

Seconds became minutes and Greg's arms grew loose and heavy, and his breathing evened. I smiled at the plain white wall in front of me, because—whether at home in Chicago or on the run in Nigeria— listening to the soft sounds of my husband's slumber and the feel of his weight, warmth, and strength at my back was a luxury. I relaxed as well, and was nearly asleep, when Greg inhaled sharply and his body spasmed.

Nightmares.

Greg was susceptible to them. Especially during times of high stress.

"Are you okay?" I glanced over my shoulder.

He looked at me, his eyes glassy and disoriented. Obviously, he was still caught in a web of sleep inertia.

I turned completely so we were face to face and placed my hand on his cheek. "Hey. Are you okay?"

"Yes." Greg swallowed, his handsome features marred by a severe frown.

I was about to question him further, but he cut me off by tugging me forward. Greg brought me flush against him, binding me in a constricting hug.

"We have to get out of here," he whispered. His warm breath on my neck paired with his despairing tone made me tense.

"I know. We will. We'll sleep, move the money, drive to the airfield, and leave at midnight."

He nodded, squeezing me again. After several moments I recognized that he had no plans to let me go. I tucked my arms between us and snuggled into the warmth of his body. Eventually, curled within his protective embrace, I dozed off.

I slept so hard I didn't have any dreams—at least none that I could remember.

Then I heard Greg say, "Don't be mad."

I frowned, as I was mostly asleep. I felt his fingers on my hair at my temples. Blinking, I opened my drowsy eyes, and found him bending over me. Now I was disoriented because I thought he was next to me on the bed. Based on the sunlight filtering through the window, I realized I'd been asleep for several hours, though it felt like two minutes.

He'd shaved. He looked thinner, tired. He also looked guilty.

I reached for him.

Let me amend that. I tried to reach for him, but couldn't. And the reason I couldn't—I quickly discovered—was because my wrists had been tied to the metal bars of the bed. I attempted to bend my knees and found my ankles had also been bound.

I was now fully awake and glaring at my husband.

And the goddamn fire ants were back in my brain, pouring scalding formic acid all over the place.

"Christ, you're scary sometimes." He sat back suddenly, like he was afraid I might bite. This was intelligent of him because the thought had crossed my mind.

"What did you do?" My tone was misleadingly calm.

"You can't come." He frowned at his hands and cleared his throat. "You're, uh, too much of a distraction."

"You have to be kidding me."

"For once, I am not kidding. I could barely sleep. I kept waking up to nightmares of you being captured." His voice was gentle and sincere, and he was gazing at me with a haunted expression. "They are not kind to women who are captured."

I believed him about the dreams.

But I was still pissed off he thought he could leave me behind. I was a CIA field agent. What the hell?

"How is it my fault that I'm a distraction for you? Maybe you need to sort through your issues instead of tying me to a bed."

"Darling, you'll always be a distraction. No amount of singing Kumbaya or bullshit getting in touch with my inner goddess is going to change that." Now his tone was flat, considerably less gentle, and his dark eyes flashed with intensity.

"Unbelievable," I said to the ceiling, tempering my urge to scream at him by reminding myself where we were, and that I couldn't afford to reprimand him loudly.

He stood and turned, grabbing the weapons bag from the floor. "I've left you the SIG X-Five and," he slapped a stack of hundred-dollar bills on a table by the door, "here is some cash if you need it."

"Where did you get that?"

"I stole it from the house last night. I figured it might come in handy in case of an emergency, and they weren't going to miss a measly ten thousand dollars. Listen, I'll move the rest of the money, and if I'm not back by tomorrow morning, go to the US consulate in Lagos. Hitch a ride with Dr. Evans. Just, wait until it's safe."

I tested the binding at my wrists. He'd used gauze and hadn't made them tight. I would be able to escape the restraints in thirty minutes, thirty-five tops.

"I know what you're thinking." He gave me a knowing look. "Don't do it. Don't follow me."

"This is you discounting me. Again. This is you being a bully and not respecting my contribution. Again."

"No. This is me overwhelmed with crippling panic at the idea of something happening to my wife."

"Thank you for proving my point. You think you have the right to make unilateral decisions for both of us, for our family, and then you wonder why I go around your irrational mandates. If you don't want me to freeze you out, then you have to recognize that my opinion matters!"

"Of course your opinion matters." He lifted his hands and let them fall to his thighs, like he was exasperated at having to point out the obvious. The proceeding pause and reflection was almost cartoonish before he added, "Just not about this."

I growled, losing my cool, because he was still trying to put me off with humor. "I swear to God, Greg Archer, if you leave without me I will . . ." I stopped, wondering what I should threaten, what I was willing to deliver—because I refused to bluff.

He stilled and stared at me, waiting for me to finish, as though sensing the seriousness of the moment.

"What will you do?" he asked, not taunting but rather bracing for my ultimatum. "Because I would rather you hate me than watch you suffer or die."

"I won't hate you. I will never hate you." I never would. "But it would hurt me, deeply. And I don't know how long it would take for me to forgive you."

Greg hesitated and I could see him warring with himself, which was progress. But I didn't want him to make the right decision because he dreaded my threat. I wanted him to make the right decision because he respected me, saw me as his partner, and recognized the value of my contribution.

I tried a different approach.

"Remember when you found out I was a CIA field agent?"

His eyes sliced to mine and he grimaced. He didn't answer at first, but the flare of intensity behind his gaze told me everything I needed to know.

At length he said, "I promised I would never bring it up. And I haven't."

Despite his terse, caustic reply, I pushed. "Remember how angry you were?"

Everything about him grew rigid.

He didn't respond, so I reminded him. "You felt betrayed. You trusted me and I had let you down. But when all was said and done, you understood. You didn't demand that I quit. Rather, you made me promise I would never take chances with my life, knowingly put myself in a position beyond my abilities. You asked me to consider you, and your feelings in all of my decisions. To carry you with me."

"I remember." He sounded significantly less cantankerous.

"I did as you asked. And when situations escalated, approached my limits, I quit. I didn't quit for me, for my safety. I quit for both of us. Because when we married, I gave you that power over me, I gave you the right to have an opinion about my life and my decisions. I'm sorry I've been freezing you out. I'm sorry."

He was teetering. I could tell because his dark eyes had kindled with anger, his mouth was clamped shut, and he was staring at the wall behind me. Indecision was a heavy cloak around his shoulders.

"I told you then and I'm telling you now: your opinion matters," I continued softly, meaning the words. "But we have to stop this cycle of shutting each other out. I can't mandate that you untie me any more than you can mandate that Grace play soccer."

"She should play soccer."

"Then convince her with logic, with love, with sincerity. Not with threats and mandates. And not by punishing Jack in the process."

Swallowing thickly, his gaze pierced mine. We'd reached a staring stalemate. It was plain to see he was at war with himself. His desire to keep me safe in direct contradiction with what he knew to be right. I could read his thoughts clearly, as though he were speaking them aloud.

And when he finally did speak, his voice was thick with emotion. "Please don't ask me do this. Please don't ask me to put you in harm's way. I'd rather break my own arm."

My heart constricted, because I could see he was truly torn, tortured by the possibility. "You have to trust me."

"I trust you, I do." He crossed back to me, holding my eyes; his were beseeching. "But you are the mother of my children. You are my wife. You are my better half—you are my better whole."

"I know what I'm doing. I'm good at this."

"You're good at everything, darling. You're extraordinary. I stood by for two years while you risked your extraordinary life. Every time you came home from an assignment I wanted to beg you to quit. I didn't bind you in bubble wrap and I didn't lock you in an ivory tower, but I wanted to."

This was all news to me. I stared at him with incredulous astonishment before I finally sputtered, "Why didn't you say anything? Why didn't you tell me? Why didn't you ask me to quit?"

"Because I knew you loved your work and I didn't want to take that from you. However," he let the bag he was holding fall back to the floor and he knelt beside the bed, "I can't go back there, to that as my reality. Just the thought of you . . ." He shook his head, his resolve firming. "I need you too much."

And I saw that I'd lost. He was going to leave me.

He cleared his throat, his eyes moving over my face with meticulous care, as though memorizing it. "Our children are extraordinary, and that's because of you. One of us has to make it back home—for Grace and Jack—one of us has to leave here—"

"Greg—"

"And I don't say that as a manipulation. It's the truth. You are a phenomenal mother. You've been playing the role of parent for both of us—"

Ice entered my veins and my brain was screaming *Don't do this! Please, please, please!*

"Greg, don't do this."

"I can't untie you. You might be upset and angry, and, God willing, if we both make it back to Chicago, I'll understand." He wove his fingers in my hair at my temples and kissed my forehead. "But at least you'll be safe."

CHAPTER 16

Dear R,

Tell me you love me. I don't think I could ever hear that enough. I know you do, but I've never minded hearing it.

-Ted
Letter
Serving in Iraq
Married 7 years

~10 years ago~
Greg

I USUALLY LIKED Fiona's friends. Although, it took me a while to warm up to the concept of her having friends. After four years of marriage, but without her explicitly saying so, I realized community was as essential to Fiona as reading and running were to me.

Therefore, wherever my job took us, Fiona surrounded herself with community. And I encouraged it.

When I was stationed in Alaska, she acquainted herself with the local muskox producer's co-op, infiltrated their knitting circle, and learned the exotic ways of qiviut-fiber harvesting. When I accepted an assignment in Iceland, she assimilated easily into the culture, deciphering the secrets of Fair Isle knitting, and taking me to all the top-secret geothermal sites and hot springs known only to natives.

Her ability to observe and discover the most tightly held secrets of the locals, assimilate herself as a part of any culture, and gain the trust and friendship of anyone she chose should have been a red flag. Instead, I admired her for it.

Maybe I had been blinded by my relief. We were finally together (most of the time). After a three-year long-distance relationship during our engagement, and an additional two years of separation after our hasty city hall marriage, the last twenty-four months had been the happiest of my life.

So perhaps I ought to forgive myself for not realizing immediately that my wife was a spy.

I knew she worked for the State Department. I *thought* she was a consulting engineer. It had been a natural progression of events after her prolonged internship with the Department of Defense throughout her undergrad and postgrad studies in Iowa. Her work seemed to consist of short, random business trips and pouring over engineering schematics.

Seemed legit.

The only friend of hers I didn't like was one of her business associates at the "State Department," Spenser Banks. He was, by all accounts, an insufferable twat.

Admittedly, the fervor and depth of my dislike for Spenser Banks was built upon his being in lust with my wife. He made no secret about the fact that he wanted to fuck her. And that pissed me off.

Obviously I'm not opposed to other men admiring Fiona. I've never been the jealous sort, and I trusted Fe. But having to witness his nauseating infatuation on more than one occasion, being subjected to his trailing, lingering looks of tortured longing made me want to remove his head from his neck, Marine Corps-style.

The insufferable twat found every reason imaginable to visit wherever we were in the world. He was always popping up and swinging by during convenient business trips to backwoods Alaska or nowhere Iceland.

But even if he'd been ambivalent to Fiona, I still would've detested the man. He'd drunk the "my government can do no wrong" Kool-Aid, as it were. Any and all discussions with him were excruciating and intolerable.

I might say, "Lovely weather we're having."

And he'd respond with, "You would never have this nice weather without The United States of America."

No arguing with that logic . . .

Thankfully, I hadn't been subjected to Spenser Banks in over three months.

On the morning of the reveal, I'd made coffee and sat down to thumb through the newspaper. Ironically, an article about the Scooter Libby/Valerie Plame debacle—wherein Valerie Plame, aka Valerie Wilson, was outed as a CIA operative by the State Department—covered that morning's front page of *The New York Times*.

I skimmed the article, frowning, irritated by what I found. Disgusted, I turned to the arts and culture section. Nothing like a little art and culture to remedy reality.

Fe drifted into the kitchen a short time later, having returned from her quick forty-eight-hour business trip late the night before. I didn't look up, but I did smile. I never heard her footsteps, she moved without sound. But I knew she'd entered the room because, as inexplicable as it might be, I felt her.

"Good morning, darling."

"Morning, handsome." Her voice was rough, like she'd been shouting too much or had a cold.

I glanced over my shoulder, finding her in a white tank top and panties, and nothing else. I sighed happily, already making plans to devour her before breakfast, but then my eyes caught on a large purple mark on one side of her lower back, only visible because she was reaching for a coffee cup.

"What's that?" I gestured to her back.

She glanced at me, her short hair in sexy disarray, pillow creases still on her cheek, and then twisted to search her skin.

She found the mark and stiffened. Straightened. Stilled. Stared forward, now apparently completely awake.

"Fe?" I prompted when she remained silent.

Her eyes cut to mine and I saw that her teeth were clenched. She swallowed thickly.

I gave her a slight smile even as the hairs on the back of my neck rose with unease. "Did you get a tattoo?"

I knew it wasn't a tattoo. It was a bruise. My mind flicked through all possibilities as to the cause. Wherever we went, and whenever feasible, she trained in a mixed martial arts studio. She'd been a black belt in Brazilian Jiu-Jutsu and Kendo since finishing college. I decided the most likely reason for her bruise was an accident during class.

But I couldn't figure out why she was so tense about it.

I tried to ease her discomfort. "Did you get hurt during a sparring session?"

She shook her head, her eyes still on me. "Not really."

"Not really?"

"Not precisely."

I lifted an eyebrow at her odd answer. "Then how, precisely, did you get that bruise?"

She swallowed again and I recognized she was engaged in a weighty internal debate.

I was just about to assure her that, no matter what, I wouldn't be angry or upset, when she blurted, "I got it while extracting a high-level target in Mosul yesterday."

Frowning at her, the sunny kitchen fell into a confused, strained silence as I tried to untangle her words.

When I wasn't able to make any sense of her statement, I asked, "Pardon me?"

"Greg, I have something to tell you." Fe placed the cup she'd just retrieved on the counter and rushed over to me, taking the seat next to mine. "I'm CIA. I'm a CIA operative. I'm part of an elite extraction team. And I'm not supposed to tell you this, but I promised myself I would never overtly lie. I promised myself that, if you ever asked—about the trips or anything else—I would tell you the truth. So," she swallowed again, leaning back in her chair as though exhausted, "I'm telling you now. I'm telling you the truth."

I continued to stare at her silently. Seconds became minutes while disbelief and acceptance warred within my psyche.

In the end, it was the steady determination and sorrow so evident in her expression that convinced me.

"You are CIA," I repeated, as much to confirm as to try the words on for size. "You're a spy."

"That's right. I'm an operative, a field agent."

"And you're also part of an elite team?"

"Yes. An extraction team. We're sent into sensitive areas and—"

"Like war-torn Iraq?"

She sighed, nodded, and I abruptly realized her eyes were rimmed red. She was close to tears.

I experienced a jumble of odd thoughts just then.

Pride.

Anger.

Fear.

Concern.

More pride.

Fear again.

Panic.

I stood from the table, the feet of my chair scraping against the wooden floor, and paced to the coffee maker. I was intimately acquainted with the violence of war. I'd tried to cloak the darkest parts of my past because I didn't want her to know the reality and brutality. Visions of her—mangled, burned, shot—played through my forebrain, a ghastly slideshow of horror.

Dangerous. What she's doing is dangerous. I can't lose her . . .

"Say something," she spoke to my back. I didn't miss the desperate edge to her voice.

"I suppose I should apologize," I said, the words sounding far away, as though someone else were speaking.

"For what?"

"Obviously, if I'd expressed more interest in your career prior to now, asked more pointed questions, then you might have told me the truth years ago. For that, I apologize."

She released a pained sigh. "Greg, no. No, this is not your fault. This is-"

"I told you, before we were married, why I only served three years in the Marines." Again, I heard my words as though from a distance.

"Yes. Because you were injured. Because of. . ." she hesitated and her voice was low, near a whisper when she continued. "Because of the burns."

The burns. On my arm, chest, and neck. The infections, the skin grafts, the scars, the loss of muscle function. The area still hurt from time to time, mostly when I awoke from dreams that were equal part memory and nightmare.

With enough practice, even near constant pain can be ignored.

"I told you my best friend died, during a forgotten war in Africa. We joined the Marines together, as a way to pay for college, and as a way to make a difference in the world."

"Yes." She placed her hand on my back.

"But what I haven't yet told you is that the day I was burned was the same day he died."

Her arms quickly came around my waist, she pressed her front to my back.

"I've lost everyone," I murmured, mostly to myself.

"Greg, I'm not going to die."

You don't know that. You can't know for sure.

Without facing her, I asked, "Why didn't you tell me?"

"Technically, I shouldn't have told you at all. Since 9/11, all operatives have been disallowed from sharing their status, even with spouses."

I had the sudden sensation of a rod being shoved down my spine.

Turning, I forced her to release me as I examined her, seeing my wife through a new lens.

A liar.

And a hero.

"How long . . . ?" I couldn't finish the question, because her stricken expression told me everything, and I knew the answer before she admitted the truth.

"Since my sophomore year of college."

"Since your sophomore year?" All the air left my lungs in a whoosh. "How is that possible?"

"They sought me out. They needed someone with a very specific set of skills, my past as a gymnast, and the research I was doing with the Department of Defense meant that I was an ideal candidate. But I couldn't tell you then, because we weren't married."

To her credit, what she didn't say out loud was, *And we weren't married because you wanted to wait.*

Now her constant propositions to elope while we were engaged made complete sense.

She held her palms face up between us, beseeching. "Right after we were married, I applied for clearance to tell you. And it was denied. 9/11 changed everything. It meant I couldn't tell you, but it also meant I was needed more than before. My country needed me, and I've been able to help in a way few people have. I didn't want to resign; I wanted to help. But," she bit her bottom lip and tears shimmered in her eyes, "I hated not telling you."

I felt how difficult this had been for her, how she must've been tortured by shame and guilt. How she hated herself for lying by omission.

"I'm so sorry." The tears spilled over and her throat worked, like she was trying to swallow. "I don't know how to make this right. Tell me what to do."

I wanted to reach out and soothe her, but before I could I needed to know, "Is there anything else? Have you been lying to me about anything else?"

She shook her head. "No. Everything, all my secrets relate to my operative status."

"You mean your *spy* status."

Her eyes dropped to the floor and remorse hit me like a fist to the stomach.

I can't lose her.

Frustrated—with her and with myself—I closed the two steps separating us and gathered her in my arms, saying, "Goddammit."

Her arms wrapped around me tentatively, as though she were afraid my embrace was a trick. I hated her reluctance, I hated that—because of her forced and gallant duplicity—trust had been broken between us.

I was angry.

I was afraid.

I would need time to move past this.

But mostly I felt desperate to ensure she was safe and nothing substantive altered in our commitment to each other. I didn't want her noble intentions to fracture what we'd built. Nothing was more important to me than her safety and my love for her. I wouldn't allow anything, not even our country, to ruin our future together.

"I haven't yet, because I need time, but eventually—probably sometime today—I'm going to forgive you, Fe."

The tension left her muscles and she began crying in earnest, holding on to me as though she'd almost lost me.

I wasn't finished.

"I want to know everything. However, I don't want you to tell me everything. Tell me only what is necessary, tell me nothing that will jeopardize you or your career."

"Oh Greg," she sobbed, holding me tighter.

"Also," I cut her off, needing to finish my thought, "I need you to promise me that you'll never take crazy risks. You'll never try to do more than you're capable of. I need you to promise me that you'll take us into consideration. Your safety has to be a priority. You don't need to discuss your assignments with me, as I know you can't. So I will have to trust you in this."

"Okay, okay," she agreed too quickly; later I would have to ensure she understood. I needed her to consider us before taking any unnecessary (or necessary) risks.

"And, lastly. Once I forgive you, once we've worked through all the issues and ramifications of your decision, I promise you, I will never bring this up again. I promise I will not tuck this away and wave it around whenever we argue, or use it as some secret weapon against you."

She titled her head back, a wrinkle forming between her eyebrows, a silent question.

I gathered her precious face between my palms and placed a soft, reverent kiss on her mouth before explaining, "I watched my parents gather dossiers of each other's mistakes for their arsenal, nuclear proliferation of emotional weaponry. You and I . . . we must always forgive *and* forget. But most importantly, we must never take each other's forgiveness for granted."

CHAPTER 17

Dear Future Spouse,

I miss you sometimes. It may be weird, since we haven't met yet, but it's true. I miss you. I miss holding your hand, I miss kissing you, those little, cute, gentle kisses on the tip of the nose. Or the temple. I miss looking into your eyes and feeling like I belong. I miss cuddling under a blanket to watch a movie. I miss just doing my own stuff, knowing that you're close by and I can come hug you anytime I want. I know I'm lucky to have a really great family, but mom hugs are not the same...

-Ana
Letter
Poland

~Present Day~
Fiona

I FREED MYSELF in less than fifteen minutes.

Determined to catch up with him, I quickly donned my holster, dressed in the scrubs over my bodysuit, and went in search of the truck. But it didn't matter. I couldn't find Greg or the mobile clinic unit. The truck was also gone.

Thirty minutes later, and feeling desperate, I sought out Dr. Evans in the hospital. I found her in the room off the loading dock.

"Hey." I gave her a tight-lipped smile. "Do you have a moment?"

"You haven't left yet?" Her eyes were wide as they moved over me.

"No. Greg left without me."

"Why would he do that? Aren't you like an ex-CIA super spy?"

"Something like that. Listen, I was hoping I could borrow the Ducati I saw parked out back last night."

Her eyebrows bounced on her forehead and I could see I'd confused her. "I-well, I mean-I guess so. Yes. Sure. Use the bike. But why did he leave without you? And why didn't he take the mobile clinic?"

Her last question blindsided me. "He didn't take the mobile clinic?"

"No. He moved it to the hangar at the back and covered it with vinyl tarp."

My stare moved beyond her as I considered this new information. "Why wouldn't he take the mobile clinic . . . ?"

"I don't know. I gave him the keys, so I thought he'd taken it. But I saw it a few minutes ago. Like I said, it's covered with the vinyl tarp. The keys were in the ignition."

"So he moved it, covered it, and left it?"

"That's right."

"He must've taken the truck."

"It appears so."

Greg had to have figured out a different way to move the money. That was the only possible explanation. I was relieved—because using the mobile clinic came with many risks—but I was also irritated, because moving two pallets of money was no simple task and he'd opted to do it on his own.

Idiot.

"Like I said, take the bike. The helmet is on the handle. It's good for getting around town, but I wouldn't take it too far out into the country side."

I nodded distractedly, agreeing with her. Taking the bike two hours north to trail Greg was one thing, but I wouldn't be able to use it to reach the airfield.

The day's end had one of three possible outcomes:

Either I would find him at the sentinel house and help him move the money.

Or I'd have to return here and wait him out; then we'd leave for the airfield together.

Or he wouldn't return. I'd be forced to go to the US consulate and risk being arrested for treason.

Sigh.

Life would be a whole lot easier if husbands would just listen to their wives.

***

I HADN'T BEEN on a motorcycle in over ten years; but as I suspected, it was just like riding a bike (no pun intended).

With a range of less than one hundred and forty miles, I wouldn't be able to make a return trip unless I brought additional gas. I jimmy-rigged a saddle with bladder bags to carry the extra fuel—double what I needed, just in case—borrowing the necessary gallons by siphoning it from the mobile clinic. I stunk of gasoline and motorcycle grease, and my headache was back as a result.

I passed a shawarma delicatessen on my way out of town. Aroma of mixed grilled meats and spices made my mouth water, and my stomach growled again, reminding me that I hadn't eaten since the First Strike rations from the night before.

As soon as I made it back to Chicago, I was going to eat a giant plate of shrimp and shawarma.

And then I was going to tie up my husband, because both of us were going to make it back alive; I was determined that this would be the case. Once we were safe at home, I would insist he do all the laundry for six months. And organize Grace's collection of Barbie doll shoes.

Perhaps then he'd be more cognizant of my contributions and time.

I headed south, knowing the greatest obstacle would be finding the turnoff Greg had taken the night before. My suspicions were confirmed when I realized I'd driven a half-hour longer than we had on the previous evening. Every sign I passed looked unfamiliar. Cursing under my breath, I turned around, driving under the speed limit, and kept my eyes peeled for the turn off.

After another forty-five minutes I knew I wasn't going to be able to find the road Greg had taken. Resigned, I drove another ten minutes south, pulled off, and backed the Ducati between thick hedgerows. If I couldn't find him, I'd just have to wait until he passed by.

I waited. And waited.

And waited.

And it was hot.

My Kevlar-LYCRA bodysuit made sense for flexibility and utility, but it wasn't as breathable as, let's say, linen.

Each minute spent in solo-limbo felt like an eternity. One hour passed. Then another. I rationalized that it would take him several hours to load that much money, by himself, into whichever vehicle he was using. I refilled the gas tank, noting that I still had five gallons of fuel left.

But when the fourth hour ticked by with no sign of him, my stomach sank to my feet.

I wasn't going to find him.

Gone, out of my reach, and I had no means to communicate—not with him, not with Alex, not with Quinn or Marie or Dan.

I was on my own.

And the real kicker was, I hated being on my own.

I'd always hated being on my own and I didn't want to be on my own anymore.

I wanted to share my damn burdens!

I was married, wasn't I?

We'd pledged our troth (or something like it), hadn't we?

So why the hell am I doing everything on my own?

Grinding my teeth and scowling at my watch, I made note of the time. It would take me approximately two hours to make it back to the hospital. If Greg wasn't there by sundown, then we were going to miss the flight home and I would have to figure out a way to make it to the US consulate in Lagos, several hours west, by car.

But I refused to think about that or even contemplate the possibility of traveling across Nigeria without Greg.

He would return by nightfall.

We would leave Nigeria together.

And when we returned to Chicago, he was never leaving me again.

Cursing under my breath, I started the engine and rolled forward so I could see around the thicket. My mouth fell open.

What looked like our truck—the vehicle Alex had arranged and Greg had absconded with this morning—was approaching from the north. I squinted at the cab, trying to determine who was behind the wheel as it passed.

A spike of alarm had me straightening my spine when I recognized Greg was driving the truck, but he wasn't alone. A second man—white male, stocky build, head turned away—was in the cab with him. Greg was driving too fast for me to make out the passenger's features.

The man with Greg could be an ally, or an enemy. I had no way of knowing, at least not yet.

Quickly considering my options, I counted to ten before pushing onto the road, following the truck from an innocuous distance. The bed of the vehicle was empty. He wasn't using it to move the money, but I wasn't going to worry about that now. I needed to focus on how to extract Greg from the truck.

Giving Greg a heads-up that I was behind him and ready to help wasn't a priority. Based on his earlier behavior—tricking me the night before, his nightmares, tying me up and leaving me—I knew my presence would only serve to distract him. Therefore, with my heart thumping like mad and my throat tight and scratchy with anxious irritation, I stealthily followed from a distance.

He was taking major roads back to Enugu. Traffic was a problem in the city. Still, I was surprised when he took the bypass route instead of heading directly back to the hospital. Nervously, I checked my gasoline gauge. I only had fifty miles left until I would need to refuel.

Sixty-two minutes later, just after Greg took the turn off for the main highway leading to Lagos, the Ducati ran out of gas. I rushed to refill the tank and quickly did the math in my head. If Greg was heading to Lagos instead of returning to Enugu, then I had another five and a half hours of riding ahead of me.

And I was at least four gallons short on gas.

***

SIX HOURS LATER my body ached.

I felt every one of my thirty-six years—in my joints, in my bones, in my muscles—and my thoughts were narrowed on two goals: rescuing Greg and murdering Greg.

My fuel problem turned out to be easily remedied. Between the westbound and eastbound lanes of traffic on many major highways in Nigeria are dirt paths, which are used mostly by commercial motorcyclists. Also, traffic in the country and road upkeep are a real problem.

Both the dirt motorcycle paths and the shoddy civil infrastructure worked to my advantage.

We encountered a traffic jam in Benin City just as I was starting to sweat my dwindling supply of gasoline. Greg and his companion were stuck on the road. I was not. I considered attempting a rescue, but decided against it. I wasn't rescuing anyone without more fuel.

I used their delayed status to weave through traffic and exit the highway in search of a gas station. Keeping my helmet and gloves on, and thankful for the baggy scrubs covering my black bodysuit and holster, I used one of the stolen hundred-dollar bills Greg had left for me at the hospital to pay for the gas.

I told the attendant to keep the change after showing him my gun. Doubled the incentive to *not* fuck with me.

Once I topped up the tank and bladder bags, I sped back to the highway, spotting Greg's truck just two miles farther along, amidst traffic just beginning to clear. My anxiety eased considerably now I'd secured enough fuel should Greg and his companion be leading me to Lagos.

Now, hours later, that's where we were headed. And once we exited on to the Lekki-Epe Expressway for Victoria Island, a nagging feeling prickled my hot skin and made the hairs on the back of my neck rise in warning.

I'd studied the cities of Enugu and Lagos in great detail while en-route to Nigeria, so I knew the US consulate was at the western end of Victoria Island.

But what I couldn't fathom was why Greg would be headed there, especially if his companion was a hostile.

This realization—that his car mate was on our side, someone Greg trusted—made me feel both better and worse. Obviously better because he was safe. But worse because he'd left me in Enugu. He'd accepted help from someone else. He'd cut me out, made plans without me. The sun was going down. He would never have made it back to Enugu in time for us to leave.

Now was not the time for me to feel hurt by all this, but I was. As inconvenient, and perhaps irrational, as the feelings were, hurt and anger settled like a granite boulder in my chest, making it difficult to breathe and focus.

However, much like baseball, there is no crying in espionage. So I remained focused.

The Lekki-Epe Expressway became Ozumba Mbadiwe Avenue, and swanky buildings rose before me, the sign for the Radisson Blu Anchorage Hotel visible in the distance. The waterfront was an oasis of clean white buildings and well-maintained roads on a shimmering blue lagoon, and the sight made my stomach turn sour.

I tailed Greg as he exited Ozumba Mbadiwe Avenue for a side street, still keeping my distance, but perhaps not as diligently as before. Both the truck and the old Ducati stuck out like sore thumbs, hugely conspicuous against the surrounding backdrop of privilege and wealth.

Greg pulled onto the road adjacent to the consulate, and I was relieved. Now that we were both here, we might as well walk into the building together. I didn't even care at this point if I were arrested. So be it.

I might even yell upon entering, *Arrest me for treason! And please point me toward a bath and a blessedly air-conditioned jail cell.*

I was so tired. He was safe. I was in one piece. The adrenaline I'd been running on for the last twenty-four hours—heck, the last four days—was almost depleted.

Therefore, imagine my confused astonishment when, instead of parking near the consulate, he parked three blocks away. I switched off the ignition and eyeballed my husband as he exited the truck and stood stretching in front of it. He then glanced back and forth down the road. He sauntered in the opposite direction of the consulate, crossing to the wrong side of the road, then leaned against a lamppost.

I frowned, watching him.

It was as though he were in no hurry to leave the streets of Lagos— which was crazy because the longer he dawdled, the more opportunity he gave anyone and everyone who might be staking out the building to pick him up off the streets.

If any of his captors were milling about, hoping he'd show up and be stupid enough to loiter, then they would not be disappointed. He would be easy to abduct . . .

And the longer he loitered, the more I became certain he *wanted* to be abducted.

. . . *that motherfucking sonofabitch.*

My mouth went dry and my heart was lodged back in my throat. Determination to force him on the back of my motorcycle, or die trying, flooded through my veins with a new overwhelming violence. I wished he'd left me the Ketamine dart gun, because I'd give him a thorough poking.

I moved to start the motorcycle with shaking fingers, intent on beating him senseless, when two strong hands grabbed me from behind and yanked me off the bike.

Obviously, I hadn't been paying enough attention to my surroundings as I'd been so entirely focused on my dumbass husband, strolling around in front of the US consulate in Lagos, Nigeria, dressed in a godforsaken alternate reality *St. Louis Cardinals 2004 World Series Champions* T-shirt!

THAT MOTHERFUCKING SONOFABITCH!

Regardless, the man now holding me with a muscled arm around my waist and a large palm over the front of my helmet was about to be the recipient of my frantic rage. Quite easily, I hooked my leg around his and kicked forward, tripping him and bringing us both to the ground. As a consequence, his hold on me faltered and I used the opportunity to whip my head back, bringing the hard surface of the helmet to his nose with a satisfying crunch.

An unhappy and sharp curse met my ears as the man's hands flew to his face. I turned, intent on breaking his nose if it wasn't already broken, or delivering a tight throat punch, but then faltered when I identified my assailant as none other than Dan the Security Man.

"What the hell?" I breathed out, frowning at him and pushing the windshield of my helmet up so I could see him better. Blood was gushing from his nose and his eyes were closed tight.

"I think you boke my nose," he groaned, laughing a little. "Fuck a duck, that hurts!"

My eyes moved over his form as I knelt next to him, checking for additional injuries; two pedestrians walked around us like we weren't even there. "Dan? What were you thinking? And what the hell is going on?"

"I was thinking I needed to stop you from swooping in and trying to save Greg." His voice was tight and nasally as he tested his nose. "I was also thinking I need to get you off the street as soon as possible, but I forgot you're a fucking ninja."

Remembering the original source of my fury, I twisted over my shoulder looking for my husband. I turned just in time to see a black Mercedes SUV pull away from the sidewalk where he'd been standing and speed away.

He was no longer there.

I gasped for air. Tears of frustration gathered in my eyes as I desperately searched the now-empty corner.

But it was no use.

I felt it in my bones.

He'd been taken. Again.

He'd left me behind. *Again.*

CHAPTER 18

Dear Wife,

The thought of losing you is unbearable; please believe in me. Always remember that no matter how dark things may seem, there is always a little sunshine for you in my heart. Love you today, tomorrow, and forever.

-J
Letter
California, USA
Married 29.5 years

~Present Day~
Fiona

"TALK TO ME, Quinn. Tell me what's going on."

If Quinn had been surprised by my sudden presence in the surveillance vehicle, he made no outward sign of it. For my part, I was incapable of being shocked or surprised by anything as my mind was singularly focused on one goal: finding Greg.

When Dan led me to the oil tanker and gestured for me to climb inside the huge cylinder that would typically house and transport gallons of oil, I did so without question.

When my feet landed on carpet and my gaze landed on Quinn's straight back, standing in front of a series of screens mounted to the far wall, surrounded by what appeared to be the latest in espionage gadgetry, I barely blinked.

The floor, ceiling, and walls were carpeted—dark blue and granite grey—the extra padding had likely been added to absorb sound and ensure the interior remained at a constant temperature of sixty degrees Fahrenheit. Server racks stood beneath a long counter sitting at hip level, hence the chilly temperature. Computing servers are at peak functionality when they're kept cool, the temperature of the space alerting me to the reality that this vehicle was capable of substantial computing power, a mobile data processing center.

"How much do you know?" Quinn asked, glancing over his shoulder. He then did a double take, his eyes moving over Dan's face. "What happened to you?"

"Fiona Archer, if that is her real name."

Quinn lifted his chin and nodded once. "He pissed you off?"

"Not precisely," Dan volunteered, walking past us both toward the front of the vehicle. "I made the mistake of grabbing her from behind. She didn't know it was me, so she defended herself."

"I'm sorry, Dan. I never would have—" I shook my head, my fingers coming to my forehead. I had a pounding headache.

"Are you all right?"

I felt the weight of Quinn's gaze, his cool, assessing inspection reminded me of a surveillance drone.

I ignored his question because I wasn't all right. "Where's Marie?"

"She's here."

"Here?" This was unexpected news. "You mean *here* here? In the tanker?"

"Yeah. We borrowed this thing from my colleague who is providing our security. He loaned me the driver and armed escort at the front, good guys, anxious to do right. I didn't want to take a chance and leave Marie back at the hotel."

"She's our ace in the hole, our secret weapon," Dan added, talking around his busted nose.

"Marie is back there, asleep. She was up for over twenty-four hours, working against a deadline for tomorrow's paper." Quinn tossed his thumb over his shoulder, indicating a narrow door which must've led to an additional room of some sort.

"This thing is like an RV, surveillance van, and bunker all rolled into one." Dan straightened from where he'd been bent over, bringing a bag of ice to his nose. "And it's perfect for this country. I've seen more oil tankers on the roads here in the last three days than I've seen over the course of my life in the States."

Unable to stem my insatiable panic any longer, I blurted, "Who took Greg? And why? And where is he? And—"

"Okay, I'll tell you everything." Quinn held his hands up and crossed to me in three quick strides, likely sensing my impending hysteria. His steadying hands wrapped around my upper arms as I swayed, and he guided me to a seat. "Let me get you some water."

"Start talking. Please." My request sounded shaky, but I couldn't help it. "Please. I need to know what's going on."

"Fine." He took the chair next to mine; both were swivel chairs and had been bolted to the floor. "Greg called Alex early this morning while you were still asleep to check on the status of the hostages."

"Alex hasn't been able to locate them. He knows they're in Lagos, someplace, but he can't pinpoint where." Dan settled on the counter behind him.

"Your buddy at the CIA, Banks?"

I stiffened. "Spenser Banks, yes. What about him?"

"He's down here at the US consulate in Lagos. Did you hear about the articles Marie has been writing?"

"Alex filled us in yesterday, or was it the day before . . . ?" The days were blurring together.

"They've been effective, putting pressure on the right people to act. Marie has been interviewing the families of the other hostages as well, putting images of their children next to photographs of desolated villages here, ruined by Big Oil."

"Nautical Oil doesn't like the press," Dan added, chuckling lightly. "Oil is money, and money makes all the difference."

"So Buhari's new government asked the UK and the US to step in and assist with the hostage situation. Nigeria's relationship with Nautical Oil has been strained for years due to the government corruption and ecological damage done by the oil companies. Buhari is trying to change that, clean up their image, clean up Nigeria, forge a new partnership."

"This all happened since we last spoke to Alex?" I asked, incredulous.

"Nautical Oil's shares have dropped every day since Marie ran her first article." Dan removed the ice and touched the bridge of his nose gingerly. "Loud, angry shareholders and bad press is a language they speak."

This was all fascinating, but it still didn't address my main question. "So, where is Greg?"

Quinn studied me for a long moment, then sighed before responding, "Alex put Greg in touch with Banks."

"Spenser and Greg spoke?" If I weren't already pushed beyond my limit, this information would have floored me. Greg did not like Spenser, and the feeling was mutual.

"That's right." Quinn nodded, his gaze once again probing. "Greg explained about the money and the acetone, how we're dealing with one hundred million dollars or more, instead of a few million."

"The money—or rather, the *amount* of money—changed everything," Dan added dryly. "The CIA is now fully invested, instead of just making a show of it in order to patronize Nautical Oil and Buhari."

I guessed the Agency's reasoning. "That kind of money is typically associated with terrorist cells, not small illegal oil refineries."

"Exactly." Dan nodded once, grabbing a water bottle behind him, leaning forward and handing it to me. "The CIA doesn't want to lose track of the money trail."

"Greg and Banks came up with a revised plan, since Greg was already on the ground, had the Intel, and time is of the essence," Quinn explained.

"What is the plan?" I became aware that the tanker was moving, thus we were being transported somewhere. I gripped the counter at my left, bracing my weight against it. "And why did the Agency rope you guys in? Don't they have their own people on the ground?"

Quinn continued, "The CIA isn't happy about our involvement, but it was one of Greg's stipulations for agreeing to his part. As I understand it, the basics haven't changed from the original plan you and Greg devised with Alex: use the threat of the exploding refinery as a distraction, move the mysterious pile of illegally begotten money to a safe location, ransom for the hostages using the stolen money."

Dan cut in, "Except, since neither Alex nor the CIA can find the hostages, and it was decided that determining their location and rescuing them is the highest priority, Greg agreed to be taken."

"That makes no sense!" I surged to my feet, growling.

"No. It does." Dan's tone softened. "He's being tracked, and he's wired. Quinn has the earpiece in right now, and you can listen too if you want. We can hear everything he hears; we know exactly where he is."

"And we're not the only ones. He's being tracked by the CIA, and a unit of Special Forces," Quinn added.

"But that doesn't guarantee his safety. You're using him as a beacon to find the others, but they could- they could—" *they could easily kill him.* I couldn't bring myself to say the words.

Quinn reached forward and took my hand, encouraging me to sit down again. "Fiona, we don't believe they'll harm him. First of all, they know he's been sent in by Buhari, the US, and Nautical Oil to conduct the negotiations."

"Who are they, anyway? Who are we dealing with?" I was grasping at straws, but if I knew the enemy then I would better understand what they were capable of.

"Alex believes this group is spearheaded by Abayomi Contee, the former oil minister of Nigeria, who was deposed when Buhari came into power. Contee had been working in conjunction with Boko Haram and was responsible for . . . well, let's just say many atrocities."

As Dan would say, *Well, fuck a duck.* We were dealing with psychopaths and terrorists. Just great.

Dan's big eyes were rimmed with compassion despite the fact that I almost broke his nose. "Don't forget about the hundred million, Fiona. Once Greg and I secured it, Banks sent Contee's people a message. Contee knows we have her money."

"And Alex believes the money is a payoff for Boko Haram, their portion of the illegal refineries' profit," Quinn added evenly. "Abayomi Contee needs that money, or else Boko Haram will come after her family, her people. Contee won't do anything to Greg or the hostages until she has that money in hand."

"Where is the money?" I narrowed my eyes on Dan. "How did you and Greg move it so quickly?"

"I took a helicopter this morning, then drove from Enugu and met Greg at the guard house."

"You mean the sentinel house? Where we found the money last night?"

"That's right. It was a sonofabitch to find. I had to follow the pipeline." Dan covered his nose with the ice again. "We moved it into one of the dry pipes."

"You put the cash into the dry pipes . . ." And that's why Greg didn't need the mobile clinic. Hiding the money was just as effective as moving it, assuming Greg and Dan were successful at covering their tracks.

"Greg has it rigged to explode if anything should happen to him. He has to speak certain phrases every hour into a transmitter Alex had me bring over this morning."

"They could torture the information out of him," I hypothesized, but even as I said the words I knew them to be false.

"Yeah. That's unlikely." Quinn's words echoed my thoughts. Greg was a former Marine. He'd been trained to withstand torture as only Marines can—with a single-minded, brutal focus.

I watched Quinn press two fingers against his ear, adjusting his earpiece; so I asked expectantly, "Did Greg say something? What are you hearing?"

He shook his head. "Greg hasn't said much yet, just made some joke about the fuel efficiency of their car. They ignored him. They're still en-route to . . . well, wherever they're going."

"Have they hurt him?" I asked haltingly, needing to know but dreading the answer. I wanted to listen in . . . but I didn't. But I did.

"Not from what I've heard so far. But they did blindfold him." Quinn's humorless smile looked more like a grimace.

"Good. That's good." Blindfolding was good; no reason to blindfold someone if you knew they weren't going to live. My attention refocused on Dan. "Why didn't you and Greg take the helicopter back to Lagos? Instead of driving?"

Dan already sounded less pained. "We didn't want to give Contee's people any clues as to where we hid the money. If we flew out of Enugu, then she'd know it was in the vicinity. The way it stands now, she has no idea whether it's in Lagos or in Tom Brady's deflated balls—so to speak."

"So what's the plan now? What happens from here?"

Quinn straightened, pressing the earpiece again with two fingers. "Hopefully, Contee doesn't know we're following her people. We track Greg until their destination is reached, confirm the hostages are on sight, then Special Forces goes in and extracts both Greg and the hostages. After that, Buhari's police arrive, Contee and her people are arrested."

I nodded, absorbing this information, and endeavoring to sort out how I could insinuate myself into the extraction team.

"How can I help?" I glanced between Greg and Dan.

They shared a look, but neither spoke for a long moment.

Eventually, Quinn said, "There's something else you should know. Banks is aware you're in Nigeria, he's known the whole time. He used your presence here to push Greg into using himself as bait."

My jaw opened and closed as I struggled to force my mouth to form words. "He what?"

"Banks threatened to have you arrested for treason if and when you made it back to Chicago, unless Greg cooperated, helped the CIA get their hands on the money and free the hostages." Dan gave me a humorless smile.

"Fiona, I think he would have agreed to free the hostages. But, you should know," Quinn waited until I gave him my full attention before continuing, "Greg negotiated amnesty for you as part of the deal."

***

BOTH QUINN AND Dan hovered over me until I ate a sandwich and drank a liter of water. I listened to the wire feed for about half an hour.

Nothing was happening. Nothing was said. But I could hear Greg breathe every once in a while. Or sigh. Or the rustle of his clothes. Each sound made my heart twist painfully and was followed by completely unhelpful thoughts like, *What if this is the last time I hear him breathe?*

Dan and Quinn held a quiet conference in one corner while I obsessed about the sounds of Greg's oxygen intake.

Eventually, Dan walked over and said, "You stink. Go take a shower, catch a nap. This could take hours."

I appreciated Dan's approach, his blunt speech, his lack of sympathy and coddling. If he'd coddled me or patronized me or promised me everything would work out, I think I might have kidney-punched him.

Therefore, I acquiesced, mostly because nothing was happening. I was making myself crazy, and my body needed rest and a hot shower. He steered me to the back room. It was a small space, no more than seven feet by eight feet. Marie was passed out asleep; she was on the bottom bunk of a stacked cot. I made a beeline to the bathroom facilities, but made Quinn and Dan promise to get me once Greg and his captors arrived at the hostage site.

Numbly, I took a shower and washed both myself and my bodysuit as much as I was able. Then I rifled through Marie's bag for some clean clothes, knowing she wouldn't mind. I settled on a pair of black yoga pants and tank top. She was taller than me, but we were usually the same size. Now the clothes were a little baggy.

I tried lying down on the top cot, resting, handing over my husband's fate to a team of Special Forces who didn't know him. People who didn't know me or our children, and how much we needed Greg. I tried. It didn't work. I couldn't turn my brain off.

"I can hear you thinking," Marie's sleepy voice pulled me out of my chaotic musings. "It's as loud as Sandra's snoring."

I smiled wanly at the dark, carpeted ceiling. "I'm wearing your clothes."

"I'll file that statement under things I don't mind hearing from my girlfriends, but I wouldn't be thrilled about hearing from a boyfriend."

"Wait. I thought you dated a cross-dresser in college and thought it was sexy?"

"I did. But I don't want some man stretching out my favorite pair of yoga pants and sexy underwear. I don't care if he's wearing a thong, it just better not be mine."

I smirked. Even so, the curve of my mouth felt sad. Everything about me felt sad, forlorn, helpless. I hated the helplessness most of all.

"What am I going to do, Marie? How can I just sit here and do nothing?"

I heard her exhale, but she said nothing for a long time. I pressed the base of my palms into my eye sockets and rubbed.

"Sometimes," she started, stopped, exhaled again. "Sometimes doing nothing is what we're called to do, I think. Does that make sense? In any relationship, sometimes we play the lead, and sometimes we follow."

"He left me," I said to the dark, and it sounded like a confession. I added, speaking mostly to myself, "He's always leaving me."

"Why does he leave you?"

"He would say he left me for my own good, to protect me. But I don't need his protection."

She was quiet for a moment, then asked, "What do you need? From him?"

I huffed a laugh. "You mean other than for him to live so I can murder him?"

"Yes. Other than that. I know you love him, but what do you need from him?"

So much, I wanted to say. *So much more than he is giving me.*

Instead I said, "Why do you ask?"

"Because he said something this morning—"

"Wait, you talked to Greg too?"

"No. I listened in on his call with Alex and that CIA prick, Spenser Banks—what a fuckwad. What's his deal anyway?"

I ignored her dislike for my former handler. "What did Greg say?"

"When Alex asked Greg why he didn't want you to help move the money and accompany him and Dan to Lagos, Greg said, 'I need her much more than she needs me.'"

I closed my eyes, a heavy weight settling on my chest, my eyes stinging. "How can he be so clueless?"

"Have you told him?"

"What?" I asked, my throat dry and my stomach in knots.

"That you need him?"

I started to say, *Yes, all the time.* But then I stopped myself. Because I couldn't remember the last time I'd admitted to my husband, *I need you.*

I remembered the last time he'd said it, just this morning at the hospital in Enugu. Before that, he'd said it at least twice while we were in Chicago. In fact, he was always saying it. This realization made me feel miserable.

Finally, I answered Marie's question. "Not enough. I haven't told him enough."

After my admission, we were silent for a time. I promised myself the first words out of my mouth to Greg the next time I saw him were going to be, *I need you.*

"I think David left me because I was too independent," Marie said. She was referring to her ex-boyfriend. If memory served, they'd been together for seven or more years. He'd left her last spring after she wrote an article about body builders and their small penises.

"Some men need that, I think. They need a woman to need them, depend on them for all decisions, crave their approval and praise."

"Perhaps some men prefer to nurture rather than be nurtured." My offered thought was an echo of Greg's earlier wisdom.

"Exactly. David was a nurturer. I didn't need constant nurturing."

"Because you're a nurturer, too?"

"Maybe . . ."

"What do you need, Marie?"

"I don't know . . . I know what I'd like, but I have no idea what I need." She sighed loudly and the cot below me creaked. We were quiet for a moment before Marie blurted, "I was worried about you, Fiona."

I smiled into the darkness. "I was worried about you, too. Thank you for coming down here, for all your help."

"I don't know how much I've helped." She laughed self-deprecatingly and then stretched. "Can we hug now? I think I need a hug."

I was already climbing down from the top bunk when I answered, "Sure."

Marie stood and we reached for each other, nearly bumping noses. I was soon enveloped in the soft warmth of my friend's embrace. She always gave high-quality hugs—lingering tight squeezes with her entire body. I leaned into her, recognizing almost at once how badly I needed to be held by someone who loved me.

A decision formed and was instantaneously ratified by my brain. I would stop rationing my needs and wants. I would no longer use cake to rationalize calling Janie for a car when faced with blizzard conditions. If I needed a hug, I would announce to my people, *I need a hug!* And then I would accept a hug. Or perhaps several hugs.

And I wouldn't feel guilty about it.

Just as Marie and I separated, but before I could thank her for the embrace, a succinct knock sounded on the narrow door leading to the surveillance space.

Dan stuck his head into the room, saying in a rush, "Fiona, they've arrived, Greg is talking."

CHAPTER 19

Dear Wife,
I'm sorry I'm the worst. I love you.

<3 -*Your Husband*
Letter
Alabama, USA
Married 3.5 years

~Present Day~
Fiona

"**WHAT HAPPENED TO** the transmission?" I glanced between Dan and Quinn. "Why can't I hear anything?"

"We just had it," Quinn cursed, fiddling with the frequency settings.

"All we're getting is static." Sitting next to me, Marie pulled the headphones from her ears.

As soon as Dan had made his announcement, Marie and I had sprinted from the room where we'd been resting and grabbed for the headphones, but were met with only the sound of crackles and hissing.

"It's Banks. He's scrambling the feed." Quinn was seething, rubbing his forehead with intense frustration.

"What? Why?"

"He didn't want us involved in the first place." Dan said this mostly to Marie. "I'm surprised he let us listen in as long as he did."

"Can't Alex fix it? Can't we get him back?" Marie asked.

"I'm messaging Alex now." Dan had already whipped out his phone.

Just then we heard a series of shots over the feed followed by a short pause, then more rapid gunfire, quick popping of several semiautomatic weapons being discharged. Each shot sent a jarring spike of panic down my neck to the base of my spine, chasing away the day's aches and pains with a surge of restless adrenaline.

I paced back and forth in the tight space of the surveillance area, barely conquering my desire to run outside and jump into the fray. I needed to think, to consider. Rushing into an active combat zone would be stupid at best, madness at worst.

"Hey, Alex. Are you hearing what we're hearing? Because we have nothing." Dan swiveled toward me and stared unseeingly forward, listening to our friend on the other end.

Quinn stood and crossed to stand next to me, hovering at my shoulder as we both watched and listened to Dan's side of the conversation. "Can't you get it back?"

Quinn made a sound in the back of his throat, a frustrated sound, then said, "I didn't want to say this earlier, but I don't trust Banks."

My attention moved to the big man next to me. "Why?"

Quinn's ice blue eyes slid to mine. "He doesn't like your husband."

"He doesn't. But whether he likes him or not isn't relevant when there's a job to do."

"It should be . . ." Quinn's tone and expression grew assessing. "Why doesn't he like Greg?"

"They met once or twice when I was in service and just never got along." I shrugged. "Greg can be abrasive and Banks plays it close to the vest. Greg was always trying to get a rise out of him."

"That's not it. I think Banks is envious."

"Envious of Greg? No, as far as I know, Spenser never married, has no kids. He's a career soldier, not a family man. The CIA is his first love."

"Or," Quinn's piercing glare moved over my face, "the CIA is his second love."

Nonplussed, I gaped at his evaluation of the situation. But before I could spare a minute to think on this statement, Quinn turned away and pulled out his phone, swiping his thumb across the screen to accept a call.

"Hello?"

I scanned his expression for any sign of who he was speaking to. Seeing the intensity of my anxiety, Quinn lifted his chin and answered my unspoken question.

"Oluwa and Zaki upfront, the drivers. Special Forces guys have entered the building."

"Can they show us?"

Quinn nodded once, addressing his next question to his phone. "Can you turn on video?"

Marie, Quinn, and I were soon huddled around Quinn's screen, watching with tense expectation the blurry video of soldiers dressed in black against the darkening sky. As day became night the Special Forces agents would become invisible. But the bright strobes of light in tandem with the sound of gunfire gave away their approximate location.

Minutes felt like hours.

Eventually there was a pause in both sound and any visible activity.

I held my breath.

I was aware of Dan somewhere behind me, still on the phone with Alex, and Marie's hand in mine, our fingers threaded together.

Cautious relief had me exhaling in a whoosh when several dark shadows were visible carrying what looked like injured hostages out of the building. I tried to pinpoint Greg, but it was no use. Dusk had descended. It was too dark. The figures were too blurry.

"Fiona."

I turned from Quinn's phone and faced Dan. "What?"

"Alex has Banks on the line for you, on the con." Dan lifted his chin to the headphones I'd discarded earlier.

With shaking fingers, I brought them to my ears, adjusting the microphone piece. "Spenser, it's Fiona. What's happening?"

"Why did you come? I told you not to come to Nigeria." He sounded oddly angry.

I didn't have time for his random and aggressive show of feelings, not when I had no idea what was going on with my husband. "Where is Greg, Spenser? Did you get him out?"

"We have the rest of the hostages."

"And Greg?"

The line was quiet for several seconds. Each moment that passed sent my heart rate doubling. "Spenser? What about Greg?"

"He's still in there." Just as he said this, a single shot rang out. Spenser rushed to add, "We couldn't reach him."

My stomach and throat switched positions and red filled my vision; I spoke without thinking, "You goddamn sonofabitch."

"Fiona, he's holding his own. He still might make it out."

"Send your team back in."

"I can't do that, not for one person. They wouldn't be able to distinguish his friendly fire from hostile. You understand."

"Spenser . . ."

Quinn tapped me on the shoulder and showed me the video feed. Spenser and his Special Forces vehicles were retreating, two of Contee's Humvees were in pursuit. He was leaving.

My ex-handler's voice turned to steel. "It's not going to happen. He's on his own. You understand."

"No. I do not understand. But you understand this: if I ever see you again I am going to rip your entrails out of your ass. Then I'm going to cut off your balls and feed them to your cat. Do you hear me? Do you fucking understand *that*, you dickless jackass?"

"Fi—"

I flipped the com switch off then slammed my headphones on the counter, flexing my fingers and marching away from the communications terminal toward the small weapons locker I'd spied earlier.

I felt rather than saw Dan tentatively approach. "What are you going to do?"

"I'm going to go get him." I selected a SIG MK25 and checked the chamber. "Where are the extra magazines for this?"

"Fiona—"

"Don't try to stop me."

"Wasn't going to." Dan reached for a .45 and passed me two extra magazines for my SIG. "Let me suit up."

***

MARIE AND QUINN remained in the converted tanker and provided what tactical support they could manage.

Purposeful or not, Spenser's abandonment of the building had drawn most of the guards away. We needed eyes inside the building, but the best we could manage was a heat signature feed and a quick survey of the building's schematics, both courtesy of Alex. Based on what we could hastily discern, Greg was on the top floor, backed into a corner. His assailants were likely waiting for him to run out of ammunition. They still needed him alive.

Two minutes later, with a hasty plan of action defined, Dan and I were on the move. We approached from the opposite side Spenser's team had left. I easily scaled the fence and offered Dan a hand over. He was heavy and my arms were tired, but it didn't matter. He seemed to need the small amount of leverage and no more.

I liked Dan. I didn't want him hurt. So I'd agreed he could join me if and only if he provided cover. He reluctantly agreed. The thing was, Dan was big, strong, and would be great in a fistfight. But I was little, light, and great in a stealth attack.

We entered the bottom floor of the warehouse, quickly navigating through the maze of pallets leading to a central, exposed stairway. I bounced soundlessly up the steps while Dan stayed behind, providing cover until I reached the top. Then I provided his cover as he mounted the steps, his shoes like a hammer on the metal slats.

I motioned for him to follow. My feet were silent on the linoleum floor, but it didn't matter. Bursts of gunshots pierced the air. I was grateful for the sound. If shots were still being fired then Greg was still alive.

We encountered no hostiles on our route to the room where Greg was being held, therefore it didn't take us long to reach it. I peeked through the glass window in one of the swinging doors, confirming the heat signatures I'd counted earlier. Greg was swapping bullets with seven combatants, and all of them had lousy aim.

Or, I realized, they wanted him alive.

Of course they did. He knew where the money was buried.

But then, so did Banks. And now Banks had the rest of the hostages and could retrieve the money no problem, looking like a big hero . . . he'd probably get a promotion.

I was definitely going to remove him from his ball sack at some point.

Greg shot twice at a cluster of three guards. I gave Dan a sign to proceed as I skipped away and toward one corner of the hallway.

Dan pushed the swinging door open three inches with his shoulder, aimed, and fired. I heard several combatants fall to the ground immediately, and one yell out what I assumed to be a curse. Dan let the door swing shut just in time. As soon as he closed the door a rain of bullets pounded into it on the other side.

I jumped and started to climb the wall leading to the AC vent above. Heavy footsteps, frantic shouting, the sound of metal against metal reverberated from behind the partitions.

And then Greg's voice calling, "They have you surrounded and your comrades are off on a goose chase. Surrender."

The earsplitting rata-tat-tat of a semiautomatic elicited an involuntary flinch, but I used the sounds of the machine gun as cover for removing the vent grate, pulling myself up and into the ventilation system.

A spray of ammunition, shouting, and furniture being moved—likely as a barricade—continued below me as I snaked through the narrow box. I wouldn't be able to back out, and that was fine. Greg and I wouldn't be leaving via the vent.

What Greg apparently didn't know, but what Dan and I could see from the building schematics, was that there was a dumb waiter—a hauling manual elevator—just ten feet from where he was trapped. It led to the first floor, close to where Dan and I had entered the building.

Dan would continue drawing fire. Meanwhile, I would drop from the ceiling. Greg and I would escape via the chute just as Dan tossed tear gas into the holding room. Greg and I would provide cover for Dan as he descended the stairs. We would all leave together.

Easy-peasy.

"Almost there," I whispered, catching sight of the top of Greg's head through the slats of the vent; the rest of him was hidden behind a pallet of stacked cardboard boxes. A few more feet and I'd be able to drop through the next vent.

"Fiona, I hear footsteps approaching from behind." Dan's voice was strained and interrupted by continuing gunfire. "I need to throw the tear gas in now. It's now or never."

"Fine. Do it." I pulled myself forward with my aching arms, then punched the vent open with the butt of my gun. "I'm dropping in now."

I had a mere moment to aim my drop, falling head first, flipping, and landing on my feet on top of the pallet—well, mostly on my feet. I stumbled one step back and failed my dismount.

Greg's face shot up and so did his weapon just as the first clanging, rolling tear gas cans sounded from behind me.

Our eyes met.

His registered shock.

I leapt off the pallet.

This time I landed the dismount.

I turned to him.

He faced me with wide eyes and an open mouth.

I wanted to kiss him.

And place him in a chokehold.

And wrap my arms around him.

And never let him go.

. . . but also place him in a chokehold.

Instead, I whispered harshly, "I need you."

He continued to stare at me, dumbfounded, as though trying to makes sense of my words. "What?"

"Follow me!"

His hand shot out to my wrist and he pulled me back and against him. "Bloody hell," he growled against my ear, crouching us both to the ground. "I'm going to murder you, Fe. What the fuck were you thinking?"

I turned in his grasp, grabbing the front of his shirt with my free hand and bringing his mouth within an inch of mine. His eyes were flashing fire down at me, his jaw working, and I saw that he was both panicked and irate.

"I know the way out," I shouted to be heard, because our assailants were now also shouting, and tear gas was filling the room. "You have to trust me, Greg."

Without waiting to gauge his reaction, I twisted my wrist such that I held his hand in mine and pulled him forward toward the chute.

This time he didn't stop me.

He followed where I led.

Granted, it was only ten feet and away from bullets and tear gas, but he still followed.

So, progress.

We made it to where the manual elevator should have been, but encountered several large empty pallets set on one end and leaning against the wall.

"Help me move these."

"Where?"

"Anywhere. Just away from the wall."

With one fierce push, Greg shoved them forward, revealing the hatch for the chute. I glanced down the vertical tunnel, estimated the drop to be sixty or more feet, concrete floor at the bottom. We'd confirmed earlier it was wide enough for Greg's large frame.

"You'll have to brace yourself against the sides and crawl down. It's concrete floor at the bottom, so be careful."

"You should go first—" he started to say, but then thought better of it, shaking his head. He stepped forward, dropped his semiautomatic down the chute, and leveraged himself inside. He used his hands and feet to brace himself and slide slowly toward the bottom floor. Once his head cleared the opening, I climbed in after him; the acrid smell of tear gas faint but growing stronger.

I slid down the walls, using my rubber soles and the palms of my hands to slow my descent. Even so, my arms were shaking and my legs were on fire. I was losing my grip. The weight of the day and week was pulling me under. I didn't have enough strength left to scale the inside of the chute and soon I wouldn't be able to hold on.

"Drop and I'll catch you." I heard Greg's voice call from below.

I glanced down just as my arms gave way, sucking in a bracing breath. I had to trust him to catch me, because I was falling and couldn't stop myself.

And he did.

He caught me with an "Oomph!" but his arms were strong and sure, and he recovered quickly.

I twisted out of his grip, my legs feeling like lead as my feet hit the ground. "This way. Dan should be on his way down."

"I'm here." I heard Dan's voice through my earpiece. "I'm by the entrance and I've got you both covered. You're clear to the door."

I didn't get a chance to repeat Dan's words to Greg because just at that moment, Quinn spoke over the com. "You need to get out of there now. Buhari's military police just arrived and I don't think they plan to leave any survivors."

"Explain," I said, handing Greg my semi-automatic pistol and motioning him to follow me to the entrance. I was too tired to be a reliable shot. My body was exhausted and my brain was fried.

"They're setting up a repeating grenade launcher. I'm guessing they plan to blow up the building."

"Fuck a fucking fuck!" Dan growled. I saw him shift on his feet impatiently. He was waiting for us, but his eyes were trained on some point behind us. "Move! They're coming down the stairs."

I moved. And I didn't stop moving. I ran straight out of the building and jumped for the fence, sparing a split-second glance over my shoulder to make sure Greg and Dan were behind me. They were. Greg ran for the fence as Dan shoved a pipe into the handles of the door, trapping the remaining hostiles inside. I sat on the top of fence and offered a hand up to Greg first, then Dan in turn. As soon as they cleared the chain link, I again dropped into Greg's arms—this time without him asking or me requesting.

We sprinted for the tanker. And when we reached it, Dan climbed the ladder first, Greg handing me up hastily, then climbed up after.

Just as Greg wrapped his arms around me, our chests heaving, gasping for breath, I heard the first explosion. The tanker trembled, but the sound was muted thanks to the steel walls and insulation.

Yet, even if it hadn't been muted, I don't think I would have registered it. Not really. Because finally, *finally* we were together and we were safe.

Echoing my thoughts, Greg repeated over and over, "You're safe. You're safe." Kissing every inch of my face and squeezing me to him with punishing strength.

"Greg—"

"Why? Fe? Why would you do that?" he demanded, shaking, his whole body caught in adrenaline withdrawal.

Seeing stars, I blinked against the blackness encroaching on the edges of my vision. Streaks of pain, hot and stabbing, pierced my temples and the back of my eyes. "You left me—"

"Because I needed you to be safe. Because I need you."

"I need you, too." I closed my eyes and the sound of my heart thumping—my blood whooshing—filled my ears.

He was still berating me, his voice fierce and irate, but I couldn't hear him. Everything went black, and for the second time in a week, I passed out in my husband's arms.

CHAPTER 20

Dearest Husband,
You are an endless source of patience to my crazy.

-Jenny
Letter
California, USA
Married 19 years

~Present Day~
Fiona

I WOKE UP to the sound of arguing voices.

Specifically, Greg and Spenser's arguing voices.

". . . swear to God, if you so much as touch her—"

"Making threats against a federal agent is an arrestable offense."

"Your face should be an arrestable offense."

"Boys. Boys. Enough." This came from Marie. I hadn't opened my eyes yet, mostly because my eyelids felt glued shut, but I could approximate each of their locations based on the proximity of their voices.

Greg was standing next to me, to my left. Marie was directly in front of me. Spenser was farther away and to the right. If I had to guess, I would say Marie was standing between him and Greg, likely trying to keep them from ripping into each other.

"Now I repeat, my client has nothing to say to you. Partly because she's unconscious and partly because if she sees you, as she mentioned earlier today, she might cut your balls off."

"Not likely, since she's cuffed to the bed."

At the mention of the restraints I felt the cold metal pressing against my wrists. I fought a frown.

"Yes, *likely*. Because your boss gave me the keys to the handcuffs." Presumably Marie was waving the keys around, because I heard them jingle. "And I'm just about to un-cuff my client, as per the amnesty agreement signed off by both you, and your boss, and your boss's boss, and recorded for prosperity by me. You have no grounds for arresting Mrs. Archer."

Spenser's voice turned gruff as he asked disbelievingly, "How can you be an AP reporter and a lawyer?"

"And how can you look yourself in the mirror after leaving my client to die, Agent Banks?"

He muttered a few choice words under his breath, after which the room fell into a tense silence.

"Time to go." Marie clapped once, and heals clicked on the floor as she moved away from me. I heard a door open. After a beat, I heard Banks's retreating footsteps.

Greg, obviously unable to restrain himself, added just before the door clicked shut, "Yes, better get back to it. Your inconsequential, lonely life isn't going to live itself."

Spenser growled something inaudible in response, but it was too late. Marie locked the door as Spenser banged on it once, causing her to huff loudly at Greg's incendiary statement.

"Really, Greg? Really? While you're at it, why don't you poke him in the eye?"

"I have no desire to poke Spenser Banks," he grumbled, fitting his hand in mine and fingering the metal around my wrist. "Will you please take these off her? Every time I look at them I want to vomit."

"Well, I think the feeling is mutual. Especially since you promised one hundred million dollars and the CIA only recovered ten from the dry pipe outside of Enugu."

"I must have miscounted."

I could almost see my husband's shoulders shrug as he made this comment.

I listened as Marie approached, lifting my eyebrows in preparation for opening my eyes. My limbs felt sluggish and weighted, sore. She reached for the hand Greg wasn't holding, and the cuff made a clicking sound as the lock was released.

I blinked once, finding my eyeballs scratchy, my eyelids heavy, and my vision blurred.

Greg's hand tightened on mine. "Fe?"

"Hmm."

"How much of that did you hear?"

"Just the end," I croaked. My lips were dry. I tried to moisten them. "Where are we?"

Greg pushed shaking fingers into my hair. "We're at the US consulate in Lagos."

"What are we doing here?" I tried to blink again, but only managed to squint.

"The plan was always to return here after the hostages were secure. When you fainted, we decided it was the safest place to go. They have medical staff on call."

"We didn't expect them to arrest you," Marie added, moving to Greg's side and insinuating herself so she could release the cuff.

"Why was I arrested?"

"For treason, but it was just Agent Banks trying to throw his weight around. Let me get you some water." Marie carried the cuffs away, placing them on a side counter with a *thunk*, and poured water from a pitcher.

"I thought Greg negotiated amnesty for me?" I could see better now, but my headache was returning, pounding between my temples.

"I did."

I shifted my attention to him. He was leaning forward, his thumb brushing back and forth over my cheek, his fingers curled around my jaw and neck.

"I've taken care of everything. All charges have been dropped. But Banks tried to renege when we arrived."

I blinked once, my mind slowly working through this information. "Why would he do that?"

"Because he's a dickless jackass?" Greg smirked, quoting my words from earlier.

"You heard that?"

"I heard every word." He nodded once, his smirk growing into a warm, wonderful smile.

Marie cleared her throat meaningfully as she walked toward me, carrying the glass, and handed it to me. "Or . . ."

I took a sip of water, thankful for the cool, soothing liquid, and studied my friend. She was staring pointedly at Greg. I studied Greg. His wonderful smile grew crooked and mischievous, and his eyes fell to where he was holding my hand.

When no one spoke I asked, "Or?"

Marie *tsked* when Greg didn't continue. "Do you want to tell her?"

He shrugged. "Nah."

"Fine. I'll tell her." Marie didn't sound angry, she sounded reluctantly amused, as though it were against her better judgment.

"Tell me what?" I took another sip of water and then rested the glass on my belly.

"The refinery exploded."

Greg wasn't looking at either of us, instead he was smirking at nothing as he said, "Big kaboom."

"Oh dear Lord." Marie huff-chuckled.

His unrepentant eyes bounced between us. "Technically, I had no way to stop the explosion. I told Banks that."

"Yes. You did," Marie agreed. "He just didn't believe you until the *big kaboom*."

"That's on him," my husband insisted. "His resultant demotion isn't my problem."

"What? Banks was demoted?" I was trying to keep up.

"Banks was demoted because he's a gar-belching guttersnipe," Greg muttered.

Marie ignored the odd insult and explained. "Yes, Banks was demoted. I suspect that's why he tried to have you arrested, because he's quite spiteful and irrational."

I could only imagine Banks' level of distress and dismay. The Agency was his life. He would not react well to a demotion.

"They demoted him because of the exploding refinery?" I asked.

"The exploding refinery was part of it." Marie pursed her lips, then added flatly as she glared at my husband, "And the money was the other part."

Greg grinned and refocused his attention on our linked fingers. "I don't know what you're talking about."

Marie kept her eyes fastened to my husband but addressed her next comment to me. "Greg moved the money."

It took me a moment to catch on, to remember what money she was referring to. "Wait, no he didn't. He left it in a dry pipe."

"Yes. That's right. I left it in a dry pipe." Greg nodded, still studying our joined hands.

"And yet, when the CIA went to retrieve the money it wasn't in the dry pipe."

Greg shrugged again. "Meh."

Obviously unable to contain herself, she laughed tiredly, but with true amusement. "How did you manage to move ninety million dollars while you were being held captive?"

"Exactly. It's not possible," Greg said cheerfully.

Marie was about to challenge him further when a knock sounded on the door. She gave him a suspicious glare and moved to answer the door.

"Who is it?"

"Dan the Security Man."

"Oh." She unlocked it quickly and motioned him to enter. "Come in."

I tried to sit up in the bed, but Greg placed his hand on my shoulder to ease me back.

"How is your nose?" I asked, anxious and feeling guilty that I might have caused my friend harm.

"Fine. It's not broken. Thank God for that. It would be the fourth time, and I really like the job the last guy did resetting it."

I could see it wasn't broken. He didn't have black eyes and the swelling was minimal. "I'm so sorry, Dan."

He waved me off, loitering by the door. "No big deal." Dan's eyes flickered to Marie and he pointed at her. "We need you for a minute."

She turned to me. "I'll be right back, okay?"

"Sure." I nodded once and took a large gulp of my water.

Dan opened the door for Marie and she filed out; just before he left he glanced over his shoulder and gave me a conspiratorial grin. "You were pretty great in there, Archer. Let me know if you're ever interested in consulting with Cypher Systems, because we could use some of your badass skills."

I gave him a soft smile in return. "Thanks. You were pretty great yourself."

Dan lingered, still grinning at me, until Greg snapped his fingers between us and ordered, "Okay, that's enough. No prolonged stares appreciating my wife for her skills."

Dan cocked an eyebrow at my husband, his mouth flattening into an unimpressed line. "Someone needs to appreciate Fiona for her badass skills, Greg. Because they are fucking awesome."

And with that, he turned and marched out the door.

For a long moment I stared at the spot where Dan had disappeared, then slid my gaze to the side as I tried to assess Greg's reaction. The movement hurt, so I closed my eyes and leaned back into my pillow. After a moment, I felt Greg remove the glass from my grip and heard him set it on a side table.

"Are we going to talk about it?" I asked, not knowing how I wanted him to answer the question. I was so tired. My muscles were sore, and so was my heart.

"The doctors said you passed out due to exhaustion and dehydration,

Fe." His voice was dark, unhappy, but restrained.

I nodded once. "I believe it."

"I think we should wait to talk about everything until after you've rested."

"I agree," I replied numbly.

"But we *will* talk about it."

I didn't respond, instead opting to ask, "Did they give me any medicine?"

"Yes. Just acetaminophen and IV fluids. You've only been out for three hours."

I flexed my hand, recognizing for the first time I had a needle stuck in my arm.

We were quiet for a while, and then I thought and said, "Will you lay with me?"

"Yes," he answered at once, sounding relieved.

Instead of allowing me to scooch over on my own, Greg lifted me with infinite gentleness. He then climbed into the bed next to me and gingerly tucked me against his chest, my head over his heart.

"I miss the sound of your heartbeat," I said, loving the feel of him, relatively unscathed, warm and real. I decided to be angry with him later, because right now I wanted to enjoy that he was alive.

Greg smiled against my hair. "The last time you said that was a week and three days ago, when we were in Chicago."

A week and three days ago felt like an eternity.

"But I think it all the time," I mumbled against his shirt.

He swallowed, and from the feel of it he did so with difficulty.

"I think about you all the time." I snuggled closer. "You know how much I need you."

"Do you?" he asked roughly, his hand squeezing my waist.

"Yes. I need you."

His heart rate increased and I sensed a shift in his breathing; yet all he said was, "Sleep, my darling. You need your rest."

I nodded, but then a thought occurred to me. "Greg, what happened to the money?"

His chest rose with a large inhale and I knew he was smiling again. "Let's just say, your idea of using the mobile clinic was genius, and Dr. Evans is a brilliant co-conspirator."

I frowned my confusion. "But I thought you rigged the money to explode."

"Yes. Everyone did."

"So she moved it?"

"I presume so."

"What will she do with it?"

Greg paused, apparently considering my question, then responded on a sigh, "I don't know. But I do feel certain our dear Dr. Evans will do more good with the funds than Boko Haram, the present government, or the CIA."

I couldn't help but agree with his statement. I decided, in a pinch, giving a hundred million ill-begotten dollars to Doctors Without Borders was a good plan.

"Also," he continued, "she emailed me a picture of her sitting on a throne of hundred-dollar bills."

I laughed lightly, tilting my head back so I could see him. "Jealous?"

"Yes." He kissed my forehead. "I've always wanted a throne of money."

"I know."

"And yet you never get it for me for Christmas, though it's on my list every year."

"I'm a constant source of disappointment," I added sarcastically, yawning.

"Tell me about it. All I ask is for a throne of money, constant praise, and naked pictures."

"How you've managed to survive all these years is miraculous."

"I know." He squeezed me again, adding on a sigh, "I'm basically a saint. Saint Greg, the Manly."

I grinned against his chest, feeling warm and loved. Bantering with

Greg was foreplay for my brain. My head already felt better.

***

"ARE YOU REALLY a lawyer?"

"Sure." Marie shrugged, settling into her seat on the private jet Quinn decided to charter. I tried to talk him out of the expense, to no avail. Now that we were all heading home, I recognized how much I'd asked of my friends and had no idea how I would be able to repay them.

Dan and I had rescued Greg less than twelve hours ago, and it was now midmorning the day after. Quinn had said, and we'd all agreed, the sooner we left the better.

"Sure? What does that mean? *Sure?*" Dan grinned at Marie, like he found her fascinating and funny.

"It means, sometimes I'm a lawyer."

"You went to law school?" Greg asked as he claimed the seat next to mine. The jet was relatively small, with seats and leather benches lining each side, facing each other.

"No. But I did pass the bar in California and Vermont."

"You passed the bar without going to law school?" Quinn asked from his spot at the back of the plane. I knew he must've been anxious about Janie. He'd spread out papers, his laptop, and two additional monitors around him. Obviously he was going to use the flight home to get some work done and distract himself from worrying about his newly-pregnant wife.

"That's the beauty of being a lawyer. Anyone can be a lawyer. You can just wake up one day and decide you want to do it. It's not like being a ballerina, or a spy, or a petroleum engineer, where you have to train or hone a skill, practice. The law is a set of rules. If you can read, memorize, and think critically, then you're basically ninety percent there. The other ten percent is pretending you know what you're talking about, and having a deep abiding love for paperwork and bureaucracy."

"You mean bullshitting," Greg supplied.

"Exactly. Bullshitters make excellent lawyers. In fact, they make the best lawyers."

"So, what you're saying is, Greg would make the world's greatest lawyer?" Dan kept his tone and expression serious.

"Dan, I didn't know you cared. I'm touched." Greg bit his bottom lip in mock sentimentality, causing Dan to snort.

"The only place you're touched is in the head."

This earned Dan a round of chuckles, including a quick smile and head shake from Greg. "I should have seen that coming."

It felt remarkably good to laugh. But also surreal.

I zoned out during the takeoff, opting to rest my head against the crook of Greg's shoulder, his arm around me holding me close. I was still tired, but it was more than that. My brain was a cascading fog of dichotomous emotions, all of which were extreme.

I was still angry with Greg.

I was also tremendously grateful we were in one piece, together, and going home.

I was also anxious about the future, Greg leaving again, coping with the loss of him.

Unable to decide which was the priority, I instead opted to dwell in feelings limbo.

"What are we going to do about Jack?"

I blinked away from the window I'd been staring out, realizing we'd taken off some time ago, and brought Greg into focus. "Jack?"

"Yes. What are we going to do about Jack and his mysterious case of musical prodigy-ism?" He gave me his charming crooked smile, his expression open and solicitous.

I felt like I was staring at him through a concealing screen. I couldn't see him or his charming half-smile, the one I'd loved and cherished, because—and quite abruptly—I was looking at him through a lens of anger and distrust.

Instead of thawing, I sighed tiredly, preparing myself for a mandate, one I would ignore just as soon as Greg left for his next godforsaken assignment.

"Fine. Tell me. What do you want to do about Jack?" I asked.

Greg's lips flattened, then curved downward into a frown, his eyes flickering over my expression as his eyebrows pulled low on his forehead. After a long moment of unhappily studying me, he leaned forward and whispered, "Am I really that bad, Fe?"

I stared at him blankly and didn't answer.

Since leaving the consulate, every so often I would feel overcome with the urge to scream at him, accuse him of breaking my heart, wonder once again if I would be able to move past his abandonment of me, tying me to a hospital bed in Enugu and placing himself in harm's way, rejecting me and my help over and over.

Logically, I knew the situation was a good deal more complicated than the oversimplification insisted upon by my feelings. I knew he'd been terrified to lose me. I knew he'd felt responsible for lying about the assignment in Nigeria in the first place.

Logically, I knew this.

But I just couldn't bring myself to care.

At least not yet.

I rejected the hurt behind his features. I was too lost in the labyrinth of my own trampled feelings to spare any energy for his.

So I stared at him blankly for another moment. And then I turned my attention back to the window, to the blue sky above dark clouds.

A storm raged below. Strobes of lightning flickered at intervals, angrily striking the earth. But from our place above the clouds, the storm was mostly hidden, and virtually soundless.

***

WE DIDN'T SPEAK to each other again during the remainder of the flight. It was long and our friends surrounded us. I don't think either of us wanted to sort through our issues in front of an audience.

When we landed in Chicago, I was still numbly cruising on autopilot. One of Quinn's cars drove us home.

Wordlessly, Greg carried our bags—really, just his bags since I'd brought nothing to Nigeria but a Kevlar bodysuit and weapons—into the apartment building while I walked ahead and called the elevator. We boarded the elevator in silence. We rode the elevator in silence. We departed the elevator in silence.

Suspension of conversation continued as he unlocked the apartment and opened the door for me to enter. I almost immediately tripped over a pile of Grace's laundry, the pile Greg and the kids had dumped into the living room nearly two weeks ago when he'd been home for a day, and I'd been so careful about keeping the apartment clean.

How long ago that felt.

Everything and nothing was different.

Except . . . I was out of sorts. I *felt* out of sorts. Something was wrong with me, really wrong. Physically wrong. I was not myself.

After a twenty-three-hour flight, I should have been tired, but I also should have been ready to move forward and plot a way through our latest marriage turbulence. I wasn't a grudge-holder. As Buddha said, "Holding a grudge is like drinking poison and expecting the other person to die." I was not that person.

I *knew* this. I should have been ready talk, to listen. But I wasn't. I remained greedy of my feelings even though I knew my irrationality could not persist.

Greg walked by me, carrying his suitcase into our bedroom while I picked up my cell phone from where I'd left it charging on the entryway table.

I had missed calls from each of the knitting girls, and several text messages welcoming me home. As well, there were several missed calls from my oncologist. In fact, there were a lot of missed calls from my oncologist. Seven to be exact.

An unpleasant and dark sensation, like inhaling smoke, crept into my chest and made breathing somewhat difficult.

Before I left for Nigeria to save Greg I'd been in denial about so many things. Bottling my feelings in the hopes that everything would just eventually work out was paramount on the list of my mistakes. Ignoring the headaches and loss of appetite had been monumentally stupid.

I did remember what it was like to have a brain tumor. It sucked. But living in denial wasn't rent-free. Eventually it required a balloon payment, usually in the form of misery and pain.

Stiffening my spine, I pressed play on the last voicemail left by my oncologist's office and braced myself for whatever news they'd been frantic to share with me.

"Mrs. Archer, this is Liz from Dr. Daud's office again. I realize I've left you an ungodly number of messages, but I cannot impress upon you enough how vitally important it is for you to call me back as soon as possible. Please do not attempt to schedule an MRI with the hospital or elsewhere until you speak to Dr. Daud or me. The office number is . . ."

My hand was shaking slightly as I removed the cell from my ear, though I smiled at my phone—a humorless, bitter smile. My stomach was dually in my throat and at my feet, but waiting would accomplish nothing.

I heard Greg's light movements from our bedroom, sounds that were usually comforting, but presently were not. I was caught in a spiral of self-pity and intense aggravation, with a chant resembling: *Your apartment is a disastrous mess, so is your marriage, and so is your mind.*

Perversely, I decided to rip off the band-aid rather than prolong the unknown.

I hit the return call option with my thumb and brought the phone to my ear. It rang three times. Someone picked up.

"Dr. Daud's office, Alison speaking. How can I direct your call?"

"The nurse please, Liz Schaffer." I was surprised by the sound of my voice, so cool and aloof.

"Just a moment."

The line clicked, signaling my call was being transferred. So I waited. And waited.

And waited.

Eventually, the line was answered. "Liz Schaffer speaking."

"Hi Liz, it's Fiona Archer. I'm sorry I didn't call back earlier, but we just got back in town and walked through the door. I'm just seeing your messages now."

"Oh! Mrs. Archer. I am so glad you called. I was so worried you would try to reschedule the MRI without contacting us first."

"No. I was just out of town. I haven't rescheduled the MRI yet."

"Thank goodness."

I cleared my throat, trying to relieve some of the tightness, and turned away from where Greg hovered inside our room, plainly eavesdropping. "Does Dr. Daud need something else? Instead of an MRI?"

"Goodness, no. Your screening panels all came back great, that's the good news. The bad news—although I'm not sure it's necessarily bad news—is that your MRI will have to wait a few months."

"A few months? Why?"

"Mrs. Archer, your HGB test came back positive."

"What does that mean?" I whispered, bracing myself for the worst.

"It means you're pregnant."

"I . . ."

Time stopped.

Sound halted first, then all movement external to my person. Every atom stood still in the entire universe and I existed in a singular moment where nothing existed except my consciousness and the meaning of the words *you're pregnant.*

I stared at the words.

They stared back.

Then they waved and smiled and shrugged—like, *We'll be keeping you company for a while, so you might as well invite us in so we can give you cankles, and cravings for beef jerky and pickles dipped in mustard.*

I wanted to push those words off a cliff.

Nothing about her statement made sense. I couldn't be pregnant. Greg had been fixed five years ago because I knew, after having Grace, that I would lose my mind if we had any more children.

"Fiona?"

I started, shaking myself at the close proximity of Greg's voice. I glanced over my shoulder, finding him standing directly behind me. His dark eyes told me he was near panicked.

"Is that your oncologist?" he pressed.

I shook my head and held up my finger, trying to keep up with Liz's gushing flow from the other end and re-entered her one-sided conversation mid-sentence. ". . . so happy for you both. I couldn't wait to tell you. I still remember when you and Mr. Archer came in together for the first time, such a handsome couple, and so in love. You two are—"

"I'm sorry, Liz? Liz, could you back up for a minute. Did you just say—"

"Yes. You're pregnant. Yay."

In my mind's eye I could almost see Liz do her happy little dance, her white nurse's shoes squeaking on the linoleum floor behind the reception desk.

"I see," I said, not seeing at all.

My gaze lifted to Greg for a quick moment. It was clear he hadn't heard the news and was obviously trying his best to *not* snatch the phone out of my hand and demand Liz give him all the answers immediately. I wasn't finished processing the baby reveal, but I knew I needed to put him out of his misery as soon as possible.

"So, the screening panel, the doctor is certain I'm still in remission? No sign of cancer?"

Greg visibly relaxed, stumbling back a step and releasing a giant exhale.

"Yes! Still in remission, though you'll need an MRI as soon as the new baby arrives."

"Of course," I said numbly, but when the words came out of my mouth they sounded weird, like I was being sarcastic. I fought the sudden urge to laugh hysterically.

After a few more pleasantries, all of which I coasted through, we hung up.

Greg stepped forward, opening his mouth as though preparing to lecture me. But before he could, Grace burst through our front door and came running toward us. Greg's smile was instantaneous as he gathered her in his embrace. Jack wasn't far behind, his exuberance surprisingly unfettered.

"I missed you so much," Jack said, throwing his arms around me and speaking against my neck.

I rejoiced in the warm strength of my sweet boy, his fierce hug. A tremendous wave of emotion—relief, guilt, gratefulness—swept up and around me, stinging my eyes and sending me off balance.

"I missed you, too." I leaned back to study his face and my heart lodged in my throat. Greg and I were Jack and Grace's world. Sending up a quiet prayer of thanks for bringing us home unharmed, I fought to conquer my urge to bawl against Jack's shirt.

"Next time, can we do video calls?"

Unable to speak, I simply nodded and smiled, pulling him into another tight hug.

Elizabeth and Nico strolled in seconds later. Welcome homes and long embraces were handed out liberally. And through it all I forced a tired smile, falling back into my necessary and familiar pattern of dealing with inconvenient feelings at some later, undefined point.

But this time the decision chaffed, though I knew logically it was best for everyone. Grace and Jack didn't need to see their parents fighting as soon as they walked in the door. They'd missed us. I could wait. My feelings could wait. The argument could wait . . .

And like so many important conversations, whatever Greg was about to say would also have to wait until our company left and the kids were asleep. When the time came, we would have to speak quietly so as not to wake them with our argument.

Marriage with children is a study in delayed everything—delayed conversation, delayed resolutions, and delayed gratification.

And I wasn't certain I could deal with the delays any longer.

CHAPTER 21

Dear Husband,
I know there is a part of you that wanted children, but has remained
with me even knowing I can never give them to you. I also know you
realize that I am lying when I say I never wanted them. You see the pain
and yet you let me lie anyway...

-B.
Letter
USA
Married 11 years

~9 years ago~
Greg

WE WERE IN a Wal-Mart on the outskirts of Chicago, standing in the
checkout line, and I was silently debating which was worse: waiting in a
Wal-Mart checkout line, having my backside spanked with a tire iron, or
giving myself a root canal.

Seemingly out of nowhere, Fiona started to cry.

My eyes cut to her. She was making every attempt to hide her tears.
Her back to me, she stood as though she were a statue. Still, I heard the
sniffles.

"Fe?"

She shook her head then lowered her chin to her chest.

I lifted an eyebrow at her shaking shoulders. My wife was not a crier.

Yes, she cried. She wasn't a robot. Had she been one of those birds who cried during fabric softener commercials, I might have offered a consoling pat on the back. But, as it was, her tears were so infrequent I wasn't physically capable of shrugging them off.

Loading our seven items back into the shopping cart, I wrapped my arm around her, steering her and our unpurchased goods into the greeting card aisle. Thankfully, it was empty.

"Hey." I turned and pressed her against my chest, alarm and worry making me squeeze her more tightly than usual. I had a sense she needed to be held together. "What's going on? Are you all right?"

She shook her head. "I'm fine."

"You're not fine. You're crying. Crying is the opposite of fine. Tell me what's wrong."

She sniffled again. "I don't want to tell you here."

"Why not."

"Because it's important."

I tucked my fingers under her chin and lifted her face to mine, stealing a kiss; true distress clawed at my chest, traveled like a spike down my spine. I didn't want to guess, or entertain any possibilities. Inevitably, my mind always jumped to the worst possible conclusion whenever I saw her inexplicably sad (i.e. brain tumor).

Even so, I attempted to keep my tone level and calm. "What could be too important for the greeting card aisle? It's the perfect place to tell me anything and everything. There's likely a card we can buy afterward for the occasion."

She huffed a laugh, laughed a bit more, and then began crying again.

Her laughter was a good sign, so I went with it.

"Let's see . . ." I shuffled us both to the rack and plucked a greeting card from it. "You tell me if this one describes your situation." I cleared my throat and began to read, "*Dear Brother, Many blessings on your fortieth birthday. May your girlfriend bring home that hot girl she works with and suggest a three-way.*"

Fiona began laughing in earnest, burying her face against my chest.

I returned the original card, walked us a few steps farther down the aisle, and selected another card at random. "Here's another. *Dear Friend, Thank you for your thoughtfulness. I am so lucky to have you in my life, especially after that time I hit you with my car and salted the earth around your house.*

I cracked a smile as I grabbed another card. She was laughing so hard she could barely breathe.

"*Dear Co-worker, Get well soon. Sorry about the scorpions in your bed. And the leprosy. And the chlamydia.*"

"Stop! I can't- I can't breathe." Fiona gripped the front of my shirt as though she needed my solid frame to remain upright.

I took one more step and picked a new card. "*Dear Dad, Happy Father's Day. I know I'm not your favorite child, but I hope you will . . . you will . . .*" I stopped reading because Fiona had stopped laughing.

In fact, she'd grown eerily still, though her fists remained anchored in my shirt. I don't think she was even breathing.

"Fe?"

She released an audible exhale—as though bracing herself—and titled her head back. New tears shone in her eyes and she looked . . . emotional.

Not sad. Not worried or scared. Just emotional.

And I knew.

"I'm going to be a dad," I said.

She nodded, her mouth wanting to smile but her eyes betraying the disordered chaos of her thoughts.

I had no idea what she was thinking.

I had no idea what I was thinking.

But I felt like I'd just been punched, slapped across the face. And it felt scary. And good.

I felt like I was the king of the universe, the luckiest man alive.

I felt panic, because I didn't know how to be a dad, at least not the kind I wanted to be.

I felt a bizarre surge of pride, of accomplishment.

I felt a heady wave of possessiveness, for this woman I loved, for the child we'd made. I felt responsible.

But I did not feel burdened.

And I knew nothing would ever be the same.

CHAPTER 22

Dear Wife,
I walked over to you and asked, "You want to go get a doughnut?"
Yep, that was the best line I had.
Lucky for me you liked Krispy Kreme. Although we didn't know it then, that night was the beginning of happily ever after. Now, 21 years and 6 kids later, it's still happily ever after.

-G.
Letter
USA
Married 21 years

~Present Day~
Fiona

AFTER ELIZABETH AND Nico left, Greg, Jack, Grace, and I went out for pizza. Evading Greg's searching gaze, I was mostly quiet, listening with all outward expression of rapt attention as Grace and Jack described their many adventures over the course of our absence.

During the early afternoon dinner, I excused myself to the ladies' room and called my OB's office, catching them just before close. I made an appointment for the next day.

When dinner was over, we took a walk in the snow. Arriving home, both Greg and I laid the kids down together. And then Grace got up seven times for a variety of reasons: she needed water, she was too hot, she was too cold, she lost her bunny, the bunny was too noisy, the bunny was too quiet, the bunny was mad at her.

After the fifth bunny update, Greg offered to intervene with Grace, lay with her until she fell asleep, and I passed out before he came back to bed.

When I awoke the next morning, I went through the motions of getting the kids ready for school, encouraging Greg to sleep in. I knew he figured I'd return after taking them in and we would finally talk, but that's not what happened.

I dropped Grace and Jack off to school, and then I took the train to my OB's office.

I had a sonogram, during which I gaped with renewed numbness and shock at the tiny person in my uterus, the beating heart, the tiny alien profile curled forward, tiny hands just visible. And then I was ushered into an exam room. I didn't have much time with my jumbled thoughts or the glossy print-out pictures of my new little person before Dr. Freeman knocked, then strolled into the room.

"Mrs. Archer, congratulations on your happy news," he said, all cheerful and efficient smiles. "Eva is preparing your prenatal paperwork and payment schedule. Do you have any questions for me? I know you're a veteran mom at this point, and very little has changed in the last five years since you had Grace."

My doctor bustled around the room, washing his hands, drying them, wheeling his stool over to the side of the exam table, sitting down, crossing his legs, smiling at me. "The kiddos still pop out at nine months with ten fingers and ten toes. The only difference I see now is that you're over thirty-five. That means you're of advanced maternal age, so we'll need to do a few more tests."

I ignored the reference to my advanced age and asked the big question. "I don't understand how this is possible."

My doctor lifted his eyebrows, as though I'd just capitulated to being ignorant of reproductive organs and how babies are made, so I sought to clarify. "Greg was fixed—er, snipped, had a vasectomy—five years ago, right after Grace was born."

Dr. Freeman tilted his chin, signaling his understanding of my confusion. "Ah. I see. Did he get the snip or the clamp?"

"I don't know."

"Hmm. Well, there have been cases of spontaneous reversal."

"Which means?"

"When was the last time he had his sperm count checked?"

I glanced around the exam room, wrestling with my memory. "I don't know. At least three years ago."

"It appears your husband's plumbing has righted itself. And now you're pregnant." He smiled merrily, as though this news should delight me.

I glared at Dr. Freeman, not feeling cheerful. I didn't feel at all cheerful. I was not at all delighted.

His smile fizzled. He cleared his throat. "So . . ."

"So . . ." I repeated, still glaring at him.

He cleared his throat again and glanced at the screen to his left, where my electronic chart presumably detailed my status, and walk-wheeled himself over to the computer. "When was the start of your last cycle?"

I struggled to remember the date. "It must've been December."

"That sounds about right. Are your periods regular?"

"No. They've never been regular. Sometimes I go months without."

His eyes moved over me appraisingly. "Do you exercise a lot?"

"Yes."

"Well, the sonogram has you at fourteen weeks."

"I'm fourteen weeks." Again I echoed, my throat tightening around the words.

"We need to schedule you for the eighteen-week sonogram with the perinatal group. Again, due to your advanced age, we'll treat you as high risk until we rule out complications."

If he mentioned my advanced age of thirty-six one more time I was prepared to knock him out.

"Also, you're due for some blood tests, but the panel they sent over as part of your oncology screening looks good. Assuming nothing has changed, your counts are great."

I squirmed in my paper gown, thinking back over the last week and all the risky—and outright dangerous—behaviors I'd engaged in. The big issue floated once again to the surface of my mind.

"I do have a question." I paused, waited for his gaze to meet mine before continuing. "I may have been dosed with Ketamine last week, enough to put me under for about fourteen hours."

He blinked at my statement, his eyebrows disappearing into his hairline. "You *may* have been dosed with Ketamine? Did you have surgery?"

"No."

"What happened?"

I struggled for a minute, releasing a pained sigh. "It's a really long story."

Dr. Freeman stared at me, obviously waiting for me to continue.

Figuring *what the hell*, I explained, "I rescued my husband last week from an illegal oil refinery in Nigeria and he drugged me with Ketamine in order to force me to leave without freeing the remaining hostages."

Dr. Freeman's expression didn't change, but he gave me two slow blinks before replying dryly, "Riiight. You don't have to tell me what happened if you don't want to."

Sigh.

Stupid Greg and his stupid poking. Both the poking and the *poking* had landed me in this debacle of a conversation.

Dr. Freeman turned back to the electronic medical record and typed as he spoke. "First I'd like to know the dose and have a sample of the drug if you have it. And we should do some additional blood tests. But, since the baby's heart rate looks good, a one-time dose of Ketamine isn't a disaster."

Something hot and panicky—a weight I'd been carrying, an albatross of guilt and worry—eased, and I took a full breath for the first time since being told I was pregnant. "So the baby should be fine?"

"It's likely, but I'd like to be sure," he hedged. "I believe Ketamine is a class B drug. Since there are no controlled data in human pregnancy, it's generally contraindicated. However, it can and is used as anesthesia while pregnant, which—from the sound of it—might be a similar dose to the one you took. I know of no case studies describing adverse effects to the fetus from a one-time dose."

Unthinkingly, I placed my hand over my abdomen and nodded. "That's good news."

He considered me with a slanted frown. "In Asia, Ketamine is abused as a recreational drug and is correlated with full-term low birth weight. But that's when it's abused daily or weekly. You're not abusing it daily or weekly, are you?"

I shook my head. "No. It should be a one-time poking."

"A what?"

"A one-time thing. I have no plans to be dosed with Ketamine ever again."

"Good. That's good. Don't use any other drugs, either." He didn't sound judgmental per se, but he wasn't his normal cheerful self either. "Maybe focus on taking a prenatal vitamin should the urge grip you. I'll leave a script for you at the front."

I tried not to roll my eyes and barely resisted the urge to respond with, *So, no meth?*

Great. Now my obstetrician thought I was a recreational drug user. I was now branded as an advanced, maternal-aged recreational drug user.

How lovely.

***

ICE CREAM.

It wasn't that I was simply craving ice cream. Rather, my soul required it.

On the way home I picked up four different flavors, unable to settle on just one. I also ordered shawarma from a takeout place near our apartment. It was another soul-deep necessity.

I arrived home just past 11 a.m. to a grim-faced Greg. He greeted me with a stoic glower, hands on his hips. I ignored him—not because I was playing games or trying to make him suffer. Not at all. Rather, I ignored him because I wasn't yet ready to engage. Not until I fed my soul some ice cream and shawarma.

Avoiding his gaze, I walked past him to the kitchen and deposited my bags on the counter. He trailed after me. I felt his eyes track my movements as I pulled a bowl from the cabinet, a spoon from the drawer, and turned back to the ice cream and spiced meat.

The kitchen was silent for several moments save for the sound of me spooning food onto my plate until Greg demanded, "Didn't you get my messages?"

"No." I took a bite of my shawarma, followed by a spoonful of ice cream. "I turned my phone off."

"Why would you do that?" He sounded aggrieved, which part of me found ironic. He was perfectly fine leaving me tied up in Enugu while planning to hand himself over to goons, whereas I couldn't leave him for two hours in Chicago without him throwing a glower-party.

I sighed, still not looking at him. "Because I needed some time."

He waited a beat before pressing, "Fe, we just arrived home yesterday. We haven't spoken—not really, not with any gravity—about what happened. And then you disappear this morning."

"And now I'm back."

"You can't just leave like that, not without a note or a text, not after everything that's happened."

I lifted my gaze to his, my movements stilling. "I'm sorry, did I worry you?" The words were out before I could stop them, dripping with accusatory sarcasm. "How incredibly thoughtless and selfish of me."

Greg glared at me, straightening his back and crossing his arms. "So, passive-aggressive is how you're going to play this?"

"Well, it's either that or *aggressive* aggressive. And I'd prefer not to be arrested for domestic violence today. Maybe tomorrow."

"I know you're angry—"

"You have *no clue* how angry I am," I hissed before taking another bite of ice cream.

"But I'm not sorry I left you in Enugu. I can't be sorry for wanting to keep you safe."

I scoffed, rolling my eyes. "You are arrogant and selfish—"

Greg held up his hands, his tone turning severe and unapologetic, "Hey, I've never claimed to be otherwise. When it comes to you and your safety, I will always be selfish."

I stared at him for a long moment, not knowing what I wanted to say first, the weight of his disregard and duplicity weighing on my chest like an anvil, the force of it chaotically propelling me down an uncertain path.

He claimed to have left me because he wanted to keep me safe, and I believed him. That was certainly part of it. But the other part—the part with which I was struggling—was his complete disregard for my abilities, talents, contributions. Never mind what I wanted or needed.

If the tables had been turned, I wouldn't have left him behind. Not because I loved him less, but because I respected him more.

But it hadn't always been this way.

"What about Jack and Grace? Hmm? What about soccer?"

The muscle at his jaw jumped, his teeth clenched as he scrutinized me. "Do you want to talk about that now?"

"No. I want to resolve that now. Because when you leave again—because you always leave—I want you to know I'll be taking Jack to soccer every Monday, Wednesday, and Friday."

"We're not discussing Jack and soccer, because what you really want to discuss is me leaving."

"Is that so?"

"Yes, that's so. Because why else would you say, 'because you always leave'?" Greg adopted a sotto voice as though to mimic me.

I narrowed my eyes at him, dropping the spoon to the ice cream because it suddenly felt like a weapon in my hands. "I do not sound like that."

"You're right, you don't sound like that. But then, I don't always leave, either."

"That's bullshit. You always leave. You're always leaving. And I don't want you to leave anymore. As of right now, no more leaving." I was being completely irrational. . . fuck it.

Embrace the irrationality!

"And how do you propose we make money, Fe? Do you have a magical money tree growing on the balcony? Perhaps a tiny leprechaun hiding in your purse?"

Frustration growing, I decided to skip past all my little gripes to the sum of their parts. When taken all together, his actions left me at a loss, so I asked the big question. "Tell me the truth. Are you really happy? With us? With kids and a wife? Or are you looking for a way out?"

Greg flinched as though I'd struck him; his expression equal parts incredulous and irate when he responded, his voice raised to a dangerous pitch, "That's like asking me, 'Are you happy your heart beats?'"

I glared at him for a long moment, seeing he believed his words, though I still doubted them. I doubted he wanted a partner.

So I pushed, "Then why did you do it? Why did you accept the assignment? And don't tell me it was for the money, so you could spend more time at home, because that's not the whole reason. You knew for a fact that it was dangerous. Kidnapping of oil workers in Nigeria happens all the time. Why did you risk so much, why risk yourself when your family needs you?"

He made a loud sound of disbelief. "My family needs me? Really?"

"Of course!"

"Not *of course,* Fiona!" He charged me, backing me up until my bottom connected with the counter, shouting, losing all premise of control. "When have you *ever* needed me?"

"Greg—"

"You don't need me. When I'm at home, I might as well be . . I might as well be fucking furniture!" He gestured to the kitchen table with a flick of his wrist.

"Are you serious?"

"As a brain tumor," he said through gritted teeth, and his eyes flashed with malice.

My mouth dropped open and a sound of strangled shock forced itself from my throat.

I squeaked my outrage for several seconds before he interrupted me with his tirade. "By the way, if you had another tumor, would you have told me? Or would I find out about it from the shirtless boy wonder next door?"

"You're still mad I didn't tell you about the headaches?"

"No. Of course not. I'm not allowed to be angry with you about anything. I'm not even fucking needed here!"

"You are."

"Then tell me to stay. Tell me you need me. Lie to me." He was all sarcasm and bitterness.

I set my hands on my waist and squinted, because my eyes were stinging with the same hot rage ballooning in my chest. "You want to be needed? Fine. Poof. You're needed! In fact, I need you right now. I *need* you to do your breakfast dishes." I gestured to the pot he'd used to make oatmeal, still caked with residual oats and left to soak on the counter.

"Oh, so very amusing, darling," he spat spitefully, his voice a dangerous growl.

I stuck my chin out. "You think I'm joking? Because I'm not."

"For your information, I've left the pot to soak on the counter *on purpose* and with every intention of cleaning it later. If you'd taken a moment to look around, you'd see that all the other dishes are done and I've wiped down the counter."

I lifted my hands and gave him three slow claps, knowing I was being insufferable but lacking the mental energy to care. "Congratulations. You've wiped down the counters for the first time in over fourteen years of marriage. What do you want? A cookie?"

Greg responded through gritted teeth. "No, Fe. I don't require treats for good deeds. But I would *like* some acknowledgement that I have been listening to you, and I am trying to do better. Yet all I'm hearing is that I'm needed only for the most mundane of tasks. Thank you for clarifying how desperately I'm needed." He moved to turn away, hurt written on his features, so I gripped his wrist to stop him and yanked him back.

"That's right, Greg. I need you for the most mundane of tasks, because *that's* what marriage and parenting is. It's the mundane. It's the everyday. It's the showing up and being there and supporting each other in a million different small ways that add up to a colossal commitment. It's consistency."

"Because you have everything else under control, right?" His words were laced with resentment, and based on the venom in his voice and the accusatory daggers shooting from his eyes, he was expecting me to answer with a *Yes. I do. I have everything sorted, except the soaking oatmeal dish.*

Instead I said, "No. I don't. I'm a complete mess. I'm frantic for you. Yet I feel abandoned when you leave for your assignments. But I can forgive you for that. What I can no longer forgive or overlook is that you abandon me even when we're together. You abandoned me in Enugu, and you abandon me when you're here."

He swallowed thickly, his eyes flickering between mine, and when he spoke the sentiment was jagged and rough. "Then tell me what to do. Tell me how I can help in a way that's meaningful."

"I don't want to tell you; I want you to just do it without me having to spell it out all the time!"

"Too bad. I'm not a fucking mind reader. You can't expect me to know without some direction. At this point I'll even accept Morse code."

"Fine." I folded my arms over my chest and lifted my chin stubbornly. "I need you to help with the laundry. Fold it. And put it away, neatly, where it belongs."

He opened his mouth as though he were going to give me a sarcastic retort, but then stopped himself. His eyes narrowed on me, examining my upturned face, and he blinked three times in rapid succession. "Wait a minute. This isn't about the laundry, or the dishes, or the vacuuming."

"Yes, it is. And it's also about you leaving your socks all over the place, and your inability to find things or put them back where they belong, and—"

"It is, but it isn't. Something has happened. Something has changed."

I pressed my lips together and swallowed with effort, meeting his searching gaze. "I've changed. You leaving me in Enugu while you risked your life—without even discussing it with me, as though my contributions and abilities were meaningless—changed me."

Greg gathered a deep breath and his voice was raw and ragged with blunt honesty. "I don't know how to be sorry for that. I honestly don't. But you must know, your contributions and abilities, they're not meaningless to me. Rather, I hope one day you'll understand my fear of losing you—or Jack, or Grace—my desire to keep you all safe surpasses even my respect for your feelings. And I don't know how to change that about myself. I don't know if I can, or that I want to."

I stared at him for a beat, seeing this desire in him to keep his family safe at all costs as both wonderful and counterproductive. Any decision founded solely in fear, with no regard for evidence or common sense, is ultimately destructive. We needed to find a balance.

Before I could voice these thoughts, he asked, "Does it matter to you what I want?"

I thought about his question for exactly two seconds, then responded with honesty fueled by fury, my throat constricting with each word spoken. "Yes. It matters to me what you want, but I honestly don't think I can do anything about it anymore. I am at the end of my rope. So, no. No, it doesn't matter what you want. And it doesn't matter what I want. Because, guess what? I'm pregnant!"

I paired the words "I'm pregnant" with frenetic jazz hands, a strangled and hysterical laugh, and two fat tears running down my cheeks. I sniffled, wiping the moisture away with shaking fingers.

Greg's features, so inflexible and determined just moments ago, grew almost comically confused—as though I'd just announced I was a twelve-toed honey badger with a penchant for rose-scented drawer satchels. I continued to glare at him, watching the play of emotions wreak havoc behind his eyes as his mouth worked but no sound arrived.

At last he said, "I don't understand." I was fairly certain he wasn't speaking to me, but rather was addressing the universe.

"When's the last time you had your sperm count checked, Greg?"

He gaped.

I huffed another humorless laugh; I was shouting now, and I didn't care one bit. "Of course. Of course you have autocratic sperm. Of course you have mandate-making semen. Because that's who you are. You show up here, after being gone for months, and you make a giant mess of everything. You have no respect for my time, for what I do, for how hard I work. I may not be working sixteen-hour shifts on an oil rig, saving the world. I may be doing the "most mundane of tasks" as you call it. But guess what? I work twenty-four-hour shifts raising our children, managing the accounts, the household, cooking, cleaning, and loving you even though it's unbearably lonely. Not just because you're gone, but because when we're together, you don't see me as a full partner."

"When did you find out?" Apparently, he was still stuck on the baby reveal. I couldn't blame him. I was also still in shock.

"Yesterday on the phone with Liz, confirmed just this morning at Dr. Freeman's office. And, by the way, thank you for drugging me with Ketamine in Nigeria. He now thinks I'm a recreational drug user."

"You're . . . welcome?" He seemed to have difficulty moving beyond the pregnancy news, so I gave him a moment to reflect, watched his handsome face as he watched me with an unfocused gaze, plainly prioritizing his cornucopia of questions.

Eventually, with wide and worried eyes, he settled on, "The baby is okay? Did I . . . did I—"

"Yes. The baby appears to be fine. The doctor said there shouldn't be any adverse effects from the Ketamine, though he's planning to run some additional tests." I split my attention between him and my shawarma, suddenly no longer hungry for it.

Greg said nothing and the fire behind his eyes had mellowed. He watched me, like I was something new and volatile and wonderful, like he was considering how best to handle me. I could see he was excited by the idea of a new addition to our family and, strangely, his excitement both eased and irritated me.

Eased because I needed him to be happy about this. If he'd been upset, I would have lost my mind, gone into full ninja mode, and destroyed the apartment.

Irritated because he wasn't the one who would be pregnant, deal with mood swings, weight gain, medical tests, back pain, labor, struggle through breastfeeding, and juggle Grace and Jack's needs as well.

And lose myself a little more in the process. . .

I scoffed at his cautiously exuberant expression and posed his question back to him. "How about you? Do you care at all what I want? What I need?"

"What do you need, Fe?" he asked, his voice quiet and curious, bracing.

"I need a partner," I blurted, swallowing a sob, my eyes still stinging with stubborn tears. "I meant what I said. I need you here. Alive. Active and involved and helping, every day. I need you to look for ways to help, not wait for me to make you a list. I need you to listen and not discount my point of view or contributions despite your feverish caveman need to keep me safe. I need you to clean the apartment, and pick up your goddamn socks, and stop making mindless messes—like we have magical cleaning fairies who orgasm every time they do the laundry."

He cracked a rueful smile at the last bit, but quickly pressed his lips together.

Despite the just-spoken sarcasm and humor, my voice wobbled as I added earnestly and gently, "Let me remind you of some words a very wise man once said to me. 'A relationship is made up of many burdens, and the two people within the relationship have different strengths and weaknesses, abilities and talents. Burdens are weightless, worlds change, and love endures when both people are contributing their maximum.'"

Greg set his jaw, his eyes narrowing, but I could tell his temper had lost its steam. "That guy sounds like a pretentious asshole."

I pressed my lips together, partly to keep my chin from wobbling, and partly because I was fighting a smile.

Pulling him into my arms for a tight hug, because I needed to touch him—I needed his strength—I lifted my chin and whispered against his ear. "I'd like to amend that wisdom to include: burdens are weightless, worlds change, and love endures when both people are *allowed* to contribute their maximum."

"Now *you* sound like a pretentious asshole," he grumbled, but I could tell it was false grouchiness because his arms came around me and held me to him with a tight, possessive embrace.

I had to take a couple deep breaths before I admitted brokenly, "I need you to stop leaving me behind."

He paused for maybe a full minute, then squeezed me and nodded. "Okay. Okay." His hand soothed up and down my back as new tears leaked out of my eyes, tears of relief and tears of panic.

"I'm serious, Greg. You can't do that to me anymore. You can't—"

"I know. And . . . I'll do my best. I might require reminding, but I'll do my best. And, in return, I need something from you."

"I don't know if I have anything left to give." I was so exhausted and overwhelmed and honestly scared. I couldn't fathom having any energy to spare.

"I need you to tell me I'm wanted."

"Of course you are—"

"And needed—"

"Yes," my arms tightened around him as his lips came to my neck, "more than you know."

"And you're desperate for me."

"I'm beyond desperate for you."

"Good." Greg placed a wet kiss just below my ear, biting me, and whispering, "Because I'm desperate for you—and not just your intoxicating warmth and body. I'm desperate for your beautiful heart and brilliant mind. I'm desperate for you to need me as I need you— insatiably, completely, eternally." He punctuated each of his last three words with a kiss, a lick, and a nibble, sending lovely spikes of melting affection and ardor through my limbs, flushed heat to my cheeks.

"I do," I admitted breathlessly, leaning my head back so I could catch his eyes, so he could see both the veracity and importance of my words. "I belong to you, Greg. And I demand you take better care of me. And not just because I'm pregnant—"

"No, darling. We belong to each other. I shall require reminding and some patience if you can spare it, but I intend to take *the best* care of you. And not because you're pregnant."

I gave him a disbelieving glare.

His mouth tugged to one side. "Well, not *just* because you're pregnant. But rather, I shall take the best care of you because it's no less than you deserve—pregnant or not."

My eyes were still leaking water, but I let the tears come, I allowed them to fall freely without wiping them away. "I'll remind you."

"Good."

"And you have to remind me not to bottle things up, you have to remind me to ask for what I need."

"I will. And thank you."

I sniffled. "For what?"

He kissed the wet streaks on both of my cheeks and smoothed his hand from my shoulder to my bottom. A huge smile split his face as his gaze moved over me with what I knew to be worshipful adoration.

Thank God! Because, at that moment, what I needed and wanted most was worshipful adoration, even if it was only a band-aid until backed up by consistency and actions.

"Thank you for always taking the best care of me, even when I'm undeserving."

I tsked, and when I spoke my voice was nasally and thick. "Haven't you realized yet? You do deserve me. We deserve each other."

CHAPTER 23

Dearest Husband,
I love you for who you are and who you have become. I am thankful
that you accept me for what I am and who I have become. I am grateful
you joined me in this ride, that you wanted me too.

-M.
Email
Indiana, USA
Married 15 years

~Present Day~
Fiona

"I JUST WANT him to put the colander back where it belongs. Is that too much to ask?" Janie was crocheting with the fervor of a woman who had just received fifty colanders from her husband. "I don't want one colander for every closet and cabinet in our apartment, I want one colander. Period. One! And I want him to put it where it belongs."

"Why can't men put the dishes away correctly?" Sandra addressed this question to Nico and Greg. "Because Quinn isn't special in this. As far as I know, inability to correctly unload the dishwasher is something from which all men suffer."

"Maybe we just like watching our wives bend over while they search cabinets." Nico grinned.

I lifted my gaze from my knitting and it immediately tangled with Greg's. We shared a secretive smile. He wagged his eyebrows. I rolled my eyes.

Two weeks had passed since we'd returned home from Nigeria. Two weeks of Greg being home. Two weeks of us clumsily trying on these new roles, new costumes in our relationship. Every so often I'd trip on my proverbial hem, or he'd rip a hypothetical seam, and we'd have to patch things up.

Ten days ago he'd washed the laundry, not separating the whites from the colors, and turned all of our socks pale pink. We'd argued. He'd researched and discovered a solution online. The socks were saved.

Eight days ago he'd caught me, awake in the middle of the night, re-washing the pots and pans he'd done after dinner. We'd argued. He'd worn a pot on his head and pretended to be a robot. I'd laughed. He'd kissed me. I'd instructed him regarding the appropriate method for cleaning the Dutch oven and seasoning cast iron skillets. He was very patient and receptive to my instruction, so we had sex afterward.

Four days ago I stuffed his pillowcase full of the dirty socks he'd left around the house. We'd argued. We'd argued some more. We'd whisper-yelled at each other until 11:30 p.m. The next morning I apologized for my passive-aggressive actions. He apologized for leaving his socks around the house. We made out in our bedroom closet while the kids watched *Big Hero 6* in the other room.

Earlier in the day he'd received a call from his contract supervisor at Nautical Oil. He let the call go to voicemail, then returned it later in the day out of my earshot. We hadn't had a moment to discuss it.

As well, I'd received a call from Quinn. He'd offered me a job. He wanted me to consult on his corporate contracts, to work full-time. Greg wasn't aware of the job offer yet because we hadn't had a moment to discuss that either.

I didn't know what Greg wanted to do about Nautical Oil—whether he was planning on eventually leaving for another assignment or turning them down and looking elsewhere—but one thing was for certain: no matter what he wanted or had planned, I would be vocal about it. I would be vocal about my feelings regardless of whether the feelings were convenient or timely.

Or at least I would try my best.

"Finding things." Elizabeth poked her husband with her elbow. "Nico does a pretty good job with the dishes, but he can't find things even when they're right in front of him. I once sent him to the Asian market to pick up soba noodles. He called me three times from the store, asking if ramen would suffice. Finally, I had to send him a picture and it turns out there were seven different kinds, and he was standing right in front of them."

He smirked and nodded. "This is true. The same thing happens when I go to the hardware store."

"At least Nicoletta can admit it," Ashley said. She'd joined us from Tennessee via Skype and her image, on Elizabeth's laptop, was sitting on the side table next to me. "If Drew goes to the hardware store without me, it takes him four hours of screwing around to find what he's looking for. But if I'm with him, he's in and out in ten minutes."

"That's probably because he'd rather be doing a different kind of screwing when you're around." Marie wagged her eyebrows and sipped her lemon drop cocktail.

"Is this what you ladies do during knit night?" Greg frowned at the room. "You corrupt my wife with your drinking, gossiping, and double entendre?"

Janie blinked at him then looked to Ashley. Ashley set her knitting down and glanced at Elizabeth. Elizabeth swapped a stare with Kat while Nico smirked at the baby blanket he was making. Marie and I exchanged a quick grin.

"Basically? Yes," Nico answered . . . for all of us.

Greg shoved a handful of popcorn in his mouth and proceeded to talk around it, his words hilariously garbled, a few kernels spewing forth for added grossness and drama. "Why didn't you tell me this was so much fun? I've always wanted to learn how to make lace—for collars and such—and here I could have been tatting whilst championing lewd comments and imbibing girl-drinks."

Kat, Marie, Sandra, and Elizabeth were giggling by the time he'd finished.

"Tatting?" Janie frowned at my husband, like the strangest thing he'd referenced during his tirade was tatting.

"Lemon drops aren't girl-drinks, Mr. Fiona." Sandra wrinkled her nose at him. "Not the way I make them."

"No offense implied, Sandra. I equate girl-drinks to anything that tastes good, like a woman's lady closet. Whereas man-drinks taste of sweat and toe jam, like a man's cock."

Marie made a gagging sound while Nico and Elizabeth outright guffawed.

Nico took out a little notebook and began jotting something down. "I'm stealing that for my show, Greg."

"Feel free. You can send the royalty payments to my lawyer." Greg lifted his chin toward Marie, and Marie lifted her glass in response.

Janie was still frowning in confusion. "What is tatting?"

"According to Wikipedia, tatting is a technique for handcrafting a particularly durable lace from a series of knots and loops. One uses an implement called a shuttle for the construction." Greg shoved another handful of popcorn into his mouth, smiling and munching.

Janie's frown deepened. "I did not know that."

We all took a moment to be appropriately shocked someone knew a random factoid unknown to Janie. It was a momentous occasion.

Sandra broke the stunted silence. "If Greg joins us he'll need a new name, like Nicoletta." She addressed this statement to me. "Gregwina?"

"Gregarious?" Marie offered.

"No. Auntie Gregina," I said with a smile aimed at my husband. "Think of him as a girl in a man's body. He's got the brain of a woman."

He nodded, returning my smile and remembering our private joke from our pre-dating college days. "That's right: shrewd, calculating, resilient, ruthless."

"Sounds about right." Sandra took another gulp of her drink. "Too bad you've got a man's body, because apparently us women are delicious."

"David never went down on me," Marie admitted flatly, her cocktail suspended in front of her, staring forward as though in a trance. The room fell into a surprised hush as everyone—sans Marie—exchanged wide-eyed glances. I doubted she realized she'd spoken out loud.

Greg frowned at our friend, true astonishment written all over his features. I don't know what he thought we talked about during knit night, but Marie's comment was fairly tame. If he wanted to be regularly included then he would have to put up with the oversharing.

I was just about to tell him this when he surprised me by prompting Marie, "Tell Auntie Gregina all about it."

Her gaze cut to his, her features blank but her tone clearly aggrieved as she said, "The good ones are like unicorns."

"The good ones?"

"Men."

Greg studied her for a beat, then he set his popcorn aside. Leaning forward, elbows on his knees. He gave her one of his soft, compassionate smiles; the ones he used liberally with Grace when she was hurt—even if he didn't realize it—and with me when I encountered disappointment or non-Greg-related distress. It always made my heart do wonderful things.

"I never liked David," he said solemnly. "He was a wanker."

"I didn't either," Kat blurted, frowning, drawing our collective attention to her. "I'm sorry I never said anything."

Marie issued Kat and Greg a small smile of wonder, her curiosity piqued. "Why didn't you like him?"

"He thought his food was delicious." Greg paired this odd declaration with a flick of his wrist, as though David, a chef, finding his own food delicious was unforgivable.

"His food *was* delicious." Marie's statement was the truth.

"Yes, but he was always talking about it, about how he cooked the most delicious eye of newt, or some such doldrums. And he was obsessed with cuts of meat."

"That's true." Elizabeth pointed at Greg. "Remember that one time he yelled at me for mixing up a prime rib with a fillet?"

"Yes." Greg snapped once and nodded vigorously. "You'd just worked a really long shift—"

"Thirty-six hours," Elizabeth supplied.

"And you didn't even know your own name. And then he left the table because you said the fillet smelled really good."

"I remember that." Kat was also nodding vigorously.

Sandra lifted her drink to the room and added, "Also, balls."

"Balls are no joke," Nico agreed, not looking up from his crochet.

Marie shook her head but was clearly trying not to laugh. "Not this again."

"I suppose what I'm saying—dearest, lawyerest, blondest Marie—is that any man who speaks about the deliciousness of his own cooking, but has no taste for your lady closet, is completely undeserving of you. One must work diligently to be deserving, placing one's partner above oneself, especially one's fears and ambitions. As such, David is undeserving." Greg's words were met with head nods of agreement from both Nicoletta and the ladies gathered.

Meanwhile, I studied my husband openly. His statement might have been seen as a show of support by our friends, but to me it sounded like a realization, a crystallization of finally appreciating my perspective. Hope and wonder blossomed in my chest, a warm spreading consciousness, both lifting my heart and soothing some of my anxieties.

"I know that. I just wish I could get over it. It's been a year and I'm still . . ." Marie sipped her drink and sighed again, her tone more resolute as she found her desired train of thought. "It's not David. I don't miss *him*. I miss having a person. I miss having someone to laugh with, someone to talk to, someone to care for. I miss having a man's body close by, the strength of it. I miss the sound of a male voice in the morning. And I miss kissing."

"Kissing is nice." Now Kat was staring unseeingly forward and sounded like she was in a trance.

I smirked at Kat's dreamy-sounding statement, because I was fairly certain she was thinking of one man's kisses in particular.

Marie ignored Kat and continued, "I want what you and Fiona have. I look at the two of you and, honestly, it gives me hope. I want someone I can rely on, but who knows me well enough to give me space when I need it, forgiveness when I ask for it. I want unconditional love and support. I want someone who fits me, is the yin to my yang." Marie met Greg's gaze head on, her voice steady and sure. "I want enduring love. And, if people are honest with themselves, I think that's what everyone wants."

Greg and I traded smiles; I both felt and saw the warmth behind his gaze, the adoration, desire, and promise.

Still looking at me, a grin still whispering over his lips, he said, "Being the yin to someone's yang takes work."

"Relationships are the ultimate work in progress," I agreed. "Think of being in a committed relationship like knitting a scarf that never ends, with lots of mistakes and dropped stitches."

"That sounds frustrating and expensive," Kat chuckled, but I could tell she was trying to infuse some humor into the discussion. "Think about all that yarn you'd have to buy."

Greg picked up on Kat's attempt and ran with it. "That's right. If the good ones are like unicorns, just think about how expensive his upkeep would be. What does one feed a unicorn?"

"Fillet, not prime rib," Elizabeth suggested, making her husband laugh.

"A steady diet of lady closet," Sandra recommended with a twinkle in her eye.

"Rhinoceroses are probably the closest non-mythical animal to a unicorn, and—contrary to popular belief—they're vegetarians. Black rhinos get most of their sustenance from eating trees and bushes. But white rhinos graze on grasses, walking with their enormous heads lowered to the ground," Janie said, obviously the only one who was giving the matter of feeding unicorns any serious thought.

Not missing a beat, Greg nodded at Janie's information share as though it were exceptionally fascinating—because it was—and added, "But just remember, Marie, it doesn't really matter what you end up feeding the unicorn when he is found. Because here's the take-home message: there's a man unicorn out there, right now, who cannot wait to dine on your lady closet and give you the horn in his pants."

***

"WE SHOULD HAVE named Jack 'The Hague.'"

I caught the tail end of Greg's eye-roll as he threw some balled-up item into our laundry basket and walked past where I sat perched on the bed.

"What? Why?"

"He's so judgy," he responded from inside the bathroom, then poked his head out and glared at me. "I blame you and your choice in college major."

"What are you talking about? My major was electrical engineering."

"No. You majored in being a hot piece of ass."

Charmed by his remark in spite of myself, I forced myself to glower—especially since I knew he was just trying to get a rise out of me.

He held his hands up, walking back into our bedroom and not fighting his smile. "It's funny because you're brilliant. If you were stupid then it wouldn't be funny, it would be true."

"It's not funny at all."

"It's a little funny."

"Whatever. Back to Jack. What happened?"

"He won't wear the Miami Dolphins 1984 Super Bowl Championship shirt I brought him back from Nigeria."

"Probably because the Miami Dolphins lost the 1984 Super Bowl."

As soon as we were home, and our babysitter had been paid and sent away, Jack had come out of his room with a scowl pointed at his father. I left the two of them to it and sauntered into the bedroom to undress.

Now Greg closed the door to our room and pulled off his sweater. "He should be rejoicing in the oddity of it rather than focusing on its veracity."

I smirked as I unfastened my sweater, saying nothing. Jack and Greg were a lot alike. It would be interesting to see how Greg handled a teenage version of himself.

We both disrobed in silence, lost to our thoughts, and my mind wandered. We still had so much to discuss, to talk about. The issues with soccer and Jack and Grace hadn't been resolved, nor had we figured out what to do about Jack's musical talent. Plus our retirement accounts. Plus the baby . . .

Our list of to-do discussion items felt endless. At this point I was going to have to make an agenda and hold him hostage until we'd agreed to an action plan for the most pressing items.

Greg cut through my musings by saying, "I need your help."

"Sure," I responded automatically, "how can I help?"

I expected him to follow up with something like,

I can't find my cell phone—will you help me find it?

I can't find my keys—will you help me find them?

I can't find this very-random-piece-of-paper-with-a-number-written-on-it—will you help me find it?

Because those requests were typical and he knew I didn't mind helping. Losing a thing was always made more frustrating when no one would help you find it.

Imagine my surprise when he said none of those things, but instead replied with a solemn, "Help me figure out what to do next."

I'd been removing my leggings when he made his request, so I stopped mid-movement and shifted my attention to my husband. He stood in front of me, not quite frowning.

"What do you mean?"

Greg sat next to me on the bed, his fingers slipping between my legs to rest on the newly bared skin of my thigh. "I received a call from John at Nautical Oil this afternoon."

"Your contracting agent?"

"That's right. They're offering a settlement, to me and the other hostages, for the gaps in security that allowed us to be kidnapped in the first place. Marie—who is now one of my favorite people in the entire world—discovered during the digging she was doing for the Associated Press that my contract guaranteed a certain level of security, teams and the like, while I was stationed in Nigeria. You know how we all have insurance policies? Owned by the company and the life insurance we pay into? Well the life insurance policy is contingent on the security protocols being followed."

Now I was not-quite frowning. "I didn't know that."

"I just found out. Our life insurance was cancelled last week. Forfeit."

My mouth fell open and I struggled to speak for a moment before blurting, "How can they do that? It's a whole life insurance policy, that money is ours."

"No, my darling. It was ours, as long as Nautical Oil was providing the security they'd promised. Since they didn't, and I was kidnapped as a result, the whole life policy was forfeit. Which brings us to the settlement." Greg pulled my legs over his lap, his fingers inching higher on my thighs.

"Okay . . . ?" I finished removing my leggings and straddled him—since I knew that's what he really wanted—and dipped my head to the side in a questioning movement. "They want to make a settlement?"

He nodded. "That's right, obviously for the entire amount of the whole life insurance policy, plus a tidy sum for pain and suffering."

"How much?"

"Not enough to build a throne of money," he mock-scowled, "more like a kitchen chair of money. Not enough that we can live quite comfortably, as long as we invest wisely."

My immediate reaction, before giving the matter any thought, was ecstatic enthusiasm. Greg would be home more. He'd have more freedom to pick the assignments he wanted rather than accepting dangerous assignments for increased money.

This was excellent news, just as long as . . .

"Will you let me? Invest the money wisely?"

Greg gathered a large inhale, studying my features, and then gave me a quick kiss. "I've been thinking on that, the retirement and such, and I see now that you were right. After . . . everything that's happened, I see that it has been a huge effort and time-drain for you. I signed the papers and sent them into Mr. Jackson yesterday."

I was surprised, and relieved, and feeling all manner of warm feelings for my husband. "You did?"

He nodded once. "Yes. Though, if we accept this money, this settlement, I'd like to work with Mr. Jackson on picking the fund portfolios—not because I don't trust you, but because I don't want you to waste your time playing monkey-in-the-middle anymore."

"Thank you." I pressed another quick kiss to his lips. "That actually sounds really good to me."

He eyeballed me for a long moment, sighed, and flexed his fingers on my thighs. "Fe, if we accept this settlement then I won't be able to work as a petroleum engineer for at least ten years."

"You mean you won't *have* to work anymore."

"No." He shook his head. "No, it means I would be disallowed from accepting work—contract or full-time or consulting—as a petroleum engineer from any publicly traded competitor of Nautical Oil for the period of ten years. It's stipulated in the settlement. I might get a job doing something else, but all the major oil firms are publicly traded. And it's unlikely Nautical Oil would hire me either."

Stunned, I gaped at Greg.

But after my mind was able to move past my surprise, the first word I thought and said was, "No."

"Fe—"

"No. Absolutely not. No. Tell them no. We'll sue them instead, then you can work for whoever you want *and* we'll get the money."

"No, we won't. We wouldn't get the money, at least not nearly as much. And it would take years, and be stressful, and time-consuming."

I wanted to argue, but I didn't. Instead I studied my husband. Really looked at him, and saw how bone-deep fatigued he was. I knew Greg wasn't infallible—Lord, I knew that—but part of me had always assumed he was indestructible. He was my superhero, a much more sarcastic version of Captain America, larger than life, able to withstand any test or burden.

I'd seen him tired before, exhausted after pulling weeks of sixteen-hour shifts on an oil rig and traveling over twenty-four hours to make it home, but he'd never looked resigned. He'd never before looked like he wanted to settle.

"I miss you, my darling." His eyes—drowsy and anxious—caressed my features, his hands rubbing circles on my thighs. "I miss you, and Grace, and Jack. And I'm tired. Maybe I'll regret taking the settlement a few years from now . . . but I doubt it."

"Greg, I don't want you to give up this part of yourself. You make a difference in the world, you—"

"Perhaps it's time I started making more of a difference to my family. Perhaps it's time I let the world fend for itself."

Though my chest felt blissfully light and airy at his words, I issued him a questioning look. He would be no good to our family if he spent all his days at home miserable.

But then one of his hands moved to rest on my lower belly. "Pretty soon you'll be gloriously round with our new person, craving all sorts of disgusting foods at all times of the day and night—but mostly night. Perhaps I want to eat cheese steak and peanut butter sandwiches with you."

"I ate those with Grace three times a week."

"I know. You told me, but I wasn't here to procure them for you," he reminded me, clearly unhappy, and placed a soft, wet, sliding kiss on my lips.

"Greg, you shouldn't use the baby as a reason to stay home."

"I'm not. But I'd be lying if I said she wasn't part of the reason I want to stay home."

"She?"

"Yes. She. And she'll love playing soccer and eschew all things forced upon her by outdated societal constructs."

I huff-laughed at him. "She or he will be her or his own person and we will love that person no matter what."

"That's what I just said." His eyes danced mischievously.

"Okay. So, what's the other reason?"

"I am. I'm the reason. I'm tired and . . ." Greg slipped his hands into the fabric of my underwear and gripped my bottom, squeezing and pulling me more firmly against him. His head dipped to my neck and he nipped my ear, whispering hotly, "I miss you. And I'm tired of missing you. I'm tired of missing Jack and Grace."

"I miss you," I said on a sigh. "But I think we should talk about this more before we decide anything. I don't want you giving up something so important to you without being thorough and thoughtful about it."

"Fine." His arms wrapped around me, holding me close. "You sleep on it and I'll sleep on you."

I chuckled, returning his embrace. "Thank you for including me in this decision. Thank you for asking me for help."

"Of course. This is our life."

We held each other and I allowed the possibility of what the settlement would mean to take hold. I imagined what life would be like with Greg at home, every day. I could finally get rid of those hot water bottle cozies and stop spraying his cologne everywhere like a weirdo.

A life with an accessible husband . . .

I abruptly recalled that I had my own news to share as well.

"Quinn called earlier today."

Greg said nothing for a beat, then asked, "He did? What did he want?"

"He offered me a job."

My husband stiffened, just infinitesimally, likely due to surprise. "Doing what?"

"Security consulting for his private clients. It would mean some travel, not a ton, and mostly to Europe, Canada, and Australia."

"Do you want to take it?"

"I need your help." Echoing his earlier words, I pulled far enough away to capture his almond-shaped brown eyes, now a little lighter than they'd been when we first met. A whiskey instead of a Kahlua . . . I might have been craving liquor.

"Help me figure out what to do next."

A slow grin spread over his features as he studied me. It was crooked as it always was—sexy and thrilling and wonderful.

Clearing his throat cartoonishly, his eyes dancing with mischief, Greg placed a single kiss on my collarbone. "Tell Quinn you want his office. I'd love to be there for that conversation."

I barked a laugh. "Yeah . . . no."

"And a pony."

I smacked Greg on the shoulder. "Be serious."

"Okay. Okay." He cleared his throat again, seriously this time. "As you said, we should be thorough and thoughtful about it. But honestly," he shrugged, "if you want to do it, you should."

I narrowed my eyes on him. "And the kids?"

"I can take care of them. Maybe I'll even enlist Man-Child Matt from time to time. We'll be fine."

When I continued to glare at him he quickly added, "Mind you, I likely won't do as good of a job as you. And I can't promise the house will always be clean. Or that we won't weld. Or launch rockets."

"Launch rockets?"

"If they don't learn about launching rockets at home, then they'll just learn about it on the streets."

I glowered at him. "That sounds like something Hitler would say."

Greg chuckled and shook his head. "Well done, Mrs. Archer. There's no arguing with that."

"Thank you. I try."

A smile lingered over his lips as he examined me. "The point is, we'll figure it out. We always do. We can't resolve everything now, because— as you so eloquently pointed out to your knitting group earlier—this marriage thing is a work in progress."

My heart skipped, bouncing around the walls of my chest, because in this moment I was happy.

We were together. We were safe. The future was unknown. However, I'd learned over the last fourteen years that there was no such thing as a happily ever after.

"Fe." Greg slipped his fingers under my shirt, his big palms massaging my breasts suggestively, sending spikes of lovely warmth and coiled want to my belly, fingertips, and toes.

"Yes?"

"My heart keeps discovering new ways to love you," he whispered, like it was a secret. A magnificent, beautiful, perfect secret.

My smile was immense and immediate. A rush of emotion stung my eyes. Because sometimes marriage to this man was wonderful.

But sometimes it was a chore.

Love was never enough, not without mutual respect and a great deal of drudgery and effort. And even then, it wasn't enough. Wanting each other, being open to change, pushing each other to improve and grow— for the better—working to deserve each other, was the key.

I loved him and I always would. But that was the easy part. Working to deserve him and demanding that he work to deserve me, everyday—that was hard.

But he was worth it.

And I was worth it.

"Thank you, Greg. I love you so much, and I'm so grateful we found each other."

"Me too, my darling." He held my eyes captive, prolonging the romance of the moment, reminding me of why I married him in the first place.

But then, after a minute, he squeezed my boobs and asked, "Are we going to have sex tonight? I have stuff to do and it's already nine thirty."

~The End~

About the Author

Penny Reid's days are spent writing federal grant proposals for biomedical research; her evenings are either spent playing dress-up and mad-scientist with her three people-children (boy-8, girl-5, infant dictator- 5 months), or knitting with her knitting group at the local coffee shop. Please feel free to drop her a line. She'd be happy to hijack your thoughts!

Come find Penny-

Mailing list signup: http://reidromance.blogspot.com/p/mailing-list-sign-up.html

Email: pennreid@gmail.com …hey, you! Email me ;-)

Blog: http://reidromance.blogspot.com/

Twitter: https://twitter.com/ReidRomance

Ravelry: http://www.ravelry.com/people/ReidRomance (if you crochet or knit…!)

Goodreads: http://www.goodreads.com/ReidRomance

"The Facebook": http://www.facebook.com/PennyReidWriter

Please, write a review!

If you liked this book (and, more importantly perhaps, if you didn't like it) please take a moment to post a review someplace (Amazon, Goodreads, your blog, on a bathroom stall wall, in a letter to your mother, etc.). This helps society more than you know when you make your voice heard; reviews force us to move towards a true meritocracy.

Read on for:

Penny Reid's **Booklist** (current and planned publications)

Other books by Penny Reid

Knitting in the City Series
(Contemporary Romantic Comedy)
Neanderthal Seeks Human: A Smart Romance (#1)
Neanderthal Marries Human: A Smarter Romance (#1.5)
Friends without Benefits: An Unrequited Romance (#2)
Love Hacked: A Reluctant Romance (#3)
Beauty and the Mustache: A Philosophical Romance (#4)
Happily Ever Ninja: A Married Romance (#5, coming Fall 2015)
Book #6 – TBD 2016
Book #7 – TBD 2017

Winston Brother Series
(Contemporary Romantic Comedy, spinoff of *Beauty and the Mustache*)
Truth or Beard (#1)
Grin and Beard It (#2, coming 2016)
Beard Science (#3, coming 2017)
Book #4 – TBD 2017
Book #5 – TBD 2018
Book #6 – TBD 2018

Hypothesis Series
(New Adult Romantic Comedy)
The Elements of Chemistry: ATTRACTION, HEAT, and
CAPTURE (#1)
Book #2 – TBD 2016
Book #3 – TBD 2017

Irish Players (Rugby) Series – by L.H. Cosway and Penny Reid
(Contemporary Sports Romance)
The Hooker and the Hermit (#1)
The Pixie and the Player (#2, coming 2016)
Book #3 – TBD 2017

Made in the USA
Middletown, DE
16 January 2016